THE HOUR BETWEEN ONE AND TWO

THOMAS TIMMINS

THE HOUR
BETWEEN
ONE AND TWO

A mystery in three books

THOMAS TIMMINS

Zoëtown Media
Haydenville, Massachusetts

ZOËTOWN MEDIA

The Hour Between One and Two

Copyright © 2014 by Thomas Timmins

Cover: Tom Dudley

Zoëtown Media
ISBN (pb): 978-0-9893283-6-4
ISBN (e): 978-0-9893283-7-1

Printed in the United States of America

Disclaimer

The author admits to taking a decade-long trip through the humid world of tofu making and marketing. He met countless inspired, industrious, good and eccentric people as he and his cohorts transformed soybeans into food for human beings. While some may wish to attribute familiar identities to some of the characters, living or dead, this is not a memoir. It is a work of fiction, arising from the author's imagination. Like all tall tales, it has at best a metaphoric relationship with what we perceive as the everyday world. If you find truth and pleasure in this book, they are yours to enjoy. That would make the author happy as the tofu master who, after stirring endless circles in a cauldron of hot soymilk, whips up a tasty batch of tofu he can serve to the world.

ACKNOWLEDGEMENTS:

Joe Timmins, David Grant, Angela Borda, Nancy Shobe, Barbara Sachs, Judith Rubenstein, Amy Swisher, Thomas Dudley all had sensitive and caring hands in the making of this book. Without Judith Roberts, Richard and Kathy Leviton, Madeleine Fox, Jon Lee, Vinny Natale, Maggie Stebbins, Cory Greenberg, Donnie Nelson, Mary Houghton and hundreds of crew members and thousands of imaginative and intrepid tofu aficionados, the author could never have made the astonishing journey from soybean slinger to tofu tale teller. I thank each one of you.

Contents

THE HOUR BETWEEN ONE AND TWO: BOOK ONE

A DARK COMIC MYSTERY
BLOOD
MEDICINE
THOMAS TIMMINS
TOFU NOIR

Prologue

Promotional Brochure
from the American Tofu Company

The Year of the Monkey

This is the year to say "Yes!" and expect miracles. Mimic the agile Monkey who won't stop till he swings from every branch and tests every angle. You'll land on your feet with a happy surprise in your hands and a smile on your face.

Enjoy this year as one big poker game. The one who gets the best deal will be the one who outsmarts the other. If you lose a hand, laugh. Monkeys shrug off their mistakes and find amusement everywhere.

Don't even try to keep track of who's ahead: the Monkey's left hand rarely knows what the right hand is up to. Not to worry—it's a year of huge rewards.

Help comes from the oddest places. Astonishing gifts arrive by coincidence, even from your enemies. Go ahead, say "Yes, Yes, Yes!" Be unpredictable, stretch and swing far. Have fun and you can leave the low-hanging fruit for the groundlings. Seriously, it's playtime.

From The Year of the Monkey
Chinese New Year Promotional Brochure
American Tofu, Inc., Clement, New York
www.AmericanTofu.com

Chapter One

Becky MacDaniel

MY "BIG 3–0"

I jumped into his car as excited and happy as I'd ever been. He kissed me quick and bit my lip. He smelled like he'd put away as many Margaritas as I had.

It's sad or crazy or love, but every time I see him, I can't resist touching him. I shouldn't, but ... Like I can't control myself. He's not good for me, I know. But what else can I do?

We drove out of town, down a gravel road that followed the river, bumping along under a forest canopy drizzling with moonlight, my fingers caressing his bare hairy arm. Warm breeze from the river seeped into the car as we crept lights out toward wherever we were going.

What a birthday today. First, a surprise breakfast made with all the love my kids could give their mom. Lumpy pancakes and soggy bacon all drowned in maple syrup, just the way I like it. And perfect coffee—half milk, half sugar.

Then, tonight, thirty rowdy friends at my house ringing in my big 3–0. Nobody will ever forget that party, even if I did send everybody home early. They all believed my excuse that I had to be at work by four.

Now, celebrating in the full moon night with him. We might stay up all night. Before we climbed out of the truck, I touched his cheek and asked, "Don't you feel like a fish tonight?"

Wrinkling his nose, he said, "Not really." He raised his thick eyebrows and poked his fingers at my ribs. "More like a stallion."

I caught his fingers in my fists and held them in mid-air. "No, seriously. See those shadows? How they wiggle between the moon-beams? Like we're sitting in a three-dimensional fish net made of light and dark."

He grunted, "Yeah," and that's all, like he had something else on his mind. I knew what that was.

I uncapped my thermos of frozen margaritas and we sat drinking and toasting each other. Before long, we started laughing and shrieking like idiots. We'd both had plenty to drink before we came out to the river.

We hopped down the root-stairs on the riverbank and stood in the pale shade of an enormous oak.

"Let's cross the river," he said. "I want to give you a present in style."

"I have a present for you, too," I whispered, kissing his ear.

He ogled my breasts like he always did and said, "I bet you do." I slapped his cheek, maybe a little too hard. He smiled. "Not that, " I said.

A jumble of rocks and boulders lay exposed above the shallow August stream. "It looks slippery," I said.

"That's shadows, not water. I can cross with my eyes closed."

My feet stayed planted so he pointed across the water. "See that patch of moonlight? I want to see my princess dressed in just her new present."

He dug into his pants pocket and brought out a velvety little box. Flipping the lid back, he showed me two tiny green jewels glowing like stars in his moonlit hand. I reached for them, but he shut the lid and stuffed the box back into his pocket.

"That's all you want me to wear?" I couldn't believe he'd buy me something so expensive.

"You don't need anything else." He held out his arms. "Jump on. I'll carry you over."

"Like a groom?"

"Like a stallion."

We laughed until we bent over, bouncing off each other. I leapt up and swung my legs around his waist. Embracing his neck with both arms, I threw my head back and howled.

"Mmmm. You're heavy," he said, adjusting his grip. "Too much cake?"

"You're weak." I teased him back. I love those extra-strong stringy muscles in his arms and back.

He threw me up into a moonbeam slanting through the trees and flipped me around and settled me across his arms where I lay like a bride.

"Nobody ever called me weak before." Laughing, he tossed me up and down as he stretched his leg across the gap between the shore and a flat boulder in the river. Stopping on a flat boulder near the middle of the river, he slipped a little and hugged me tight to his chest while he stopped, regaining his balance.

I kissed him on the nose. "These rocks. Watch out. They're slippery." He didn't move for a moment. "Are you awake?" I said.

In answer, he nibbled my neck and mumbled, "Gotta be careful of moss. It bites."

Placid water trickled around luminous round rocks that lay scattered randomly between the banks the way my daughter drops biscuits onto a baking sheet. Below the surface, sharp rocks and pebbles fluttered like leaves in a breeze.

"Let me down. I can walk." I arched my back, trying to twist out of his arms.

"Hey, stop that. I got you."

"I want down."

"Quit wiggling like that, I might drop you."

I straightened my legs and pushed against his chest with the heels of my palms.

"Take it easy," he said, swaying back and forth. "please."

"Let go. You're too soused to carry me."

He took another step. As his foot touched down, he wobbled, stretched between two rocks.

"You want down? Be careful." My toes touched the boulder while he held onto my shoulders. He lost his balance and his leg skidded out and shot across the rock. His hands flew apart, flailing, he tipped backwards, my body slid away.

He shouted, "Becky! No! Becky!"

He tried to catch me, but when his fingers clutched at my back, I fell, face-first, through a moonbeam, into dark ... the rock ... oh ...

Chapter Two

Charlie Greer

DEATH SPEAKS ALL LANGUAGES

midnight phone ringing
who else but Benko?
the call that shattered my dream

I was sailing in the Caribbean. Warm silky water flowed between my toes as I lay dangling my feet in a turquoise sea. Playful steel drum melodies drifted across the yacht from the Jamaican group playing on the stern, lolling me into euphoria.

Without warning, the wind shifted. The boat shuddered and the sail whipped, cracking the air inches from my head. The drums clanged, showering sharp, cold notes into my naked ears.

The phone rang four times before Nora got it.

"Charlie, wake up. It's Benko."

"What time is it?"

"Three fifty two."

She poked me in the shoulder with the phone.

"OK. OK."

I took the phone. Nora usually slept through middle-of-thenight calls from my tofu factory, but she woke up for this one. Her intuition must have told her that this was that dreaded call everybody gets sometime.

Benko wouldn't call if it was just a brown-out or production error. He was the best production manager I'd ever had and I totally trusted his judgment. I figured it wasn't a tragedy, because the police come to your door to tell you about that.

"Charlie," Benko growled in his heavy Russian accent, "Trouble, we got. Big."

"What's up, Benko? It's four in the morning." Half-asleep, I felt more annoyed than worried.

"Better get over here. Little problem it's not. Too much for me. I don't know what to do."

"Slow down. I can't understand you."

"Sorry. Cops. Cops I called." His normally confident voice trembled, frightening me. Sometimes I'm just paranoid, always worried about someone behind my back, but this time my radar was right.

"Somebody died."

"My God. Who?"

"Good-looking redhead? Becky. Cook, you know."

I jumped up out of bed. "What? What? Shit? Damn! How? God!"

Her eyes wide, Nora asked, "What?"

"Something bad happened at the factory."

I spoke into the phone.

"Benko, where is she?"

"Right here. I'm looking at body. Laying on floor by big tank."

"I'm out the door. Leave everything alone."

"Don't worry, Charlie. I got all covered."

Flashing blue and red lights, a patrol car and an ambulance idled in front of the American Tofu Company. The colors of blood pulsed in and out of the low office building's windows. The three-story factory loomed overhead, pale and gleaming in the security lights.

I approached the cop at the front door. "I'm the owner. Let me in." He started to ask me something but I rushed past him.

I ran through the dim offices lit only by streetlights shining in the windows and opened the swinging doors to the plant and smelled the musty odor of soybeans cooking. The scent distracted me for a second with a sense of comforting normalcy—the tofu factory chugging along.

On the far side of the fluorescence-bleached production room, another cop, some EMTs, my production manager Benko, and the half-dozen or so morning production workers dressed in white uniforms and caps stood in a circle staring at a body on the green floor. No one spoke. Steam billowed against the slick walls of the processing room where rows of tall, stainless steel caldrons and pipes glistened. Every few seconds, the tofu machinery pumped out loud booms followed by rhythmic hisses in the otherwise silent factory

The dead woman sprawled on the tile. It was Becky MacDaniel, a woman too familiar, intimately familiar, but nobody else was aware of that, I hoped. Seeing her there lying dead on the floor weakened my knees.

Water from the processing area flowed constantly across the green production room tiles. It pooled against one side of the body . I stared at her hand as the fingers bobbed up and down. Chilly water soaked my pants from my knees down to my socks.

Tough luck, Greer. You should have known better than to fish off the company pier .

I know. I know. My personal Jiminy Cricket never lets me off the hook. I can't shut him up, even if I try.

"Becky," Benko said in his gravely tones. "Morning shift bean cook." He put his arm around my shoulder.

"I see that." My neck relaxing against the grip of his muscular fingers. "Jesus, Benko. Your goddam accent on the phone confused me. I thought you said our chef—Gen, Genevieve."

"Shit, Charlie. Becky I said. Becky."

I shrugged off his arm and shouted. "Christ, Benko. You almost gave me a heart attack. I thought it was Genevieve." Genevieve O'Connor—we all depended on her to make the sales that paid the bills. Everyone knew how devoted I was to her.

One of the EMT's or cops mumbled, "He thought it was somebody else."

Good, they see it as a simple accident. That we can handle. I knelt down on the wet floor next to the body, my staged relief that it wasn't Genevieve fading in the harsh light of the dead Becky laid out on the floor

I wanted to pick Becky up and carry her out into the night and send everybody home and start the night over. Go back to the time before the company party months ago when I drove her home when she was drunk and I stayed too long.

She was the prettiest tofu worker in the company, but lying dead, she had the swollen face of a teenager who spent too much time in front of the TV set nibblng chips and chocolate.

Greer, you've got ice in your veins. You'll need it now. You're in for nothing but pain.

Sometimes you have to be cold. Don't need to get distracted by the pain, mine or anybody's. Benko squatted down beside me.

"Checking beans in tank, she slipped on platform." Keeping his voice low. "Knocked her head on the edge of tank. She had big birthday party last night. Could be she's still drunk this morning? Everything else in the factory ship-shop-shape. Right?"

"Thanks, Benko. You're probably right. All the cleanup records straight?" I stared at him hard. He had to make sure our records were in order. A blizzard of investigations would come our way police, state worker health and safety board, state food manufacturing inspectors, insurance companies.

Benko nodded at me. "Records in good shape. I make sure."

I nodded and exhaled for the first time since his call. He'd handle it.

The young policeman squatted beside me. He held his hat in his hand. "You the boss?"

"Yeah."

"Chief Buhrman's on his way. We gotta investigate."

"Sure. We don't have many accidents. My God, we have safety training. This is awful." Tears began to leak down my cheeks, surprising me with their volume and warmth. With the cop beside me, I said to Benko, "I thought she worked on the loading dock?"

"First week on new job. She wanted out of warehouse. So try cooking I told her. Chen found her upside down in tank. Called me." He nodded toward Chen, the tofu maker we'd hired from our New York City network of Chinese migrant workers. "Pump wouldn't draw beans so he checked tank. There she was. Head stuck in drain. He dragged her out. Called me. Like crazy man I ran here."

Empty-headed, I stared at the body. The shadow of black bra and panties on pink skin showed through her soaked uniform. A wave of dizziness rolled through me. After less than an hour of sleep, I'd raced here, my adrenaline pumping and blood sugar going nuts.

"Cops I call from home," Benko added. "I run here hoping she's knocked out maybe. Right away I see she's dead so I call you."

Benko had followed proper protocol. Thank God for him. His cool head hadn't failed me yet. He handled problems easily, fixed any machine, got production done on schedule and within budget. A good-looking guy, he smiled a lot, charmed me when he first stepped into my office, grinning like a kid. He reminded me of me if I were a mechanic. He could handle seventy production workers like they were his little kids. Especially the women, most of our crew.

I glanced up at Chen, the somber Chinese worker, for confirmation of Benko's story. His English almost non-existent, he shrugged. His whites were pressed and clean, except for a tan smudge across his chest. He must have crushed beans against himself when he dragged Becky out of the tank.

The other Chinese and the Latino production workers avoided my eyes, not wanting to volunteer any information, in English, Chinese, or Spanish.

But death speaks all languages. At that minute, everybody in the room was reading everybody else's mind. I emptied my mind of any thoughts about Becky, except the fact that she was dead and I was the boss and I had to keep myself and everybody else under control.

Chapter Three

Charlie

DOUBLE MURDER?

*buried in soaking beans,
she forgot to wash her hands—
bloody fingernails*

The afternoon after Becky died, Police Chief Aaron Buhrman asked to see me in my office at the factory. "Got some pretty serious questions for you. Can't do it on the phone. You available now?"

My heart nearly stopped. Did he find something? I distracted myself with making phone calls to assure some of our vendors that all was all right with American Tofu, sad, but we'd bumble through, doing our best for the family and our employees.

By nine this morning, the street in front of the factory was jammed with vans, cars, pickups, and journalists insisting on talking with me. Channel 13 and Channel 10 and three other channels, reporters from five radio stations—even the university station every newspaper from Syracuse to Buffalo including *The Shoppers* clamored to get me to say something I'd regret.

I'll never know how, but that day's *New York Daily News* online led with a sickening headline "Suspicious Death in Upstate Tofu Factory." Rumors flew among our customers and competitors. Several of my friendliest competitors had called me to "express concern" about what this scandal-mongering would do to our sales. I even got a call from Xanadu Tofu in the Bay Area. Messages swamped the company's Facebook page. I considered taking it down.

I hoped the story would become a simple industrial accident before the *Enquirer* published something humiliating and sensational about us. I prayed that in a day or two, TV news would squeeze all the family tragedy they could out of the death and give up its coverage of American Tofu.

Despite the storm of bad publicity, my business mind wondered if, after the media calmed down, the constant repetition of American Tofu in the news would have a positive effect on sales. The old saying, any publicity is good publicity. I hoped so.

Genevieve O'Connor, my faithful and brilliant marketing director, called all of our customers before Channel 13 and the others broadcast the news around the region. She assured them that it was an accident, a tragic loss of one of our treasured employees, but it was not due to poor working conditions or mismanagement. She told them about our sterling safety record—tops in our industry.

Our customers trusted Genevieve so they pitied us and stuck with us, despite reducing their orders for tofu. No one could fault them for that—we're all practical business people.

Without Genevieve, I don't know how I'd have managed. Her warm and professional manner assured Becky's shocked factory friends the company would do its best to take care of Becky's family. She focused on how sad we all were, and made sure Becky's children were tended to by family and a minister.

I offered to call off production for the day, but the workers insisted on working. "Becky'd want us to." Even when I said it would be a paid day off, they persisted in wanting to work. Smart, down-to-earth folks. Keep the routine going to lessen their pain.

Gen managed Facebook with her usual brilliance and aplomb and tweeted all our followers with the news, condolences to the family, and notice of the foundation I told her we'd set up.

She set up a memorial page for Becky and her family with pictures and sympathetic comments from Becky's co-workers. She made a short video for Facebook of the company meeting I called, zooming in on the women's tears and the men's helpless expressions. Gen aimed the camera at my face, caught me sobbing, then quickly sobering up to show the staff how strong we all had to be.

Gen handled Twitter messages by posting empathetic notes and updates as any news came in. I referred the local media to her when I was finished answering their questions.

Before officially meeting with Chief Buhrman, I planned to give him the blue ribbon tour of the factory. At my office door his small hard hand gripped mine while he challenged me with his glassy brown eyes.

Buhrman was six inches shorter than me, trim and fit. He wore his navy blue uniform with padded shoulders. From the collar of his starched blue shirt to the cuffs of his pants, his outfit brooked no creases or lint. A polished brass badge jutted from his breast and a smaller badge rode just above the glossy brim of his hat.

Up close, decked out in full regalia, he reminded me of a Manhattan limo driver. But the fierce glare he shot at me from close-set eyes under beetled eyebrows warned me not to expect any servitude.

The herringboned mahogany butt of Buhrman's pistol bulged off his hip in a gleaming but aged and scarred black leather holster. Heightening the threat of the gun, he wore a shiny wide belt with a German Shepherd's narrow-eyed face embossed on the silver buckle.

A squalling cigarette pack-sized radio competed with a jangling ring of silver and brass keys to give his measured stride a clashing noise that reminded me of a school janitor's benign jingling as he pushed his broom.

All bluff and bluster, but see his billy club? It's been used. Careful, buster.

Trying to lighten up the encounter and gain a little power in this new relationship, I grinned. "We never had so much ordnance in our tofu factory before. We're mostly pacifists here."

He frowned and drew himself up.

"Just joking. Glad you're here."

He said, "We met before."

"I remember," I said.

"That Boys and Girls club fundraiser. You ran it, right?"
"Yeah. It was the YMCA."

Buhrman frowned.

"We raised almost a million dollars for the new therapy pool." I remembered how the guys at the Rotary Club joked how Buhrman insisted on being called "Chief."

The Chief nodded, pursing his lips.

"For the elderly. You know, lots of old folks get arthritis, need to work out in the water. It's easier on the bones." I wasn't getting through to him.

"Disabled kids, too. My kids are healthy but I felt getting that pool into town was a pretty important mission."

The Chief scratched his neck and said, "Yeah. My mother-in-law goes there every week. Does some kind of water acrobiotics." I grinned.

He stared into my eyes. "You know, we got us a pretty important mission right now, Mr. Greer."

Nodding, feeling that sinking feeling I get when things start to get out of control, I agreed. "We sure do. Gotta take care of that poor little family."

I noticed the Chief stood three feet from me, but his glare made it feel like he was about to crush against me.

Stretching a hairnet down over my ears and offering him one, I changed the subject, curbed his intrusion into my mindspace. I'd stick to my plan of impressing him with our professionalism and attention to details.

"Sanitation's our number one focus, Chief."

Buhrman grumbled "Food plant, it better be," and tugged the net down over his neatly parted brown hair.

We started with viewing the three forty-foot tall silos at-tached to our building where we stored up to three hundred thousand pounds of soybeans.

Inside the factory, we traced the route the beans followed as our machines processed them into tofu, past the soaking tanks where they found Becky, down the processing line to the cooking and the slurry area, to the extracting, where bean juice becomes 'soymilk.' We watched our state-of-the-art machinery change the soymilk into curds and whey.

"It's sort of like making cheese," I said. "We make curds and press them together into a soft cake."

He scowled. "Wouldn't catch me eating this stuff, especial-ly not for dessert."

"It's not that kind of cake, Aaron." I laughed, always pleased to explain my unusual way of earning a living by making and selling a strange oriental food. "Some people do make pies and desserts out of it. We mostly eat it like meat—same way the Asian people do."

"Big place you got here, Charlie."

"Yeah. About an acre under one roof, with storage and of-fices." "Lotta places for somebody to hide."

He's not here to grieve. Something up his sleeve.

Waving off my suggestion that he wear earplugs, the Chief had also refused my offer of rubber boots. I in my galoshes, the Chief in his spit-polished, round-toed shoes, we sloshed through water that flowed half an inch deep across the produc-tion room floor.

Heavy soy-scented mist swirled around the cooking room and cold fog rose off the tanks where we iced down the finished tofu. The machine noise of bean grinding and the high-pressure steam-injection drowned out my words. Buhrman wasn't in a listening mood anyway. He moved slowly and stopped every few yards to observe.

"Did you notice the rows of panels on our roof?" I asked.

"Yeah. Solar. Must be tough to get enough sun this far north."

"You'd be surprised," I said. "We use it for hot water. Warms up the well water before it goes into the boiler. Energy efficiency. Saves money. Good for the future. I'm in this business for the good of society." I lowered my voice. "Want my kids and every kid to have a good future."

The Chief grunted, circled his finger in the air, motioned for us to carry on with our tour.

After circling past the chilling tanks and following the filled cases of tofu into the cooler, we stood on the loading dock watching a fork lift driver zip in and out of shipping trailers with pallets of tofu.

The Chief nodded his chin and flipped the hair net up in back, as if he finally understood something that had bothered him. "We'll get the photographers over. I want to see all your records, who came and went the other night."

'Getting the photographers over' meant hiring the only professional photographer in town away from his wedding and high school yearbook business. Later, when this thing blew over, maybe we could use some of the shots in our brochures or the web site.

You better get real, or Buhrman will bury American Tofu. How will if feel when you go down, too?

"Sure thing," I said. "We'll check the time clock records. Would you like to speak with the workers?" It made sense to take a cooperative stance. In my business dealings, I practiced win-win negotiation, and the Chief clearly had to win something here.

He said, "You bet. I hope they speak English."

"We have translators. Spanish, Chinese, Vietnamese. Our Cambodian workers speak English."

"Good. I need to talk with everybody."

"We've always had an international crew, the way it is nowadays. Globalism, you know."

"Yeah. That's smart. Get 'em cheap. Illegals, too, I bet."

"No illegals here, Aaron." I smiled. "When I started the company, we had Zen monks working here. Best workers I ever had."

Buhrman furrowed his brows. "You got monkeys working here?"

"No, no," I laughed. "Monks, Aaron. Not monkeys. Zen's a Japanese religion. Monks. Tofu is a big industry in Japan."

"Monks? Oh, yeah, like priests. Ever heard of 'anchorites'? Monks who live in the desert."

'Anchorites?' He was a Bible reader.

"I'm Catholic myself," he said. "We have monks, y'know. Call 'em Trappists. Famous for their jams and honey and things. The wife's on a kick lately, spreads blueberry jam from the monastery on my Sunday pancakes. Ever try that?"

"Sounds tasty."

"After Mass, with a cuppa joe? Mmm." Ambling along the loading dock like old friends talking, Buhrman stopped in the shadow at the corner of the building and squinted up at me and said, "What was that you said? Japs?"

"Yes. Japanese."

"Thought so."

"Japanese taught us how to make tofu. They've made it for centuries in shops and factories. To them it's like milk or cheese. Big business over there. Tofu is like their dairy industry."

Buhrman challenged me again. "I always thought Japs looked like monkeys. Little squirts hopping around in swarms, squeaking, taking pictures. Best thing Harry Truman ever did. I've seen all the Hiroshima clips on the History Channel. Too bad they're black and white."

He was feeding me, testing my politics, testing my will with his belligerence. He'd gone right at the core of my belief that we have to open up to every culture if we're going to save the human race from itself. Amicable as any Chamber of Commerce member talking to the town's only security force, I grinned and said, "You mean The Bomb."

"That's it. The Big One."

Shaking my head, I wondered how to adapt my progressive attitudes to this racist yokel. I had to take his guff, no matter what, stay on his side. If I upset him, he might want to make an example of me. Still, I had to appear spontaneous and natural. He'd made it clear that he expected me to be at least a little odd.

He turned away and examined the cars and pickups in the parking lot, then turned deliberately. "Anything else you wanna show me, Charlie?"

"That's about it."

"What's out back?" he asked.

"Oh, I forgot. Didn't think it could have anything to do with the accident."

"You never know."

Outside, the temperature had already climbed to the high seventies and the oaks that circled the industrial park showed early scars of tans among their deep green leaves.

Sun-glistened corn stalks ripened in the nearby fields waiting for the combines to strip and chop them into silage for the county's abundant cattle.

Since cooperation was my only strategy until he revealed his intentions, I guided him toward the rear of the factory. "Beautiful day. Indian summer's early this year. Hope it stays like this for the funeral."

"Never a nice day for a young person's funeral." The Chief sounded angry.

"Yeah. It was sad. Horrible for the kids. We're doing everything we can for the family but, you know, we gotta keep the business moving if we're gonna help anybody. It's really sad," I said, unable to stop my voice from wavering.

Greer, he's a snoop. Don't show him your feelings. He's not your dupe.

I'm not his dupe, either.

At the rail line behind the plant, six black open-topped rail cars hunkered in a line, waiting to be filled with ground-up soy pulp.

"When I look at these rail cars, they seem like hogs the size of dinosaurs queuing up for feed," I said.

Buhrman grunted.

Beyond the tracks, our five-acre sludge pond filtered the gray water before sending it into the town's sewage disposal system.

"We call it the 'Blue Lagoon,'" I said, my voice firm again. He didn't get the joking old movie reference.

"See those rail cars, Aaron? They're one of my biggest profit centers. See that stainless steel pipe coming out of the side of the building and the yellowish stuff dropping out? That's *okara*, ground soy pulp, the waste from production."

He squatted and picked up a moist clump and sniffed it.

I said, "Crushed soybeans with the soymilk removed. We fill the cars with okara and send them to a ConAgra hog farm a couple of hours downstate. They empty the cars and we get a nice price for it. The profit from okara pays employee Christmas bonuses."

We watched the okara drizzle out of the pipe and disappear like wet tan snow into the rail car.

"Smart, Greer," he said. "Waste not, want not."

Squeezing the clump of soy pulp between his thumb and fingers, Buhrman said, "I always thought soybeans were animal food. My cousin feeds his hogs and cattle soy and corn."

"Yeah, well, the factory hog farm mixes the okara with corn and vitamins and antibiotics, anything else hogs need. Once the okara leaves here, no human touches it again before the hogs chow down. Feed's all mixed together underground and conveyed to the hogs on a continuous belt. It's an infinite swill trough. They call it 'Hog Heaven.'"

Buhrman shook his head. "Never knew where your bacon comes from."

"I thought about investing in hogs, I said. "You only need one man to supervise two thousand hogs. The least labor intensive manufacturing business you can imagine."

The Chief turned away from the rail line and started back toward the front of the factory. "To each his own. I'm not really much interested in livestock. I like my animals in the wild, like deer. You hunt, Charlie?"

"When I was a kid. Not since."

"Been shooting since I was five. Always loved it. Those gun control idiots in Washington never had the pleasure of eating meat they spent all day tracking in the freezing woods." Buhrman raised his hand to his nose and jerked his head, indicating the rear of the plant. "Stinks back there."

"Yeah. Okara decays fast, especially in warm weather.

He raised his eyebrows and wrinkled his forehead. "Like this case. The longer it sits around, the rottener it smells."

***

After walking the loop around the property line, we returned to my office to have our real talk.

"Good tour, Charlie," he said. "I always wondered what went on up here. But, goddam it, my feet're soaked."

Instead of reminding him that he'd refused the boots, I tossed him the towel and a pair of thick cotton socks from my travel kit in the closet. He dried between his toes and pulled on the socks. We wiped off his soggy shoes and flicked drops off the glossy toes with the towel.

"You know I don't want to cause you any trouble," he said bending over his laces.

My heart sank.

"We found some strange things. I have to come up with answers," he said, tying equal and precisely balanced bows that stood out perpendicular to the sides of the shoes. Sitting up and staring at me with his bulging eyes, he said, "I never investigated a murder before."

"Murder!" I said. "Who says it's murder?" Panic lanced my stomach. My thighs clenched and I had to grip the chair to stop myself from leaping up and bouncing around the room.

"Nobody—yet. Some things about the body don't add up to just a little accident."

"Like what?" I said, breathing deep to stifle my fear. Employing one of my sales techniques, I tried to act like his co-investigator so he'd feel I was on his side.

"Cause of death. Bludgeon by a blunt instrument. Coulda drove a chunk of skull right into her brain. As it was, she hemorrhaged."

I thought a minute and said, avoiding the mistake of defensiveness, "That's news. We thought she drowned."

Buhrman grunted. "Not only that. Her stomach was full of tofu. I mean, crammed full. Like someone shoveled it down her throat. Mixed with alcohol, beef, nuts. Big appetite for a little lady."

"Oh," I chuckled, "the tofu in her stomach, that's easy. The first shift sautés up a batch of scrambled tofu. It looks and tastes like scrambled eggs. No cholesterol, though. Did you ever try it?"

I gush about my favorite subjects when I'm nervous, but I caught myself and snapped back to my objective executive posture. "Most of our people take advantage of our free tofu breakfast policy. She probably ate some. Or else she had it at her party the night before." "No way I'll ever try that. I like my eggs real, over easy. Cholesterol doesn't worry me. Not like murder."

Buhrman's melodrama pissed me off. "Aaron, this is not *CSI Miami*. You're looking into small town, small factory industrial accident. I want to help you as much as I can. Please. Don't act like some uptight city cop. We can figure this out. You have my total support."

My tough CEO side, the serious businessman who could see through everybody's act, permitted no silliness. At the same time, he had to see that I was a solid citizen, thoroughly behind the efforts of our town's diligent investigator: him. All the time my nerves tingled and the muscles in my legs twitched.

"Relax, Charlie. So she had too much tofu for breakfast. I hear the stuff gives you gas. Do you think her own farts made her dizzy and she fell on her face?" Buhrman cackled.

Stone-faced, gritting my teeth, I thought, what do you expect from the police in a town named Clement? "Chief, if you don't have anything more serious ... How can I help you now?"

Burhman's eyes darted around the room, taking in the details. He'd never been anywhere decorated with so many exotic statues and fabrics and souvenirs.

He thinks you're weird. Makes him suspicious. You better act calm, normal, and gracious.

"Do I need to call my lawyer?"

"No. Take it easy." He smiled and leaned back, extending his legs and fiddling with a souvenir teacup from my stay in the Miyamasi Hotel in Tokyo. "Just looking for ideas here. We have to examine at every angle. We found a high level of THC and alcohol in her blood. No Ecstasy or crystal meth. I suspected that when I first heard about the death, but no."

I didn't want to discuss drugs, unless I could discover how important they were in his assessment of Becky's death. I knew we had a problem, especially with the immigrant workers and the part-time high school kids, but Becky had told me she never got involved with it. "Yeah. We're all for abstinence," I said.

Buhrman raised his eyebrows.

"Drugs, I mean." He nodded and relaxed his face. "We make our annual donation to the police department's Drug & Alcohol Prevention program. Gotta keep the kids sober. You cops do the best job you can."

He coughed. "Keep everybody sober. Keep your money coming, Charlie. Between you and me? Fighting drugs is a losing battle." "What?"

"Keeps two men I need on the payroll is why the government keeps the program in town. Still, if it stops one kid from getting hooked, it's worth it."

Everyone knew that about Clement's D&AP, but the Chief's disclosure to a business taxpayer about its futility sounded like negotiation. An honest man who wasn't afraid to reveal personal opinions different from the usual ones expected revelations about my reality. That made him a dangerous man to lead an investigation that was bound to implicate me, if he got some breaks. I'd have to get to his supervisor somehow. I gave Bill Murphy on the town council a decent contribution last election. He might help.

Taking the lead, I moved our talk back to Becky. "Scuttlebutt here says she was probably still high from her birthday when she came to work. Drugs and alcohol: main cause of industrial accidents."

"Yeah. If it was an accident."

"Anything else in her blood?"

"Like what?"

I risked self-exposure. "HIV, or something?"

He sat back. "Why?"

"I don't know. Maybe clues about the kind of life she lived?" "What do you want us to do? Check everybody who has HIV in the state and see if she slept with them? But good point. Any lovers of hers are suspect. Do you know who she was, uh, going out with?" I kept my face blank, unblinking.

"Y'know, illicit relations. Screwing." He looked away when he said "screwing" as if embarrassed.

"No idea." I wasn't really worried about HIV because I'd always used a condom, but you never know if you can get it from kissing. I never thought about it when I was with her, our whole affair felt so natural and wholesome—a calling from the goddess of love that nothing bad could touch.

That goddess of love is one scary dame. Lets you feel divine, then drops you into a tank of shame.

Now came my chance to find out what Buhrman knew, if anything, about her and me. The question could backfire. "Did you find anything at her house that gave you any clues?"

He didn't answer for a long minute, his cheeks flat and his eyes cold as he held mine.

"Charlie, I know you're used to being the boss, but this is my investigation. You can help by keeping your nose out of it unless I ask you something."

"Hold it, Aaron. I'm trying to help here." I waited for him to speak but we sat staring at each other for an uncomfortable silent minute so I changed the subject back to drugs. "As long as my workers come to work and produce, I never wanted them to have those mandatory urine tests. Maybe I should start."

"Yeah. They all smoke and drink. We know it. You don't have to test for that. I'm sure you watch out for speed these days. What worries me is the bump on her head. Big as my thumb. Like someone clubbed her."

"Most likely she fell and banged her head on the tank," I said. "They lift sixty pound bushel bags of beans and carry them up the ladder. It's kind of a steep ladder. She lost her balance and slipped."

"Could be." He paused. "It's, well, we have some problems."

I waited.

"Coroner says the woman had been dead at least two hours before they found her."

I'd thought about that and had my answer ready, but held back. Speaking slowly in a puzzled tone, I said "Day crew gets started between two and three. She was the first one on the schedule. She could have come in at two, and been dead in ten minutes. They found her at what? Four?"

"Give or take." He stared at me. "What about her wet clothes." "Wet clothes? You'd have wet clothes if you were laying in a tank of beans that soaked all night in water."

"This is no joke. I mean the clothes in her locker. Had some moss on the seat of her shorts. Mud. Pieces of leaves in the elastic. Twigs."

"Mmm," I mumbled as if considering what he might think it meant. "Must have sat on the ground at her party?"

"Hey, good idea, Charlie. They told me you were sharp. I'll check it out."

Who told him that? I let it go. "Pretty thorough investigation." "Background. You know. Gotta have something to go on before the D. A. gives me the full steam go-ahead. Warrants and such."

District Attorney? This was serious. Buhrman was the type of cop who'd love grandstanding to his higher-ups whether he had anything substantial or not.

Leaning forward and resting his elbows on his knees, Buhrman propped his jaw on thumbs. Speaking through folded fingers, he said , "You know what's got me stumped? Maybe you have another idea here."

I waited for what felt like a full minute. Losing patience, I almost said, You should try out for the new reality TV show. *Big Chiefs*. You have the flair.

He said, "I wonder where she got the skin we found under her fingernails."

"God." I got up. I pace when I'm thinking something out, walk in tight circles if I'm in the office, take a few trips around the neighborhood if I have to think really hard. Buhrman watched me with a thin smile on his face.

"What skin? When did you find that?"

"We had it all along. We'll wait till after the funeral. Respect for the family, it's how we handle this type of thing in Clement. Hold off the formal investigation so people can mourn and have their services without the commotion of a murder."

Besides, I thought, he needed the time to get his ducks in a row. I sensed he was propping me up in his shooting gallery, the big mallard drake whose iridescent green neck begged for the bullet.

"Charlie, this may not be *CSI Miami* but we got the same kinda problems. Y'know, once we find the motive? We're good as found the killer."

"We don't know if it's a murder." He couldn't bully me.

"Explain this." He leaned forward and jutted out his lower lip while he spoke. "She was dead at least two hours. Somebody could have killed her, then dumped her body in the factory. That wasn't soybeans under her nails, unless you tell me your beans bleed."

"Sure," I said, chuckling, trying to lighten him up. "We make 'em bleed. Soymilk, not blood."

"Yeah, well, we gotta check everyone's bodies here. See who's got any strange scratches before they heal. Anybody's got scratches, we'll do a DNA test real quick. Lab downstate handles this kind of thing. Top priority." He studied me through narrowed, triumphant eyes.

"If she didn't try to fight off her killer, scratch the hell out of him, I'll bet my badge! We'll know everything in two, three weeks."

Buhrman found something to make his career. Just make sure it ain't you, Greer.

He was in his late thirties and he obviously thought himself capable of far more than supervising little Clement's Saturday night drunk driving traps and domestic abuse patrols. Just being involved in a murder investigation would sharpen up his résumé and if this happened to be a crime and he happened to solve it, his future was secure. He could go anywhere in the state.

I had to use every ounce of sales skill I'd developed over the years to keep Buhrman under control. "Aaron," I said, casually sitting down beside him, "do you know what you're getting into here? This town has eighty-three jobs riding on American Tofu. Eighty-three jobs that weren't here a few years ago. I'm proud of those jobs."

He nodded and licked his lips.

"Didn't we help your niece out when she got pregnant? Now she's in college! A lot of people start out working in the factory here. We move them up fast as we can." I paused, letting him think, then continued. "I'm glad to help. We both want the same thing. If we have a murderer out there, let's get him. But all you have is a theory. For God's sake, let's keep it calm and quiet until we have something we can prove."

He edged away from me. "No problem, Charlie. It's to all our benefits. But don't bring my family up—"

"It's all our families—"

"It's not about families. It's about murder." His face reddened and he stood up. "Maybe your family's next!" Striding across the office, he stumbled on a crease in the rug I'd brought back from Istanbul.

"You think I'm having fun here? You may be playing around with your barrel of monkeys up here in Tofuland, but you know what? There's plenty of folks in town—taxpayers on the town council who wouldn't mind if your tofu business left Clement." Contempt tinged his voice. "They wouldn't have to pay for the new sewage plant to take care of all the crap you flush out of your slush pond."

"Sludge pond, Aaron. Lagoon! Blue Lagoon." The news about the town council surprised me, though I had a pretty good idea that the council needed someone to blame for the property tax increase they just voted in this year. Not only that, Buhrman probably wanted to buy a new patrol car and the council told him he had to wait.

"So, let me ask you this," Buhrman went on, a tight smile cutting his face. "Will you be the first to let us inspect your skin? I already cleared time with Doc Wallace at the clinic. Whad'ya say?"

"Sure," I fumbled.

Becky scratched me the last time we made love. I remember yelping and jerking as she dug her fingernails into my shoulders.

Sometimes, she played a little rough, growling and biting me and she liked me to pinch her nipples hard. When we first started sleeping together, I had to tell her to back off with the nails on my ass and back. I didn't want marks on my body in case Nora might notice them.

After that, when she started to scratch, she'd ask me if it hurt. But the night before she died, she was wilder than ever. Could traces of my skin have stuck under her nails? If they did, no matter what I'd done to cover my trail, I didn't have a chance.

The Chief shifted in his chair and said, "Well? It won't take long."

As I considered what to tell him, my eyebrows lifted and my shoulders shrugged in innocence. I had to be imagining it but Becky's scratch burned across my shoulder hot as a brand. It should have faded by now. I'd have to check it in the mirror.

Everybody knows a guilty mind can cause physical symptoms and guilt was not on my mental agenda. It was love and if you have to feel guilty about love, you might as well give up your citizenship.

Still, if the doctor mentioned the scratch to the Chief, my reaction would be embarrassment. Nora hadn't touched me all summer, but if the Chief asked me about it, I'd tell him to leave my bedroom out of this.

Stalling, for no good reason, I said, "Why me, Aaron. I was home in bed. Ask my wife."

"Sorry, Charlie. You're the big cheese. Oh, excuse me," he said with a sarcastic downturn to his lips, "the big tofu. You volunteer and everyone else follows. The best motive we've come up with is jealousy or her boyfriend beating her up. Happens all the time."

He was right. That's usually the case.

"We don't know who she was sleeping with yet. Maybe he was trying to shut her up about something. Who knows? I can think of half a dozen reasons. We're checking everybody."

I stood up and walked toward the door, eager to end the interview. "No problem. I'll head over. Have my secretary tell everybody they can get half an hour's pay."

"You don't have to do that."

"Least I can do."

"All right. It's your money." He stopped at the door. "I have to say, Charlie, you were so fired up by this, you're making me wonder a little bit. A man who runs a company and wears a diamond earring and has a cube of tofu tattooed on is arm is just a little bit peculiar and worth checking out, don't you think?"

He smiled as if he were teasing me the way your best friend would kid you when he knew you were fibbing.

I couldn't tell whether Buhrman wanted to intimidate me or not but I already knew he was not the kind of man who joked around. Coming after his sinister comment about dropping the atomic bomb on Japan, his remark about my earring didn't faze me. A Clement, New York, police chief would define conservative in any dictionary.

"What's that scratch on your chin, Charlie? About three days old?" The smile stayed on his face, but his eyes squinted with real interest.

My hand shot to my face to feel the inch-long scab that grew on the underside of my chin.

"Playing with my kids." I spoke too quickly, as if I'd prepared, and I had.

Stammering, I went on, "What? You really think I had something to do with it?" I modulated my outrage, not wanting to alienate him, but making sure he knew he was out of bounds.

"Naw, not yet, anyway. Still, I'm not sure you were nowhere near the factory that night? I heard you work late sometimes, real late."

"Don't mess with me, Aaron. You want a successful business, you work all hours of the day and night."

He smiled again, without sarcasm or any kind of pleasure. "I'm not 'messing up' anybody. It's Investigation 101 here: Everybody who had anything to do with MacDaniel better have a good alibi."

"In that case: I didn't work late that night. Check with my wife. Sound asleep, same bed."

"I'm gonna. Don't worry. We gotta start somewhere. See where she was at that night."

"I told you. Why are you being so aggressive, Aaron?" I raised my voice. "Because my wife and I own the company and you think we're to blame for an accident?"

"Take it easy. All in the day's work. Besides, there's rumors around town about you and women."

"Ridiculous. Rumors don't get far in court. I bet there are plenty of rumors about you and women, too. Any man who's anybody in a small town like this gets gossiped about."

He glared at me and I saw the mistake I made, giving him an opening to distance himself.

"Don't worry, Chief," I said, cooling off my pique and playing it safe, giving his ego the respect it needed to render me a somewhat neutral character in the murder drama he was concocting. "I'll head over to Doc Wallace's right away. I have nothing to hide."

"I'm afraid I have to ask you to get all your employees over to the clinic, right away. It's already been three days too many. We gotta check everybody before their scabs heal up. By the way," he said, flipping his Chief's hat onto his head, his eyes glittering. He tossed out his trump. "Did you know she was pregnant?"

"What?"

"Yeah. Two, three months. Now we have a double murder."

"Double murder?"

"Two people died, that's double. One adult. One child. That's how we think in Clement, anyhow. It's New York law."

Double your trouble. Double his fun.

I stared at him, my stomach rumbling and my lungs beginning to wheeze.

"One more thing. From now on, I gotta ask you to let me know when you or your people go out of town."

"What? Are we all suspects? You don't have any evidence this is anything more than an accident. Somebody's always on the road. I can't be calling you and asking permission to run my business."

"Well, just for courtesy's sake."

"What do you mean?"

"Work with me on this. That's all."

"All right. Aaron," I said, "in the spirit of getting this behind us. I already told you I'd work with you. But you should know I'm leaving the country for a couple of weeks."

"Leaving the country? I don't know. How long you had this planned?"

"Since June. Relax, Aaron. I'm going to Taiwan—business."

"Oh. You go overseas a lot?"

"Not really. This is a big trip. Bought my Taipei tickets last spring."

Buhrman's eyebrows lifted slightly as if he was thinking, 'Hey, maybe Greer set something up here.'

Don't protest. He could guess the rest.

My Jiminy Cricket voice was right. My view of Buhrman's abilities as an interviewer, and my apprehension, climbed inch by inch up my own alertness monitor.

Finally, he said, "Leave me your Taipei number in case I need you."

"I was planning on it. I hope you'll keep me informed of anything you find."

"You'll hear plenty. You know, I never went to China. Wife and I went to Rome a few years ago with the NYCPA. Catholic Policemen's Association? Beautiful city. Loved every minute. Know what I remember best?"

I breathed easier. "Never been there. What?"

"The catacombs."

I shook my head and smiled. "Bones," I said. "You liked the bones."

"You know why? Because that's what it's all about. This life is a bone yard and we're all cemetery keepers."

"That's depressing."

"Maybe. But think about it. I do."

"Yeah, you're right. We all end up the same place but I don't think about it much." He waited and I changed the subject back to our mutual interest. "I'm glad to help however I can," I said. "Let's get this thing done and move on."

He perked up. "Great. One little thing you can do? I'm going to send someone over to pick up copies of your personnel records for the last couple of years. Everybody's file, payroll, that stuff."

"You better get a legal order. Employment files are private and confidential."

"I'll do what I have to do."

I nodded.

"Last thing. We might need other records. Email, bonuses, profits, taxes. That kind of thing."

"You'll definitely need a subpoena or warrant or something. I'm not giving you my private business information just to satisfy your curiosity. Call Harold Fierst at his office if you want to talk to him about anything legal."

"Yeah, well. I'll wait on that. If I need anything, I'm sure Judge Kreppel will pave the way. Meantime, round up your troops and send them over to Wallace. We gotta see who the victim scratched." He grinned at me, his eyes sparkling with excitement. "I'll have a man over at Wallace's. He'll take everybody's prints."

"Prints? Fingerprints?"

Buhrman nodded and pursed his lips.

"Is it legal?"

"Of course. Easier that way. Get all the nuts 'n bolts outta the way in one place."

***

After the Chief left, I walked down the semi-rural street in front of the factory. Locusts were sawing at the old oaks and the air dripped with summer's best effort at dissolving everything into soggy sponges.

I had no idea Becky was pregnant. Did she know she was knocked up before she seduced me that night? If she did, she was playing me for a sucker ... but I don't think so. For one thing, she was too honest, too real with me to hide something like that. She always wanted to use a rubber. That couldn't have been an act, but wouldn't I have seen her body morphing, her breasts and nipples getting bigger, maybe some belly showing.

It's not like I haven't had two kids myself and seen exactly how a woman's body changes. Becky's baby wasn't mine. But what if one of the rubbers had split and we didn't notice. If it did and that baby's mine, I'm screwed.

You're a business guy with skin in the game. You didn't use a skin and it's gonna prove your blame.

That skin under Becky's nails? She had to have washed a dozen times since we made love, done dishes, soaked her fingers while she was at work the day she died. For that matter, while she lay in the tank that night, her hands were under the wet beans a foot below the surface. It was amazing that after all that, Buhrman found something stuck under them.

If it was somebody else's skin—who else? I started wondering if she was fooling around with somebody besides me. No, not possible. Could have been food or dirt—she liked to garden. Maybe playing frisbee or volleyball at her party.

I worried most about the DNA test, but that was only one of Buhrman's attack plans. He would pry into every aspect of my life and my family's and everybody's in the company. I'd stonewall if he had a legitimate idea or lead and if not, I'd continue to cooperate, to keep him off balance.

His threats about forcing me to supply confidential company information gave me a good idea. I went back to the office and called Adam.

Adam had computerized the company a few years back when I hired him as an intern from RPI . He did so much for us that whenever we needed computer help, we brought him in.

The one person you have to trust in business is your computer guy. I trusted Adam. He'd taught me everything I knew about computers and I'd taught him a few things about business. The basic policy we conducted our relationship on was discretion, at all times. What went on between him and me and the computers nobody needed to know, but us, and neither of us asked why.

I asked Adam to meet me at the Wendy's across from Doc Wallace's clinic. I was sure he could teach me to route copies of everybody's internet and intranet emails, searches, downloads, and anything else to my home computer. The last thing I could afford to do with my time was to spy on my employees, but right then, I had to prepare for anything and everything. If I didn't, Charlie Greer and American Tofu could be history. The kind of history you want to forget and can't: the bloody kind.

Chapter Four

Genevieve O'Connor

GEN'S FIVE MEN AND A FUNERAL

Charlie called me at six in the morning the day they found Becky MacDaniel floating in the soybean soaking vat. He mumbled something like he thought it was me and thank God it wasn't but now we had to take care of business. He rambled on until he said, "Call Nora at home. She'll tell you what happened. I'll call you in an hour. We got a lot of work to do today. Thank you, Genevieve. Stay alive. Don't do anything stupid."

What was he was talking about? Becky MacDaniel was a plant worker who I knew slightly. She had a couple of kids in my son Liam's school, and I felt immediately how terrible her death would be to them. The only worse thing than losing your child is losing your parent as a kid. I know. I lost my mother when I was ten.

Nora told me the story of how the morning start-up crew found the body. "Damn Benko," she said. "He called to tell us and first he said it was you. Then we found out it was that poor woman Becky. She must have slipped and hit her head on the tank."

"I barely knew her."

"I half-remember her from the company picnic, but ... what a horrible way to die." Her voice trembled.

"Don't think about it."

"We have to talk." Nora's voice trembled. "Do something for the family, not just flowers. She had two kids. Single mom, y'know."

"Relax, Nora. I'm taking care of it. Meantime, help Charlie relax. He's freaked."

"Like if I wasn't?" she said. "We never dealt with anything like this before."

Before he left for school I told my son, Liam, what happened. "A lot of your friends have parents who work at American Tofu. They'll be upset about the accident."

"Good thing you don't work in the factory," Liam said, two tiny wrinkles crossing his twelve-year old forehead.

"The office is safe, safest place in town, sweetie. People will be talking at school, but don't worry. Call me if you need to, otherwise, we'll talk when I get home. Maybe we'll go out for pizza."

"It's not Friday," he said, protecting our ritual week-ending meal at the Monster Pizza Patch.

"O.K., honey. How about Dori's Dairy Diner?"

"Good idea. I'm gonna have their Fatty Fat Burger."

"No fries if you order that."

"C'mon, Mom. I need the calories for swim team. See you tonight." He gave me a quick hug and ran out the door.

I watched him ride his bike up the street, dreading what I was sure to face in the office: Charlie frazzled, Benko wondering what to do, frightened factory workers, calculating customers whose confidence in us I had to maintain. All the bad publicity could wreck all the work I did to make the company as successful as it is.

Plenty of problems had come my way in the last couple of years, but this one burned in my stomach. We were too close to being totally out of control.

***

At work by eight, I braced for the grueling job of fielding calls from the media and explaining to customers what happened. Almost before I sat down, Benko stepped into my office and locked the door behind him.

"Did you hear?" he said.

"Of course. Charlie called me at six. What do you think I've been doing since then?"

He sighed. "Yeah."

"Charlie told me you found her."

His eyes flashed. "Chen did. I called cops, ran here, called Charlie. I was sound sleeping."

He reeked of sweat and his breath stank of garlic and booze. The odor of his musky sweat usually excited me, but that morning it was sour.

Benko was the handsomest men I'd ever met. Two inches taller than my five eleven, he wore his thick ash-blond hair in a long crew cut. The straight hair flopped sideways on his head, giving his lined face an odd boyish look, a hurt but brave boy. Thin, somewhat narrow shoulders, but enormous hands hung off muscular arms like paws. Long wide fingers sprouted from broad meaty palms. Somewhere in his forties, he probably had a dozen years on my thirty two.

The first time I saw Benko, he gripped a large pipe wrench like a baton. Pale and hairless, the back of his hand was boldly sculpted with bulging veins risen like blue ridges crossing his thick wrist. I watched the hands maneuver the wrench around motors and pumps in the factory, tightening bolts, loosening buckles, testing joints, the heavy wrench slow-dancing with the steel machinery

He spotted me watching, then smiled the warmest, openest smile. "You like my tool?" He waggled the wrench like a magic wand. "Monkey wrench. Makes loose and tight any nut you got." I smiled at his crude flirtation and waved without replying and walked on to pick up tofu samples from the cooler, wondering if his eyes were brown or blue.

I found out a few days later when I stopped in the factory at six o'clock one morning to organize my day's sales presentations. We met in the company kitchen. In a gruff voice, Benko introduced himself

He said he knew who I was and he understood I was the most important person in the company, " ... because, we learned in Russia from Americans. Only with sale, business starts."

Of course, when anyone reminded me that all my hard work meant something besides my rent check and Liam's new shoes, my ego cheered. Now, Benko gave me more than appreciation for my sales work.

Nobody else knew about our late-night dates and I intended to keep it that way. And I didn't like talking to him behind a closed and locked door—too many curious eyes and flapping mouths in the office, even in the emergency of Becky's death. When I reached for the door handle to unlock and open it, he clenched my wrist.

"Ow." I knocked his hand away. "What's the matter with you?"

"Not yet. Lock for now."

"Why?

"Will they come after me?" Benko's eyes narrowed and his fleshy lips pursed. "They will, I know."

Letting the doorknob go I turned to him, putting my hands on his shoulders. "Sit down, Benko. Relax. Why would they come after you? Becky tripped and fell. Charlie thinks she was probably still drunk from last night. Her birthday party. Everyone knows she's a party girl."

He shuddered. "I was there with her, celebrating. They find out and blame me. I gave her Azteca. Expensive tequila. Big bottle. They find some way to lock me in."

"Wait a minute, Benko. This isn't the old days in Russia. We still don't lock people up because they went to a party with someone who accidentally died."

He slumped into a chair, shaking his head. I went to him and held him, caressing his damp forehead

"Baby, take it easy. I'll cover for you. Nobody can come after you just because you're a foreigner. Half the plant is immigrants."

"You wait," he growled and reached around me and pulled my belly to his cheek

His unexpected fear softened my heart as I rubbed his steel-cable shoulders. "Let's go to dinner tonight, just us," I said. "It's good if people see us together now. Colleagues."

He perked up. "You come over after?"

"We'll see," I winked.

He stood at the door, his eyes narrowed and his jaw set. He turned to leave and opened the door, then looked back.

"I got bad feelings. Real bad."

I waited.

"About Charlie."

My mouth dropped. "What?"

"He's in this somehow."

"What? Impossible."

"Don't know, Gen. What you call it, 'Gut pain?'" His hand circled his abdomen. "Down here something I know."

Benko stepped into the hall and stood still. His head and shoulders sagged forward and his long arms hung down nearly to his knees, his prehensile fingers curling. For a moment I thought he might drop to the carpet and keen.

He poised himself, bouncing on his toes. His back to me, he raised his head, jutting his chin, and hulked down the hall, his arms swinging front to back.

I watched him go then closed and locked the door, and went to work.

***

Charlie had hired Benko Gladonov a few months before Becky died. He said that Benko needed a chance to expand his good work record in the States, and he'd worked in a food company overseas as well as in Albany.

"Immigrants usually work for reasonable pay," Charlie told the staff during a management meeting. "We help them launch themselves into the mainstream. It's a win-win." Charlie's altruism always included a business arrangement favorable to him.

That summer I found myself spending several pleasant, diverting evenings with Benko. We walked around the sidewalks of my neighborhood or sat on my porch swing and talked about tofu and business and he told me his life story.

As a suspected Jew in Russia, he endured beatings and ostracism. Benko laughed when he said, "It should be easy. I pull my pants down and show my natural thing, but my father was hygiene man. Expert, so he had me cut." Benko grew up the child of the manager of a large dairy commune so he knew farms and milk processing as his second nature, but, "My heart," he thumped himself on the chest, "is true Russian: heart of rebel, not farmer.

Because he didn't perform to his father's or the commune's standards, he was expelled and joined the army. A fistfight with an officer in the army landed him in prison for six months and kept him out of Afghanistan. He spent his twenties on the streets of Moscow begging and stealing and running errands for whoever would pay him anything, tempted to join a gang

Before glasnost made wealthy entrepreneurs of his criminal cohorts, Benko had fled to London where he parlayed his early experience on the farm into a job in a mincemeat pie factory. He got married and had two children before he divorced

"Should have joined gang in Moscow," he mused one night as we rocked on my porch swing. "I'd be rich man now. Boss. I miss my Brit babies. All time, I think how I fly them to Daddy."

"Why don't you?"

"Mother. Brit bitch. She has court papers. Me? They put me in jail I try to see my babies."

I let the subject of his children slide because I wasn't ready to get serious with any man. Still, Benko's eagerness to be with me was flattering. He acted like an adoring teenager trying to impress a favorite teacher he has a crush on, and I was at least ten years younger than he.

"Those puppy-dog eyes are almost irresistible, Benko. Is that how men flirt in Russia?"

"I never flirt," he said. "In Russia, you feel something, you don't do flirt."

"Here you flirt to have fun. It doesn't mean anything."

"You teach me to flirt," he winked.

"That's good," I grinned and winked back.

I always maintained a policy of no personal involvement with my fellow employees, and I made that clear to Benko the first time we had dinner. He said he agreed with me totally

"Except," he said, "in Russia, passion rules principles. But, this is America. You're my boss, Genevieve. Whatever you say, I will do."

He glanced away then looked up and held my stare. If I wanted him, he was mine.

Benko growled "Genevieve." Four syllables rumbling directly out of his chest siezed my name like one of his wrenches, turning it between his tongue and teeth as if it were a piece of soft metal. Soon enough, we all learned that Benko was a master of torque.

***

I had to call Gianni Giordano, my best customer and my ex-lover. Since we'd broken up a year ago, I'd avoided him, until now.

He still wanted to sleep with me and we were still best friends, as far as he was concerned. From his traditional Italian male position as the head of a long line of patriarchs and successful businessmen, he saw no reason we shouldn't be lovers. I fell for him as hard as he fell for me, but a mistress role with him or anyone was out of the question.

I told his secretary it was an emergency. Gianni didn't need to work, but he showed up every day by dawn at his produce business as he had for twenty-five years.

"Hello, beautiful," he said. "Wait a minute. I have to get off the other line. It's the Pope, but he can call back."

I laughed and held the line.

Nervous but excited to hear his voice, when he came back on the line, I said, "Let's do FaceTime."

In a few seconds, his gorgeous face bloomed onto the phone. He was tanner than usual, and his smile melted my heart. He beamed and waved, mouthing a kiss. My stomach flipped.

"Gianni, I have some bad news."

He sat up. I could only see his chin for a minute.

"Are you all right? What can I do?"

"I'm fine. It's not me. It's about American Tofu."

"It can't be that bad."

"Somebody died. A woman. One of our workers died in the factory."

"I'm sorry." He fell silent. I knew he was considering how the death could affect his business. "Unfortunately people die in factories all the time."

"She had kids, a boy and a girl. Liam knows them."

"I'll send something for the funeral. What about a fund for the kids?"

"We just heard about the death. We haven't thought about anything." Except holding back chaos.

"Charlie?"

"He's a mess."

"Tell him to relax. This happens all the time. I lost a man to a fork lift ... years ago, but ... It's a war wound—if you have employees, sometimes you lose them. It happens to everybody in this business. Where are you?"

"In the office."

"Call me later. If you run into anybody who gives you trouble, tell them American Tofu has one hundred percent support from Giordano. Tell them whatever Genevieve says, it's the truth and that's all there is to it."

"Thanks. That'll help." I would do anything for him, except sleep with him now.

"Good luck. Call whenever. I miss you. I want to see you."

"Maybe when the uproar is over. I'll be in New York some-time in the next couple of months. How about having lunch?"

"That's the best invitation I've had since the last time you took me out."

"Stop it, Gianni." We both laughed. "Right now I have to concentrate on work."

"It's all right," he said. "I miss you that's all. You miss me, too." He wanted me to respond, but the MacDaniel woman's death distracted me, even from Gianni's flirtations.

He went on. "Take care of yourself. You know you can get hold of me anytime you need me."

He never gave up. A dense silence rose between us

After a minute he said, "Genevieve. You know how it is."

"I've got a problem right now, Gianni. It's the only thing on my mind."

His voice softened. "I love you." He raised his eyebrows, smiled, and stretched his arms out toward me.

"I love you, too. Thanks for all your help." I mouthed a kiss and touched End. I stared at the phone, then called Charlie.

"Giordano's not worried and he said you shouldn't either. It happens to every employer. He suggested setting up a fund for Becky's kids."

"God, Gen, that's the first positive thought I've heard all day. Thanks. I'll call the bank and open an account. I'll call Giordano and tell him thanks."

"Good idea, Charlie. I've gotta go now. My customers are already at their desks. If I get through to them now, I can get it over with before the news becomes gossip."

I made and fielded more than fifty calls that day. Custom-ers, friends, Charlie every half hour, *The Clement Observer*, our local paper, Channel 13 out of Rochester, even freakin' *WRUR* public radio.

Jim Keough at the *Observer* had my cell number as a matter of course. I didn't want to, but I had to talk to him, my former boss. As he interviewed me, I cringed. I'd quit his paper one af-

ternoon before I started at American Tofu, when his hand circled around my back and landed on my breast while I worked
at the computer. I immediately deleted his entire weekly color
ad supplement and walked out.

The interview about the death was the first time I'd spoken with him since. I'd enveloped myself with such anger and
distaste for him, that even in this one supermarket town, I'd
evaded him. Now, for the dead woman's sake, and for AT, I acted civil toward him. I told him I didn't know the woman, but I
was shocked and sad, and the company would do everything it
could for her family.

"I don't know any details. Call Charlie." Then my disgust at
him got the best of me.

"Don't call me back you creep if you know what's good for
you." I slammed the phone down. I'd never told anybody about
his roving hand, but the way I felt now, nothing would stop me
if he gave me or AT any bad press.

I called our customers. To a man and the two women, they
were sympathetic and expressed their concern. I told them
about the fund the company had set up to take care of the funeral expenses and to start an education account for the kids.

"That's the kind of thing I like about you, Genevieve," more
than one customer told me. "Always watching out for everyone.
Don't worry. We'll stick with you." I prayed they would, or we
were all finished with tofu.

***

I arrived home late that night, wiped out, to find Liam waiting
up, not happy that I'd canceled our dinner date.

"Mom, I walked into school today and everybody stared at
me like it was you who died."

"You told them I was fine?"

"Yeah. But I had to go to the principal's office. She asked me
if I wanted to take the day off. I said 'Sure' but she changed her
mind when I told her you wouldn't be home."

We talked about how sad everyone was. He knew one of the MacDaniel kids from his soccer league.

"Half the girls in school were crying all day," he said.

"Work is always dangerous, honey. Accidents happen all the time. All we can do now is try to help the family." Too late, I heard how Liam might think I was telling him I could have a bad accident just by being on the job.

He squirmed and his voice quavered. "Is it dangerous where you work? Ashley's dad got hurt at his place and has to sit in a wheelchair now."

I backpedaled to assure him I was always safe, but I wouldn't lie to him. He and I never misled each other.

"My job's the safest one in the company. I'm on the highway or in offices. When I'm in the car, I drive slow. When I'm in the office, I make sure I stay out of the way of people when they rush out the door at five o'clock."

He missed my poor excuse for humor and lay his head back on the couch. I sat next to him, pulled him against me, and lay my head back. We sat, our fingers interlaced, now and then squeezing reassurance to each other, giggling. How I love that boy.

***

At the funeral reception, Charlie played his usual Big Gorilla, strutting around like he was in charge of everybody's mourning, striding down the aisle between Becky's sisters, hugging them against his ribs as tight as he could, agony on his face. He and Nora and their children sat in the front row with Becky's family. Dozens of bouquets drenched the little church with a nauseating fragrance. Charlie had spent at least a thousand dollars on flowers.

I brought my camera to document the funeral for the family. Of all the sad gatherings I'd shot in my ten years of semi-professional photography, none were as gloomy as this.

We shut the factory down for the day and lowered the flag in honor of Becky. All our employees and their families showed up for the service, filling the pews with more worshipers than the church had seen for years.

The minister obviously didn't know Becky any better than I did. He mentioned her 'lively spirit' and 'enthusiasm for life' but he couldn't help moralizing with 'As you reap, so you sow," no doubt referring to her reputation as a party girl. Several heads nodded in agreement with the preacher.

After the service, the friends and family convened at the Grange for the reception. Charlie and Nora had spent another couple of thousand dollars on food and booze for the mourners, most of whom were morose tofu workers and their families. In American Tofu, the multicultural crew somehow formed bonds tighter than many families. Charlie's inclusive nature had something to do with it, the stability of the workforce helped.

Charlie sat at the head table trying to entice Becky's children to talk, but they kept their chins on their chests and barely moved.

After everyone had served themselves from the gourmet buffet I'd cajoled from Wegmans, our top supermarket customer, Charlie stood up. Dinner was a hit: the mourners had cleaned the platter of tofu-stuffed mushrooms with double Parmesan.

"This is the saddest time we can imagine. One of our own, a dear friend and a mother and a beautiful woman, not to mention a great worker and a dear friend."

He stammered and began to cry. I snatched a glimpse of Benko, one of the few in the room with dry eyes. He raised his brushy eyebrows and wiggled them at me and I smiled and looked away, feeling a confusing mix of sadness for Becky's kids and impatience with the whole scene.

You could almost taste pumpkin and cinnamon in the light and my body longed to leave with Benko and make the most of an afternoon off work. The police chief and his wife sat by themselves at a table near the door, watching everything, either keeping themselves at the border of the group so they could see everybody better, or paying their respects as official, but disinterested, town officials.

Charlie sipped something tan. Ginger ale? Whiskey? "The only thing that matters is that she comes back and we know we can't have that ..."

He drank again and I noticed many arms in the audience lifting glasses nearly in unison with Charlie.

"I'm not gonna speak a long time. All of you have a lot to say. Nora and I just want to announce a fund we're gonna start for Jolanda and Jonah. The Becky MacDaniel Children's Education Trust."

People nodded in appreciation. A few started clapping.

"No, no. Wait. We'll get the ball rolling with ten thousand dollars ... and ... Genevieve O'Connor. You all know her?" He pointed at me. "The greatest tofu saleswoman in history."

I wanted to scream at Charlie for his stupid badly-timed flattery, but when I smiled glumly and looked around with my lips turned down, real smiles came back at me from the women, along with flirty smirks from some of the men.

Half a dozen men winked at me. One of the warehouse guys raised his half-full glass, tipped it my way, and downed it, his eyes never leaving my face. I pinched my lips, raised my eyebrows, and shook my head, intending to express my sadness while showing him my appreciation for his salute, but keeping my distance.

Charlie continued. "Genevieve'll convince our customers to donate many more thousands for these beautiful little children here to go to college."

Charlie wavered again and pulled out his handkerchief. The two secretaries who sat beside me offered me tissue too so I could wipe my eyes.

A thunder of nose-blowing rolled through the room with a couple of extended booms. A large woman in her twenties wearing a scarlet and gold running suit blew a long set of tortured bass notes and rolled her head back and wailed.

Her friends leapt up from their seats and surrounded her, hugging her, shushing her but she resisted and howled louder.

Except for her weeping, the room fell silent. The woman moaned the words "Jo-nah" and "Jo-laaaan-da" over and over.

My eyes and everyone else's latched onto Becky's children. They both stared at the mourner with dry, hard eyes until Jolanda ran across the room, folding herself into the sobbing woman who wrapped her arms around the calm child and, shrieking one more time, buried her face in the little girl's neck.

I turned to check on Benko. He slouched in his chair, gazing straight ahead, his hands grasping his glass on the tabletop, ignoring the scene.

Becky's daughter ran back to her seat at the head table near Charlie and snuggled into her aunt's arms and the room came alive with a buzz of conversation.

"One more thing," Charlie said, almost shouting, "we're all pretty upset, but the most important thing for these kids, for our American Tofu family, we have to stick together, take care of each other. Remember. We're a family here."

A few voices called out "Yeah."

"Right, Charlie."

"Family."

Charlie raised both hands. "That's all from me. Now you all say beautiful things you have to say about our sad lost friend. Be good to each other."

Charlie sat down and put his head in his hands. The room went totally silent until someone started clapping again. Charlie's head bobbed up and he clapped back to the audience like a performer.

After a half-hour of speeches by Becky's friends, I said good-bye to the family. They held my arms and hands so tightly, thanking me as if I was going to make everything all right for them now that nothing would be right for a long time. The kids' faces held so much confusion and anger, I had to turn away before tears poured down my cheeks. I tried to smile at them and left the hall, avoiding any employees.

Nora followed me outside. We hugged and held each other for a moment.

"You holding up, Gen?"

"Yeah, all right. Did you see those kids? What will happen to them now?"

"Live with her sister, y'know, till they figure something out."

"You and Charlie are generous," I said, meaning it. They paid the best wages in the area and gave better benefits than any other business in town.

"We can't really afford it right now, but what can we do? Thank you for your help with the fund."

"It was Giordano's idea. I called him again and he gave another five thousand."

"How was that?" she asked, referring to my lingering feelings for Gianni.

"He still wants me. I miss him, but that's a past life. He accepts being my friend."

"Good. He's one of the company's best friends, too," she said. "Thanks to you." Tightening her lips, she went on, "Let me know if you need any help raising money for the kids' fund, all right?"

Nora, the boss's wife. Maybe the real boss, but I respected her. Charlie never faced any problems head-on. He would hint that something bothered him, or make some passive-aggressive remark, if he was upset with me. But Nora always spoke her mind, even if she was flaky as often as she was sharp.

"Thanks," I said. "Gotta go."

"By the way, thanks for taking pictures. I'm sure the family will be grateful."

"Maybe. They may not want these memories, but I'm sure our production staff will. They want to make a memorial."

We hugged good-bye and I drove home to meet Benko for an afternoon rendezvous, before Liam came home from school. We had two hours to play on a perfect afternoon.

Chapter Five

Charlie

THE CHIEF AND
THE EMPEROR

I'm not worried now
I talked with everybody
no one knows a thing

By the night following the medical exams ordered by Buhrman, all but one of our workers and managers had shown up and given fingerprints. Embarrassing scratches showed up on the backs and bottoms of three single women and one married man, but they obviously had nothing to do with Becky.

The scratch on my back had blurred but Buhrman insisted on sampling my DNA along with the others, but if I objected he'd point to my chin and elevate me to the top of his suspect list. The workers and I joked about our "love tattoos" and I think they held me in high regard for being not only a boss but for still having a lively sex life.

"Too bad but, my scratches have nothing to do with sex," I told the group of four as we sat around waiting for instructions.

"Sure, Mr. Greer," Stanley Pucánski said. "Nothing at all." The women tittered.

"I wish it did." I almost leered, getting into the spirit with them. "Well the one on my back, maybe. Twelve years of marriage, still having fun."

Everybody laughed, thrilled to hear such self-revelation from their boss. "The other one? My daughter punched her old man in the chin."

They stopped smiling.

"Wrestling with my kids." Everybody relaxed. "This whole thing's way too sad," I said.

"Wasn't nobody's fault," one of the women said. "The Chief's gone bonkers. It's the stupidest thing I ever heard of." Everyone agreed.

The newspaper came out the next morning with a chronicle of events since the death, steaming with lurid speculation about the flesh under Becky's fingernails and false sorrow about the fetus. The owners published an op-ed piece by one of the local ministers who decried the horrors of violence to the unborn, while ignoring the loss Becky's living children would have to endure.

Photos of our four scratched employees appeared under the caption "Ferocious Lovers Implicated in Death at American Tofu." The caption mentioned that the owner of the company was also examined for cuts and scrapes, but he declined to have his photo taken.

When I read that article and especially when I saw the pictures, I went berserk. I offered to help the workers sue the paper for infamy or libel or anything they wanted, it didn't matter how much it would cost.

None of them wanted to sue. They'd denied that the scratches had anything to do with lovemaking, but after talking it over, they decided they liked being known as "Ferocious Lovers." The photo and the caption appeared in several newspapers around the state.

One of the women searched every publication and web site in the country for signs of the picture. She posted a couple of dozen images from newspapers as far away as Vancouver, British Columbia on the internal company web site, printed them out, and pinned them to the employee bulletin board. Another Google search yielded the same photo in a Japanese business paper. The translated caption read "Tofu Transforms American Workers into Lovers with Appetites Like Man-eating Tigers."

Watching their *Ferocious Lovers* fame expand around the world distracted our employees for a little while from the serious business of Becky's death and the murder investigation. The DNA reports were delayed, but Buhrman cleared all but one of our workers of any connection with the death, though he said new information could change his mind.

As soon as Nora saw the photo and read the caption, she called me, furious that I hadn't told her about the exam and how my scratches had implicated me.

"You know what a DNA test for you means?"

"It's nothing. Protocol. I told you the Chief is riding his high horse. Nobody thinks it was a murder. You know as well as anybody."

"Wake up, Charlie. He's as good as accusing you."

"Of what? Nora, he's playing an intimidation game, is all. I go along with him, show no resistance, he calms down. I've got nothing to hide."

Her voice went flat. "Are you sure?"

"Of course I'm sure. What do you mean by that?"

"Where did you get the scratches?"

"Now you're accusing me?"

"I'm not accusing you. Just, like, where'd you get them?"

"Rissi bopped me on the chin while we were fooling around. Remember, I put them to bed so you could play cards at the club or whatever you do?"

She ignored my sarcasm. "What about the ones on your back?" "Oh, Jesus. Are you getting jealous?"

"I heard you told your workers I scratched you. Your hot little wifey."

"What am I supposed to tell them? I got kinky because my wife's never home?"

"We haven't touched each other for weeks, months. Why lie?"

"For God's sake. I was out in the country bushwacking. You know, I hike into the woods, pretend I'm lost, find my way back. You never want to go with me. Too many bugs."

"Oh. The woods. What happened?"

"I ran into one of those pines with broken low branches sticking out of the trunk. Lucky it jabbed the shoulder and not the eye."

She knows something strange went down. Will she play along? She knows you're no hero. She thinks you're a clown.

We didn't speak for a minute, both of us thinking over the story.

Finally, Nora said, "Whatever. You have to keep me informed about everything. Don't go off on some Charlie Greer crusade on this one. We have too much to lose."

"I'm taking it real easy. I'll let you know whatever happens. Don't worry."

"Way too much at stake, Charlie. The kids, the house. I'm in this with you. She was *our* employee, not just yours, y'know."

"Thanks, sweetie. You're the greatest. We'll let Buhrman play his game and the whole thing will blow over. When it's done, let's take a trip, maybe the Jazz festival in New Orleans like we always dream about. Your mom can stay with the kids—"

"We'll talk about it."

Neither of us spoke for a minute, not sure we wanted to go away with each other.

Nora broke the silence. "Call me before you make any big decisions about the Chief."

I hung up and sagged in my chair wondering whether I could really trust her to be with me, one hundred percent, no matter what happened now. She was my partner, more my business partner and my parenting partner, but no longer my romantic partner, but whatever happened would affect us equally. Except if anyone found out about Becky and me, I could lose everything unless I put it in Nora's name, and soon. Not yet.

For now, I had an employee who died and an ambitious cop trying to make something of a factory accident, and that's all anyone needed to know.

At least now Nora and I had the story about my scratches straight between us.

***

The one employee who didn't pass Buhrman's scrutiny was Chen, the Chinese tofu specialist. He became the main suspect by default—he disappeared two days after Becky died without letting his body be examined or giving fingerprints.

A huge sense of relief settled into the factory when Chen became Buhrman's suspect, even though most of the workers thought Becky had slipped because she was probably high. Buhrman continued his investigation by probing into every-body's private lives, even the semi-retired women who did nothing but the laundry two hours every night. Everybody started acting nervous. I'd walk through the factory and notice no smiles, everyone head-down, grim-mouthed, making tofu.

I called Benko into my office to learn what I could about Buhrman's interrogations.

"What's he asking our people? He may be stepping on our people's rights. Cops always think they can get away with that."

"Yeah. He don't ask much," Benko said. "Where we were. Did we know her. He asks all the men if they ever 'had relations' with her."

"Did anybody?" I'd heard rumors that she was a party girl, but I really doubted them. Becky liked to drink and dance, but she wasn't the type to sleep around.

"No. Nobody admitted it. The Chief's wants her boy-friend— he's prime suspect. More than Chen, I think. Lucky for her ex." "What do you mean?"

"Her last guy. Moved. Cleveland. Works nights at IBM. Good alibi."

"Anybody say anything that got the Chief's attention?" Even though he promised to keep me informed, Buhrman would never tell me the results of the interviews.

"Who knows? One thing, boss? Hate to say. He asked the women if Becky ever said anything about you. Positive. Negative. Anything."

I cleared my throat and sipped some Pelegrino. I kept a case of the water in my office while I tried to get off coffee. Didn't work but I liked the light bubbly feeling in my throat. I raised my eyebrows.

He said, "They all told him she liked you."

"Shit. I mean, of course she liked me. Everyone likes me."

"Take it easy, boss. That's right. They all like you, 'specially the women. Nice fizzy you drink."

"Did they tell Buhrman that?" I felt like a guilty politician for a minute, checking my poll ratings to see how far I could go before I lost ground with my people.

"Yeah."

I told Benko thanks and gave him a liter of Pelegrino to take back to his office. He'd told me a few things. Buhrman suspected me of some connection, but my employees—definitely the women would back me up.

Oddly, during Buhrman's inquiry, our factory productivity climbed like it never had. Waste material declined and our pounds produced per hour skyrocketed. I guess the workers tried harder than ever to be good for fear of becoming suspects or scapegoats of gossip.

My secretary buzzed my line and I answered the Chief's daily call.

"Greer, you've got to help turn the Chink up. He's gotta be the one. Why else would he disappear?"

"He might be," I said. "Chen worked here for a year and we never had any trouble from him, but it does seem strange." If Buhrman wanted a murder, Chen was the perfect suspect as far as I was concerned, especially since he'd be impossible to find. "Chinese workers come and go all the time. They circulate in and out of New York on something like an underground rail-road."

"They have papers?"

"Sure, they're all legal. I mean they have some kind of shuttle. They work here, on farms, restaurants all over the state. Chen came on recommendation of a customer of mine. Maybe you should call some Chinese cops."

"I did already. They've put the word on the street in New York. Soon as he gets a paycheck, we'll grab him. I've got his social security tagged. By the way, we're checking your employee records. I hope everything's ship-shape."

The Chief's tough guy act wore on me but I had to put up with it. My lawyer told me to keep notes of everything Buhrman said or did in case any real trouble showed up.

Maybe I could catch him in a good old-fashioned procedural mistake.

The Chief's no screw-up. He's a crime engineer, making sure every angle trues up.

***

Making tofu is a hot, wet, messy business. Workers wear tall rubber boots, rubber aprons, rubber gloves, and ear plugs. Water flows constantly across the floor, steam pours out of kettles and coagulators sometimes rendering the production room into a tropical fog, while grinding and banging noises fill the air with a rolling thunder.

Despite the fact we paid wages twenty percent higher than other businesses in the whole of Upstate New York, we had trouble finding and keeping good production workers.

Chen had been the eighth or ninth tofu worker I'd hired on the recommendation of Chang Meng, the owner of Meng Produce, our second largest customer, and one of my mentors in business. All the workers were excellent, though they usually didn't stay in Clement for more than a few months.

Meng was one of the most powerful men in the New York produce market. At the office, we referred to him as "The Emperor of Hunts Point." He was more than a customer: He was an elder who planned to take me to Taiwan and who treated me like a relative; I knew his daughter very well; most importantly, he'd implied in his ambiguous way that he wanted to buy American Tofu, should I ever want to sell. I couldn't afford to jeopardize my relationship with Meng.

Each of the Chinese tofu-makers Meng sent me had been meticulous and hard-working and obedient. I liked them on the cleanup crew because they had a natural bent for sanitation. They never dirtied their uniforms. They seemed to float through the night-long soap and scalding water routine like albino ducks.

I gave Meng a call.

"Charlie, I don't know where he is. He could be in LA or Mexico City by now. I'll try to find out. Don't expect much. These guys have an underground railroad that I don't get involved in."

This was a real underground railroad, shifting illegals from city to city, state to state, no doubt for a percentage of their pay.

The next day, Meng called me with bad news about Chen. "We think he's in San Francisco already."

I felt the first relief I'd felt in weeks. We had a live suspect to engage the Chief.

"You'll never get him back," Meng said. "First, he's an illegal. He had all the right papers, but his name is not Chen. Nobody knows what it is. I'm sure he has a different name and new papers now."

"If you could find him, why can't the police?" I asked. "They'll have their contacts, too, won't they?"

"I found his trail, not him. If he wants to disappear," Meng pointed out, "it's the easiest thing in the world. See it from his point of view—he's an illegal. Doesn't speak English. Those farmers up where you live would love to hang a Chinaman. All the good jobs in the country are moving overseas—godless Chinks are easy to blame."

"Wait a minute, Meng," I said. "There's justice in the courts. He'd get a fair trial."

"Charlie, whether he killed the woman or not, you're on a wild goose chase. If you get too close, they just fly up into the sky and become stars." Meng's chuckle came through the phone like a cough. He was referring to my favorite Chinese fairy tale, the one my kids had memorized.

***

A few hours after I spoke with Meng, Buhrman showed up. If he didn't call, he'd taken to dropping by unannounced almost every day.

"Guess what?" he said, beaming a satisfied smile. "Chen's looking like our boy more and more. Did you check his papers real careful when you hired him?"

"We followed the legal procedure to the T," I said. "We're a professional company, Aaron. Maybe you think we make a strange product, but we have bank loans, a government con-tract. We pay as well as anybody in town. We do it right."

"Bet you do," he said, ignoring me. "Chen used false papers. Hsi Shin Chen of Long Island City, New York, is not the Chen you had in your factory. The deceased Mr. H. S. Chen ran a fu-neral home. Your boy stole his name and social security num-ber." The Chief brayed out the information like a hound snap-ping at the heels of his prey.

If Chen's illegal, Chief's caught you in a little crime. He's building his case on you, thinks it's just a matter of time.

I played dumb. His information sounded solid, but the ca-sual assertion that I knew Chen was an illegal let me know that Buhrman wanted to involve me. "How was I supposed to know his social security number is false?" I asked. "He showed us his card, we took his photo ID, he signed the papers. You can leave us out of this, Chief. Go find Chen if you think he did it."

"I'm doing everything I can. But why would he kill her? You have a reputation for getting to know your workers. What do you know about him?"

"I'm too busy to know everybody."

"Don't hide anything now. What about the dead woman. Mac-Daniel. You know her very well?"

He surprised me by the abrupt turn from talking about Chen. Where was he headed? I kept the conversation flowing, concealing my discomfort and playing along. "If they stay long enough, I talk to them at lunch or at our parties. She was a good worker. Talk to Gladonov if you want to know more."

"Every time I talk to him, I almost have to have a translator. These Russkies. Smart? Don't know right from wrong? Don't care either. Power hungry ex-commies. If I was you? I wouldn't trust him farther than you can throw a soybean." He laughed at his joke and clapped me on the shoulder.

"He's the best production manager I've had."

The Chief watched me through his laugh-wrinkles, expecting me to defend Benko's heritage so we could have an argument that I'd end up losing. I had to stop the Chief's immigrant-baiting. "As far as I can tell, he's honest and hard-working. Comes in all hours if we have a machine problem."

"Yeah. He might be the exception." The Chief blinked as if he had something in his eye, then shrugged. "I have to go down to Hunts Point tomorrow. Visit your Chink distributor. Maybe see Giordano, too." He sneered and stood up. "Good Italian company. Connected?"

If he thought he could force me to lose my temper and reveal something, I was not that dense. Giordano Brothers was our largest customer by far, a fifth-generation family-owned company. I had no idea if they were connected to the Mafia. I doubted it. Everything about them was far too elegant, especially Giordano himself. When did a Mafia don ever graduate from Princeton with an MBA from Harvard?

Maybe Buhrman thought old-fashioned orneriness went along with the hassle of a small-town murder investigation. Without replying to his insinuation about the ethics of my customers, I rose and came around from behind my desk to escort him out.

"You got yourself sleeping with some strange bedfellows, Greer," he said. "Makes you wonder how you keep the riffraff out of Clem when you can't even trust your employers. Not that I don't trust you, understand. I'm going over to immigration when I'm in the city. Maybe the FBI."

The FBI? They can make a happy man cry.

Panic surged in my chest. "Why get the FBI into this? I heard they're a bunch of clutzes when it comes to small town stuff. Fat Bureaucracy of Idiots."

Ignoring my sarcasm, he said, "Can't help it. Things're moving fast. Maybe some drug connection here. Chinese Mafia. Italian. Crossing state lines. Double murder. Everything. It's a big mess. Do you think I like spending my time this way?"

Buhrman grinned like a teenage boy who couldn't help bragging to his pals about last night's conquest in the back seat of his father's car.

I changed the subject. "By the way, Aaron. Whatever happened with the DNA analysis?"

He stared at me for a minute before he replied. "Had some problems with the equipment. Unreliable high tech stuff. DNA's fragile, y'know. Can't take heat, can't take too much pressure, but we'll get it. Moved it over to Cornell where they handle the big cases. I'll let you know, when we get something concrete. We'll find out whose baby it was."

"That'd be a good clue."

"That'd be the whole story, Greer." Burhman put his Chief's cap on and looked at the floor, thinking. My full-specturm fluorescent ceiling light glinted off the shiny ebony of the bill.

"Didn't you go to Loyola University?" he asked.

"Yeah. In Chicago."

"Know where the FBI gets most of its agents?"

"Where."

"Good Catholic schools in the Midwest. Notre Dame. Loyola. Hey, you might even get to see some of your own classmates when they come to town."

I laughed. "It's all about right and wrong."

***

As soon as Buhrman left, I called Meng, as a friend, to warn him. Even though Giordano Brothers was my biggest customer, I never felt as comfortable with Gianni Giordano as I did with Meng, especially since I never paid much attention to Giordano until Genevieve joined the company. She accepted my challenge and built his sales up from almost nothing to the cash cow that drives our profits.

With Meng's recent overtures about buying the company and our upcoming Taiwan trip, he'd become more than my business ally. He even sent his daughter, Shu Ling, to make an industrial film with American Tofu and me in the starring roles—we were nearly family.

Meng wanted our whole New York market, all of Giordano's business as well as the Asian part he handled and I didn't blame him, but I couldn't allow that unless he bought the whole company.

I treated him like a respected uncle without whose business my company would lose thirty percent of its sales and most of our profits. I had a dozen good reasons to warn him about Buhrman. Not only that, I had a moral obligation to call him.

"Ridiculous," Meng said. "I don't have time to waste with a petty investigation. You don't want him digging too deep here, anyway. Shu Ling wouldn't like it either."

Shu Ling? Did Meng know about me and his daughter? She'd promised he'd never find out about our slightly more than Platonic dalliance. We were always discreet, but he could know something. I had nothing to hide from him about her, except my lus,t and since when was unconsummated desire for a stunning woman unusual? Just because it was his daughter I was supposed to shut off my appreciation of female beauty?

I kept my mouth shut about Shu Ling. If I lied and denied a relationship with her, he'd lose respect for me, respect I'd worked hard to gain. If I admitted to anything other than business, Meng might have to forbid me to see her. American Tofu would be the loser.

We were in a fragile position. If I was him, right now with all the ruckus around the death, I would find another source of tofu, for a back-up supply. A simpler one, one he could control, or one he could use to control me.

Becky's death had given the Canadian company that had snapped at our heels for months a wide open door to our market. The only way I knew to keep the customers in our fold was to suck up to them ten times more than we already did. "Nurture the relationships," something Genevieve was a master of.

"I'll do what I can," I told Meng, pointedly not responding to his mention of Shu Ling.

Dealing with Buhrman had primed me for handling other interrogators. "Don't take Buhrman too seriously. American Tofu's personnel records are in perfect condition. T's crossed, i's dotted, every capital letter capitalized. The Chief has to huff and puff to show he's on the case. It'll blow over," I said. "By the way. How is Shu Ling's film coming along?"

"You know better than I do, Charlie," he said, sounding exasperated. "Let's hope your Chief backs off soon. Chinese companies don't operate the same as Americans. He may have a little trouble understanding that."

"He's country, but he works hard." Why was I defending Buhrman to the most important man in American Tofu's, and by obvious extension, my life?

"I don't have to tell you Meng Produce doesn't enjoy annoyances like these."

With that phone call, my relationship with Meng became way too complicated. About two months before, his daughter and I cooled a strange non-affair that, the more I thought about it, the more I believed that Meng probably knew about. Worse, I had to assume, he may even have orchestrated it.

Meng had introduced Shu Ling to me, suggested that he'd help finance her film about the tofu business in the United

States, and he'd arranged for its distribution in the Orient if I allowed her to shoot some footage in my factory.

Selling me on the idea, he said, "Good for everybody's business, Charlie. More people know about you and tofu, the more sell." Reflecting on that, I realized he tried too hard to sell me on something obvious and that made me nervous.

Shu Ling flew into Clement last spring like the Chinese princess she was, and I fell for her as soon as she walked in my office door. She was about the same height as her father, about a foot shorter than me, but her gleaming black cowboy boots made her feel tall and graceful as a ballerina. She astonished me with her ebony eyes and her red suede jacket and deerskin pants.

Her round face loomed out of a thin, ebony halo of hair that seemed to lengthen her neck and lift her head slightly off her trim body. A long French braid pulled her hair back and emphasized her wide cheeks and broad chin. A tiny ruby nose stud told me that she was a totally modern American woman, independent from her family tradition.

The first thing I said after "Pleased to meet you" was something like "Hey, your nose stud matches the one in my ear." I heard myself speaking idiocy and knew I was lost.

She came to make a film for her class at NYU grad school and I thought I was supposed to be the star with star privileges but she wouldn't let me touch her. She flirted continuously, we went skinny dipping a couple times, she even stayed overnight at my house one night when Nora was home. But we never came closer than light hugs hello or good-bye, yet my entire body ached and hummed with desire for her.

My paranoid analysis of Meng's purpose in introducing Shu Ling to me: He wanted to own my business some day and get his hands on the millions of tofu dollars that flowed through my bank account every year. Meng knew I was married, not totally happy, but married. Still, he could possibly get me as a son-in-law, if certain things went his way. If I was him, and wanted to

acquire a major piece of business, I'd have a few different strategies in place.

It all fit, too well. I expected our trip to Taiwan to reveal all,
or at least the essence of his plan. Until then, I had to keep the
Chief out of Meng's way.

***

Harold Fierst, my company attorney, had the reputation as the
toughest business attorney in central upstate. He'd never lost
a major case against the IRS or any state agency, and he had
deep influence in Albany. His brother owned a New York City
investment banking firm specializing in oddball but legitimate
initial public offerings. If we stayed on our growth curve, they'd
take our company public in five years and I'd never have to
work again.

Harold had always taken care of not only our legal filings
and contracts, but he made policy recommendations and over-
saw our risk coverage. Next to me and Genevieve, he brought
home American Tofu's biggest checks, worth every penny. The
day after Becky died, he'd sent a man to interview all the employees about her and to take photographs of the accident site
and the surroundings.

In his office a few days later, he advised, "Prudence, Charlie.
We make a case of the MacDaniel woman as a careless worker,
somebody who partied big the night before, a known drinker
and pot smoker and who knows what heavy drugs. Didn't they
bust a crystal meth lab out your way last year?"

"That was a down by the Finger Lakes, Harold. Long way
from Clement."

"Close enough. Hell, we can almost prove she was so stoned
out of her mind that she dived into that tank of beans just to
enjoy the experience!"

He laughed but he didn't smile when he saw the disapproving scowl on my face. He cleared his throat.

"Sad business, but we gotta protect the company. I've seen
ten million dollar settlements on less harmful industrial acci-

dents. Somebody lost his big toe, for Christ's sake. Ten million bucks, the jury award."

I must have looked stunned because he followed with, "Don't worry. We appealed and got it down to four."

"Christ, Harold. Let's make sure all our i's are dotted, you know. Do what's right, what we have to."

"We got it covered, don't worry." He steepled his fingers, resting his chin on his thumbs.

"Do her kids get anything?" This was one of the main reasons I'd driven all the way to his office for a confidential, unrecorded talk.

"This is where you're brilliant, Mr. Greer," he said, sitting up straight in the cracked leather chair he'd inherited from his grandfather. "Remember those term life policies on your staff I suggested and you said, go for it?"

"Yeah? That was a good idea. We have terrific benefits."

"Her kids will get $50,000 each and the company gets $100,000 to cover legal and other expenses."

"Great news, Harold. I'd never have remembered that." The truth was, the memory of that policy had come to me like the breath of an angel. Due to the nature of the accident, the insurance company would pay out and everyone would see how much we cared for our employees. Any possible suspicion would slide away from me. The insurance payouts would also take care of Harold as he stymied any lawsuits Becky's relatives might feel tempted to file.

"We'll make sure the news gets out about what a caring and responsible employer AT is," he said.

That's you, Chuck. So caring, especially when it's your body you're sharing.

"That's true as you're the most expensive firm in Syracuse." I grinned at him. "Just for the heck of it, Harold, what will your fees be in this case?"

He steepled his fingers again, tensed them, and leaned forward. "I think you have enough. Unless we get into a protracted court case. I know you don't want that."

"Let's get this done."

"She was a drunk and a druggie and an incompetent mother. She partied when she had to go to work in two hours. No jury would award a penny to the family, especially since the company has always taken care of its own."

I cringed, acid crept up into my throat. He portrayed one of the sweetest women I'd ever known as some low-life bitch, and he'd never met her. She liked to party, but she always took care of her kids first. As far as I knew, anyway.

"One little collateral thing." He leaned back in his chair. "You'll have a premium increase but hey ... your umbrella policy covers you for most contingencies."

"Let's do what we have to do." I was in no mood to worry about a premium increase no matter how big. "By the way," I said, getting to the real purpose of my visit, "what did the District Attorney say about Buhrman's investigation?"

"Well, John's a friend, you know, and I can't ask for too many favors."

"I don't want any favors, Harold. Just fair treatment. We don't have a murder here. We have an industrial accident and a berserk cop who's trying to make a name for himself!" I stood up and started my patented pacing. "On my back!"

"Take it easy, Charlie. Sit down."

"I can't."

"John's not gonna give Buhrman any more resources. He thinks the case doesn't have enough merit."

"All right." The first good news I'd had.

"But he won't pull him off the investigation."

"Outrageous. Why not?"

Fierst sat back, smiling at me like I was a naive kid. "Buhrman's got a good reputation and John likes to give the nose to his up-and-comers. Remember that schoolteacher kiddie porn bust a few years back? John says if it wasn't for Buhrman, if he hadn't stuck with it when everyone else was ready to hang it up, they'd never have found the main guy behind it—that scumbag preacher in Troy."

"What's that have to do with anything? Buhrman's out there fucking with my business, calling in the FBI, harassing my customers. That's gotta stop."

"Take it easy, Charlie. Here's how it lays: If Buhrman makes a fool of himself, you're the good guy. The long-suffering employer who goes all out to do everything possible for the family of the deceased. Besides, Buhrman's doing all the work for us if it ever comes to trial." He leaned forward, his hands flat on his desk like a pastor issuing dogma. "Buhrman's got a future, and he knows it. He's not gonna go out on any limbs that could short-circuit his path up. Calm down, Charlie. You're taking this guy way too seriously."

Buhrman's finding the 'main guy behind it all' scared me more than anything. I knew he was stubborn and clever, in his fake-Columbo way, and he was building his reputation on obstinacy, the one thing I feared most. As long as Buhrman kept beating the bushes, you never know who would show up or what could trap me. That's how you get results in business or anywhere: keep knocking on doors.

Fierst broke into my thoughts "You pay me for advice, right?" I nodded.

"I don't give it unless I think you need it, you know that." I nodded again.

"You're a problem-solver, Charlie, but don't turn this into a problem. Be neutral, concerned, but don't get involved. See no evil, hear no evil, say no evil. Be a good guy and Buhrman will back off pretty soon."

I left Fierst's office more vulnerable to Buhrman than when I thought he was just a bumbling, ambitious cop building his ego and his exit strategy from Clement. My life, my marriage, my business had become as wobbly as cubes of tofu floating in a bowl of hot and sour soup.

Chapter Six

Charlie

THE ART OF "MONKEY LOVE"

even if it's the only way
you can love me,
whisper me a dream

News of Becky's pregnancy drove my mind out of my body. I walked around in a constant state of hyperventilation. If my DNA matched the baby's, so long Charlie Greer. It wouldn't prove murder, or even manslaughter, but it would prove the end of everything. Even Clinton wouldn't have survived if Monica had died for any reason.

We'd only slept together a half a dozen times or so and the baby couldn't have been mine. I always used a condom, except maybe the first time, and I'm sure I did, too, even if I can't remember. I remember talking about AIDS, so I'm sure I used a rubber. Her old boyfriend must have knocked her up before they split.

Anyway, the timing was off for me to be the father, close, but Becky and I didn't start our affair until the end of June, after Shu Ling made it clear she'd never be my lover. When Becky came along, I found the perfect stand-in for Shu Ling and the necessary release valve for my horniness.

I really don't know how this whole thing could happen to me. When I puzzle it out, I want someone to blame: First, Nora, for shutting me out, then Meng, for setting me up with Shu Ling who heated me up to volcanic melt so when somebody like Becky showed up, somebody who shouldn't have started fooling around with her boss, I lost it.

The real cause of it all? Me, myself, I, the bumbling stud who let my craving for love—face it—for sex, turn me into an ape in a tree, my tail dangling, feeling for any branch to swing on or crotch to land on—if only Shu Ling had not been such a tease.

***

What started as a once-in-a-lifetime opportunity—having my company publicized all across American and Asia—ended up with me in love with the film-maker daughter of my favorite customer, in an obsessive lust that led me to make the stupidest decision of my life.

By the time Shu Ling finished shooting the footage she needed for her segment on American Tofu, testosterone ran my show. Any reasonable person, even me in my lucid moments, would tell me to grow up and keep my barn door closed, but sometimes, one thing builds on another and events take on a life of their own.

First, one humid spring night in Albany, Genevieve charged me up with about 400 amps of lust. The night she told me about her failed affair with Giordano was the night I almost wrecked my entire relationship with her. She probably would have left the company and taken half our customers with her if I'd insisted on getting what my little brain wanted.

That started when I challenged her to a tofu-selling contest. For five years, I'd been the greatest tofu salesman in America, I'm sure, because AT grew faster than any other tofu company, and not because we had the most capital behind us. I beat the bushes, cut deals, came up with half-brained marketing schemes that, with luck, worked. I spent thousands on tickets and dinners for my customers and their wives while I built AT's solid foundation of customers.

I tried not to show it, but I felt proud I'd created a company, but more. Before AT, people thought tofu was an esoteric inedible thing that came out of roach-ridden basement factories in Chinatown, probably made by serfs. My goal was to change all that, and change it I did.

Genevieve had early sales successes and I wanted her to become better than me—so I could take a break. I concocted a scheme: I told her if she sold more than me in a year, I'd send her on a trip anywhere she wanted to go. She agreed, on the condition that whoever lost had to do ten housekeeping chores for the other. Typical female humor, but my office always needed cleaning.

At the end of the year, she'd torched me, outsold me by fifty percent and the company made more money than I'd dreamed of. I suspected she did it by inviting Gianni Giordano into her bed in exchange for his becoming our biggest customer. She claimed they fell in love and the sales jump had nothing to do with their relationship, but I can't believe that. The guy's gonna return the favor, unless he's a cold bastard.

So, one night last spring, on an after-dinner stroll along the swollen river in Cleveland, she told me about their affair and their break-up. I half-expected the purpose of her revealing her affair was that she wanted me to replace him somehow.

Stupid as a teenager after two beers, I came on to her in the hotel room. She kissed me and let me graze her fully-clothed breast, but once I got serious, she shot me down. Later, she admitted that she encouraged me, 'allowed me,' she said, out of loneliness.

"I need comfort, Charlie," she said. "Not sex. Besides, what about Nora?"

"Nora and I don't sleep together any more," I said.

"You don't?"

"Twelve years of the same old person, I guess. Let's not go into it. I'm sorry about tonight."

"Forget it, Charlie."

I'm glad she stopped me. Nora's never yet questioned my relationship with Genevieve, so I counted on Genevieve to keep quiet. What would she have to gain by talking anyway? Still, from that watershed night on, my sexual longings sprouted like a field of dandelions just waiting for somebody like Shu Ling to meander by and pick them.

From the first day I met the Chinese woman, she teased me incessantly, calling me 'my Nobleman from the North Country,' insisting I treat the 'Peach Blossom Princess' like a 'tender bloom,' but she wouldn't let me close enough to show her how sensitive my fingers could be.

My infatuation with film stardom vanished to make room for my lust for her. On impulse, a few days into filming, while we sipped coffee after lunch, I said, "Shu Ling, I want to be your lover."

Her anthracite eyes bored into mine and she didn't smile. "My lover or just make love to me?"

That confused me. "Why not both?"

"I have a lover, Charlie. I don't need two."

I blurted out "I have a wife, I don't need two."

"You didn't ask me to marry you, did you?"

"You make me crazy. Nobody's ever twisted me up like this."

Shu Ling reached over and lay her cool fingers on the back of my hand, circling her nails in the hairs, sending shivers up my arm and over my shoulder into my skull and out the top of my scalp. I jumped an inch off my chair.

"Charlie, I like you a lot. We have chemistry, but wait a while. When the time comes, the film's done, we know each other a little better—I can teach you some special ways of being with a woman."

My boldness almost always worked. "What do you mean?"

"Ancient Chinese love teaching. *The Art of Monkey Love.* I'm no Adept, but I know enough."

I laughed. Things were moving my way. "Monkey love? I thought all monkeys did was play with themselves for the tourists at the zoo?"

She removed her fingers from my hand.

"I get it. This is the Year of the Monkey and it's something the Chinese do to celebrate?"

Shu Ling shook her head no, taking my question seriously.

My mind spun out, like it always does when I'm nervous, clowning around. "Do you have a different art for every year? After we do the 'Monkey,' can we go for the 'Dragon.' That's gotta be hot and heavenly."

"What are you talking about?"

"Just wondering if this art of love is why China has so many people?"

"I don't think so, Charlie. You know what? You're not ready."

Shu Ling stiffened her shoulders. "I shouldn't have brought it up." "What? I'm sorry. What did I do? I was just joking around." "You're näive, Charlie, but I'm not upset. You wait and maybe, if we still like each other—"

"We'll like each other."

Shu Ling slid her chair back and came around the table, holding her tiny hand out, summoning me up. Taking it in both of mine, I drew myself close to her, inhaling her compelling fragrance, a heady mix of gardenia and spicy incense.

"Patience, Charlie. Waiting is the number one Taoist virtue." She laughed and let my hand drop and turned toward the exit. "Let's go back to work."

I believed she'd follow through with her promise so I had no choice but to enjoy the delay. I'd call it subtle lingering foreplay.

"No problem, Shu Ling. I get it. The first step in Monkey Love is called 'Filling the Reservoir.'"

She laughed and slapped my arm. "Not really, but if that works for you."

"It's rising fast. I'll let you know when we have to open the sluice."

The regular and only lightning rod for my sexual charge for all these years of marriage was Nora, and I'd done a damn good job of repressing my natural longings for other women. But lately her moods had become so changeable and our lovemaking, as mind-blowing as it sometimes was, happened so erratically I couldn't depend on her at all that summer. Now, my infatuation with Shu Ling prevented me from courting Nora the way I should have, if I really wanted her as badly as I claimed in our couples therapy.

Shu Ling and I talked on the phone daily the two weeks after her first visit. We talked so often that I began to feel closer to her in some ways than I was to Nora. But she let my lust rage unrequited, until too late, she gave me some hope of respite. By then, my patience worn thin, my reservoir overflowing and threatening to flood the whole valley, I started monkeying around with Becky.

***

My folly with Becky started the night after our annual American Tofu summer solstice party. I'd name the party after whatever Chinese Year we were in. This year, I invited the AT employees to come out to the park for an afternoon to "Monkey Around with Tofu."

We passed an afternoon at the local state park swimming, playing softball and Frisbee, eating endless forms of tofu salads and hot dogs, cakes and cookies. I'd ordered special desserts from our local ice cream shop: tofu ice cream banana splits drizzled with hot fudge and salted peanuts. We called them "Monkey Tails." The crew polished off the keg of beer and, at sunset, they migrated to the office manager's house for dancing and more drinking.

Nora went home with the kids, but I felt it was my duty as owner to continue sharing the fun with my employees. I'd paced my drinking so, at midnight, when the party dissolved, I volunteered to be a designated driver. Four inebriated workers, led by Becky MacDaniel, staggered to my car. I dropped the other three off first.

Becky had partly sobered up by the time we arrived at her yard. She invited me in for a nightcap and I accepted, sober and feeling the good feeling you get as leader of a clan that knows how to party together.

She offered me some hashish she'd just received from her cousin in Montreal. I didn't want to appear stodgy, so, following my policy of appreciating one's employees and in the entre-preneurial spirit of venturing into unexplored territories where you never knew what opportunities you'd find, I accepted.

She was a cute redhead, a little wide in the hips, but hard-working and cheerful. Sweet. She was one of the women I'd no-ticed and cultivated a collegial relationship with, in hopes that she'd seek a promotion inside the company. Keeping employees was much cheaper and better for the long-term morale than al-ways hiring new people.

Still, I hesitated. "You can't get addicted to this, can you?"

"C'mon, Charlie, it's hash. Everybody knows it's medicine. Good for you. I wouldn't touch ice or crack. Nothing hard." She glanced at my lap when she said this and Mr. Jones got the sig-nal to stand up and wave, but I crossed my legs. Still, her husky voice lured me, as if she knew about things I didn't, things I needed to learn.

She'll teach you how to play. But how much d'you wanna pay?

"I've never even smoked cigarettes," I said.

"Hash's smoother than cigarettes, if you take it easy." She inhaled from a polished wooden tube with a dull black bowl on the end. "Your turn."

'Your turn.' You wanna burn?

I accepted the pipe and sipped sweet smoke, letting it roll over my tongue and down my throat.

Becky coughed a cloud of smoke into my face and doubled over, laughing. "Don't be a sniffer like a puppy, Charlie. Drag it in deep and hold it down like a big dog." She hooted.

I sucked and held smoke in for what seemed like half an hour. I'd never smoked hashish before. Like everyone, I'd had plenty of chances, but booze got me high enough, and I knew how to control my alcohol buzz.

Becky put some drum music on her CD player, sat me down on the floor of the living room, and we passed the pipe back and forth. After three puffs, her face became radiant, more beautiful than Shu Ling and Nora put together.

Her skin looked silky and creamy, tinted with peach and strawberry. Her eyes twinkled and invited me to come closer. The entire universe shrunk down to the sapphire color of those eyes. I lost myself staring into them for an hour or an eternity. Never before in my life had I had the experience of seeing into someone's soul.

She touched my cheek with her fingers and the next thing I knew, we were rolling naked on the floor, laughing and hollering, pounding our fists into the carpet in time to the drumming on the CD. For a moment, I wondered where my clothes went and I scanned the room for them. My aloha shirt and cut-offs lay piled in a mound with her crimson blouse and leopard panties, shimmering tropical blossoms all tangled up and lit with animal light.

Becky tugged me into her room and we tumbled onto the bed. I had no protection with me. The hashish had burned off all my inhibitions but I knew enough to check with her.

"Do you have condoms?" I asked.

"Sure thing."

I said, "Don't worry. My annual physical included an HIV test and I was negative, I mean, I passed."

She laughed and said, "Me, too. So far, so good."

The "so far" scared me a little but I got it and we belly-laughed and pounded the bed. Afterward, I told Becky that the sex with her had been my best ever. The next morning, however, all I remembered was the oniony smell of her breath in my mouth as I listened to myself sneaking up the squeaky back stairs to my house while an owl hooted in the woods out back. I didn't remember disposing of a condom.

I came back to her several times during the summer, for laughs, wine, hashish, and sex. She must have learned by August that she was pregnant, but she never offered to skip the rubber. I wouldn't have, anyway.

***

During my affair with Becky, and after, no one in the company's warehouse or factory ever regarded me with anything other than respect, so I presumed that she'd kept our secret. I'd bought her a few candles and some things for her kitchen, but nothing personal or with my name on it.

Her kids were never home when I visited and they didn't recognize me at the funeral. I worried a little about my fingerprints, but we spent so little time at her place. If Buhrman dusted everywhere in her house for fingerprints, I might have a problem, but I hoped that Becky's birthday bash the night before she died would have smeared over any evidence of my presence.

***

At first, I thought the only reason I'd made love to Becky was for sexual release. When we got closer, I realized I needed a companion, someone to talk to, to let down my guard with. Becky and I had an honest relationship, no pretenses, no demands, and we had so much fun. Not like the other two women in my intimate life.

Shu Ling's flirting had tortured me and Nora was barely available. Her new passion for golf kept her at the country club most afternoons and late into many nights, drinking and playing cards with her golfing pals.

But as long as Nora was happy, I had my freedom. She received her share of the abundant funds American Tofu earned and she had total control of our family checkbook. I didn't need it because the business paid almost all of my expenses and gave me plenty of "walk-around" money. The talks Nora and I had in therapy compensated for that summer's absence of regular conversation and physical contact. We both seemed happy.

****

One sweltering night that July, a few weeks after I had taken up with Becky, I had to stay in New York the night before an early meeting. Shu Ling invited me over to view updates of film segments she'd shot on a recent trip to California, the real center of the tofu industry.

"You're calm, Charlie. I like you when you're not so hyped up," she said. "Did you start meditating?"

"Sort of." Sleeping with Becky helped keep me poised around other women, especially Shu Ling. I was tempted for a minute to tell her about Becky to add spritz to the evening. If I let her know that I was taking care of my sexual self quite well, thank you, perhaps she'd desire me more.

Don't trust her. All you can count on is your lust for her.

True, so far. But I'm an optimist, if I'm anything.

I kept my mouth shut about my new lover. That proved to be one of my wisest decisions ever. "I told myself I'm going to love you no matter whether we go to bed or not," I said. "I don't need to prove anything. I don't need anything from you. I enjoy being with you. Mature, isn't it?"

"I guess," she said. "Sounds boring. Did you give up on me?" She scooted close to me and, putting her arm around my neck, she kissed me on the ear.

I turned to kiss her, but she pulled back.

"No. I like it fraternal. It's got fizz that way. I have a boyfriend, Charlie. He wouldn't like it if we did anything."

I stood up. "Why are you teasing me then?"

"Let's just play," she said, ignoring my irritation. "Same ground rules as when we go swimming—naked but no fondling. Touching's allowed. No intercourse. You don't need penetration to really express and receive love."

"You ever hear of the Chinese Water torture? This is worse."

"Shut up. It's all part of Monkey Love. You should pay better attention—I've been teaching you all along. It's all about communication, connection."

"I wish I'd known."

"You knew. You got the essence, the non-verbal part."

"I get it. That's the Monkey part. The non-verbal," I said, puffing out my upper lip and mimicking monkey squeals.

"Could be."

I tried to tickle her but she shifted away. Scooting after her, I said, "I googled Monkey Love and I came up with some web sites I didn't want traces of on my computer."

"It's not about sex with animals. Give me a break."

"It's about the fact that chimpanzees and humans have 99.4% the same DNA. We're kissing cousins. The bonobos, too. You know, the monkeys who make love, not war? Every bonobo does it with all the others. They're not the shy types like me when it comes to sex."

"You're a gas, Charlie."

"Just the facts, ma'am. Just the facts."

Shu Ling wrinkled her nose as if she couldn't believe me. "Good research. You're a natural student."

I grinned, half-embarrassed, half-enthusiastic. I didn't know whether she was putting me down or teasing until she stood up and held out her hand.

"You want to stay here and jabber or do you want to come into my room and learn about real communication?"

I'd been waiting for that invitation ever since she soared into my office in the spring. I followed her hand-in-hand like her toy, a willing, salivating pet. I was out of control and I didn't care.

We sat down side by side on her black silk-quilted bed, our thighs brushing. I reached out to unbutton her blouse and she flicked my hand away.

"Wait." She turned to me and said, her voice dry and serious, "I'm going to teach you to make love without touching genitals, with clothes on."

I slumped and pouted, intentionally melodramatic. Hoping to inject light-heartedness into what was becoming schoolish, I said "We call that foreplay."

"Do you call it foreplay when you explode in ecstasy?"

"Do you mean, come?"

"Mmmm, yes ... " she hesitated. "Sometimes that's part of it. I think of orgasm as more of a distraction."

"I don't get it, but let's go."

"Patience. Tonight I'm going to teach you 'Marmoset Ears.' If that works out, the next time you can learn about 'Orangutan Toes.' If you're still a good boy ... I'll show you 'Bonobo Bellies.'"

"Bonobos? I knew I was onto something. Research pays." I tried to tickle her again but she wiggled away. "Let's start with them. I already know something about bellies."

She put her finger to my lips, shushing me. "Those aren't the Chinese names, Charlie. I made them up just now."

"They work for me."

"Relax. Nothing urgent here. Anyway, you're a virgin."

"I wish—"

"I don't want to hurt you."

We never did see her film clips because for the next hour, Shu Ling elevated the game of monkey play to a fine aural erotic art: pinches, nips, groans, flickering licks and countless other touches with her teeth and tongue stimulated my lobes and whorls and inner recesses in a way that hyper-sensitized my entire body.

"Your ears are like a woman's secret parts," she whispered. "Silky, moist, tremulous."

She strummed toneless string instruments that sounded like telephone wires buzzing and murmured love poems in Chinese. She demonstrated acupressure-point nibbling and writhed and moaned when I practiced my new learning on her.

I didn't arrive at any explosion, but when I left for my hotel at midnight, city night sounds sang in a symphony of horns tooting, tires fluting, voices harmonizing a cappella. My body hummed a summer melody that was part steam, part melted butterscotch. I gasped awake in the middle of the night, a chorus of birds and blowing leaves tingling in my ears, my pelvis shuddering. I called Shu Ling immediately, gasping my thanks into her voice mail.

When I checked my own voice mail the next morning, she'd left me a puzzling message, some Taoist teaching, no doubt.

"Sorry you lost it," she said in her breathy accent. "I didn't mean to go overboard. Next time I'll remember you're still a fledgling. Ciao, little gander."

We didn't find the time or place in August to have the next session on 'Orangutan Toes and Simian Soles.' She was traveling and frankly, I'd lost interest: Becky had become primal woman enough for me.

***

Three months after Shu Ling and I played Marmoset and five weeks after Becky died, I felt mugged by the Chief's investigation. It often felt more like a persecution: browbeating calls to me, demands on my staff, intimations in the local paper about a "highly placed" suspect.

One morning, I aimed my car south and slogged down the Interstate toward an advertising meeting in New York and dinner with Shu Ling. I braved the lashings of the tail of an autumn Caribbean hurricane that kept all but the most desperate drivers off the road.

The highway flooded with streams and puddles, rocking my Cherokee like a small outboard on a windy lake. Confused thoughts splattered across my mind while muddy water splashed over my windshield and rain blurred headlights into haloes too dim to illuminate the lane markers.

By the time I arrived at Shu Ling's apartment on Mott Street, the rain had stopped and the city basked in a balmy fall blessing. The New York air sparkled and the traffic whistled by like it was carrying people eager to get to a spontaneous city-wide party.

I looked forward to an afternoon of relaxation with the Princess. I needed to blank out my fears and worries, even the facts, from my mind. I'd told Shu Ling about the death right after it happened, and during the weeks since the investigation began, we talked a half-dozen times. She was always caring and her words never failed to strengthen my resolve.

I rang her bell and sped up the stairs the second she buzzed me in. Pushing open her unlocked door, I found her in the kitchen and we hugged each other chest-to-chest and thigh-to-thigh. I grinned at her, even as she pushed me gently away, pointing me to the living room.

She'd ordered in ravioli and salad for lunch and we opened a bottle of Chianti, a prelude, I thought, to one of her arcane love lessons where all was pleasure and bliss. We sat down on her couch to an indoor picnic.

"I think it's going to be all right," I said between mouthfuls of mesclun spiced with lots of raddichio. We sat close to each other, our plates on the glass coffee table. "Your father and our other customers aren't too worried."

"I'm worried, though. I'm worried for you," she said, putting her plate down and scanning my face, as if checking for signs of deterioration.

"I'll survive."

"You'll survive. But what about your family and everyone else? Did you know your police chief called my father a bunch of times? He says the death was no accident."

"When did Buhrman call again?" My body went cold at the news. One of my knees started shaking. "Why didn't you tell me?"

"I don't know. Yesterday? My father mentioned it last night. He called just to say hello and talk about the film. He said 'Things look sticky for Charlie.'"

"Buhrman pisses me off. He's making everybody nervous."
"What will you do if it is a murder?"

Shu Ling's interest tempted me to tell her then and there about my affair with Becky.

If Meng finds out, bye bye American Tofu pie. He'll wreck your business and suck you dry.

Jiminy's words rang true, as usual. This time I listened. I swallowed and changed the focus of our talk.

"I don't know," I said, not looking directly at Shu Ling. "Do you think your father had anything to do with this?"

"Charlie! Are you crazy? He's rough, but he'd never get involved. What's the matter with you?"

"I don't know. I'm really confused." Telling her that little obvious truth made me feel better.

"I guess you are. You'd better talk to my father. He's probably your best ally. Maybe he can help."

"How?"

"He's got contacts everywhere."

"I'll talk to him about it on our trip. It's only two weeks before we leave."

Either she had no clue that her father would do anything to achieve his business goals or her acting could win her awards. Of all the businessmen I knew, I'd identified Meng as the one whose style I could mimic to help get me through the Buhrman crisis: Play it close to the vest, stay above the fray.

"Can we preview your film?"

She inserted the DVD and, relieved to stop thinking about Meng, I watched.

Shu Ling had done everything to make her straightforward industrial film as upbeat and entertaining as possible, but as we watched the final segments showing California and Canadian tofu factories, I started feeling depressed.

I should have waited until the cloud of the investigation cleared, because I was in no mood to face the realities of my company's true inferiority in the harsh world of the tofu wars.

The huge factories all had modern high-tech equipment and energetic, Asian, robotic, sanitized workers. I suspected that they could make tofu a lot cheaper, and probably with better quality, than we could, ship it east, and take most of American Tofu's business if we showed the slightest vulnerability in our position or reputation.

I desperately needed a bottle of hot sake and a lesson in "Orangutan Toes," but Shu Ling said I was too upset. Besides, she had a dinner date.

I dragged myself to my hotel, ordered room service, and ate a tasteless meal. I lay unable to sleep, wondering if Shu Ling would forgive me for accusing her father.

By late evening, the hurricane circled back around Manhattan, pouring dense sheets of water onto the night city. They snaked across my hotel room window like thick vines probing the sash, seeking a way inside.

Chapter Seven

Charlie

HOTEL DELIGHT

in scarlet Taipei
slave girl barbers rub
bald heads—all shapes, all sizes

Meng and I left from JFK for Taipei two weeks later on a Taiwan Airlines 747. This would be my first chance to immerse myself in Chinese culture. Ever since I read Sun Tzu's *The Art of War* and applied its lessons to running my business with incredible success, ancient China has obsessed my thinking.

Its ancient discovery, tofu, supports my family and dozens of others, bringing health to hearts and hot-flash free menopause to women. Its drugless medicine—acupuncture, herbs, qi gong thousands of years of healing without government boards approving treatments, and without doctors becoming rich on the pain of their patients. Ancient Chinese wisdom can't be compared with our modern thinking. They practiced *wu wei*, non-action. As I understand it, you wait until the thing you want happens by itself. You have to get your mind in the right place, but once it's there, you're in the flow, and the flow is the way the universe operates. I've heard it said you have to surf the flow.

Wu wei worked in my negotiations. If somebody objected to something I proposed, I'd wait. If the flow washed their acceptance my way, I soaked it up and we moved on. If not, I'd leave the table, until they called me back with an offer.

But since Becky died, my flow had run underground and I had just enough energy to focus all my *wu wei* on avoiding the Chief's suspicions.

Relaxing in comfortable first class seats as the plane rose over the North Atlantic, heading over the top of the world, Meng and I sat side by side. I wanted to impress Meng with the scope of my business ambition, so I revealed my hopes and dreams.

"Henry Ford was one of the greatest businessmen America ever produced," I said. "He created the assembly line. He was clever. Did you know he demanded that parts be shipped to him in a certain kind of box? When the box arrived, he dismantled it and bolted it to the car for running boards?"

"He sounds Chinese," Meng said, chuckling, setting down his Taipei newspaper and raising his leather recliner from nap position.

"He made one kind of car in one color for years. It was cheap, simple, everyone could have one. That's how he single-handedly created the auto industry. The whole economy of the world can thank him."

"True. Everyone wants a car."

"Yeah. Think about the oil and gas companies. What about the steel and rubber and glass and computer companies. The people who build and maintain roads. Advertising agencies. TV. Government. Everything."

"He did appear at a point of high industrial leverage in America," Meng said, sounding like a professor.

"Well, the point is not about his cars. It's about soybeans. He made a car entirely out of soybeans. Soybean oil, I mean, turned into plastic."

Meng listened carefully, focusing on my eyes.

"In 1934, at the World's Fair in Chicago, he served a 13-course dinner. Everything was made from soy. Appetizers, milk, meat, dessert. Everybody raved."

"Genius doesn't confine itself to one field, does it?" Meng said. "Some of my heroes were rulers, poets, swordsmen, inventors. Flowers of human evolution. I myself only dabble in painting and piano."

"I don't do much else besides business," I admitted. "A little poetry. My dream is to carry on Henry Ford's vision. Right now, I make one color, one flavor, two sizes of tofu. It's cheap. Everyone can use it. It's democracy's ideal food. The Model A of the dining room table."

"Good luck. Maybe your research in Taiwan will help you become the Henry Ford of tofu. Excuse me," he smiled, "I should say the Charlie Greer of tofu. You'll bring soy to the whole world, just like Ford brought cars."

A flash zinged through my mind—the flash I'd been waiting for. *Soy to the whole world.* Right there on the 747, the future of American Tofu popped into my head. *Wu wei* in action. Oops, I mean, non-action.

We'd combine modern American farming and food processing technology with ancient Chinese healing cuisine and military strategy. Using the most creative, flamboyant marketing talent in New York, American Tofu would make its way onto every table in the U.S., and beyond.

We'd call our marketing campaign "Soy to the World." I'd copyright the words and create TV ads no one could forget. The trip had already paid for itself.

Soy to the world? Not your idea. It came from the dead girl.

He's right. I'd buried the idea with Becky. It started with her asking me a question.

She had a day off, the kids were at school until 3. I took a long lunch at her house. We made love and lay there in bliss. Becky turned over on her back beside me and said, "What's your biggest dream? What would you do if you weren't afraid to fail?"

She was always reading self-help books and practicing their techniques on me. Usually I'd tease her about trying to change me or hypnotize me to have me under her control.

She'd laugh. "Don't worry. I'd never do that. Besides, I already have you under my control." I'd scrunch up my face like I was mad and tickle her until she'd squirm and kick and break free.

This time, I took her seriously. I thought about two seconds and blurted, "People all over the planet would eat tofu. Maybe not American Tofu. Maybe Kenyan or Brazilian. I'd set up factories everywhere, hire millions of people. It would change everything."

"That's pretty big. Tofu everywhere. Wow. I would never think up such a thing."

"You know, if you thought about tofu twenty four seven the way I do, you'd probably want to see everybody in the world eating tofu. We'd make lots of other soy foods and drinks. Soy all over would solve war, climate change, no more haves and have-nots."

Becky lay silent for a moment, then said, "Soy all over the world. Hmmm." She turned her head to me, her lush brown eyes twinkling. "Soy to the world."

"That's it," I said, taking her seriously. "Soy to the world." "Sounds like the Christmas song. 'Joy to the world.'"

Her rhyming got me going. "Hey. Cool. Want to write the song? 'Soy to the world.' We could make it American Tofu's anthem." "You're ambitious, Mr. Greer," she said.

Becky was a teaser, too. She called me "Mr. Greer" whenever she wanted to mock my upperclass standing. She called us "Mr. Greer and Little Becky."

When Becky called me "Mr. Greer," she was inviting me to play the game where she became the boss and I worked for her, doing whatever she commanded—from doing her dishes to trying something taboo in bed. This time, the idea of international tofu factories held my full attention.

"I guess I'm ambitious," I said. "I don't think of it that way. It's a mission. It's purpose. Something bigger than me."

Becky sat up and crossed her legs. She looked me in the eyes. "So you have been listening to me—you have a purpose, just like the CD said."

When I remember her sitting that way, naked, her lips pursed, her hair disheveled, her eyes focused on mine like she was trying to understand, nodding her head, my throat thickens. I feel tears rising behind my eyes. She was the most perfect gift of a woman I'd ever met. I missed her in my whole soul, like I'd never missed anybody.

I had to stand up and make my way to the plane's water closet where I sat on the lid of the toilet seat and let the tears pour out. I cried and groaned for a minute or two, then splashed water on my face. Once my eyes cleared up, I strode back to my seat.

At that minute, 37,000 feet in the air, somewhere over the Pacific, I decided the most important thing I could do with my life was to make "Soy to the world" come true. It would change the world, make a lot of money, assure my kids and her kids a happy future. And Becky would be at the heart of it.

Before she died, I wrote the song "Soy to the world" and sang it to her, off key but it sounded nice, she said. We sang a couple of duets and were starting to get good.

At Becky's memorial service, I handed out copies of the song to everyone, telling them Becky had composed it and given it me a week before she died. Everyone thought it was a perfect memorial all of us could share.

"It's beautiful." somebody said. "So sad."

***

Like all my dealings with Meng, the Taiwan trip became a mixed blessing. When we landed, I lifted my hundred pound case of samples onto a pushcart. A sharp pain stabbed me in my kidneys and I went to my knees. I staggered upright, but my lower back hurt so badly that I could barely walk.

Once I limped through customs, a perfunctory stamping of both our passports, Meng deposited me at the "Hotel Delight" in downtown Taipei. We made a date for dinner the next night, but he called an hour later and postponed dinner for a week. "I'm sorry, Charlie. I have to go down south and meet with some new suppliers. They're having problems with a project we're counting on."

"I'm sorry, too, Meng. I don't know what I'll do."

"I told William Woo Ai to be on call for you, if you need anything. Reach him through my Taipei office. You're enterprising, I'm not worried about you."

"Good luck with your suppliers, Meng. See you in a week."

"I'll call in a few days. Till then, enjoy yourself. Make sure you try The Golden Dragon restaurant. They have the most delicious dim sum I've ever eaten."

"Looking forward to that," I said. "Next week then?"

"Good, Charlie. Enjoy yourself. You might be surprised what a good time you can have in Taipei."

Meng had given me a guidebook and a list written in Chinese of restaurants, museums, and temples. He told me to show any cab driver the list if I needed help. Maybe I could buy a Chinese/English phrase book and surprise Meng with my language facility when we got together for dinner.

A sour taste of panic at being alone for so long rose into my mouth, but I washed it back with a Dong Qi beer from the refrigerator. I didn't really want a week of solitude, but I decided I ought to take advantage of it to get a perspective on things, maybe come up with some inspiration about how to move the Chief to give up the case.

When I rolled out of bed the next morning, my body immediately jackknifed, falling hard onto the floor. My head slammed into my knees, my stomach retching as a violent spasm jolted my lower back. I worked an hour to relax the muscles and to crawl back into bed.

I'd told Meng I wanted to stay in a hotel that natives used. Since I couldn't speak or read Chinese when I groaned into the desk service phone, none of the hotel staff understood what I wanted. I dialed Meng's Taipei office but hung up before his secretary answered. No need to play a weakling.

The back pain, the muggy Taiwanese weather, my exhaustion from the trip, and the spasms every time I moved sapped my will. I lay in bed staring at the lone American TV channel and swallowing whatever food the staff left at my door.

I didn't feel like calling the factory and complaining. They needed to think I was out conquering the Orient for American Tofu. Nora had taken the kids hiking in the mountains while I was gone, so I couldn't call her.

I could have called Nora's cell phone, I guess. I didn't want her to know I was hurting as bad as I was. At that point in our marriage, I was pretty sure she didn't have much comfort in her heart for me anyway. I wondered if she had sniffed out something about my relationship with Becky. I'd never let on I'd had anything to do with Becky, but Nora seemed angry with me all the time. She was the one person I should be able to count on, but she kept her distance.

I lay on my back there in the Delight Hotel, listening to tropical showers drizzle off and on, half-paralyzed, alone as a beached whale. I had nothing to do except worry that somebody would come forward to the Chief with the news that they saw me with Becky the night she died. Or they'd seen us together sometime, anytime. It didn't make a difference which because I'd denied knowing her as anyone other than an employee. Still, in a small town, you bump into people you know in the grocery store or at the gas station all the time. So what if someone saw us together once or twice?

***

Nora called the second day of my incarceration in the hotel room. I groaned when I turned over to pick up the phone.

"How's it going, Charlie?"

For some reason I didn't want to tell her I was hurt. I wondered if I waited on purpose to throw my back out until I was half a world away from Nora. If I did it at home, she'd either ignore me or make such a big deal of taking care of me, I'd feel guilty for feeling bad.

"Not much happening so far. Meng's been busy so I just hang out, waiting."

"How's Taipei?"

"Noisy. What's going on with the Chief? Did he close the case yet?"

"Naw. He's called everybody in for a second round of interviews. I can't believe it, y'know. I'm scheduled for tomorrow."

"Jesus. Think he's up to something now I'm out of town?"
"Why would he? Guess what? I think he's, like, a dry drunk on a binge. An investigation binge."

I laughed. "Good insight. I hope you're right."

"Seriously. Deborah thinks so."

"The hundred fifty dollar an hour therapist? I guess she knows what she's talking about," I said, not eager to get into therapy-talk.

"She thinks we're under too much stress, y'know."

"Nothing that getting the Chief off my back won't solve. Howie the kids? I miss them."

"Rissi got a part in her kindergarten play, 'Three Billy Goats Gruff.' She's our little starlet, running around the house screaming and fainting, expecting me to clap every time she falls down."

"What do you mean?"

Nora laughed. "She's the little baby goat the trolls scare. All she has to do is scream and swoon."

"I can't wait to see the play. Tell her I'll be there. What's Chuckie up to?"

"Should I tell you? He's so proud he wanted to be the one to tell you he won the second grade spelling prize."

Thank God. Kids' lives go on no matter what hurricanes blow through the parent world. "You tell me and he can tell me, too, when I call on Saturday."

"Well, he was the only kid in his class who could spell 'friend.' Everyone else transposed the i and the e."

"Wow. Good thing he's your son, Nora. I'm not sure I could spell it right today."

"You could, Charlie. Are you taking care of yourself?"

"Best I can. I always do, you know."

"I mean, the stress and all. You've been a wreck."

Nora was right but, despite the pain, I was feeling a lot calmer than before I left Clement. "It's a good break here. I'll tell you all about it when I get back. How are you doing?" I asked, feeling real concern and wanting her to hear it.

"I'm fine. Too rainy for much golf these days, but I'm working with Genevieve on some projects." Nora sounded tired.

"Good. How's she? How're sales holding up?"

"Business is fine," she said. "Gen's got sales under control. Benko says things have never been smoother. The kids miss you."

"I miss them a lot. Give them big hugs. You, too, honey."

"Take care of yourself, Charlie. Bye."

She didn't say she missed you. When's the last time she really kissed you?

I think she half-missed me and was half-glad to have some time alone. Nora was the smartest woman I ever knew. She had the vocabulary of a college English professor and she could talk numbers and taxes well enough to impress my accountant. She was my board of directors for the company, and any of my business associates who met her always told me that I was lucky to have such a business partner. But when it came to marriage, is she smart? I don't think so. Am I smart? No way.

Deborah, the infallible therapist, said one of the 'spousal parties' is the change agent and one is the stabilizer. Nora's definitely the change agent for our relationship. I didn't have the time or the energy for that. I put all my change agency into running a business and trying to make money so I practice *wu wei* with my wife. Non-action. Let if flow.

Except, lately, I tiptoed around Nora—I could never give her quite what she wanted. She's the one who should have felt guilty. I didn't have an affair in public like she did with her painting teacher. Somehow she blamed me for her fling, and I believed her, to a degree. If I'd had time to give her all the attention she said she needed, I'd never get any work done. She and I went over it a hundred times: She slept with the guy because he made her feel special, and I didn't. Have we been married too long? I've never stopped loving her, though.

She pissed me off so much I thought about leaving, but I'd never let her know how much it hurt me that she slept with that goose-necked Picasso wannabe. She'll never learn that he left town a month after I found out about her and him because I called in a private eye from Syracuse who got some nice shots of him with two other women. I should have shown them around, but I'd never bring shame into my family by exposing Nora's idiocy.

I called him up, told him to meet me for lunch. He sat down and I laid the pictures out in front of him on the tablecloth, and said, "You've got 24 hours to lose yourself."

"What are you talking about? This is bullshit."

I glared at him with my narrowest Jack Nicholson eyes and laughed. I never felt better than when I saw the expression on his face as he threw down a twenty to pay for my lunch and ran to his car.

Therapy made it clear that I didn't want to leave Nora and she didn't want to leave me for him. Anybody can give into temptation, and I don't have a double standard here.

She'd said I neglected her soul but I still have no idea what she means. Maybe she'd feel I cared for her soul if I asked her to get more involved in the day-to-day business. She'd share the angst in the moment, rather than listening to my second-hand tales, which always sounded like griping. She already worked with Genevieve whenever she wanted to and she was in charge of the company's Human Resources. I hung her art in the office and we had a big celebration when she sold her first painting to the woman Genevieve introduced her to.

When I said that her soul would feel a lot more taken care of if she worried less about it, she screamed at me, "What about you? I know you fuck around on all those sales trips."

I screamed back, "The hell I do. I've had plenty of chances, but I don't. I take our marriage seriously."

She broke down when I said that and she pushed herself out of her chair across the therapist's office and gave me a huge hug.

I said, "Take the opposite of what you feel now. That's how I feel about you fucking around."

She snapped her head back and raised her palm, but she didn't strike. She's a passionate woman and I love her for it but how long I put up with her passion for somebody else is another story.

Maybe if I'd forgiven her in the spring after the painter split town and if Nora told me how sorry she was, I'd never have noticed Becky, much less slept with her. I was so angry with her for having an affair, I guess I tried to get even with her.

***

Last winter, worn out from our huge Year of the Monkey sales push, enervated but innocent of any inkling that death and doom waited only a few months ahead, Nora and I decided to reward ourselves with a Caribbean vacation. Deborah, the know-it-all therapist, encouraged us to go so we reserved two weeks in a small resort in the Dominican Republic.

Four days after we arrived, I came down with food poisoning or mild sunstroke. Whatever it was laid me low and kept me in bed for a week where I sweat through the sheets every afternoon. I tried swimming at dusk, but my legs dragged across the sand to the shore where I would lay, half-submerged in crystalline eighty-plus degree water, shivering.

At first, Nora was angry with me. "Why didn't you wear that beautiful straw hat I bought you? You don't have to prove you're Tarzan."

"Hey."

"You don't. You didn't have to devour those mangoes without washing them, either. Or papayas."

"Maybe it was the lettuce at the resort salad bar." I had no strength to fight with her.

"I ate the lettuce. I'm fine. You wanted this trip. Now you're ruining it."

I couldn't handle her energy level. I wasn't going to take the blame for her disappointment, so I said, "You go have fun, for both of us."

She did.

I stayed in the little room, lying on the bathroom floor in front of the fan, vomiting, drinking gallons of bottled water, crawling in and out of soggy sheets, sleeping fifteen hours a day while Nora rode horses, snorkeled, sailed, learned the merengue, and turned as brown as the natives.

She rejuvenated herself into the gorgeous babe she was when I first met her, but I had no libido, so I couldn't appreciate her the way she deserved, or the way I deserved. For a whole week my skin prickled whenever she touched me. I wanted to go home before we'd used half our reservation, but I kept quiet.

With my first breath of frigid air when we got off the plane at home, a thrill ran through me as if I'd just won a marathon or deposited a million dollars in the bank. I couldn't believe how the snow heaped along the runway excited and welcomed me.

Nora and I might have traveled to two different places—she to a tropical paradise where she became bronzed and beautiful, me to an indoor diet clinic where I lost ten pounds I didn't need to lose and stayed pale as a worm.

When we discussed our experience with Deborah, I suspected that Nora enjoyed the heat in ways I didn't want to think about. She laughed about how warm and friendly the people were and how one of the guys dived fifty feet down without oxygen to pluck off a branch of elkhorn coral for her.

When she told Deborah about the merengue dances and mambos the resort held every night and the Spanish she'd learned, her voice crackled with excitement. I may have been paranoid, or jealous, but I asked her why she was so enthusiastic when she talked about the trip with Deborah.

"Charlie, sweetie, I had a great time. Thank you for taking me." "We took ourselves," I grumbled.

"I didn't want to upset you anymore than you were."

That sounded true enough, and I appreciated her sensitivity. I told her how glad I was that she had so much fun. I admitted that she did check on me often when I was sick, brought me water, washed the mangoes and lettuces when I could eat them, and brought me beer from the cabaña when I could drink it.

But a couple of weeks after we returned, Nora brought up the subject of "restructuring our relationship."

Now I got mad. "What the hell do you mean?" I shouted. My voice was so loud that I glanced at Deborah to make sure I was playing by therapy rules. She just nodded her head, encouraging me.

Nora said she just didn't know for sure that monogamy was always good for every couple.

"You go down that road," I said, "you go alone. I'm not interested. Who are you fucking now?"

"I'm not fucking anybody! I just think we should open up the way we think about marriage. Be mature about it. It doesn't have to mean sleeping with other people."

Jesus, I thought. She's been reading those New Age books about opening up our thinking about everything like we were old blankets that needed airing out.

"You guys are really getting somewhere, Charlie. Nora is still playing her role as your change agent, while you're opting for stability, keeping your marriage anchored. You're talking about things together that will really take you deep. Everything is right on track."

You got a one-way ticket to Cuckoldville. Your therapist sounds like Nora's shill.

But that night, Nora and I made the fiercest love we'd made for years, since before Chuckie was born. We agreed as we drifted off to sleep that maybe this shouting and fighting in therapy was working after all.

***

Lying there nearly comatose in the Delight Hotel, as I meditated on the state of my marriage, a state I might not long reside in, I tried to recall that night with Nora. I felt a little sputtering of desire, but my back hurt too much to jerk off, so I lay there steeping in fantasies of what might have been, wishing my aching body would dissolve in the tropical drizzle.

***

I was chewing the ice of my third Johnny Black of the night, courtesy of the Delight Hotel or Hotel Delight, feeling numb and drowsy when the room phone rang. Eleven thirty, already a half hour past my Taipei bedtime. I hoped it was Nora again, because I doubted I could have a rational conversation with anybody else.

"Hello Charlie? Charlie Greer?"

My God, what did he want? "Aaron. You found me."

"Not too hard. Tried three times then got smart. Called the international operator and she put me right through."

"What can I do for you, Aaron? I was almost asleep."

"Oh, what is it, yeah, middle of the night over there. How's the jet lag?"

"Bad. I hurt my back. All I do is lay around my room."

"Sorry about that. Try ibuprofen. Keeps the swelling down and chases the bad chemicals away. Doc Wallace told me about it." "That's what I'm doing."

"This call's expensive so I'll get right to it. I'd Skype but I don't have time right now."

"That's all right, Aaron. I'd have to turn on my iPad."

"Sure. No problem." He paused.

I heard him take a deep breath.

"Two things. Somebody says they saw your car in the Mac-Daniel neighborhood."

I jerked straight up in bed with no pain. "What do you mean? When? I was in the neighborhood sometime. I've been in every neighborhood. Clement's small."

"A couple times. The night of the murder and a week or so before."

"Don't know how it could be, Aaron. My Jeep's not the only one in town."

"They said it was white like yours."

"So what? Lotsa white SUVs—"

"Said the driver looked just like you."

I let that sink in while I got out of bed to pace. My back spasmed and I went to my knees. I choked off my groan. "Not much evidence," I gasped, "Anybody could be driving."

"Well, maybe. The other was your rig was at Brownwell's Supermarket, two, three times. Got your license plate—*TO-FU4U.*"

"Remember I told you about my job? I visit stores to see how our tofu is selling? I also do a lot of the family shopping. Brownwell's locally owned and I support local businesses. Keep our cash in our town."

"You're a local hero, Charlie. Like the article in the paper said last year."

His praise sounded sarcastic, but I couldn't tell for sure. My B.S. detectors had almost shut down for the night under the cozy blanket of booze.

The booze shut your radar down. Turn it on or Buhrman will top you with a thorny crown.

"Wait a minute, Aaron. I gotta get comfortable." I had to lie down on the bed with my legs propped on a pillow. "I'm set." Buhrman resumed. "The other thing ..."

I didn't like it when he paused so long.

"Your fingerprint. We got it off a glass in the dead woman's place."

Shit. How did he do that? He had me in her house, drinking something. Why didn't she wash the dishes any better? I thought quickly about that last night. I didn't go inside then or anytime in the previous week. The print must be old.

"Could only be one thing," I said, adopting my co-investigator's ploy as well as I could. "'Member I told you I took her home from the comp'ny party? Musta had a glass a water or sum thin.'"

"You drinking, Charlie?"

"Had a few tonight. For the pain. Works good with the naproxen." I chuckled and he laughed, too.

"Yeah, well, maybe that explains it. You had a glass of water, you say?"

"I was the designated driver at the party, Aaron. Ask the workers. Wasn't about to drink anything else with an employee. 'Specially a woman late at night."

"Okay."

"Don't make more of this than there is. Bet you got fingerprints from two dozen people who work at the factory."

"Good guess. Twenty-seven. Talking to 'em all."

"Lotta work, Aaron. For an accident."

"Gotta go with my gut, Charlie."

"Hope the taxpayers don't run out of money paying for your gut, Aaron, I gotta go to sleep. Anything else?"

"No. Thanks for your help. Have a good trip. Make sure you come back."

I set the receiver down and threw my arms out across the bed. That dog. Good thing I already admitted I'd gone to her house, the one time that was public knowledge anyway. Surprising, he bagged my Jeep in Brownwell's parking lot. Twenty-seven sets of prints. That must have been a hell of a birthday party.

I tossed down the rest of my drink and lay in the dim light with my eyes open. He really meant it when he said he hoped my back got better. I wasn't the bad guy, yet.

***

The next morning, I rolled out of bed, clear in my head, with back pains a little dulled. I'd handled the call from Buhrman without giving away my shock. Now he'd keep himself busy interviewing the twenty-seven others for the rest of my trip, so I was free of him for a while.

After lying around until afternoon and finishing off a packet of Advil, I dragged myself downstairs and outside, and limped around Taipei's smoky streets, searching for a drugstore and more painkillers. Nobody had ibuprofen or even aspirin.

I finally found a pharmacy where I found a bottle of naproxen. I swallowed a handful of pills, then, hobbling and stopping every few steps, I trekked beyond the hotel's immediate neighborhood into a perpetual construction zone. Wrecking balls pounded incessantly against brown concrete buildings of the same size and shape as nearby buildings that seemed to rise, cloning the ruined ones as soon as they collapsed. Under the foreboding sky clogged with dust, Taipei reminded me of the black and white photos I'd seen of bombed-out Warsaw after the Second World War.

I'd come to Taipei with the romantic delusion that I'd be welcomed into a thriving modern metropolis. I expect it to be built with the refined esthetic sense of the noble refugees determined to preserve the old empire in their Taiwan island refuge. I expected to have discussions with natives about Chinese history, Mao and his place in history, their prosperous manufacturing economy, the electronic age that made them rich.

Instead of educated, informed citizens engaging me in dialogues, the din of thousands of mopeds and motor scooters rip-sawed at my eardrums and their acrid exhausts seared my eyes and nasal tissues. I retched and coughed. Finally, I stopped a pedestrian and pointed to the surgical mask he wore. He said something and rushed on so I tied my handkerchief around my face like a rustler in the movies. With my lungs somewhat protected, I relaxed a little.

Around me, manic Taipeians ignored the pollution, racing around the streets, bargaining incessantly, creating the next million dollars per hour of export surplus to the US. My businessman's calculating mind began to despair. How my sweet little American Tofu company could ever compete with the voracious twenty four seven commercial spirit of the Taiwan Tiger, the spirit that guided Meng, I couldn't conceive.

On every block, a Buddhist supplies store sold incense, herbs, cloth, prayer sheets, and other things I couldn't identify. I bought a small pack of prayer papers, delicate tan rice paper with a gold square in the center that fit into a shirt pocket—convenient replacements for bloody pig or chicken sacrifices.

After watching the locals make their offerings to Buddha, I stood outside the store and lit a few of the prayer papers over an urn in front of the store, placed on the sidewalk for the customers who had burning needs to get Buddha's attention.

Like the other devotees, I held the flaming papers while they vaporized in my fingers until the ash dropped into the urn. The smoke drifted up, mingling with the toxic motor scooter fog and the construction dust and the oily tropical mist, finding its way right into Buddha's nose.

That was probably the original purpose of the fire sacrifice— tickle the Buddha's nose with smoke and make him sneeze squalls of rain onto the rice fields.

As I headed toward the Delight and the calm of my room, I passed dozens of aromatic food carts lining the narrow alleys abutting the main shopping street. Barbecued meat and the saucy noodles and exotic fruits tempted my curiosity more than my appetite. Before I came to Taiwan, I'd met an American who lived in Taipei for two years, returned to the States, then six months later, she lost all her hair.

"Parasites," she told me. "I ate everything."

Determined to keep my hair as long as I could, I decided not to pick from the carts except for some kai, a crimson apple-shaped pear. With fantasies of importing the *kai* by the container load to feed obese Americans a crisp and juicy health snack, I carried several to my room to wash before I ate. Except for carton after carton of guava juice I picked up in little shops, I ate all my meals in the restaurants around the hotel or in my room.

That night, as I nibbled some deep-fried pork and fish combination with seaweed-flavored rice and sampled a local beer, I listened to the English-language radio station playing classical music. The music gave me a shudder of familiarity—it could have been WRUR in Rochester—and my mind cleared.

As I sat there half a world away from Clement, I saw that ever since that night I'd taken on the victim mentality.

Backtracking from the Chief, fearing his next phone call, my mind racing from calculating the consequences of every lie to imagining my future wandering the homeless streets as a smelly ex-con.

Terrified of how my family and friends would scorn me, how my whole life, all my work, was futile—if I got caught. More than my fear, I was fed up with being on the defensive. I hadn't become a success by waiting around for prosperity to tap me on the shoulder when I wasn't looking.

I ordered up a pot of Oolong tea and pulled out my laptop. I started writing the "What if" exercise I'd learned at one of the Young Presidents weekend seminars. What if I had a million dollars? What if Buhrman went away? What if I could get the whole New York State school system to buy tofu? What if the President declared October is National Tofu Month? What if scientists found that tofu not only prevented cancer but it made you feel and act ten years younger? What if I came back from Taiwan as the Tofu Tiger? What if Shu Ling invited me to live with her in New York? What if Shu Ling and I took a yearlong trip around the world?

What if the Chief finds out the truth? Now's the time to plan your escape route.

I felt regenerated and relaxed after I finished that fantasy tripping—my life was an atlas of open roads, not a maze of dead ends. Even after three cups of tea, I fell asleep and slept nine hours without getting up once.

***

I woke up the next morning with an erection in my lap and the words "Soy to the World" singing in my ears, tickling like Shu Ling's tongue, and I laughed out loud.

I headed for the shower and as I stood under the water, I noticed my back was free of pain. I bent sideways and forwards and backwards and almost had a full-range swivel. I started singing out 'Soy to the World .'

"Soy to the World, The beans have come, Let earth receive her curd."

I toweled off, musing about the lyrics—Becky said curds reminded her of Little Red Riding Hood. She got her fairy tales mixed up, but I never said anything.

I realized why I was in Taipei with no distractions until Meng returned from the south—I had the time and now the energy, at last, to create the greatest tofu promotion ever: "Soy to the World". We'd launch it with the next Chinese New Year. What better time to make a huge racket than at the dawn of the upcoming Year of the Rooster?

Lots of people ate soy these days—every supermarket had dozens of soy meats, soy cheeses, soymilks, soy this, soy that. But really, it was the same old gang that supported the industry: women worried about menopause and the natural foods mavens. They made up a tiny portion of the big picture. Soy to the World would create a whole new consciousness among the pizza gobblers, the grillmeisters, and the ninety eight percent who think "toad food" and their stomachs cramp.

All morning I paced around the room, dictating ideas into my phone. Here was the perfect chance to practice the 'Hundredth Monkey' marketing theory. Becky told me about it. Anthropologists showed that once monkeys start washing their potatoes on a remote island, when that fateful hundredth monkey scrubbed his spuds, every monkey in the world spontaneously washed their potatoes. Only my monkeys were people and my potatoes were cakes of tofu.

That night I'll call Gen and Nora and enlist them. They'd be monkeys two and three on the way to the hundred. We'd call it 'The Hundred Monkeys Campaign.' On second thought, Soy to the World had all the punch we needed and not half the silliness monkeys would bring to it.

I made my to-do list.

—Get everyone on board Soy to the World Express
—Call trademark attorney. Get the ball rolling on registration
—Bring in Rick and team from ad agency
—Start P.R. campaign to swamp the media
—Email, Facebook friends, twitter customers, suppliers, consumers
—Get everyone on board the Soy to the World Express
—Build up head of steam—no company can touch us—Canadian, Californian, Taiwanese, nobody!!!!

While writing, I realized a major side benefit. We'd have so much activity around the plant and I'd be so totally dedicated to STTW, I wouldn't worry about Buhrman. All he would see was a hard-working leader out to do the best he could for his company. Would a likely murderer throw himself into creative work like this? No, he'd worry about his secrets, get depressed, cover up his lies, sneak away if he could. I felt like Becky was an angel hovering nearby guiding me.

I faxed, emailed, and called everyone I could reach that night and the next. In three days, I broadcast the idea to every soy producer listed in the Soybean Blue Book, the industry bible. I wanted insider feedback and Genevieve's touch on the idea before we publicized it on our website, blog, facebook or on our packaging and fifty more ways. Before long, American Tofu would be the lead marketer of soy foods in the world.

After my third super-productive day of work on Soy to the World, I got a call from William Woo Ai, Meng's English-speaking Taipei liaison. Eager to speak with a friendly person, I told him about my back problem, the immense amount of work I'd accomplished and how, now, I was ready to meet some natives.

"We'll take care of you, Charlie. I have a lovely evening arranged for you. A nice massage, some local people?"

"Sounds great. Can you bring me some naproxen? I ran out of mine." I anticipated an excellent acupressure massage. I'd heard about the Chinese tradition of training blind people to become masseurs and masseuses.

"I'll pick you up tonight, Charlie."

I climbed into the taxi with William as the muggy city twilight deepened. Behind windows closed against the clouds of exhaust smoke, shutting out the 90-percent humidity and 90-degree temperature, we launched into a night aflame with pink and chartreuse bouncing off a low sky. The cab bumped down narrow cobbled streets designed and built for buggies and motor scooters. Metallic blue and orange neon, glaring and flashing lights and signs screamed for attention from a disinterested crowd.

We turned off the main road into a residential area. Crowds bumped continually against the car. At stoplights people of all ages leaned casually against it while they held conversations, as if we'd rolled into their living rooms, a kind of mobile couch.

As we inched our way through the crowd, the people banged the hood or the trunk and waved through the side windows at me in some kind of ritual. I held my back as still as I could as the taxi swerved to avoid bikes, mopeds, pedestrians. Dozens of delivery trucks jammed the street.

"The stores stay open all night," William said. "Everybody has lots of money and not enough to buy."

I was glad there were only twenty million Taiwanese in the world economy. I had a vision of the twenty-second century, when China dominated the overpopulated world with its noise and smog and hustle, I was glad I wouldn't be around. We rode in silence until the car pulled into a large courtyard where it stopped and William climbed out.

"I have an early meeting, Charlie. Lin will take care of everything," he said, nodding toward the driver. "I'll call you in the morning."

I called out the window to him. "William, where am I going?" "Lin knows, Charlie. Have a good time." He waved and disappeared into a storefront.

The driver's a thug. You shoulda stayed in and taken more drugs.

Exhaustion settled into my spirit. I'd been working long hours and I was too weak to try to control the situation. I'd just have to let happen whatever came next. I closed my eyes, to escape the lights and sounds of the city.

The car stopped on a wide street in front of a long red awning that stretched from a building out to the street. Two young men wearing black pants and starched white shirts approached the cab. Lin barked at them, tossed one the car keys, while the other opened my door quickly.

I climbed out, curious now, and we trailed the men up wide stairs carpeted in the same reddish-gray color as the awning. The rug led into a lobby where six or seven young women wearing pink skirts and peach-colored blouses lounged on plastic lawn chairs. Illuminated by tiny spotlights, three-foot tall palm trees grew out of pots placed along the walls. Responding to Lin's signal, several young women rose from their chairs and followed him down some stairs.

I waited, examining the surroundings, the first semi-private building I'd been inside in Taipei. Its old carpet was worn to the woof in spots and the rouge and black lobby walls were chipped. Some older women sitting at the bar smiled and waved their down-turned hands at me, urging me to catch up with Lin.

As I descended the stairs to the basement, a cloying bitter smell rose up like cleaning fluid or insecticide. At the bottom, I turned into a narrow hall where several doors lined the corridor. Grinning, Lin pointed to an open door and signed to go in. He pointed at his watch and at the chair behind me. I supposed he meant he'd wait there.

A wrinkled leather recliner filled most of the wood-paneled cubicle. Facing the chair, a fluorescent tube shone over a mirror at the end of the room, lighting the tiny room with chilly reflections. I climbed into the chair and lay back, expecting the masseuse to arrive any minute.

A girl no older than fifteen came in wearing the same peach and pink outfit as the women upstairs. Maybe she was older. I can't tell how old or young Chinese are.

She carried a mug of steaming water, a tea bag, and a lemon. Setting the cup down, she inserted the tea bag, and turned to me.

She smiled weakly, pointing her pinkie finger to my shoes and belt. I got up and deposited my shoes next to the wall and dropped back into the chair.

Groans and coughs came from the other cubicles. My little masseuse ignored the sounds and shook her finger at me, pointing to my belt again. She turned away, reaching into one of the drawers near the mirror.

When she faced me again, she held a large jar of Vaseline in one hand and a towel in the other. She aimed at my crotch, while she circled her fingers and wagged them up and down in the universal jerk-off motion.

Here it is, playtime for the Chinese business mob. You're in a "barbershop," where guys come for a hand job.

I stared at the girl, unsure what to do. She shrugged her shoulders and set the Vaseline jar on a table beside the chair. She reached for my belt and began to unbuckle it. I'd tightened it to the last notch because it supported my sore back, so she had to concentrate on loosening the tine from the hole, yanking it so hard my back spasmed and I cringed.

She ignored my flinching and focused on her task. Finally, she pulled the buckle free and quickly unbuttoned the top button and with a flourish of her wrist, unzipped my pants. She stuck her little hand into my boxers, sliding it further in.

Her fingers felt like cold Jell-O slipping down my belly. My penis had shrunk and retreated deep between my thighs. As she probed, her fingernails nicked my scrotum and I jerked. She stopped moving, anticipating more tremors from me. I wiggled and tilted my pelvis a little so she could have freer access.

After slithering her hand in and out of my pubic hair and across my thighs, she finally found my penis in its burrow, pinched it, and tugged it out of its hiding place. She removed her hand from my shorts and patted my penis through the cloth.

Standing beside me and reaching across my body with one hand, she grabbed the waist of my pants in both hands and began to wrestle them down over my hips.

The girl hadn't shown me her eyes since she first came into the room. She lowered her head almost to my chest and heaved, trying to lift my hips up and pull the pants down at the same time. I weighed at least twice as much as her, and must have felt like dead weight. I couldn't help her because whenever I tried to raise my butt off the chair, my back screamed.

She tugged for at least a minute without moving the pants over my hip bones. She glanced at me, bent her elbows and tugged a couple of more times and she snatched them down to my knees, exposing my legs to the air-conditioning blowing down from the ceiling. Goose bumps embossed my thighs.

The girl frowned and pointed at my boxers that lay across my pelvis like a sagging veil. She gestured for me to finish the job of exposing my parts and turned to the table.

Chilly breeze from the ceiling poured over my exposed middle. I shivered. I wanted a blanket. She could do what she wanted to me, but if I wasn't warm, I wouldn't have any fun. I turned in the chair and retrieved my jacket. Once I laid it on my stomach, I felt a lot better.

The girl, busy at the table, ignored me and squeezed the lemon into the tea cup. Facing the wall, with back to me, she lifted the cup and sipped. She bent over the table again.

As I wriggled out of my underpants, I studied her in the mirror in front of me. I watched her in profile as she pulled on a pair of surgical gloves. She stabbed her fingers into the Vaseline jar, raked a gob of grease into her palm, and turned to me.

I had my hands on my underpants with my knees bent up.

I let them go and pointed to the gloves. She shook her head up and down several times and reached for my jones. It had shriveled even further into a tiny question mark in my lap.

Check out the gloves. She's gonna give you Latex love.

I considered the gloves and thought "AIDS."

The whole scene had mesmerized me so much I forgot about AIDS. The girl probably had it. It's rampant in Asia. The only prostitutes that don't have it are the virgins. Those Japanese businessmen who travel around Thailand and Taiwan on the sex tours cruising for young girls, they must have a death wish. I didn't. Gloves or no gloves. Besides, the image of rubber gloves pumping my cock brought a giggle to my throat. I almost laughed out loud.

Shaking my head and grinning, I gripped her empty hand in both of mine and snapped the wrist band of the rubber glove. She stiffened and stared at me wide-eyed. I gesticulated with the universal hands-down, facial disgust "No" sign.

Leaving her cool gloved hand in mine, she just as vehemently rocked her head up and down.

I whipped my head back and forth and grabbed her other hand. I felt about as turned on as if I were naked in the dentist's office with the drill buzzing in my mouth. If that girl touched me with those icy rubber gloves, my penis would shrivel to the size of a toothpick.

As she tried to free her hands from mine, a clot of icy Vaseline dripped onto my navel. I let her go. With her hands in mid-air, she stood inert, almost catatonic, staring at me with her fine lips frozen into a maroon Cheerio.

My nose came to the rescue. The air conditioning blew a stink of rancid fried food laced with a pungent scent of Lysol across my face and I sneezed sharply. The girl jumped back, bumping against the wall. Rhythmic banging noises came from outside my cubicle.

I toweled the grease off my stomach and handed it to the girl. I shrugged my shoulders, and slid down out of the chair.

My back balked as I straightened up, but I managed to pull my pants up without staggering.

As I buckled my belt and began to stand up, the girl bit her lips and pushed me back into the chair with her Vaselined glove. I said "No!" and she bolted, backing into the corner.

I smiled, groaned, got to my feet. I kept shaking my head vigorously at her and saying "No." She kept shaking her head "Yes," and I kept shaking mine "No."

She ran out of the room, banging the door.

After fumbling with my shoelaces I finally tied them. Creaking my stiff back straight, I pulled out my wallet and left an American twenty-dollar bill on the seat of the chair and I made my way into the hallway.

Lin burst out of the room next to mine, shoeless, tucking his shirt into his pants, in a panic. Several doors opened and women wearing the peach blouses peeked out of every one.

I laughed and pointed to a chair in the adjoining hallway. With both hands, I signed to him to go back into his room. I showed him that I'd wait. He understood and turned around, relief on his face.

I discovered the source of the rhythmic banging and it wasn't fucking. In a little room beside the cubicles, a woman stuffed a soggy pile of hand-job cloths into a washing machine while beside her, an upright laundromat-style dryer rotated, thumping its pale load

I made my way upstairs where one of the women served me a pink guava drink. In about five minutes, Lin rushed upstairs, said something gruff to the women, and, clutching my arm, pulled me outside. The taxi hurtled out of the unlit side street into the light in front of the barbershop. I climbed into the back seat as Lin zoomed into the night.

Back in my hotel, in the scalding shower, I laughed and laughed, feeling better than ever since I arrived in Taipei. Healing through humor, I thought.

Meng called the next morning. "How are you, Charlie? Enjoying Taipei?"

I told him about my back and the hilarious mistake Woo Ai had made. "She was going to give me a massage all right. I was expecting something a little different. For my back." I chuckled. "All she wanted to do was my front."

"Many of my American friends enjoy nice Taipei haircuts, Charlie," Meng said seriously. "They're quite safe. I thought you knew about them. I'm sorry you didn't have a good time."

"I had a good time, Meng. Feel a lot better. I just didn't need a haircut."

"Perhaps because you're married?"

"I'm trying to stay married, Meng. But that's not why. I just didn't feel like it. It surprised me, I guess."

"Maybe some other time, Charlie?"

"I don't think so, Meng. That place stunk."

Watch your mouth, Greer. Meng's calling the shots here.

I suddenly understood that he'd set up the hand job for me. He might even have chosen the barbershop because it was AIDS-free. He said it was "safe." I stuck my foot deeper in. "I mean, Lysol. They used some heavy disinfectant to wash the cloths. The chairs were in the basement. Lousy ventilation. I could barely breathe."

"Sorry, Charlie. Too bad it smelled. You could have had a good Chinese time."

I reversed as fast as I could. "It wasn't all that bad, Meng. Must have been my back. You know how sometimes you have a pain in one place and it affects some other part?"

"I see. Well, that must be it, Charlie."

"Meng, one more thing. I've been working on Soy to the World. I have some great ideas I'd like to run by you. This will be the most fantastic publicity ever to hit tofu."

"No doubt it will. You have brilliant thoughts and strategies. Why don't we talk about it back in the States."

Was he brushing me off? "It's pretty hot in my mind right now, Meng. If we—"

"You're working too hard, Charlie. Too much thinking can ignite your head. Like you say, one part of our body can cause problems elsewhere. Too much heat here, not enough over there.”

“Uh, yes. I know what you mean. Gotta keep things in balance.”

“I agree. Now, relax and we’ll work really hard when we get home. What do you say?”

“Thanks, Meng.”

“William will be in touch with you in the morning. Good bye, Charlie.”

I hung up and sank onto my bed.

I like all kinds of sex. But not by some child wearing cold greasy plastic gloves in a stinking hotel basement.

You should be smarter. You won’t get another chance later.

I did what I did and it’s done.

He’ll never be your partner now. He won’t trust you. You rejected his gift. Boo hoo.

Did I just blow the chance to become one of the guys the Chinese way? I couldn’t do it any other way. Sometimes you just have to play it loose and let the chips fall where they may.

Chapter Eight

Genevieve

THE CHIEF'S INTIMATIONS

Nora and I met almost daily to organize the details of the trust fund for the MacDaniel children. She handled the legal and financial details while I raised money from customers and local business groups. Charlie had managed to raise thirty thousand dollars from his peers in the industry, so the MacDaniel orphans had a solid start on their college education.

After Charlie left for Taiwan, Nora invited me to breakfast. "Let's go to Lazy Meadows over in Whitfield," she said. "I feel like splurging on their Northern Spy apple pancakes."

"And getting out of town?" I asked.

"We can talk," she said. "Nobody knows us there."

Nora barely touched her pancakes. I'd never eaten them before and they tasted so good I offered to help.

"Take them," she said. "I haven't had much appetite lately."

"I can see it in your face. You should sleep more, Nora."

"The Chief asked me to come to his office to talk with him so I went to the city hall. I'd never been inside a police station before." "Me either."

"It gave me the creeps. Hospital green walls, cold overhead lights, black filing cabinets everywhere. He kept it neat, I'll say that for him. He had a couple of yellowing ivies and some spider plants on the windowsills, but once I stepped inside the door, I felt like I should confess."

"Confess *what*? What could he want with *you*?"

"He said he had to talk with everybody from the company. I thought he'd ask about our personnel records, maybe he found a mistake. With so many forms, who can expect our staff to cross every t?"

Nora sat still while she spoke, her lips barely moving, her fingers wrapped around her teacup but never lifting it. I didn't know if she was scared or mad.

"Anyway, he congratulated me on the records. 'Very nice company, Mrs. Greer. You seem to have everything in order. People like working there. It's clean. Except that okaroka out back.'"

"Okaroka?" I said.

Furrowing her forehead, Nora smiled without showing her teeth. "He meant okara. You know how it smells, especially in hot weather." She went on. "He wanted to talk about me and Charlie. He said he'd heard from a little birdie that a former friend of mine had left town suddenly and Charlie was the rea-son for it. When he asked, 'Was that true?' I stood up and said, 'Leave my relationship out of this. You have no right to pry into my and my husband's personal life.' I was pissed."

Nora tapped the table with one hand while she twirled her fingers in her hair with the other. I reached over and covered her hand with mine. She let her hair go and grasped my hand.

"I would be, too. That Chief has no boundaries. You'd think he'd show a little respect to you, after all you've done for the Mac-Daniel kids."

Nora sipped her tea and called the waitress over to ask for more hot water. Crisp sunlight poured through the restaurant's front window. But around my legs, the room held its chill. Nora stared out the front window.

Nora thanked the waitress and turned her eyes back to me. "My anger was an act. I don't know how I pulled it off. My heart was pounding and instead of falling apart, I got mad. The way he'd been sticking his nose in everybody's business, y'know. Did he get to you yet?"

"Not yet," I said.

"He will. I asked him if I needed an attorney and he said no. I sat down and said I wouldn't think so. But right then, y'know, I decided to call Fred Fierst. Charie told me I should if I needed help while he was in Taiwan."

"Good idea," I said.

Nora continued, tapping the table again with her free fingers. "Then Buhrman said, 'Mrs. Greer, this is just as hard for me.' He looked a little embarrassed, rosy in his cheeks and around his collar. But he'd tied his tie so tight, it could have caused the red. Maybe he was faking like me, y'know."

I nodded.

"I asked him to just call me Nora. He seemed relieved and told me I should call him Aaron. 'At the bottom here, Nora, we're just neighbors. Fellow citizens of Clement. I'm doing my job and I hope you understand that.'"

"I can see why you were creeped out. He sounds like he's trying to be bad cop and good cop at the same time."

"It turned out he was all right. I told him Charlie and I had gone through some rough times recently, like any married couple. When he heard that he blurted out, 'Me and Gloria never did.' I said, 'I'm glad you were spared the misery, 'but some people have more pressures in their lives than others.'"

"I don't like this guy," I said.

"Buhrman's a country bumpkin."

"Don't underestimate him," I said.

Nora leaned forward and I followed her into the private space above our cups.

"He was leading up to one question, y'know: Did Charlie have anything to do with Becky?"

"What does he think he's doing?" I said.

"My reaction exactly, but I played it cool. If he involves Charlie in something dicey here, we could all be in trouble. Imagine the press."

"Can't someone stop that bastard?"

"I don't know. Trying that could be worse, because only the guilty object to a careful murder investigation. Like, Catch 22."

The waitress came over to ask if we needed anything else and to clear our plates. I asked for a cup of coffee, something stronger than my peppermint tea.

Nora continued. "I told him Charlie was her boss, and we had three layers of management between him and her. But Charlie's gregarious. He knows all the workers, talks to everybody. It's one of the reasons people like to work for AT. Charlie's available."

"The Chief listens to me and sits back without saying anything, as if he could frighten me with some kind of accusative silence. Of course, I sit back and wait, too. Then he says, 'Charlie claims he didn't know her.'"

Nora sat straight in her chair and crossed her knees.

"So I say, 'I guess he didn't.'" She grinned and said, "He sat there for a minute, kinda staring at me, then he said, 'Thank you, Nora. You've been a big help.' That was it."

"That was it?"

"Well, for him, it was. He tried to cow me once more. When I got up to leave, he said, 'Would you swear to that in court?' I said, 'Sure. But what are you implying, Chief?' He said, 'Nothing. Nothing. Just following some leads.' Some leads? I said, or some trumped-up witch hunter's charges? I was furious this time."

So the Chief wants to make Charlie a suspect, I thought. But what could he be suspicious of? A woman dies in a factory and the boss is to blame? Maybe, if we had a shoddy business, but we're one of the most respected companies in upstate New York.

"Nora," I said, "we've got a crazy man wearing the police chief's hat."

"Once I got mad, he apologized. He was sorry for offending me. He gets all formal again. 'We're a small town, Mrs. Greer.' *Mrs. Greer!* 'We have to go out 110 percent. We conduct a superior investigation, nothing gets messy with the D. A.' I didn't know what he meant so I asked 'What do you mean?' He said 'Nothing unusual other agencies. The insurance company, the state health and safety board.'

"I heard that and I understood Buhrman immediately. Like I didn't already know. Who's been dealing with them. Me."

"I get it," I said. "We're supposed to cooperate, be passive, while the Chief investigates whoever he wants because he has to prove how competent he is."

"I guess. I'll tell Charlie when we talk tomorrow, but, like, I don't think we can do anything but stay cool."

For a few minutes, Nora and I sat there telling each other how angry we were, how unfair it was, but as we talked, we acknowledged the reality of accident investigations and the huge liabilities insurance companies could have.

As she opened her car door, Nora said, "Don't worry, Gen. The Chief has another month at most to clear this up. Until then, we just take care of business, y'know." She shivered and we hugged each other hard.

I drove back to Clement in a sober mood, feeling trapped in a flood of official distrust that could seep into every aspect of our lives. I was glad I'd been so careful to keep my affair with Benko a secret. I felt no guilt about it, but in the cloud of suspicion hanging over us, I was leery of someone finding out, especially the Chief. Who knows what he would make of it. Nothing good for anybody but him.

Chapter Nine

Charlie

BLOOD MEDICINE

sneezing incense, dripping blood
i slid and slipped,
gaining face at last

Twenty-four hours after the barbershop fiasco, Meng sent William to pick me up for our business dinner. I hoped we'd come to some agreement about our future joint ventures. I planned to explain Soy to the World and offer him credit for the idea. I was sure he'd have contacts in Taiwan and China who could launch the campaign in the East and make it truly global.

In gray twilight, William and I drove across the city to Keelung, Taipei's port, arriving at a block of two-story buildings situated across a wide road from several piers. No signs advertised a restaurant and the windows of the buildings were smudged with grease and soot. Before we entered, we watched dozens of cranes drag containers off the cargo ships and set them down on the piers. Under blinding lights posted along the docks, giant forklifts muscled the containers onto trucks that carted them toward us and off to whatever voracious Taiwan business needed more supplies.

"C'mon," Woo said, opening a heavy steel door. We climbed greasy concrete steps up a hallway lit with a few incandescent bulbs. For a second, I wondered if I was safe, but when I heard laughing coming from a room at the head of the stairs, I relaxed.

Meng stood up to greet me from behind a row of red and black-lacquered carvings of dragons and swans perched like familiars on pedestals in front of the table. The burnished belly of a two-foot tall "Happy Buddha" presided over the table from a shelf beside the table, encouraging the diners to enjoy the nirvana of uninhibited appetites.

"Welcome, Charlie," he said as he pumped my hand. "It's been a long time and I apologize again. Have you had a good time in Taipei?"

I was really glad to see Meng. "No problem, Meng. I got a lot done. Can't wait to tell you about it." From the table, one other man, casually dressed as was Meng, smiled and waved at me and lifted his glass. I could see that this was not the time to talk about my debacle last night—the other man must be the key contact Meng promised me, the one who'd make Soy to the World a slam dunk in the Orient.

With its bare yellow walls and high windows encrusted with grime, the small room seemed more like an empty office than a restaurant. I assumed it was converted from warehouse into a private club for harbor bosses. Indirect lighting crowded the room with shadows of the four of us and the statues, muddying the atmosphere around the table.

Meng introduced me to the man, Yi Lan Sun, apologizing also that he spoke no English, and nodded to the empty chair beside him.

I asked Meng if Yi Lan Sun was related to one of my heroes, the ancient Chinese General, Sun Tzu.

He said something to Sun and they both laughed. He turned to me and said, "Good joke, Charlie. Tonight we'll mix business and pleasure."

"Perfect." I was serious about my question, and Meng was host so I'd have to follow his lead, but I wasn't ready to handle too much 'pleasure.' Another barbershop?

A single yellow bloom rising from a crystal vase flirted with us from the center of the table. Yellow, I thought, watching for omens. The Golden Flower. Secret Taoist medical practices. Yellow. The color of the Golden Mean, the Middle Path.

Don't get high, don't fall low. Wait for Meng to make his move.

At an invisible signal, a waiter lit the Sterno flame under a stainless and crystal bowl etched with dragons and loaded with sluggish crawfish. As the broth heated up, the crustaceans began swimming in the ginger soup, their antennae waving silent cries for rescue, before drooping in feeble good-byes. We plucked them out of the broth and dipped them in a chilled sweet sauce, sucking the mild-flavored meat from the shells.

Meng called for the dinner. I'd never seen such a collection of seafood gathered onto one table. Crab stuffed into rose petals surrounding a whole baked carp draped with scales of cucumber slices. Assorted stews displayed in large red-lacquered bowls. We sampled three kinds of mussels and snails served in three kinds of shells: zebra-striped snail shells in pungent sweet sauce, tiny white oyster-like shells drenched in seaweed stock, and pink-and-yellowspotted razor-clam shells soaking in a potent alcohol soup.

After I swallowed a few spoonfuls, my nose watered, my head spun, my heart raced. I wondered if I was in some kind of eating contest, or competitive business dinner ritual where they hauled out the loser and pumped his stomach.

Meng sipped his beer and said, "How do you like the bass? Half hour ago it was swimming without a care."

"Delicious. I've never tasted anything like it."

"The chef arrived from Kaohshiung only a year ago. Already he's one of the most popular in Keelung."

Impressive. Meng was more powerful here than I'd imagined. Who else could hire one of the city's most exclusive chefs, for a private party of four, on demand?

I wanted to angle our conversation toward business but I restrained myself since Meng ate and drank in silence. I followed his example, managing to swell my belly until it bulged like the Happy Buddha's. How the Chinese stay so trim, I'll never understand.

"Our business potential is unlimited, Charlie," Meng commented after he ordered tea. "To celebrate our association," he said, as we watched the waiter pour green tea into tiny red cups painted with black dragons. "This tea costs $700.00 per ounce in Taipei. I import it to New York for some friends." He said something to our dinner partners in Chinese, getting a laugh.

I raised my glass and toasted our association. As my business grew, I said, I'd learned that it would take years and hundreds of thousands of dollars to educate the non-Oriental population of America to eat enough tofu to make me rich. At that point, a few years ago, I found Meng at Hunts Point and he agreed to distribute American Tofu to oriental markets.

The men laughed politely, then Meng set his cup down. "Things are changing, Charlie."

"It's all yin and yang?" I said. "Which way is it going now?"

"I don't know. If I did, would I be in business? I'd be in Hawaii or New Zealand." He laughed. "What about you?"

"I like business. It's something I was born for. My fate."

I risked exposing my personal philosophy to Meng in hopes that I could generate a cross-cultural respect with him based on ethical principles. If we did everything for the almighty buck, frankly, I wouldn't have a chance going against wealthy, powerful people like him. So, my strategy not only had personal meaning for me, but I felt clever as old Sun Tzu, the ancient general, when I used it.

Meng stayed silent. I wondered if he understood me or if he simply ignored my ploy. Instead, he sent the conversation in an unexpected direction. Leaning back in his chair, he said, "My company has recently developed some new markets. The demand has proven substantial, and the profits quite significant. Mr. Sun here and I need a U.S. import partner. That's why you're here."

I blinked. I'd expected to meet someone who would make tofu in Taiwan as one of our partners, or someone to open up the food distribution channels for a brand Meng and I would create. Big profits and high demand sounded wonderful, but

I was a tofu maker and if Meng insisted on my getting into a new type of business, I might have to decline. I was already cash poor from so much tofu growth and importing. I'd need a whole new department. It would cost thousands and take energy away from Soy to the World.

Turning to him, I opened my mouth to ask what we'd import when Meng said, "The real future is bringing China to the West, and I don't mean like poor people's goods in Wal-Mart. We have precious things the Westerners will buy and never ask the price. Perhaps, you can join us."

"Maybe. Let's discuss it. But there's Soy to the World, Meng. It's a great marketing idea and we can make soy the most profitable food anywhere."

Can't open up to more than one thing at a time? Meng could be offering you the chance of your lifetime.

"That's your territory, Charlie," he said, raising his hand to signal the waiter. "As for me, I always take new ideas slowly and surely, until I am absolutely positive they work."

"Soy to the World will work, I'm positive. We have to move on it though. Before the competition." Meng accepted a glass from the waiter and glanced at me with a puzzled frown on his face.

Catching on I was acting too stubborn, obviously in my own interest—a lousy negotiation technique—I said, "You're right. Let's talk about it later."

"Thank you, Charlie. Mr. Sun and I appreciate your sensitivity."

Meng called for another round of beers and the waiters brought out some dense cake. Thinking it was chocolate, I cut and chop-sticked a large slice into my mouth and almost spit the sour, rotten taste out. Grabbing my beer, I washed the 'cake' down as gracefully as I could and laid my sticks beside the plate.

"Stinky tofu, Charlie," Meng said, grinning and placing a dime-sized bit on his lips. "It's our special celebration treat. I see it's an acquired taste."

When I moved my tongue to reply, a foul odor seeped into my nostrils and I gagged. "Yes," I gasped. "I can't believe it's tofu." It smelled like two-month old rotten tofu. Which it probably was.

"Guess we'll need some special products for Western markets. We have to please our customers." Meng laughed, and repeated himself to the others, who laughed and wisecracked because all three Chinese guffawed and grinned at me, the bumbling American who thinks he can do business on equal footing with the ancient masters of trade and taste.

When the table quieted except for the sound of a ceiling fan, I said, "What are we going to import? Tea? Fruit?"

Meng translated and William cracked another one-liner that broke up Meng and Sun. Nodding his head, Meng said, "Special fruit, Charlie. Healing fruit."

Woo stood up and lectured and when he finished, Meng laughed loud. "William suggests we call the import business The Special Fruit Company." The others nearly fell off their chairs.

I missed the joke. My hosts held a long serious conversation while I sipped beer, wondering about the novel fruits I'd seen in the street markets. If we could figure out how to ship them quickly and get them onto the shelves before they spoiled, we might have a business in front of us.

I finished my beer and excused myself to go to the men's room. The waiter led me down a hallway to a luxurious apartment with floor-length windows showing the illuminated harbor. He tugged me away from the view and turned around. I headed down a narrow hall toward the bathroom. With a film of dust on its marble tiles and counters, grease blotching the glass doors to a steam bath, stacks of thick white terrycloth towels sagging on slightly rusted metal shelves, I wondered if I was the first person to use the toilet in a long time.

When I returned, Meng and the others stood waiting for me at the open door. "We'll talk more about the imports later,

Charlie. I'm sorry we have to leave you but Mr. Sun and I have to go back to the south tonight. William will drive you home."

Sensing that I disappointed him by my lack of enthusiasm for his fruit-importing venture, I said "The Special Fruit Company sounds like the future, Meng. I'm sure we can design the right system and get the ball rolling. I'm always open to new things, you know. Importing makes a lot of sense."

"Good, Charlie. That's what I like to hear." He said something in Chinese, everybody laughed again, and we all went into the night to our waiting cars. Across the street, orange and maroon trucks and cranes and forklifts glinted under racks of blinding overhead lights, driven by invisible men, unloading imports, loading exports, carrying Taiwan, like the whole of China, into the wealthy, grimy future.

***

I stayed in bed until noon the next morning. My sore back had returned so I downed a few more naproxen and walked to the street markets. I bought a dozen unfamiliar foods, not knowing the difference between a fruit and a vegetable. I planned to show Meng my research when we next met.

At eight that night, the phone rang and William laughed when I said I forgot that he was coming by. I invited him up to my room to have a drink with me before we went out.

William and I greeted each other warmly.

"Call me Woo, Charlie. After dinner last night, we know each other better."

I handed him a glass of Johnny Black, courtesy of the room's wet bar. "Here you go, Woo. Hair of the dog, we say. Gets rid of the hangover."

"Thanks," he said. "Snout of the pig." He raised his glass in a toast.

We sat for a while, saying nothing, letting the whiskey settle in our stomachs. He emptied his glass and covered it when I offered a refill. "Good time last night?"

"Yes. I loved what the chef could do. I'm sorry we couldn't talk more about business though."

"Mr. Meng takes his time."

"I see that. He told me to slow down Soy to the World. Problem is, I can't. He'll understand." I got up and paced. I needed some action, but my backache had relocated down my sacroiliac into my legs. I had to bring up the massage subject again.

"Woo, my back's feeling lousy again. I wonder if you'd make an appointment for me with one of those blind masseurs? The ones the state trains to see with their fingers?" I wanted no confusion about the type of massage I needed.

"Mr. Meng has a better idea," he said. "We believe that all physical problems start in the blood. Without fresh, pure blood, you can't be strong. Mr. Meng needs you to be strong. Tonight, we'll take some blood medicine."

***

A silver Mercedes waited in front of the hotel. Woo told me to lie across the back seat, "to rest your back," while he rode in front with the driver. The stout car rolled along the pitted streets as gently as a raft floating across a still pond.

Glossy neon light flowed across the windows in greasy rainbow colors. As we crept through the narrow streets toward Old Taipei, I lay drowsing, sunk in leather cushions, relaxed and content.

We stopped abruptly and Woo said over his shoulder, sharply, "Goddam politicians. Let's go, Charlie. We have to walk. Lin will watch the car."

Angry shouts punctuated by firecrackers popping roared into the car as Woo opened the door. People ran by waving flags and banging on trash can lids.

"It's the government. The new generation thinks it's their turn now. The old boys want to show they still get hard-ons."

"We have demonstrations in the States all the time," I said.

He gripped my arm and led me against the current of the crowd. My sense of being a pawn in someone else's game sharpened, but all I could do was play along. I might as well enjoy myself.

We crossed into an open loading lot where dozens of reeking dumpsters lined the walls on four sides of the square. A throng of men milled around in the putrid night, shouting at each other, hip-checking boxes onto pallets, pirouetting out of the way of the smut-blatting motor scooters, all at an earnest commercial pitch. My nostrils twinged as exhaust fumes assaulted my face.

"Trash sorters," Woo said, impervious to the stinking vapors. "When the shops close, they pick through the dumpsters. They sell to Beijing. Very rich men."

A wave of fatigue rolled over me. My watch said midnight. How long had I dozed in the back of the car? I wanted to go back to the hotel and sleep away my growing befuddlement. The scotch had worn off and the pain had climbed from an ache in my lower back to a knife under my shoulder blades.

Taiwan had taken my measure and I was a lot smaller here than I'd ever been back home and I felt no need to prove myself anymore. For a moment, I shocked myself with a stroke of longing to be back in Clement, volleying insinuations back and forth with the Chief, worrying about sales, dealing with the everyday problems that made my mundane business life exciting. Taipei had satisfied my appetite for the exotic and I was ready to bring the taste of the new to America with Soy to the World, at my pace, on my turf, on my terms.

I slowed down to watch the trash sorters, night buzzards who struck it rich from some deal with a government agent, no doubt. Several thin men scrambled in and out of the dumpsters, hollering at each other. An ebony BMW sat sentry in the shadows at the end of the block.

Woo picked up his pace, tugging my arm hard and drawing me out of my reverie. Turning the corner toward a chartreuse glow yawning from the wall, we stepped through an open storefront into a wide, high-ceilinged shop lit by shining neon ideographs. Glistening white tiles rose to meet wall-length mirrors reflecting so much light that most of the dozen or so people in the room wore sunglasses.

I followed Woo to the back of the shop, my leather soles clicking over the terra cotta floor tiles. The shop smelled slightly of rancid fat or old meat, reminding me of a large restaurant kitchen or the butchery in a grocery store. It was set with trestle tables.

I pointed to the many eight-inch long geckoes that perched near the corner between the walls and ceiling. Woo said, "Geckoes. Do you see any flies?"

I shook my head no.

"Geckoes," he said, dismissing further gecko talk.

Seven or eight boisterous men and a few animated women sat at the table talking. A thin bald man called out "New York!" and raised his glass and toasted me. He tossed off his deep purple wine quickly, leapt up on a chair and began chanting at me, pointing to himself, to his image in the wall mirror, and back to me.

Watching him over my shoulder, I closed the distance between Woo and myself, hoping to defuse the drunk by ignoring him. Woo stopped short and I bumped into him. I groaned an apology for my clumsiness.

"Don't pay attention to him," Woo said, dismissing my self-reproach. "There, Big Man's coming to throw him out."

The largest man I'd seen in Taiwan strolled across the room. Standing at least seven feet tall and four feet wide, he wore a black business suit, black shirt, and black headband restraining a shock of silver hair on his basketball-size head.

The giant curled a trunk of an arm around the drunk's neck and lifted him up. The surprised man twitched on the bouncer's hip, gasping and grunting and kicking as the other drinkers laughed at his predicament.

Oblivious to the commotion, Woo stared intently into a large rectangular aquarium from which, I guessed, he'd select a fish for our midnight dinner. I'd had seafood every dinner since we arrived in Taipei and each dish was exquisitely different from the next.

I edged around Woo to stand beside him, watching him as he made up his mind. The aquarium windows were dry and I couldn't see any fish. The tank's shadowy floor gleamed in the room's haze, an emerald and ivory sheen pulsing slowly, sloshing, like brackish water. I detected a sweet, pungent odor wafting out of the tank.

As Woo stared into the aquarium, I raised my eyes. Hundreds of shadowy, flat snake skins were attached to the wall behind the tank, some entwined, some laid over others, the longest of them climbing from floor to dusky ceiling and stretching out over the room, a bas relief of flat scaly vines. The widest and longest pelts hung like woven blankets, died in earthen tans and browns, patterned in diamonds and swirls, artfully connected with repeated crosshatches.

Exotic. The adventure you wanted. Be cool. Act undaunted.

I stared into the tank: the 'fish' were living, coiling snakes. The brackish water was snakes oozing over and under each other, warming themselves in the friction of scaly muscle on muscle. A field of lidless eyes sparkled as blunt heads rose and dipped, curved and turned, pausing in the air as if curious about us. The snakes had heads ranging from the size and shape of flattened ping pong balls to full oval turkey eggs.

A short man wearing an orange and blue flowered shirt draped over an ample stomach approached, smiling, speaking rapidly as he waved his arm over the tank. He reached in, brushing aside several nodding heads. He rummaged through the writhing mound like someone sorting wet laundry.

Woo barked at the man as he lifted a snake, dangling it in front of my face while letting its tail brush back and forth on the floor. I braced myself, waiting for a clue from Woo. I didn't want to make another barbershop blunder.

The man quickly tossed the snake back and bowed to Woo, glancing sideways at me. He signaled for us to follow him. We passed a large cage holding four small monkeys. I stopped Woo to ask about them.

"What are these guys doing here?"

He was so intent on following the tropical shirt, he didn't know what I meant, so I pointed.

"Oh, the monkeys. They love snake. They clean up afterwards. Every year, Danny Ren—'Big Man' in English—brings in the animal of the year. You should see it when it's Tiger year." He honked like it was the year of the Goose. "He puts a baby tiger inside and all the women in the mall want to come in to pet it. Best year for business."

"What does he do for a dragon," I asked, challenging him with a grin.

He belly-laughed and said, "Come back and see."

I might. Maybe I should imitate that idea in my office. On second thought, my office staff would resign if I had a bunch of monkeys or dogs, or God forbid, rats in cages in my office. I'd have to make do with photos or little statues in Clement. Every year, I'd give a Year of the Whatever Animal promotional statue to our customers, emblazoned with our logo.

Big thoughts. Someday maybe they'll pay off.

We pushed through clacking bamboo strips hung across a doorway into a room about the size of my office back in Clement. Behind the far wall, which was glass from floor to ceiling, was a forest scene, thick, smooth tree trunks, broad leaves, ferns, trails of moisture running down inside the glass.

The man disappeared while Woo and I sat down in thickly upholstered chairs across the room from the jungle diorama.

"Relax, Charlie," Woo said. His face shone in the dim light seeping into the room. He sat lightly in his chair, leaning forward almost eagerly.

"What's going on, Woo?"

"Our lucky night, Charlie. Mr. Meng said spare no expense. Huan went to get us the finest snake in the house."

Huan and another man emerged from the doorway beside the aquarium. Huan backed into the room, bracing himself against the floor, pulling the tongue of a long wooden wagon with three-foot high sides and wide rubber wheels. The other man bent over, his arms locked straight, palms against the rear wall, straining to push the cart ahead. Water, or some mysterious fluid, dripped from the cart's seams.

Grinning at the snake handler, Woo bounced up from his chair, and I followed him over to the cart. Inside, a huge snake lay tangled, embracing itself, bulging against the side walls, bowing the thin planks. Its body was the color of a faded red barn tattooed with rows of brown footballs. A head the size of a large cantaloupe with open silver eyes lay passively on top of the glittering mound of its body.

I'd never seen anything like it. "God, where did they get that thing?"

"They raised it. From an egg. Takes years."

"What is it? I've never heard of a snake this big."

"Anaconda. Lives in the water and eats deer and wild pigs."

The men tugged and pushed the cart toward the store's front room. Huan snapped something to the man in the rear and Woo laughed. "Stay back, Charlie. Don't get too close to the head. It could grab you with its jaws and wind itself around your neck."

I jumped back. Shades of my worst nightmare as a kid. I'm strolling along a shady sidewalk and a snake drops out of a tree and strangles me to death. As soon as I spooked, the three Chinese burst into belly laughs. More cultural confusion. As long as My Chinese associates found me funny and laughed, I didn't mind. That showed their pleasure in my company, even if in their provincial minds, they thought me an idiot.

"Just kidding, Charlie. It's not hungry," he said, between snorts. The three of them giggled like junior high girls talking with a high school hunk. "It just ate, last year." He said something in Chinese and they all burst out laughing again.

"What's so funny, Woo?"

Woo eventually settled down while the two tittering men resumed maneuvering the cart ahead and out the door. "It's not really funny, but this is the biggest snake in Taipei. None of us thought we'd ever be so lucky to taste such a wonder. We're happy."

Addiction, I thought. Some way to get high. "What do you mean, 'It ate last year'?"

"This one eats every year or two, maybe a pig, a deer. One big supper holds it for a long time."

I'd heard plenty about snake blood aphrodisiacs so I prepared myself to join in the fun with Woo. If I drank the blood, I would redeem myself with Meng. He probably thought I couldn't get it up in the barbershop. Maybe that's why he avoided serious business talk at dinner with Sun. So he sent Woo to get me a libido booster, a shot of self-confidence—this honor I would never refuse, no matter how woozy drinking blood might make me feel. I'd eaten weirder things, though there in the snake shop, I couldn't remember what they were. Fried ants and chocolate-covered African termites, once.

Woo and I entered the main room. Half the store's patrons had their arms around the snake, tugging and hoisting it onto a long wooden table. The other customers or congregants—I didn't really know which—gathered around, speaking rapidly, their voices rising. They pointed at the snake, glancing at me, everyone grinning.

"He must be twenty feet long," I said, astonished to see it stretched to full length. About ten feet from its head, a man hugged the beast against his chest, barely stretching his arms around the snake's body. "How big is he?"

Woo turned to the giant standing at the foot of the table and asked. The giant nodded, folding his hands, and stared at the animal that now lay across the table, rolling its muscles in slow shudders. One of the men picked up a pail and doused the snake with water from its tail to its head. He did it a second time. After the second pail, the snake stopped moving, except for its head that it raised and aimed straight at me.

Everyone fell still and gazed at the snake. I dragged my eyes away from it and examined my fellow snake aficionados, trying to sense what was going on. Some stared with gleams in their eyes, others seemed to be in trances, rocking back and forth on their toes.

The giant said something to Woo. He turned to me and said, "Seven meters. A hundred twenty kilos. He's in his prime."

The handlers stabilized the animal on the table, each man holding it in place with both of his hands. Huan motioned for me to come to him at the head of the table, where he held the sides of the snake's head between his palms. The snake kept its dull eyes fastened on me.

Woo nodded, encouraging me to go on. Moving to the opposite end of the table, near the giant, he clutched the snake's languid tail. Huan pointed his chin first at me, then at a stainless steel pail about the size of a two-quart blender canister. As I held the pail, it reeked of organic rot and my palms squashed moist hunks of goo that stuck to its sides.

"Stand in front of the head," Woo told me. "Hold the bucket under the edge of the table. He'll chop off the head and when it drops, you catch the blood from the neck. You might need more pails." He pointed to several stainless pails stacked on a stool beside me.

"When Huan signals, take the first drink. You're the guest of honor. Hand it around, starting with Huan."

I felt like I was on stage with the audience crowding closer, focusing on me and Huan and the anaconda while the snake and I stared, baffled round eye to passive elliptical eye. Huan raised a cleaver in both hands, stood on his tip toes and reached as high overhead as he could.

Everyone in the room inhaled roughly as the snake opened its massive jaws and squirmed, stretching its daggery mouth toward me. Its tongue flicked out, rasping my chin. I jerked back.

The cleaver fell, smashing into the table with a thunk. The anaconda's severed head shot up into the air, flipped over and landed, mouth agape, on the top of my head. I screamed, dropping the pail, digging the fingers of one hand into the snake's bleeding neck at the base of the head and pushing at its nose with the other. The snake's jaws clenched my head, its teeth stabbing into my ears. I felt the front of my pants become wet and warm. I went blind.

Shouts in Chinese erupted and Woo screamed in English. "Charlie, wait. Stop."

Someone grabbed my hands, fighting with me to pull them away from the head. The jaws let go and the snake head rose up, scraping the back of my scalp and ripping hair out. Slime and blood flowed down my forehead and cheeks and I opened my eyes into the cold blue light of the room. I turned to find a towel to wipe off my face and slipped. My feet slid out from under me flipping me onto on my back, somehow twisted halfway under the table. For an instant before a shower of blood sprayed my chest and face, running into my mouth, the lights dimmed and I felt myself lying on my back in warm water at the river with my kids splashing and laughing.

I swallowed, choking on the thick warm liquid. Scrambling and flailing, I tried to stand up.

Woo screeched and suddenly the rain of blood stopped and I was three feet in the air, hanging upside from Big Man's paws. I swabbed my eyes with my sleeve and arched my neck up. Woo knelt in a shiny pool beside the table legs, his pants and shirt stained black, steadying the bucket as it filled with blood gushing from the snake's neck.

Huan stared at me, his mouth as wide open as the snake's jaws, the cleaver raised, frozen in the air, as if he were fending off an attack. The men holding the snake's convulsing body had their eyes closed, murmuring guttural sounds over and over. The other customers stood in shocked silence, gaping, except for a woman who had the presence of mind to snatch another pail and, standing beside Woo, waited to catch the essence of the snake when Woo's pail overflowed.

The giant grunted and dropped me on my back onto one of the drinking tables, breaking the spell. The rest of the people swooped down to the floor beside the butchering table and began lapping at the puddle of blood that spread in rivulets across the tiles. Woo shouted at them but they ignored him.

Huan snatched the pail from Woo's hands and throwing his head back, he poured blood broth into his mouth, gargling before he swallowed. When he finished, blood dripping from his grinning lips, his shirt splattered, he handed the bucket to Woo.

Woo glanced at me, closed his eyes and raised the bucket to his mouth. He pulled and pulled on the blood, deep gurgling swallows. He finished, grunted and leaned back against the table, his white clothes crimsoned and soggy and offered me the pail. I raised it to my mouth and sipped.

The blood tasted like my own blood that I'd licked from cuts, but with a sweet and gamey note. It smelled a little like boiled chicken that had sat out of the refrigerator too long. I started to set the bucket on the table, but Woo signaled for me to drink more. With his head tilted to the side like a listening bird, Big Man watched me, no doubt wondering what my next strange move would be.

I lifted the pail up and tilted it against my lips. I opened my mouth and the warm soup surged against my throat, almost gagging me. I tipped the pail back to stop the flow and swallowed as gracefully as I could. Glancing at the giant, I saw him smile, and for good measure, I gulped again.

Everyone, except Woo and the giant and me, knelt on the floor. The snake had fallen off the table and its body lay like a fire hose, leaking blood out of its decapitated end. A man tried to prop a bucket under the gash, but he couldn't hold the snake in his blood-greased hands. Two women squatting at the shore of the scarlet blood pond used their hands to brush blood into wide-mouthed glasses, flicking the blood so quickly their fingers blurred.

Huan and Woo lunged toward me, reaching for the half-empty pail in my hands. Woo slipped and spun around, landing on his butt right at my feet. Huan glared, aghast, appealing to the giant to do something.

At the sight of Woo's pratfall, a roar of laughter erupted from my belly, convulsing my shoulders and neck. Big Man joined in, honking and huffing at the mess. Woo tried to jump up, slipped down again, and let himself fall into hilarious laughing at his predicament. The whole crowd screamed and howled. I'd never had such a good time in my life.

We pointed at each other and bayed, unable to stop. Woo finally got up and lurched over to me. "Are you okay?"

"Woo, you're crazy," I shouted. "This is what I've been waiting for." I was feeling drunk and free, having a wild adventure in Taipei.

He clapped me on the back in the first display of affection I'd ever felt from a Chinese man. "Mr. Meng was right about you." I placed the blood bucket on the floor.

Big Man handed me a towel and lumbered to the front of the store where a group had gathered outside to watch the gory melee. He shooed them away and rolled down the aluminum overhead door. He turned to our blood-soaked clan and muttered something. The people stopped talking.

Woo translated. "'Settle down. Stand by the wall.'"

We all watched the giant step carefully into the bloody goo already beginning to clot into a pudding. We all dreaded what could happen if he slipped onto his duff. He gracefully picked up the bucket by its handle, hefted the snake carcass onto his shoulder, laid it out straight as a post on the table, and grumbled to Huan.

Woo managed to retrieve the snake's head from the browning pool under the table. He offered it to me. The scaly flesh hung slack under dull eyes. Its jaws were jammed open showing dozens of bloody teeth with thin strings of spittle dripping from the corner of the mouth. I noticed that the strings were my hairs hanging like lo mein noodles from the decapitated head, my stomach surged and I turned away, closing my throat and holding the souring blood in my craw.

Big Man herded the other customers out of sight into the back room and returned with fresh black towels to Woo and me. Woo began stripping and told me to do the same. We swiped our bodies with the cloth, rubbing off most of the blood. A funk settled in my nose. I blew hard into the towel a half a dozen times, but the stink of fruity meaty decay clung.

Huan had stayed at the table, blood clotting on his face and clothes, butchering the snake with the same cleaver he'd use to behead it. As I toweled the blood off my back and chest, I watched him slice the snake's belly and spread the skin, revealing shiny blue-gray guts. He dug his fingers in, then slipped his arm deep into the entrails and vibrated the body. When he removed his arm, he dragged out a slithery, magenta hunk of organ meat the size of a football.

Lifting the organ in both hands like a priest raising a chalice, Huan called to the owner. The giant nodded impassively. Huan set the organ down on the table and cut off several finger-like chunks with quick expert slashes.

Woo whispered without moving his lips, "The liver."

Wrapped only in our towels, Woo and I approached the table along with the owner. Following Woo's lead, I picked up one of the julienned slices of anaconda liver, tipped back my head and gulped. I flashed back to the time when I was a boy and had swallowed an earthworm. The worm had been cold and rough, but the liver was warm and slipped down my throat like a smooth consommé of fresh tofu.

My snake-munching mates stood around the table, eyes closed, chewing, relishing the oily magic in their mouths. I wished I could enjoy the ceremony as much as they did. I felt another stomach spasm. The last thing I wanted to do was to spew and lose total face with the Chinese. I shut my eyes and counted my breaths, exhaling through my mouth.

When I'd calmed my guts down, I opened my eyes. All three Chinese, including the giant, sagged against the butcher table, their glazed eyes barely open.

They roused themselves while Huan slowly went back to the butchering. The giant offered Woo and me a pile of black silk which, when we unraveled it, became two huge robes, his own lounging gowns. We wound the silk around our bodies like swaddling blankets. I stepped into my shoes, squishing cool, clotting blood between my toes. Black anaconda goo spurted out of Woo's shoes. I mimicked his indifference, ignoring my last little discomfort for the sake of group unity in our Taoist bacchanal.

The giant escorted us to the front of the store and rolled up the door. He handed Woo a package and bowed. Chuckling, he shook our hands. He patted me on my head and tugged on my ears with both hands. A huge laugh erupted from his mouth, spraying drops of pink saliva into my face.

Woo and I laughed, politely, and, feeling energized, we nearly jogged back to the street where the Benz was parked, each musing to ourselves. I wiped the giant's spit off my face. A rancid, garlic smell had insinuated itself into the stench that occupied my nose.

"I never did anything like that before," I commented to my groggy guide who sprawled against the hood of the Benz.

"Nobody in all history ever did that before," Woo said. "I never had such fun either."

"I've been mostly a vegetarian for so long, I hope I can digest that raw meat."

"Charlie, you worry too much. The snake blood will take care of you better than drugs or health food."

As much as I love Chinese mysticism, I didn't want to get into any discussion of snake magic at two in the morning. My stomach felt queasy, my head had begun to ache, I felt dizzy, and my back throbbed. I just needed to get back to my room and sleep off the night of smoke and blood.

"What's in the package?" I said more to distract myself from my nausea than out of real curiosity.

"The liver," he hesitated. "For Mr. Meng."

I'd expected something like that.

"Mr. Meng gets half, Big Man gets one third. They give us the rest. Like profit sharing in America. Generous men."

We rode in silence for a long time. I forced myself to pay strict attention to my breathing. If I let my mind stray, I knew I'd vomit snake blood all over the back seat of the Mercedes.

"That's all Big Man eats," Woo said out of the shadows. "Boa liver, viper liver, red belly liver. He never gets soft. He can have a hundred girls and still keep going. He's number one snake man in Taiwan."

I listened, trying not to make a snide remark. Stories of the sexual powers of these men bored me. Or did they frighten me? No wonder the Chinese are so populous. Did the Taiwanese sublimate a boundless sex drive into their manic business dealing?

"Woo, forgive me for asking?" I saw his eyes open. "About how much does one anaconda like that cost?"

He grunted. "More than you and I have. Feeding the snake for so many years is very expensive. For us, this was a once in a lifetime chance."

How much could pigs and deer cost? I wondered. Should I ask him what all the snakes eat? I didn't want to know. What do I owe Meng now?

"You should know about Big Man, Charlie. He's a hero to us Taiwanese. Did you know Big Man nursed Deng Xiao Peng in his last year?"

"You mean the guy who turned China into the economic power it is? Didn't this Deng die quite a while ago?"

"Not too long by our standards, less than twenty years ago," Woo said. "All Chinese know Deng is the one who set us on the road to riches."

That sounded like the common wisdom the media touted, but what did I care?

Woo went on. "Back then, China gave the president of Taiwan permission to fly Big Man to Beijing. Very smart move for Taiwan. Big Man kept Deng alive when doctors could barely help him breathe. That was when Beijing assured Taiwan we'd always be free partners in wealth."

"Oh?" I said. "Did he bring snakes with him?"

"No. Beijing has good snakes. Big Man stayed more than a year in the Imperial Palace, treating the old man. At ninety-two, Deng died with three girls in his bed and a happy smile on his face. The last thing before he gave up his spirit, Deng held Big Man's hand and said, 'Thank you, Big Man.'

"China was so grateful for Deng's last year with Big Man, they sent Taiwan five shipping containers of ancient treasures. They're in the National Museum. It really pissed off the next generation.

"Truth is, Deng was going to live to 105 before he started getting sick when he was 90 or so. He suspected his juniors were carrying out the ancient Chinese change of dynasty ritual. That's why he called in Big Man. Snake blood neutralizes most poisons, you know."

I didn't know, but that gave me a new business idea.

I noticed my back felt better. It felt normal. I sat up straight.

What if I packaged and marketed snake blood medicine? It's a libido enhancer, a longevity producer. I could have it dried and vacuum packed. It sounds weird, but it's a perfect global business of the future.

Who'd have thought snake blood—a billion dollar business in Asia alone? Something American Tofu will never be, no matter how popular Soy to the World makes it.

Forget it, Greer. Animal rights people would have your head. First things first. Get the Chief out of your life or maybe you end up dead.

Ah, Jiminy. You're too right, too often.

I slumped down into the car seat, feeling blood medicine rumbling in my stomach. In 36 hours I'd be home, with a chance to get things back under control. We're coming into the Year of the Rooster. With a little luck, I'll be crowing my success from the rooftops of Manhattan.

Go ahead, Charlie, enjoy your bliss, forget your woes. But the Chief's still here. Better stay on your toes.

The End

Book One

Blood Medicine

THE HOUR BETWEEN ONE AND TWO: BOOK TWO
A DARK COMIC MYSTERY
THE SPECIAL FRUIT COMPANY
THOMAS TIMMINS
TOFU NOIR

Prologue

Genevieve

Tofu:
It's What You Make Of It

A Cookbook by
Genevieve Mellon O'Connor & friends

Dedication

Every recipe in this book came from a woman of the land, beginning with Amanda Ralston of Taugatuck, New York. I'd been taking photographs of wild flowers, got lost on a country road, and had a blowout at dusk. No cell phone reception, on the verge of panic. An old pickup with dim lights approached and stopped. A small woman, dressed like she just came from church, jumped out of the truck, fixed the flat, and invited me to her farm home for tea.

Well, tea turned into a long gab about food, children, families, men, art, and more food. When I told her my job was Vice President of Marketing for a tofu company, she laughed and said, "You're having dinner with us." In half an hour, she served me and her family their favorite tofu recipe: meatballs. Who'd have thought a livestock farmer from the backcountry would know about tofu?

Over dessert, we concocted the idea of a cookbook based on tofu recipes from the farms and villages and cities of America named Tofu: It's What You Make Of It. Some food marketing people are saying we've abandoned the cooking culture and joined the eating culture. My friends and I say, who's going to cook what you eat?

On my web site, you can read the life stories and see my photo portraits of my creative new friends from all across the country: From Eveline Jessup in Pine Valley, Georgia, to Betty Ann Fettig in Milford, Iowa, to Juanita Gomez in Salinas, California, thank you to the most capable women I've ever met.

This book is dedicated to all of you beautiful, ingenious, soulful women of the land, whether you live in the country or the city. You've taken your salt-of-the-earth way of life and spiced up bland old tofu into succulent dishes no hungry man, woman, or child could ever resist.

From the Introduction to:
Tofu: It's What You Make of It
Genevieve Mellon O'Connor
American Tofu, Inc., Clement, New York
www.AmericanTofu.com

Chapter One

Genevieve O'Connor

A CAREER CHANGE

By Thanksgiving of the year I joined American Tofu, my ten-year old son Liam and I were down to our last four hundred dollars. The job at the newspaper had ended when the owner's hand strayed one time too often.

I'd come to Clement the spring before because I needed a change from my old life on Cape Cod. *Winny's of Wellfleet*, my best friend's art gallery that I'd managed for five years, was closing its doors for good in March. Jason, the man who came closest to being the love of my life, left me six months earlier. I spent endless hours sitting in front of my fireplace during the lonely, barren winter, dreaming about our future, wondering what I had to do to make sure Liam had everything he needed.

Liam and I would need a bigger place soon. He needed a lot more space at home than I could give him in our one and a half bedroom apartment. But if I gave it up, I doubted that I could find an affordable year-round apartment, or, dream of dreams, a house anywhere I'd want to live on the Cape.

We moved to P-town when Liam was two. He loved the town, the people, his friends. He swam and sailed every summer and played hockey on the ponds in winter. My friends had become our family. Liam had more women uncles and men aunts than any other child I knew.

My life there had been great for seven years. When Jason split, he took my enthusiasm for P-town life with him. If *Winny's* had stayed open, maybe I'd have postponed our leaving, maybe not. If I was going, Liam was at the perfect age to make a school change, before the cliques started forming in middle school and while he was still too young to feel I'd ruin his life by forcing him to leave his friends.

I told Winny I planned to leave Provincetown.

"It's time, Winny. I can't hang around P-town forever waiting for my boat to come in. I need to try something different. Besides, Liam needs to go be a teenager in a regular town."

"Makes me too sad, Hon. I'll miss you too much."

Tears came to his eyes. I started crying and leaned into him.

"Liam in a normal town? He'll be so bored. God, G, we'd take a lot better care of Liam's manhood in P-town than those manipulative little girls and those violent little boys out there in that decadent straight world. Not to mention those slimy pedophiles sneaking around."

I laughed. He hugged me.

"You? You're another story. I love you and want you to have the maximum best this life can give you."

Whatever my motives for leaving, Winny was my friend. He persuaded his uncle in the rural upstate New York town of Clement to hire me as graphics manager for his newspaper.

"It's beautiful in upstate New York, honey," Winny said. "If you want normal, Clement's middle name is 'Boresville.' I should know. I lived there sixteen lonely years before I got the guts to let my high school drama teacher take me to the city. I never looked back."

"I could use small town boredom for a while, Winny. I'll meet somebody."

"You always do."

Winny took both my hands and put them to his cheeks. "My advice, little sis? Come back here by next summer."

I ignored Winny's pessimism. He didn't want to lose us, but I was determined to make it work out in Clement.

***

After two months in my new town, I lost the newspaper job, my first straight job in years.

When Winny's brainless and resolutely heterosexual uncle's hand brushed my breasts the second time—the first I'd let go as his clumsiness—I erased the day's advertising layout five minutes before deadline and walked out. Standing in front of the newspaper office that afternoon, all I wanted was to get in my car, pick up Liam, and flee to the Cape.

Instead, I drove to the park at the edge of town and sobbed. I had no friends, no love, and now, no job.

The inland skies over Clement barely glowed. The thin light sunk into the earth, clutched it like a fearful mother, spreading a greenish shadow over everything.

I couldn't let myself fall into self-pity. I told myself I just needed time to establish a stable life for Liam and time to find some new friends for myself.

Liam and I decided to rent a house at the lake for the summer. We'd keep our apartment in town, but spend most days and nights at the lake. We'd garden, swim, sail, and plan our next move. I calculated that my savings would last until at least the end of the year when I'd have to find a job. We moved to a three-room cabin on the lake with a view through oaks and cottonwoods out over placid blue water.

Liam said, "Mom, I'm glad we're here. We have to recharge our batteries. I like Clement, but sometimes I feel lonely. It'll take us a while to settle in. I'm sure when school starts up I'll make lots of friends."

I didn't know whether I should be grateful for having such a wise son, or sad because he'd grown up so fast and shouldn't really know his mother so well.

I'm not complaining. I'd never complain about Liam and me. Moan and groan, a little, that's healthy enough. I'm just so deeply in love with my son, it scares me. Not in any bizarre incestuous way, just a pure love that colors every corner of my life and sings to me when I'm hurting. I joy in my mothering of Liam. A lot of times I think, I don't matter, except for Liam— that scares me, too.

Still, I can't imagine a life with any less love. It's odd, backwards, somehow, but I feel this total freedom that comes from my mother love. I've never felt that kind of freedom with a man, maybe because I've never surrendered to a man the way I give in, in my bones, to mothering.

If I ever met a man who makes me feel even freer, even more myself, he's the one who will sweep me away. The one time since Liam was born the right man came close, he split. I've come to wonder if I'm too much for a man. Too independent, too free, too much a mother.

When we came to Clement, I put my desire for a man on the back burner. We'd come for Liam's teenage years, and I'd still be in my thirties when he left for college. That gave me plenty of time to meet somebody.

Maybe living in Clement, without a man calling every day, wouldn't get lonely, but I doubted that. All my life, I'd kept some relationship simmering, if for nothing more than to keep myself company. The way I could keep myself from rushing into something with a man was to accept loneliness as a regular visitor. It would be good for my character, but terrible for my sex life.

Liam and I enjoyed the lake so much that the summer disappeared before I'd had a chance to find a steady income. We rented a sailboat and sailed every day. In rain, we rowed across the lake, unless we heard thunder. I met plenty of single fathers of his lake friends and uncles and married dads' best buddies. I went out every week, but not one interested me enough to have dinner with him a second time.

***

Once we came back from the lake in time for school, I looked seriously for a job, never expecting how hard it would be. The possibility I'd end up clerking in a grocery store, office temping, pizza delivering, or night managing the downtown McDonald's depressed me enough that I almost called the jerk at the newspaper and asked for my job back.

A job managing the local frame shop and art supply store opened up in mid-November. It paid barely enough to cover our rent and food, but I needed to find something before the snow fell. They offered me the job, and I said I'd let them know after Thanksgiving.

Then I met Nora at the Salvation Army Thanksgiving Day dinner where Liam and I had volunteered to help serve the needy.

Nora was friendlier than the average Clem citizen, and she took a liking to Liam, praising him for his generosity and civic sense. Of course, he had no idea what she was talking about. As far as he knew, we were simply doing what we always did on Thanksgiving. We'd started serving up spuds and breasts at the "Salvo" five years before in Wellfleet when we had no place else to celebrate Turkey Day.

Nora was petite, raven-haired, shapely, pretty but not striking. Her face was kind, totally wrinkle-free, she looked thirty. She dressed conservatively but expensively, though you probably couldn't tell unless you knew fabric as I did. Her two most arresting features were her slightly bulging royal blue eyes that looked at you as if you were the most important person in the world. And she listened like a born therapist. When she told me that she was six years older than me, I complimented her on her complexion. She claimed it was her vegetarian diet that kept her looking so young.

As she scooped potatoes, I sliced and forked out the white meat. Liam stood proudly at the end of the table, waving his spatula and talking non-stop as he served the apple and pumpkin pies.

Usually I'm reserved with new people. In Clement, where everyone knew everyone else, reserve was a survival tactic for a single woman. But with Nora, in between filling plates and joking with the diners, I jabbered on about my money situation, my newspaper boss's fondling, my fears for Liam, my artist's life on the Cape.

She told me that she painted and asked me to look at her work sometime.

"Maybe you can you tell me if it's worth trying to sell."

"It's always worth trying," I said. "I don't have to see it to say that. I don't know if I can tell you, but I'd like to see your work. It can be great and not sell."

I was starving for the company of artistic spirits. She was the first artist I'd met since I left the Cape.

She pulled me away from the table as soon as the last guest had received her turkey and gravy. I told Liam to go ahead and sit down to eat, I'd be right back. He'd met some new kids, so while he enjoyed his first Thanksgiving away from Massachu-setts, Nora and I sat in the chaplain's office and I told an abbre-viated version of my life's story.

When I finished, she took my hand and said, "Go see my husband Monday. We have a food company and he needs a salesperson desperately. You'd be perfect, Genevieve."

My heart leapt, but I doubted the job was for me.

"I've never sold anything but art," I said.

She grinned. "Hey, if you can sell art, selling tofu's gonna be a piece of cake...tofu cheesecake." She laughed and stood up. "Let's go have our pumpkin pie. I'll tell Charlie all about you. Really. Call him."

She didn't worry about my looks, so I assumed she had a solid marriage. I hoped we would become friends. I needed a good friend.

Chapter Two

Charlie Greer

A GOURMET COOK

silver earrings, green eyes
she laughs, who could resist?
the tofu spring starts in December

"What d'you know about tofu?" I asked Genevieve O'Connor the afternoon we met almost two years before Becky MacDaniel died. "Or soybeans? Health food?"

Glancing at her résumé, I said, "Art major. Photographer. Worked in a gallery? Ever do any food photography? By the way," I said, softening my tone, "call me Charlie."

I didn't mean to confront her. When I get nervous, words flood out of my mouth. She should have been the nervous one but women like her always agitate me, especially when I'm not expecting them.

Before she walked into my office, I'd imagined an attractive and personable woman who, according to my wife, Nora, was someone who "...could help us with sales." Instead, a lovely, elegant woman sat across from me, smiling as calmly as a lioness playing with her game.

Get control, Greer. You're the boss here.

Jiminy, my inner fool. Nothing I can do about him. p"To tell the truth?" Genevieve said, showing me her sparkling teeth. "I don't know much except a few recipes I took out of magazines. Tofu's a cheese made from soybeans?"

She paused, expecting me to answer. I sat there, saying her name to myself. Genevieve. She pronounced it the French way. I said it to myself. *Zhon a vee ev. Zhon a vee ev.* Too many syllables. Thought I might as well call her Gen.

"No cholesterol. Low fat. Stops hot flashes?" she asked. "Reduces the risk of cancer in women. Men, too. The Chinese invented it thousands of years ago, right? Most Americans still don't know how to use it, do they?"

She'd done her homework. A natural sales woman, she drew me in with her questions, then she made the irresistible offer.

"I'm a good cook. Italian. Chinese. Japanese. Couple of Thai dishes everyone raves about. I'm really good at making up recipes."

She laughed nonchalantly as if she'd let me in on an embarrassing family secret. I'm a picky eater but I was already eager to taste any new dish she felt like trying out on me.

"I'll make up some tofu recipes for you. I may not be much of a salesman," she said, the two words "salesman" stressed ironically, in good humor. "I wasn't a great photographer when I started out, either."

She combed her fingers through her hair while she spoke. When people fidget, it usually means they're uncomfortable. With Genevieve, I let the gentle raking motion mesmerize me.

"At the least, Charlie, you need me for my cooking."

I needed her for some other things, too. Not for what I thought, as it turned out but, right then, I just wanted her.

Jiminy jumped into my thoughts.

Your little brain's running the tofu train.

"I may not know much about health food or soybeans," she slowed her pacing, "but I know people."

Crossing her legs, she sat back with her hands in her lap.

"I bet I can read your mind right now."

She showed me the widest smile I'd ever seen in my office.

"I'm not going to say what you're thinking."

She knew. How could I think anything else? Was she flirting or challenging? Genevieve Mellon O'Connor. Long russet hair tinged with gold flowed over the shoulders of a rich brown business suit. Her green eyes had crinkles at the corners that revealed warmth. Her eyes held mine, inviting me to search them. Silver spirals dangled from her ears gracing a sensual neck.

While she talked, I examined her. I pretended that I was a supermarket buyer observing this tall, attractive woman who wanted to sell me a low profit item. I noticed that her teeth weren't perfectly straight. They were white as a TV toothpaste model's, though. While I loved her free-flowing hair, it could use brushing or a permanent before she tried to sell anyone tofu. She had no pretentions. She was a regular guy, who happened to be a woman. As a buyer, I liked what I saw.

My observation skills had improved dramatically since I started writing haiku. It's what you have to do when you practice haiku. Basho, the ancient Japanese haiku master, teaches that truth lies in beauty seen up close. Now I can see beauty everywhere. Strange thing, since I started writing haiku, business started getting better.

"More than anything," Genevieve said, speaking in a low pitch that forced me to lean toward her to hear, "I know people. Isn't that what you really need, Charlie? Don't worry about me and the customers. I tell it like it is. I handle myself. I'm used to guys acting idiotic when they see me. I'm pretty, but not sensational, thank God. What is it? My mother gave me her spirit. I love life. I love people. I'm not afraid. Everybody likes people who love life."

I nodded. She was smart. I like intelligent women, especially if they're working for me. Genevieve sounded like she'd thought about things. Maybe I'd learn from her.

Most of what I know about life I've learned from women. I'd have to teach her about business, though.

"One thing you don't have to worry about? I don't believe in sexual harassment. I'm always in control. If I see a problem coming, I take care of it before it gets out of hand."

Where did that come from? Sexual harassment made me nervous.

Reading my mind again, she said, "It came up at my last job. He was a jerk who didn't know any better."

Her candor began to convince me she was strong enough to handle the job, because we both knew that plenty of guys would come on to her and there was nothing I could do to make it easier on her. Then she clinched it. Nora would insist I hire her when she heard what she said next.

"I'm a feminist. I have high standards. I expect to be treated respectfully."

As if waiting for me to acknowledge her conditions, she stopped speaking, raised her eyebrows and held my look.

"Of course," I said. "I respect every woman. I'm the son of a woman. I have a wife I love and respect. I have little daughter who deserves only love and respect. I'll do anything I can to make sure she gets it."

Genevieve smiled and nodded.

"You're really going to like having me around, don't you think?"

She was right, of course. I loved having her around. She not only sold more tofu in two years than any other Caucasian, living or dead, but with her brains and guts, she saved me and my family from ruin.

"You act like I made up my mind," I said, wiping any expression from my face, invoking my position as president.

"Well, haven't you?"

"Maybe," I said, grinning, reassuming my authority. "We do need people who know people. But can you sell? You've mostly worked in galleries."

Genevieve smiled. I had the oddest feeling high in my chest. A knob of energy rose into my throat that only a growl would relieve. I felt like I was back in my college fraternity again, stupid with testosterone. I began to inhale in rapid short sniffs.

Of course, Jiminy sounded off.

She's blasting you with pheromones. Stand up. Walk around. Open the window. She's gonna give you more grief than you've ever had in your life.

Jiminy always snapped at me whenever I acted the slightest bit irrational. Under the pretense of acting like my conscience, it tried to make me guilty just for throwing myself into life's possibilities.

"I'm thirty-two and I've been around. Had a lot of different jobs. I know, you can't ask me how old I am, but I can tell you. My mother died when I was twelve and I had to take care of my dad. He was a drunk. Died a few years ago. My husband left me when I was pregnant. I get zero child support and for 11 years, I've raised Liam by myself. We've never been hungry. Don't you think I can handle a little tofu?"

"What about pay?"

Enjoying her personal disclosures, sympathizing with a tough life that assured me she could handle the job, I admitted to myself that I'd hired her.

"Pay me what you'd pay any sales manager. I'm not worried. We need health insurance."

It was simple. If she sold our customers half as easily as she sold me, she'd make me king of tofu before she was through. We decided that she would start the next week. When I saw a rusty Subaru parked in front of the building, I realized I'd need to get her a car. The job called for a lot of road work.

She was a survivor, a mother, not a career path woman. I'd known a few other single mothers who had created wildly successful careers for themselves because they were motivated by their kids. It's what's called intrinsic motivation. When I hire men, I look for their I. M. that makes them want to be heroes.

Nora and I preferred to hire family people. Well, she preferred it and I did it. It all worked out because they're like us, Nora said, family. They needed jobs and they'd stick with us. We're one big family.

Instead of a family, I saw us at best as a clan. If we're a family, you can't get rid of anyone, and I've had to fire my share.

Genevieve apologized for not being used to dressing up every day to impress customers.

"Don't worry," I said, pulling up the company checkbook on the computer and printing out an advance. I took the sheet out of the printer, signed it, handed it to her.

"Three thousand dollars!"

"I know how much women's clothes cost. You should see Nora's charge card at Lord and Taylor's."

"Charlie, I can't take this. There's no way I can pay you back." "Take it. If things work out, it's an investment. If not? Well...I know you'll try as hard as you can."

She wavered. I knew she didn't want to feel indebted to me. She was too independent.

"I see it as a signing bonus. You're going to bring it back into the company in the form of a classy image and big sales. Image is what sells, you know."

She finally relented and we shook hands warmly, congratulating each other on our mutual decision. I hired her because she had desire, and she needed the job. Not to mention my desire, of a different kind, which compelled me to make a decision I'd never regret.

Some people, women usually, say that men make all their decisions with their gonads. That may be true, even unfortunate in some cases. But I say that I've made many of my best decisions because I followed the guidance of those smart fellas down below. "Los cojones" the guys in the factory say.

As she was leaving, I suggested that she read up on Chinese New Year, the best time of year to make big tofu sales. When I told her the Year of the Sheep was coming up, she laughed.

"I used to spin wool," she said, "when I lived on a farm in Connecticut.

Curious to learn as much as I could about this fascinating woman, yet not wishing to act too eager, I said, "Oh yeah?"

"Living the simple life when my son was born," she said. "It's different now. Thanks a lot, Charlie. See you soon."

We shook hands again and she clicked my office door shut behind her.

I pumped my fist into the air, whirled around, and started talking to myself. "Way to go, Greer. You lucky dog. You must be doing something right. Jee-sus! They'll never stop you now!"

Smirking to myself like a fool, I collapsed into my leather president's chair and tilted back, clenching my hands in glee. Three thousand dollars was a big advance, especially when we had ten thousand in the checkbook in those days, but true entrepreneurs know when to leap.

I knew Genevieve O'Connor was worth the risk. We needed the sales, bad. I'd just ordered state-of-the-art manufacturing equipment from Japan that we had to have, but I didn't know how we were going to pay for it. I had the feeling that Genevieve was the key to taking American Tofu up to the next level. I couldn't wait to unleash her on my customers. Big time, here we come.

Chapter Three

Genevieve O'Connor

"YUCK!"

The afternoon I left Charlie Greer's office I felt as elated as I'd felt since I left Provincetown.

I'd told him enough so he could convince himself he'd made a rational decision. He had that same look in his eyes every man has when he gets my full attention, the look that says I want you, I'll do anything to have you. I saw that he'd made up his mind to hire me the minute we met. I was the one who had to make the decision. He knew that, too.

I'm glad I did. Selling tofu wasn't my first choice of a job—nothing against tofu—I'd rather give food away. But I didn't have a choice right then.

Since I took the job, my life has never been richer, more filled with love, or more thrilling. Without the job, I'd be in some dead end relationship with a hardware store manager, living in a drafty old house on the edge of town, worrying about Liam using drugs because he couldn't find anything else to do in Clem.

Charlie is a decent man. He gave me the job and he came through in the end. He impressed me that first day when he said he gave 5% of his profits to hunger relief. He was handsome, younger-looking than his mid-forties. About my height, on the thin side, thick hair slicked up over his big head. A diamond stud in one ear. He'll never make GQ, but he's got a modern cool business image and a genuine smile. His best feature is that he comes across as sincere.

He'd decorated his office with a New Age mix of traditional oriental and high tech furnishings. We sat on a low couch, drinking herbal tea from heavy 50's-vintage white porcelain coffee mugs. I commented on the old blue and gray rug at our feet.

"It's authentic Chinese, maybe 200 years old. I found it in a garage sale in Rochester," he said.

A Japanese scroll painting with a mist-seeping-through-bamboo motif hung down one wall. Across from it and behind us, an iridescent velvet rendering of a fierce green and yellow dragon peered into the room. I almost asked him if he found it in a Chinatown bar, but when Charlie rubbed the dragon's nose, saying "My protector," I admired it.

A screensaver flock of white cubes with flapping wings drifted across a computer monitor sitting on his stainless steel and glass desk. I assumed it was tofu flying through the night. Flute music played while we talked.

"Classical bamboo," Charlie said when I asked him about it. "Might be from the Shang dynasty. Thousands of years ago."

When I noted the three avocado plants growing in red lacquered urns, he said, "I ate the fruit, sprouted the seed, cultured 'em myself. Three good friends. Mr Meng, Mr. Giordano, and Mr. MacKay. Our three best customers."

He laughed at my surprise.

"No, you don't have to shake hands. They remind me who pays the bills is all."

When I told Charlie how old I was, he flipped through a calendar with Chinese script on the cover.

"So, you're a Sheep. I should have known."

According to Chinese astrology, everybody born the same year as me was a Sheep. I mentioned my regular sign, Taurus, but he wasn't interested.

"Sheep and cows," he said. "Same thing to the Chinese. I worry a little bit about you as a sales manager. Sheep are compassionate, artistic, and peace-loving."

"That's me," I admitted.

"Can you handle the Tofu Wars?" he said. "Maybe you're a Wolf in Sheep's clothing."

He laughed. Charlie loves his own jokes.

He wanted me to ask him so I said, "What year were you born in?"

"I'm a Tiger. Tigers and Sheep work well together. My fearlessness and strength coupled with your artistry and care for people? We'll be unbeatable."

Even if Charlie'd been a jerk, I would have had to take the job. I knew he'd fall in love with me. Thank goodness, he was sweet. I planned to give him plenty of respect and appreciation. He not only expected it, he needed it. He was the kind of man who'd compete with me to give me even more esteem than I showed him, to show his superiority. Anyway, I always give more than I receive. You can never lose that way. That's why I became the best tofu salesman he ever had.

***

The money Charlie gave me the first day we met helped more than he could know. It went for winter coats and boots for Liam and me and two months' back rent. Even though I'm sure he would have let us, I couldn't ask Mr. Donahue to go another month without paying.

I dragged out some of the clothes I took home from Provincetown modeling jobs I did years ago. My figure had filled out some, but most of the clothes fit. I lowered and raised hems, sewed on a few buttons to some bright cotton blouses and polished a couple of pairs of heels. I created a wardrobe Charlie'd think I bought at Taylor's. I took my five chic gallery dresses and reworked them into a fashionable business wardrobe. I always buy quality and I stick with my colors year after year. Class and style survive the trends.

After my interview with Charlie, when I told Liam I'd taken a job selling tofu, he scrunched up his face and said, "Yuck!"

As usual, I told him I was glad he told me his true feelings, but he'd get used to tofu. I reminded him how he used to hate mushrooms until I sauteed them in butter and drizzled maple syrup over them.

"You can be my inspiration," I said. "I'll come up with some tofu recipes you won't be able to resist."

"Wanna bet?"

Chapter Four

Genevieve

WE SELL U 4 LESS

During my first two years at American Tofu, we more than doubled sales. Tofu was still the butt of a hundred jokes in the media and in the produce business. My standard was "Why did a tofu cross the road? To prove he wasn't a chicken."

I knew we had a real company as far as supermarket buyers were concerned when five different buyers told me the same crude risqué joke. "How are tofu and dildos alike? They're both meat substitutes." None of them looked me in the eye when they told the joke, but I laughed it off like one of the guys. From then on, they'd buy as much American Tofu as they could possibly sell.

I'd made new friends across the Northeast, driven 60,000 miles, and seen Liam grow into an independent middle-schooler. He still loved to snuggle with his mom while watching a movie and gobbling popcorn. It helped that I let him stir chocolate chips into the buttery, salty, soggy mass.

Nora and I had become close. She sometimes told me things about Charlie I didn't need to hear, like how lately he'd become cold in bed. He said it was because he was so worn out from working so much. But Nora said she needed a man in her bed, not a lump of tofu. She proceeded to get herself into trouble with her painting instructor, until Charlie found out and drove him out of town. I didn't really like being her marriage confidant, so I convinced them both to find a therapist. For the last few months, they've had the added pressure of the murder investigation, but they seem to be doing much better.

When our sometimes beloved, sometimes moronic, always charming CEO Charlie Greer traveled to Taiwan last month, we were all glad to get him out of sight. We had a lot of work to do in planning our next Chinese New Year of the Rooster sales promotion and Charlie's trip gave us the time we'd need to concentrate. This would be the biggest sales event we'd ever seen, and I had three people's work to handle. Mine, mine, and mine.

Jet lag must have worn Charlie out because when he returned, he seemed distracted, but he didn't say much about the trip other than Taiwan was crowded and polluted. He promised to show slides, but he never did. All he wanted to talk about was "Soy to the World."

He intended to design a logo and copyright the words then sell them to every soy farmer and company in the U.S. as well as across the globe. These new customers—"allies" Charlie called them would use the phrase and the image on their packages, their web sites, their trucks.

"Intellectual property, Gen. It's where the real value of a company is. Anybody can make tofu, but once we've copyrighted Soy to the World, we have something nobody has, nowhere. And they have to pay us to use it. Royalties."

We humored him because he became so wrapped up in his campaign that he left us alone to get our jobs done. I congratulated him on his fabulous idea but I wouldn't promise that I had time to help, at least until after the Year of the Rooster promotion.

"Wait till you read the article I wrote about my Taiwan trip. It'll be in all the trade journals—it's the next step in our STW promotion."

Charlie eventually told me about his escapade in the "barbershop." He lowered his voice, almost whispering, confessing.

"The girls were sex slaves," he said. "And Meng—he imports snake livers and dried deer penises and ground monkey balls and other aphrodisiacs."

I wasn't surprised. The Chinese diet contained all kinds of herbs and animal parts.

"He smuggles tea and who knows what all. Chinese restaurant workers? Chinatown sweatshop employees? I hope he's not into guns or drugs."

***

A couple of weeks after Charlie returned to the States, Meng called me asking if I could visit him the next time I came to New York. Meng's account was Charlie's responsibility, so I asked Meng if he wanted me to have Charlie come, too.

"No, just you, Ms. O'Connor. Please let me tell Charlie about my invitation. He's nervous about things right now and I'd like to tell him a little later."

Red alert. I'd tell Charlie right away. I wondered what Charlie had done in Taiwan to warrant a secret meeting with the Dragon of Hunts Point. Meng might be pulling me into the murky side of business way over my head.

"I wonder if you'd prefer to meet in the city? I know an excellent restaurant. Do you know the 'Adam's Rib' at the Palace?"

I almost dropped the phone. I blurted out "I'd rather meet at your place...office, I mean. It's easier."

I'd heard about the way the Chinese negotiate in the business world. They let you know your vulnerabilities right away. You know they'll do anything they have to to win your concession. During our affair, Gianni and I had made Adam's Rib our favorite restaurant and the Palace our regular hotel.

Worried about Meng's call, I rushed into Charlie's office and told him, expecting him to know what it was about.

"No idea, Gen. He's got something up his sleeve. Setting something up. Let's learn from his technique. Those Chinese know how to negotiate."

"He's your customer, Charlie. Why don't you handle it?" I didn't tell him Meng had mentioned the Palace and what that might mean. "He's giving you a big honor. They call it 'face.'"

Everybody knew about 'face.' Charlie talked about it every time he had a difficult conversation with anyone. Lately, he'd bragged how well he'd given the Chief 'face' and in return, he expected the investigation to wrap up any time.

"Tell you what. I'll go to Hunts Point with you. I'll drive so you can take a break. I'll wait for you across the Market at Giordano's."

Of course I knew where Giordano's office was even if I'd avoided it for the past few months, when Gianni was in town. I didn't want to see him but Charlie didn't need to know that. As it turned out, Gianni's schedule sent him out of town that morning but he invited Charlie to wait in his office.

"I'm on auto-pilot for you, Genevieve," he said when I called him. "Just tell me where you want me to touch down."

***

At dawn in the South Bronx, the first week of November, Charlie and I, in his midnight blue Beemer, followed a tractor-trailer emblazoned with the mud-spattered slogan "We Sell U 4 Less" toward the Hunts Point Produce Market. He pointed at the sign and groaned.

I laughed. "New York humor."

"Or bad translation," he said.

We stopped at a red light beside the truck and I snapped a photo for my collection of truck ads. The ten foot tall fence that ran beside the road had collected hundreds of plastic bags in its cross hatches. They glowed pink and lemon and gray as a light breeze inflated them like giant mushroom caps.

Charlie nodded absently as he stared out the windshield. When I saw what he saw, I said, "Poor things."

Two women, one lustrous brown, one white and deathly anemic, both wearing blonde wigs and brown trench coats and stiletto heels, stood on the curb in the mustard glow of a street light. Timing their move to our stopping, they pulled their coats open, revealing thin naked bodies. Both had ample breasts with long nipples and scrawny legs. They rolled their hips languidly. The white one stuck out a long pink tongue and wiggled it at me. They must have been so high they couldn't feel the cold on their skin. According to the car's thermometer, it was thirty-five degrees outside.

Last week it was seventy three in Clement and next week it could climb to eighty. At least with global warming, the girls of Hunts Point won't have to freeze when they show their bodies.

Charlie accelerated through the red light before they could approach the car.

"I forgot about this," he said. "Sorry."

I swung around to watch the whores. They seemed miserable. I faced forward and said, "No. I feel sorry for them. They're not dangerous. They're sisters. What's horrible is they're already good as dead."

Using my zoom, I made a portrait of the women through the car's back window. My camera kept me company on most of my sales trips and I often made portraits of the buyers and framed them for their homes or offices. They loved that. I'd keep these shots for my personal collection: "Travels for Tofu."

We rode toward the Market's main gate in silence. Every now and then Charlie glanced into his rear view mirror.

"A van stopped. One of them's getting in," he said.

"Forget them, Charlie. Let's go," I said. "I want to get off the street." Charlie gunned the accelerator and we left the women behind. We both needed to change the mood.

"Know what, boss?" I said. "I'm eager to meet Meng. I'm curious. Besides, I like foreign men."

"I know that," he chuckled. "But I don't think Meng's your type."

I laughed. "Boss is always right."

Charlie showed his pass at the gate and we cruised into the Market, entering a maze of warehouses and loading docks, heading for Aisle B-28 where the specialty produce companies had assigned berths.

We sold American Tofu to Giordano Brothers and Meng Produce and to their peers in produce distribution centers throughout the country from New York to Chicago, from Maine to Miami, from here to Los Angeles. Montreal and Vancouver were our only international markets, but Mexico City was on our radar.

Our distributors sold and delivered the tofu, along with their other produce items, to supermarkets, delis, corner stores, institutions like schools and hospitals. Some sold to the military, others made it available to health food stores. Sometimes, depending on the wishes of the supermarket chain, we sold our products directly to the retailer, avoiding the distributors.

Passing by a small warehouse that sold a little of our tofu, Charlie said, "That's where we can get those esoteric ingredients for the gourmet spaghetti sauce you told me about."

"Which one?"

"You know, the one you seduced Giordano with." Charlie couldn't resist ribbing me about Gianni. "You know you'd never have beaten me in the sales contest last year if you hadn't, you know, with Giordano."

"How many times do I have to tell you, it was not about that? Sales was a whole separate thing. Gianni doesn't make buying decisions—he runs the company." I should never have told Charlie.

"Whoever runs the company makes the buying decisions," Charlie said.

"Not at Giordano Brothers. Not even at AT. You don't make many buying decisions and you run the company."

"Still, if I was a single man and had a woman business associate hot for me, my sales would go one way: up."

"Forget it, Charlie. Just be happy you have such a successful business."

"You're right. It doesn't matter how we got there—the end justifies the mean. Machiavelli. Italian, right? Knew all about how people use their ends to get what they want. Just like any other primate. Sex."

"Shut up, Charlie. Don't be mean."

"I'm sorry. Just teasing."

For all his so-called wit, Charlie could get tiresome. He drove fast and we bounced over the potholes, rocking us from side to side and back and forth, in silence.

Charlie parked under a bare incandescent bulb the size of a gourd, the only light that shone among a dozen empty sockets at the end of the dock. We got out and veered across the greasy parking lot, avoiding puddles and slippery gray leaves and smashed brown pulp. I could see tiny movements out of the corners of my eyes.

"I hate rats," I said, clutching his coat sleeve.

"Keep moving. They'll stay in hiding."

I hoped they would. I remembered the doubts I had when I first came to the pre-dawn Market's filthy alleys crowded with idling trucks and shouting men. Now it felt as familiar and safe as a college campus. I knew dozens of guys here who'd take care of me if any little thing happened.

Behind us, a caravan of empty trailers rumbled and boomed as the tractors, belching diesel fumes, bounced from bump to pothole to bump in the access road between warehouses. Coughing, we ran to escape the slime the truck tires splashed everywhere. I still gripped Charlie's arm as we trekked between rows of parked tractor-trailers and climbed a set of rickety stairs.

Harsh voices and loud laughs echoed off the metal warehouse walls. A sour fermented smell dosed the air. Standing on the loading dock, I said, "It doesn't smell as bad as it does in the summer, like a dumpster behind a restaurant. But there's some perfume in the air, too. It's kind of rosy."

"You have a good nose," Charlie said. "Too cold for my sniffer. I can't smell the flower market and it's only in the next lane over, but you're right. In July, this place stinks like a dump."

"Let's go to Blooms 'n All after my meeting," I said. "Bring some flowers back to the office to celebrate. I'm going to have a great meeting, Charlie. I can feel it."

"Positive affirmation, Gen. Proud of you. Only way to go."

Geez, Charlie, I thought. You think everybody's your kid.

As we walked down the cement platform leading to Giordano's, men appeared wide-eyed from the backs of the long-haul rigs. The workers stopped and called my name. Truck loaders in parkas burst out from between the wide plastic strips that curtained the warehouse door. Drivers leapt the stairs two at a time from the parking lot below.

I felt like a long lost queen returning to her castle. As we reached the Giordano crew, at least a dozen men in heavy coats and dirty aprons circled around us.

"Where you been, Genny-vee-ev? We missed you."

"Hi, guys." The last time I was here I'd bought breakfast for everyone. I was so distracted by Meng I forgot to buy even bagels or donuts.

"Come to get me for brunch?" another called out.

"I been savin' that Chianti I told you about. How 'bout co-min' over after work?" That was gray-haired, sunburned Rico, my favorite.

I laughed. "Sure. What time will that be?"

The rest of the crew started pummeling Rico. He lit up and said, "You like fusilli or rigatoni with your lamb?"

"Whatever you want, sweetie. It's your party."

Everyone laughed. The men invited themselves to the party and five offered to drive me to Rico's house.

"You'll have to pick me up in Clement," I said. "Gotta see my son first."

"I'll pick you up in Roma," Rico said. Someone else hollered, "That's nothin'. I'll pick you up in a limo." Another guy climbed up on a box and threw his hands into the air. "Hey, Genny-vee-ev, get this. I'll rent a helichopper."

"Better start saving your pennies, Gary. You know what a chopper costs?" He shrugged.

"You show up in a helicopter, and I'll take the ride," I said, lifting my hand in a salute.

All the men started shouting and snapping their aprons at each other until a short young man in a Mets stocking cap hollered, "All right. All right. Cool it. Get back to work. She's here to see the boss." Nobody moved but they quieted down.

"Thank you, Donello. You know I don't mind the guys. They're sweet." I tilted my head and said, "Charlie. Remember him?" They glanced at him. "He's my boss. Gonna wait for me in Mr. Giordano's office while I go to a meeting over at the competition."

"You goin' to the Chink's?"

"Meng Produce, Bobby. Another customer," I said, maintaining my neutrality. Every ethnic company feigned hate for every other, though after work, you'd find Chinese, Salvadorans, Koreans, Italians, Croatians, Puerto Ricans, Australians, Africans, nearly every other nationality or race of men drinking together in the local bars.

"We'll take care of your boss, Genny. You just say the word."

I loved my produce warehouse guys. They made me feel like I was the only woman in the world, and in their world of trucks and boxes, I usually was. I believed they'd do just about anything for me, if I asked.

I shook hands with the men, high-fiving some, trying to remember all their names, giggling when I got it right. All the attention made me feel giddy, almost tipsy, even if it was just fooling around.

"Sell a lot of tofu!" I called as Charlie and I turned to enter the warehouse.

All the men smiled and one said, "Hey, Genny-vee-ev. Don't worry. We'll sell tofu to Donello's grandma."

Everyone laughed. "Yeah. Right."

"You d'Man, Donello."

Someone whined, "Charlie, Charlie." He turned back. "Tell me what to do, boss," the man said, kneeling down with his hands pressed in prayer. "I got a problem with somethin' beautiful."

Charlie and I laughed with them, then slipped through the plastic strip curtain hanging over the twenty-foot wide ten-foot tall doorway.

"Don't worry, Charlie," I said as we climbed the metal stairs to the main office. He followed me, pretending to shield me from the workmen's hungry eyes. "They treat me like a sister."

"If that's how brothers treat you," Charlie said, "no wonder there's a taboo against incest."

Once we entered the cool, spicy order of the warehouse, all traces of the Market's squalor disappeared. Pallets piled high with common vegetables and fruits in boxes arranged in clean, precise rows stood ready to salute.

Ugli fruits, miniature bananas, pink tangerines, white papayas, marbled grapes, mushrooms labeled with oriental script, yellow thorny vegetables, and other nameless stars of haute cuisine all waited under fluorescent lights for their chances to audition on the fine china of white table restaurants around the city. Racks of pallets lined the walls thirty feet high, holding white pails of olives, silver tins of nut butters, crimson and brass buckets filled with olive and sesame oils, and transparent five-gallon carafes of imported vinegars.

Charlie picked up one of the fruits. "Think you could make up some recipes for tofu using Ugli fruit?"

I thought a moment. "Would you really want people saying tofu and Ugli fruit in the same breath?"

"Mmm. Yeah. Didn't think about that."

"What about a salad with tofu, grapes and toasted walnuts and a tart dressing with balsamic, light on the olive oil, heavy on the garlic?"

Impressed, Charlie said, "I'd try that."

The temperature in the warehouse felt the same as outside. The whole room was a vast refrigerator. Its forty-foot ceilings extended so far back from the loading dock that we couldn't see the rear wall.

The scene moved me so much, a warm shiver passed down my back. Surrounding us was a testament to the global village. The food came from all parts of the planet. The hooded faces of Giordano employees who moved briskly around the warehouse riding electric pallet jacks, hauling boxes, shouting to each other, came in all the human colors and sizes, black, yellow, brown, white. I heard five different languages spoken as we headed toward the stairs.

I watched, amazed that our little tofus had entered the vast river of calories that flowed ceaselessly through Hunts Point out into the insatiable alimentary systems of New York.

"Awesome," I said.

"Yeah. I get a buzz every time I see this." Charlie twirled in a circle, his arm up, fingers giving a palms-up blessing to the foods. "This is why we're in the food business. Everybody's gotta eat. American Tofu is the healthiest food anyone can eat."

We climbed three flights of stairs to the office level. We knocked and Gianni's assistant opened the door, inviting us into the office. We stepped onto the bridge of a yacht. The window wrapped around the room, halfway down all four walls. The view out the back window wall over the roofs of the Market toward the Bronx on one side and the Manhattan skyline on the other made me imagine I was powering down the Harlem River, heading for sea. The entire front wall was glass through which he could watch his warehouse crew at work.

Across the carpeted office, an oval conference table gleamed under shaded wall lamps. Between the table and us, a leather couch and three chairs surrounded a lacquered coffee table. The contrast between the rubbishy Market streets outside and the Park Avenue elegance of his office always fascinated me.

"Not bad," Charlie said. "Someday I'll have an office like this."

We sat at a small table as a young man in a white coat and black pants served us. Sipping cappuccino and nibbling biscotti in silence, we watched the sun wash the shadows down Manhattan's eager skyscrapers.

"You better go," Charlie said. "Don't keep Meng waiting."
"Charlie, will you relax?"

"I can't. You know I can't, ever since Becky died. The Chief's snooping everywhere. I know that's what Meng wants to talk about."

"Take it easy. I thought you gave him so much face the only place he'll want to snoop is in the mirror." Charlie groaned. "Have a cappuccino and enjoy the view. I'll be back and we'll go buy some flowers and have a nice lunch. Want to go to Cuchi Fritos? Plantains and fried chicken. You can't do anything right now, so just sit here and accept it."

"Easy for you to say."

Charlie stood up to help me put my coat on. "Good luck." He hugged me. "Watch for any weird products at Meng's."

His face was gray and his normally trim suit was wrinkled. "Like what?"

"Snakes. Dried deer penises. Rhino horns. Like that."

"Sure thing, Charlie. I'll brush up on my Chinese on the way over."

He stared at me.

"To read the labels," I said.

***

"Hello, Mr. Meng," I said as he rose from his massive black lacquered desk. I always called him "Mr. Meng."

Not only was he nearly a foot shorter than me, but he wore a five-thousand dollar silk suit that glowed with midnight iridescence, and a diamond as big as my thumbnail adorned his little finger. As imposing as he was, despite his tiny stature, what made me most cautious was I'd entered an alien world populated by powerful men who experienced the world in ways that I would never understand.

I'd never seen a woman other than me in his warehouse, not even in the administrative office, and I assumed that everyone, except maybe Charlie, in his stubborn democratic naiveté, paid Meng a lord's deference.

In his office, Meng expected and received my complete attention and formal respect. We sat on low ivory stools at a small jade table inlaid with scenes of farmers and crops, hunters and animals, fishermen and fish.

"Fifteenth century." He nodded casually at the table and stools I was staring at. "They have more sentimental than economic value. We trace the group back to an ancestor thirty-four generations past. As you can see, it foreshadowed our interest in the food business."

I shifted on the stool like many uncomfortable servants of the Empire called to meet at this table during the last five hundred years.

He poured tea into tiny cups painted with ornate calligraphy. He said the tea set, while not really a unique work of art, also had some sentimental value because it had been in his family for ten generations.

"I enjoy serving tea, Ms. O'Connor, especially to Americans. It gives you time to slow down and relax. You all work too hard. It's something I have learned from my Japanese associates."

My eyes scanned the room and landed on a long mahogany bar next his desk. In the shadows above the bar, thick shelves carried an exhibit of whiskey bottles any four-star bar would be proud of.

He noticed my glance lingering on the bottles. "Would you prefer a whiskey instead, Ms. O'Connor? Powers Gold? Ireland's finest."

"No, thank you."

"A liqueur? Midori? Campari and soda? My daughter tells me it's her favorite."

"No, Mr. Meng. Really. I don't drink. It's kind of you, but I prefer the tea." I picked up my cup and had a tiny sip. A little smoky, spicy. "Delicious."

He asked me about my family, my background. When I told him about my previous career as a gallery manager and a photographer, he asked me to sit beside him on the couch. He showed me a fat album of family snapshots. His two sons lived in Taiwan where they ran an import-export business. Meng had dozens of photos of his grandchildren.

He smiled as he turned the pages to a series dedicated to his daughter. "She is something like you, my Shu Ling. An artist. She wants to make movies." He pointed to a broad-faced, grinning girl dressed in a white evening gown.

She was a cold and arrogant rich kid, as far as I was concerned. She'd all but ignored me while she made her film of AT. She had Charlie following her around, wagging his tail and panting like a lost puppy. Everybody in the plant made jokes about him and his 'Tokyo Rose' behind his back.

"I met her at the tofu plant. She seems very smart and competent. We're excited about the film."

"I'm proud of her," he said, "but I am not sure what will become of her. She's our 'untamed mare.' She's determined to stay in the States. She's still quite young, though she imagines she's a woman of the world."

Meng began our formal meeting, first moving us to comfortable chairs and pouring more tea. "I appreciate all you have done to increase our tofu sales, Ms. O'Connor. You have also improved sales of some of our other products."

"Thank you, Mr. Meng. Please call me Genevieve. Everybody does." I gazed down into his face, noting that he didn't resent my superior height in my heels. I wore them on purpose, a demonstration for Meng of my professional persona. "Your success is my success," I smiled. "Without you, we would have much less success."

He returned my smile and, holding my eyes, poured more tea. We drank without speaking, listening to the muffled racket of empty trucks careening and jangling down the pot-holed passages between the warehouses. I felt as relaxed as a mouse in a cheese barn, sensing the cat close by.

"A very nice tofu firm from Canada has approached me," he continued. "They call themselves 'U.S. Tofu.' Do you think that's strange?"

I agreed it was. I sipped tea and ventured, "It could even be a trademark infringement," offering him resistance and intelligence in the same breath.

I recalled one of the sales seminars Charlie had sent me to. I'd use its strategy for dealing with Meng, like I did with other men customers.

If you mirror their self-importance, they'll never know it but they'll think you're the same as them. Let them wonder later why they respect you so much.

Placing his cup on the table beside his chair, Meng smiled and went on. "The company is a division of a large dairy and marine enterprise. The son of the owner runs the tofu operation. He wants to enter this market very badly."

I settled back, but held his eye as he launched into a little lecture.

"We're now riding a wave of Asian products entering the U.S. market. The farms are finally large enough to supply an export market. From bok choy to schizandra, the supermarkets will never be the same. Even your Mr. Giordano has made a great deal of money from Oriental products. However, I don't carry Italian or even Belgian products in my warehouse."

Concealing my discomfort, I decided I'd better deflect the conversation away from references to "my" Mr. Giordano toward the business at hand.

"Mr. Meng, Charlie really should know about this."

"He knows about it, Genevieve." He pronounced my name hurriedly, as if he wanted to brush it off his lips. "I called him a few minutes before you arrived to let him know you were coming to see me. I also told him about U.S. Tofu. More tea?"

Cringing at Meng's attempt to undermine Charlie's trust in me and make me an unwitting player in some game he had going with Charlie, I set my jaw and accepted the tea. As he poured, he said "I had the feeling he knew about our meeting before I called him today."

Of course Charlie betrayed my confiding in him about the meeting. He had to let Meng know who was in control of me. Boys.

Holding the warm teapot between his palms, then setting it down beside his empty cup, Meng stood up, gracefully, but abruptly ending the meeting before I touched my freshened cup.

"I told Charlie that if any new developments happened before I saw you, I'd give you the update on the situation. He hopes you can discuss this with Mr. Giordano?"

"Of course," I said. "Thank you for the tea. It was the best I'd ever tasted. Charlie said you import the best."

Meng raised his eyebrows, furrowing his forehead in three wide equidistant arches. "I'm sorry I can't take you to lunch, Genevieve. I have to chopper to JFK. Those Brazilians never keep their freezers cold enough. If I don't inspect, I can lose a lot of money." Meng helped me on with my coat. "I promised Shu Ling I'd take you to dinner with her very soon."

"Oh." My arm caught in my sleeve and Meng let go of the coat so I could shrug it on. "I'm not in New York very much, but maybe next time I come in?"

"I'll tell Shu Ling. She knows all the places you young people like. A couple more things, Genevieve. I didn't mention this to Charlie. Mr. Buhrman called me wondering if I knew anything about Charlie's relationships with women. I said Mr. Greer is happily married, as far as I know, and he should ask Mr. Greer himself. I told him businessmen don't interfere in each other's personal lives."

So, he wanted Charlie to know the Chief suspects him of something. Charlie would be so pissed at the Chief, I wasn't sure I should tell him. He might lose his temper and get himself in trouble. The Chief often tried to rattle Charlie and it usually worked. I pulled on my left glove and extended my right hand to shake good-bye.

Meng touched my fingertips with both of his hands, holding on while he said, "Tell Charlie I thought his article on the snake blood parlor in Taiwan was charming. I told him thank you for letting me read it in rough draft form. If he publishes it anywhere, I'd appreciate it if he removes Meng Produce from mention as sponsor. In fact, Meng Produce doesn't belong in that or any other article he writes."

Meng's abrupt dismissal of public mention of our association told me it was time for me to go. I thanked him again for the tea and left. I heard him pick up the phone and speak in Chinese into it.

As I arrived at the warehouse door, a smiling man handed me a lightweight package. Gold leaf wrapping printed with scarlet Chinese ideograms. I knew it was some of the exquisite tea we'd just shared. Meng was the master of sending mixed messages.

I went out into the chilly morning light, confused and worried. I knew Charlie had sent the article off to a couple of industry trade journals and to some New Age magazine that had offered him three hundred dollars. I hoped he was holding out for more. If not, he'd better get to the editor before Meng wrings his neck and kicks AT out and invites the Canadians in.

I left Meng's office wondering what I was supposed to discuss with "my" Mr. Giordano. Was the fact that Meng knew something about Gianni and me a threat? Who was he threatening? I assumed it was a threat to American Tofu. Maybe to Giordano Brothers. Maybe to me. Did I screw up? I doubted it. The past is the past.

I hurried outside to call Gianni before I picked up Charlie and he started freaking out about Meng and the Canadians. Gianni answered on the first ring. "I don't want this to cause you any problems, Gianni. I'm way over my head. I'm sorry."

He laughed and told me not to worry about anything. "I like it when you're in trouble. It's the only time you call me anymore."

"You told me I should call if I needed to. Friends, remember?"

"Yes, yes. I just enjoy hearing your voice. Forget about Meng. The last time he intimated that he'd give me trouble, he was just crowing. He'd lost a few hundred thousand on some Hong Kong stock. He's using you to play what we call the Chinese cosmetics game," he laughed. "He's saving face, or getting new face. Something. It's not about you or even tofu. Don't worry. I'll take care of it."

***

On the ride home, I drove because I had to tell Charlie about the details of the meeting and I didn't trust him behind the wheel when he blew up. I told him Meng's bad news least to worst: the article, the Canadians, the Chief.

"He doesn't want me to mention his name in the article? Did he say why?"

"No. He doesn't like publicity."

"Yeah, that's his right. It's just Meng Produce, a real modern world business, makes such a great literary contrast to the ancient world of snake blood guzzlers. No problem. I'll fake a name."

"If I were you, I'd run it by Meng."

"I don't go for censorship, Gen. Free speech is just that."

Charlie clung to his principles at the most irrelevant times, like now when he could lock himself into offending his entree into the world's biggest tofu market: Asia.

"Don't think of it that way, Charlie. This article isn't the great American novel. Meng's a precious customer. Show him some deference." He scowled at that. "Give him respect, that's all."

Charlie folded his arms and grumbled, "All right. Not a big deal." Charlie fiddled with the radio while I drove up the interstate, barely keeping up with traffic at eighty. Settling on a classical station, he sat back and said, "Did Meng tell you about the Canadians?"

"Yes. It worries me."

"U.S. Tofu. Can you believe it? The balls to copycat us. Meng and I had a laugh about it."

"You don't think they're trouble? I do."

"Naw. Meng's solid. He wanted to let me know about the competition. That's all. He's watching my back."

Then I turned the questions back to Charlie.

"He said the Chief called, asking about you and your relationship with women."

"What?" Charlie nearly came off his seat so fast he bumped his head on the ceiling. "Ow. That son of a bitch. He asked Nora the same thing. Goddam. I try to do everything I can for him and he goes behind my back to my wife and then to my best customer."

Giordano's your best, I thought. Meng's your favorite.

"I'm gonna have an injunction ordered on him. He can't do this? He's outta control."

"Are you sure? He's probably just doing his job."

"Asking my customers about me and women!" He slammed his palm down on the dashboard. "Implying I'm fucking around! What's Meng gonna think about me and Shu Ling? Pull over. Let me out."

I pulled to the side of the road and he stepped onto the shoulder. He slammed the door and let loose a deep groan that went on and on, sounds a torture victim would make, trying to keep himself from breaking. He stopped and kicked at the shoulder of the road, hollering "Fuck, fuck, fuck, fuck" and kicking the dirt. He lost his balance, regained it, and threw his head back, howling a high-pitched scream.

I'd never seen Charlie lose control of himself like that. I rolled down the window. "You all right?"

He turned around, eyes blazing out from traffic shadows flickering across his face. "What do you think?"

"Charlie?"

"Give me a few minutes. I'll be all right."

I rolled the window up and waited with the car running. When he got back in, he was breathing hard, but quiet.

"She was really a sweet woman, Gen." His voice trembled as if he'd been crying. Leaning back into his hands folded behind his head, he stared out the windshield, oblivious to the stream of oncoming headlights. "She didn't deserve to die. Now the cops are mucking around. Where do they get the right?"

"I don't know, Charlie. Maybe he's following some lead that has nothing to do with you?"

"He doesn't have any leads. He's just on my ass." He sat back, cooled off a little. "You know how a junkie has a monkey on his back? Well, I've got a Burr-man on my back."

I couldn't respond and the joke sank. Then, in a mournful tone, Charlie said, "And I don't know if I can kick it before it sucks me dry."

"Why? Did you do something to him?"

"I don't know. Buhrman doesn't trust anybody. Me? He sees me as the convenient target. He told me he likes to take shooting practice." He'd slipped off his loafers and propped his feet on the dashboard, his eyes examining the murk out the side window. "Maybe when the workers told him Becky liked me, he got a bug up."

"They told him that?"

"They all like me, Gen. That's what Benko said, too. I know it, you know it. I like them, treat everybody right."

What was Charlie telling me? She was a 'sweet woman.' She 'liked him.'

"Charlie, what do you mean, she was a 'sweet woman?'" I waited a long second for him to answer.

"Just what I said. That's all. Nothing else." His voice tailed off so I barely heard him.

"Are you sure you don't want to tell me something?"

"What?"

"Like you knew Becky better than I thought you did?"

The sound of wind grinding past the windows was all the answer I got. We drove the last hour in silence. Charlie turned away from me and stuffing his jacket against the window, he lay his head over and fell asleep.

I knew Charlie as well as I knew any man I wasn't lovers with, probably better because I saw all his weaknesses and didn't make excuses for them,

***

I pulled into my driveway and nudged Charlie. I didn't know if he'd slept or pretended to sleep the last three hours, but I was happy to have the time to myself.

"'Night, Gen. Thanks for driving. Sorry about the tantrum."

"Forget it, Charlie. We gotta talk sometime."

"'Bout what?" he said and slid over into the driver's seat.

I held the door half open, watching him. "You know."

"Sure. Whenever. G'night."

I went inside, read a sweet note from Liam, and listened to my voice mail. Only one message, from Gianni.

"I called Meng. Told him Charlie suggested I call. It's nothing. He just wants me to get him more supermarket business for some of his own products that Giordano distributes for him. I said I'd try. He was just fishing when he guessed that we were involved. Don't worry. Let's talk soon. Ciao, mi amore."

The message sounded like poetry to me. Emotionally whipped, I lay down on the couch. I knew it was weak, an illusion, but I played Gianni's voice over and over, his words kissing, nipping, nuzzling my ears. I lay still a long time, unable to fall asleep.

Visions of Gianni's face close to mine merged into images of him making love to his wife with me standing next to their bed. As I watched them, my hand, my hand more faithful than a husband, more faithful to me than I am to myself, my hand lifted from my stomach and dropped to my lap.

My hand slipped down into my pants. Where Gianni once mounted me, my fingers began to play. Where he sang bawdy songs with his breath, my thumb began to flutter. Where he tickled me with his tongue, my hand began its familiar rhythm. Where he fed on my pomodorini rosa, I opened myself like an empty basket. Where I stretched like a mare to buck him, I tossed myself against his ghost who rose into my mind as real as if I rode him again in the flesh...and then the ghost of my ex-lover Jason rose...and the ghost of my ex-husband Robert...

and vague ghosts of men I've known and men I'll never know, ghosts who always circle me, approaching my hungry skin like servants of my delight when I pleasured myself...and the ghost of Gianni rose groaning into my face again...and the delicious ghost of Gianni whose love I felt lying across me in the bed and then the wet ghost of my own flesh rose into my palm like a wave my whole body felt rushing upwards and back and up and back and when it crashed, I cried out and tears poured out and once again seeing Benko's living ghost, feeling the warmth of his bare chest against mine, my body sagged into my pillows and I drifted off into sleep.

Chapter Five

Charlie

BENKO AND CHARLIE IN THE RING

distracted by lust
I hired the wrong guy
he did his job, I did mine

Rogelio Padilla, my production manager since I started the company, resigned about the time I met Shu Ling. He wanted to move back to Queens where he'd found a job running the night shift at a pudding factory.

We received twenty-five applications for the production manager position.

My first choice was Benko Ivanovich Gladonov, a Russian living in Albany, previously employed as a plant manager at a mincemeat pie factory in England.

I invited Gladonov into my office for a final interview. He'd be number three in the company with tremendous responsibility for every product that went out the door and authority over seventy or so plant employees. I had to make sure he could handle it before I brought him onto the team. I wanted to see how he'd react to a challenge.

"You have everything it takes for this job, Mr. Gladonov. Experience, good references, skill. Only one problem."

"Mr. Greer, yes. My favorite. Problem solving."

"This is not against you, sir. But if I have a hard time understanding you, my Latino and Chinese workers might not get a thing you say."

He laughed, tossing his head back and shaking his long blond hair. "English. Yes. Hard I study. Everything I understand. Ask my old boss. I speak just fine. People? Twenty-two people I boss now in Albany. They know everything I say. Labor? No problem."

"We have seventy in production, a lot more than twenty two," I said. "Far more complicated. What is your management style? How do you handle people who come late to work?"

"America, Mr. Greer. People come late? One time, I say three strikes and you're out. Three times, bye bye."

Tough love. That sounded reasonable to me. We didn't have a tardiness problem, but he gave a good answer.

"Somebody doesn't show up? The work I take care of it, no matter." He sat across from me as comfortably as any prospective employee I'd interviewed.

Uninvited, he said, "Children, Mr. Greer?"

"Do I have some?"

"Yes."

"Two." I pulled out a snapshot of the kids I'd taken the previous Christmas. Marissa, Little Chuck, and Nora posed beside their presents under our room-sized tree.

"Lovely," he said. "Your wife?"

"Of course."

"Beautiful." Now he smiled at me. "Lucky man."

I smiled and agreed. "I can't legally ask you about your family," I said, leading him to reveal some of his personal information.

"Family? No. I have no children. Wife in England. Ex-wife. New husband and new babies she has. Now happy." He shrugged.

I was glad to hear he had no family because the job required him to be on call twenty-four hours every day of the week. If we needed him, he had to show up. No excuses. I tested him further. "Mr. Gladonov, we need somebody we can count on. Somebody who's not afraid to work."

He interrupted me. "Work, I love. Good working, life tastes sweet. You count on me. So much energy, God gave me. Ask my boss. Two men, three men, I do all that work."

I usually paid no attention to past employer references. Due to employment laws favoring workers, no employer told the truth unless the worker was a real creep, and then they'd barely hint at it, saying "It was better for Mr. X to move on in his career." Still, I'd contacted his employer in Albany and learned that Gladonov had a stellar record. Either his Albany boss wanted to get rid of him, or he wanted to help him. He gave him an unqualified "Great worker" rating. I decided to give Gladonov a chance.

Better be sure, Chuck. You hire him, you're stuck.

"Well, Mr. Gladonov. What do you say we give it a try?"

"Good idea, Mr. Greer. I will give it the old college tryout."

"I'm thinking a three-month probation." I had some doubts about his ability to get along with the workers. On paper, he seemed good enough, but if the factory crew didn't take to him…I'd be right back where I started. "If it works out after that period, we'll hire you with an open-ended contract."

His smile faded and his eyebrows drooped. He gripped his knees with big hands, rocking his body.

"Probation? Like jail? No, I don't take that."

I laughed. "No, not like out of jail. Learning time. You learn about us, we learn about you. We like what we learn, then you're in. It's a critical job, Mr. Gladonov. I have to be careful."

"Yes, I have careful, too. I want green card. I need only less than one year, I have it. Tools, Craftsman I have. Good ones. I work hard all day for you. All night."

Using my tried and true technique of hiring people who need the work the most, I welcomed him to American Tofu with the sense that he could quickly pick up the job from the line supervisors. I could return to dedicating my time and energy to Shu Ling.

I introduced him to the office staff and Genevieve. He charmed us all with his stilted English and his easy smile. I noticed that Genevieve was especially warm to him, volunteering to show him around the plant when he started work. Everyone who met him gave him a cheerful thumbs up. For the first few months as production manager, his smiles and his tools made life in the factory run like an enchanted kitchen in a great castle.

Benko fooled us all and I have only myself to blame, because if I hadn't been so distracted, I could have seen through his "Charming Hardworking Russian Peasant" facade. The way things turned out I don't know if he was the worst or the best hire I ever made. It's no excuse, but I felt so besotted with Shu Ling, I couldn't concentrate on anything else. Her flirting and resistance to my come-ons had built up so much pressure inside me, I wanted any relief wherever I found it.

Having Gladonov in place as production manager turned out to give me the same kind of relief you get when you toss a bone to your neighbor's barking Rotweiler to get it to shut up. If you don't keep tossing it something to gnaw on, it finds its own way to get over the fence and come digging in your yard.

First you shout, then maybe you run, then you hold your ground with a stick in your hand. Then, once the dog makes a move, you do whatever it takes.

Chapter Six

Genevieve

RUSSIAN SAUSAGE

Benko and I had a summer love affair that might have lasted much longer if Becky hadn't died. Although he seemed to enjoy talking to Liam and helping him fix his bicycle, he made it clear that he had no interest in children. That suited me fine. Guys who showed as much interest in my son as in me always ended up proposing, meaning, 'mother me.'

Liam had gone camping in the Adirondacks with his swim team, so I had a luxurious mid-summer week to myself. Feeling a little lonely one afternoon, I invited Benko over that evening to try out a tofu barbecue recipe I'd developed for our seasonal tofu sales. He arrived with a sausage he'd driven two hours round-trip to Buffalo to buy. "Russian aphrodisiac," he said with a big grin.

I complimented him. "Congratulations, Benko. You're learning to flirt."

"Not really," he said. "Flirt I still don't." I showed him the grill and he went to work. "Special spice," he said as he forked the steaming sausage onto my plate.

"No sage, I hope. I'm allergic. It closes up my throat so I can barely breathe."

"No, no. Only special fennel. Opens the heart." He opened his mouth and laughed as he slid a chunk of sausage dripping with grease into his mouth.

"You can flirt, Benko. Don't tell me you can't."

"I learn fast. You like it?"

After a bottle of Chardonnay, Benko and I flopped into my backyard hammock. We swayed in the warm dusk and started kissing. In a few minutes, the mosquitoes drove us inside to a fevered interlude on the couch before we staggered into my bedroom.

Savoring the bubbles of lust that percolated through our veins, we undressed each other slowly, our eyes roaming eagerly across every revelation of the other's body. In the center of Benko's chest, he wore a tattoo of a deep red heart torn into two pieces with blue teardrops cascading down to his belly.

"Don't break my heart again," he said as he watched me examine the tattoo. "Like the others."

I followed the trail of tattoo teardrops down and saw another pink heart-shape peeking out of the elastic of his black briefs. I smiled and he grinned broadly. Benko stayed all night, proving, he said, "the power of the sausage."

"But, Benko," I retorted, "Every cook knows the secret's in the sauce."

His fingers, for all their callused mass, grazed my skin so delicately he felt like my own shadow nuzzling me. He held me gently, following my unspoken instructions perfectly, massaging lonely muscles, tickling sighs from me that I hadn't heard since I lay with Gianni.

That surprising summer night, I snuggled into the cave of Benko's long arms with my head on his chest riding the tranquil rise and fall of his breath into the dreamless night. As the first sun shined through the leaves outside my window, he climbed out of bed to go to the factory.

"Benko, let's keep this between us. Our secret," I said.

"Passion over principle," he replied, groaning tenderly.

"Our secret. Right?"

"Always. Have good dreams. At work I see you."

We saw each other again three nights that week, sleeping together two of them. Benko had enough passion for both of us, aphrodisiac or no. I started calling him 'The Amazing Russian Sausage.'

As far as I knew, Benko and I kept our affair completely quiet. His inbred paranoia coupled with my fear of small-town busybodies spreading gossip forced us to use absolute caution.

When we met at my house, he arrived late, after Liam had gone to bed, and he left before sunrise. The few nights I visited him, I followed the same regimen, showing up late, leaving early, always using his back door. For me, the threat of getting caught added a thrill to our time together.

Benko said he felt at home in our clandestine affair.

"Ferret. I know how ferret lives. Without secrecy, I don't survive," he bragged. "I lived in underground all my life. Anything you want I can teach you how. You get away easy."

I pleased him by pretending to learn every surreptitious and stealthy move from him, and I let him reveal more about himself than he wanted.

Behind his charm and bravado, Benko carried a cold, cynical view of life. He claimed to enjoy our lovemaking more than he had with any other woman, but he never made a sound. He didn't much like to kiss, and when I'd open my eyes from the throes of passion, he'd be staring at me as if he didn't dare let his guard down and surrender to the underworld where feelings rule.

When I asked him what he wanted out of life, more than anything else, he said, "This. What else? I want all I can."

"You must have a dream."

"Yeah. American citizen. Then freedom."

"What then, I mean?"

He closed his eyes and squinted, his cheeks burnished on his high cheekbones.

"Right now, you have ferret eyes," I teased. "Is that what happens when you dream."

"No dream. Thinking about dream." He opened his eyes. "Everybody wants to be movie star in America. Top of the heap, right?" "Not everybody."

"I had chance. One movie. Didn't like it, so I quit."

"You quit?"

"Big money, fame, everybody would know Benko Ivanov-ich. Gladonov...B-I-G. But nobody would know the real me."

Benko could lie with the best, and he was proud he could, but now I'd caught him. Not that I cared, but he showed what an adolescent mind he had. "What was the film? When?"

"Brit film. Long time ago, over there. Forget the name."

"You must remember the story," I said, egging him on deep-er into his fable.

"Stupid story. Oldest story of all. Boy meets girl. Girl sucks boy. Boy fucks girl."

I sat up on the bed. "You were in a porn flick?"

"One time. Not my face. They cut my face off my body. Some smart-ass gay guy, his face on my body in the movie. He never get it up with woman. Dick the size of pinky finger. I quit."

"You mean you acted in the porn and they edited out your face? You're way too cute. Your face is your second best feature."

"Shut up," he snarled, missing my humor. "You're like them. All you want is big cock. I'm not cock. I'm man."

"You're a man, yes you are. I didn't mean anything. It's teas-ing, that's all." I raised my palm to his cheek and stroked it. "C'mere. Let me kiss your beautiful man's face." I kissed him all over his face and cooed and tickled him until he smiled.

I thought he told the truth about acting in a porn film—he had the equipment—but if he quit, I doubt it was because the editor demeaned him. Benko was the kind of man who, as long as he got paid in money, admiration, attention, he'd perform for more.

I marveled at Benko's physical strength and his stamina. He worked twelve hours in the factory, made love to me for half the night, and awakened refreshed after four hours of sleep.

"Vodka," he said. "Jet fuel. Pure energy. Burns in my veins a pure sun."

My edginess about our affair sent a tiny ripple of peril through my summer. But even without our secret, one other

thing kept me really interested in Benko. He had the largest penis I'd ever seen.

It was almost too large for me, and I'm a big woman. He
acted so proud of it, especially after the first few times I praised
it. About the second week of our affair, I opened my phone and
found a text from him.

› check pic ‹

I clicked on the attached image. At first I thought it was a
shadowy rose-colored band printed diagonally from one corner
of a piece of paper to the other, but when I recognized what it
really was, I laughed. He was either showing off or enticing me
in his clumsy way, and I didn't totally discount a subtle threat.

That night, I teased him about using Photoshop to magnify
the size of his penis. He denied it.

"Prove it," I said.

He unfolded a piece of paper from his shirt, then unzipped
his pants. On a regular sheet of printer paper, he'd printed the
photo he texted me. He lay his penis against the image on the
paper. I burst into laughter.

"Funny?" he snapped. "Funny it's not."

"Oh, Benko, I don't want to hurt your feelings, but it re-
minds me of a Christmas candle. I can't believe it."

He smiled when I asked him to autograph the paper.

"It's my Christmas candle," he said. "Not always sausage."
He signed the photo with a flourish.

"Candles melt," I said, teasing.

"My candle? Never."

I never fully trusted Benko. Someone who boasted about
his ability to get away with anything was likely to deceive me,
too. In fact, I suspected him of beguiling me already. Yet, that fi-
ery image of his penis exuded a sense of hazard that exhilarated
me those summer nights.

If my intuition was right and I ever needed evidence to
thwart him, if I ever needed protection from him, perhaps I
could use the signed photo so I kept the image on file, at home.
If I wanted to continue enjoying the affair, and I did want to, I

needed to limit his feeling of power over me that his immense member gave him.

The next time he strutted his erection around my bedroom, dipping and prancing and flapping it like a branch tossing in the wind, I told him he had the thickest one I'd seen, but not the longest.

"No," he said. "Not possible."

"It sure is. Maybe half again as long." I grinned.

"I don't believe you. No one ever told me that."

"You've never been with anyone like me. They're probably just too timid to tell you."

He narrowed his eyes, wilting slightly.

"I'm not saying you've got a pencil there, Benko. Some guys have width, others have length." My knowledge or my experience, or my willingness to compare him negatively, deflated him completely. His puzzled gaze fell on his shrinking limb, rose to my eyes, dropped back. Now I could take charge, swell his cherished limb, and reinflate his confidence. "It's not the size that counts, you know."

"You think I don't know that?" he said defensively. "But most women I slept with don't know that."

"I'm not most women, Benko."

If he was anything, Benko was adaptable. He could change to get something he wanted, so he gave up the boyish bluster about his penis and learned to clown around about it.

"You can be proud of your hands," I said. "Not your cock. You do things with your hands nobody else can."

"From now on," he promised, "my hands I'll use. That's all." "You better have more moves than that," I replied, assuring him that I still appreciated his endowment.

Benko adopted me as his American angel, and I cuddled him as my Siberian bear. A note of mothering crept into my feelings for him and at the same time, a yearning to match his emotional recklessness and free myself from responsibility.

He taste-tested all my new tofu recipes, chuckling and adding vodka to half of them, and he taught me to slake my longing for Gianni. When I let drop that some of the dock men at various produce warehouses had come on to me a little too insistently, he said "You need help, any place, you tell me." With cold eyes and half-snarling, he said, "I take care of them. Nobody knows nothing. Ever."

I shrugged my shoulders.

"It's all right, Genevieve. With me now you're safe."

Chapter Seven

Genevieve

MEAT AND POTATOES

Chief Buhrman asked to see me at home so, naturally, I invited him to lunch. In the middle of November, the day was unbelievably warm—actually it was hot for any day of the year.

I hadn't had time to rake the backyard, so we walked across a crackling brown carpet of oak leaves to the picnic table.

After we commented on the heat and sat down, I explained to Buhrman that he'd entered a wild territory. Once on my property, he had to taste my new tofu recipe.

"I need non-tofu-eating men," I said. "Women like my recipes, but if the husband turns it down, there go half my sales." Charlie had told me to be careful because the Chief was clever and he always went for what he wanted, so I tried to set up a convivial tone for our talk.

"I don't like many new foods," he said politely. "I'm a meat and potatoes kinda guy, like my old man. He lived to ninety-three. I'm not worried about my diet."

He wore a yellow button-down long-sleeved shirt tucked into his khakis. He'd rolled the sleeves up to his elbows in precise folds. New blue running shoes shined on his small white-stockinged feet.

Relieved that he was off-duty, I said, matter-of-factly, "You're in great shape. You must work out."

"It's my policy at the station. All the guys work out," he said as I served him salad. "Something I've kept up since the Marines. Mmm," he murmured, tasting the tofu, "it's okay."

I'd need all my sales and negotiation skills to manage our conversation. I made sure we had plenty of fresh French bread and butter from the farmer's market. His wife had told me he loved iced mint tea so I'd made a jug that morning.

"Do you mind if I take a couple of pictures of you, Aaron? I'm a photographer and I like to shoot people I come into contact with through my job."

"Shoot people?" he said, crossing his hands over his heart in mockery.

"It doesn't hurt. When I develop the photos, I'll give you a copy for Gloria. Maybe for your office."

"I don't mind. Let's take it right now, then we can have our talk?"

"Thanks," I said, and coaxing him to smile and make faces, I took a half dozen shots. It's always amazing how taking someone's picture can loosen them up, if you do it in a spirit of fun. I put my camera back in its case and offered him more tea.

He accepted, saying "Thanks for inviting me over. Can't think of a better thing to do than have a picnic in November. Global warming. It's a good thing." He laughed at his joke. "Not that bad, Jon-a-viv," he said, forking another bite of tofu into his mouth.

He butchered my name as badly as anyone in Clement. "Call me Gen, Aaron. Most people do."

"Gen?" He didn't understand how Gen could be short for Jon-aviv. His hearing was acute, but his processor might have been slow.

"I have to ask you a few questions," he said, swallowing. "You've heard we think the MacDaniel woman was murdered?"

"I hope it's not true. You're the police, Aaron, but it sure looked like an accident."

"Looks are deceiving," he muttered, his eyes glancing away.

"She was a nice woman," I said, not wanting to confront him or his theories even though I doubted she was murdered. Who would benefit from her death? "I didn't really know her, but she was always friendly when I saw her at work."

"Did she have any enemies?"

"I have no idea."

"If you want a lawyer, you can have one," he said, speaking quickly, suddenly serious.

Caught off guard, I hesitated, then I said, "Do I need one, Aaron?" I tried to slow him down by pacing my voice and saying his name, the way I calmed Liam down when he lost his temper.

The Chief went on. "Only you know that. You can have one if you like."

When the Chief first called and asked to meet me, I phoned the Syracuse lawyer. He urged me to keep my conversation with Buhrman neighborly. If the Chief pried into my private life, deny everything, he said. Stay calm. Take notes.

I had a great memory. I wouldn't offend the Chief with taking notes in front of him.

"I'm just wondering how things are going with you and David Golman," Buhrman said.

I should have been ready but my mouth went dry. "We stopped seeing each other quite a while ago." The Chief's tack would be personal. He probably talked to every man I've dated in Clement since I moved here three years ago. Not counting Benko, Golman was the latest. He lasted two months.

"Too bad. He's a good catch. He supports the police and fire retirement fund with a nice donation every year."

"He was always respectful and generous to me."

He nodded, appearing to listen closely, wanting me to say more. "Pretty girl like you. Must be picky, Gloria says. Can't blame you these days, especially with a young boy like yours."

I stiffened. "What do you mean? He's a great kid."

"Oh, I don't mean he's not. Everybody knows he's a good kid. The principal, swim coach, everybody says he's got lots of energy, smart. He's obedient, not like some kids. You trained him real well, Jon-a-viv, I mean, Jon...uh...Gen. I mean, well, finding a man to take on somebody else's son, could be hard. That's all."

"If you were a woman you'd know that's not really a problem, Chief. Most good men prefer mothers." I let my eyes narrow and go cool.

His shoulders rose and he grimaced. "Sorry. No disrespect. Sticking my foot in my mouth again." He softened. "You must drive what, thirty five, forty thousand miles a year?"

"I fly a lot, too. We have customers in every part of the country." Charlie said Buhrman had examined all the AT personnel records. Sounds like he stayed up nights snooping into my expense accounts. Well, let him.

"I was wondering, excuse me for asking, I have to ask, just because, you know, a Chief has to ask the hard questions." He paused while he sipped his tea. He leaned back in the chair and gazed up into the tree. "Bad thing about oaks. Squirrels. I have sycamores in my yard. Squirrels stay away. They don't like the taste of sycamore seeds—stink like rotten fish."

While I waited for him to ask whatever hard question he had, I buttered a thick slab of bread and set it on his plate. He picked it up and nibbled.

Chewing slowly, he asked, "Do you think any of your customers have something against Greer or the company? I mean, any kind of grudges or plans for one of those hostile turnovers?"

"I doubt it," I said, ignoring his obvious Columbo ploy. "No customer would commit a murder to get cheaper tofu. Even if they were crazy. Tofu's not that important in the big scheme of things."

"Now you mention it, there might be a scheme here. I heard that the Chinese guy wants to buy the company. Think he'd put any pressure on Greer?"

"Not that I know of. I don't have anything to do with that side of the business." Buhrman planted a doubt in my mind. Was Charlie really thinking about selling out to Meng? It sounded like one of those buyout rumors that made the rounds of the industry every year or so.

"Charlie's a lively guy," the Chief said.

I nodded, listening.

"Done a lot of good for the town. Made some money. Pretty good reputation with the Chamber and all. You know I talk to pretty much everybody in town?" He leaned forward.

"If I were the Chief, I'd do the same," I said. "You have to know people and let them know you to gain their trust."

Buhrman frowned. "They should trust their Chief no matter what."

The Chief got up and wandered around the yard. I followed. From behind, he looked like a boxer. His wide shoulders and narrow hips and the eager way he leaned forward almost bouncing on his toes belied his laid-back investigator posture.

We meandered to my fall garden. A few stalks of kale and the last Brussels sprouts plants stood green and brave.

I handed him his mug, now filled with fresh ice cubes and tea. I began to wonder why he was really here. So far he'd only confirmed my real distance from the case.

"Ice," he said. "Who'da thought we'd be drinking iced tea, outside, in November?" He shook his head and sipped.

"Got to bring tough things up, Jon-a-viv. Clear everything up, get it out of the way, y'know."

"That's all right, Aaron. I want to help. Ask away."

"Well...did you ever hear anything about Charlie and the dead woman?

"No. Nobody's said anything." So, Charlie and Becky must have been fooling around and the Chief's sniffed it out. I'm glad I didn't ask him the other night in the car. I'm a lousy liar, and Buhrman would pick it up right away. Using an old sales trick, I reversed the focus. "Have you?"

"There's something in the wind, but no, not directly. I know he and his wife have been getting counseling for quite a while..."

"They've been under a lot of strain since the death, even before. Trying to build a unique business like this, from nothing, it's worse than a roller coaster. Charlie says he feels like he's always at war." We stood beside each other contemplating the yard.

Eventually, Buhrman said, to the side of my face, "You know him pretty well, don't you?"

"Pretty well. After him and Nora, you could say I was next in line. I love the company. He gave me a great job when I needed it and nobody else came through."

He shot a skeptic's narrow eye at me. "But if it came down to the truth or your friendship? Or your job?"

He knew I'd say "The truth, of course," and I did. I added, "It's the right way to go, isn't it." He nodded, and I said, "Safest, too."

He turned and smiled. "Truth. That's my motto. One little word. If only everybody believed in it. We'd have world peace, health, happiness, it would be heaven on earth."

He was such a dissembler—no doubt it takes a liar to catch a liar.

"Is there something you want to tell me about Charlie, Aaron?" "No, no." He avoided my eyes. "Just checking on the scuttlebutt about him and MacDaniel. Lotsa rumors flying around town."

"I haven't heard that one." Or even suspected it until the other night on the drive home from Meng's. I kept walking, pointing out my wilted white Peace roses, planning my answer. "Those roses are one of the best things about my house. They were beautiful right up to the frost we had last week."

Buhrman touched a blossom. Every petal fell, drifting to the ground, white leaves speckled with brown rot.

"Lotta nice gardens in Clement. Great town for gardens." When he straightened up he said, "I hear it's real nice down in the Berkshires this time of year..."

Maintaining my slow breathing, affecting indifferent tone, I said, "I love it over there. The hills are too flat for Alpine but cross-country skiing in the winter is wonderful. Or used to be."

He wrinkled his eyebrows and pursed his lips, obviously expecting me to tell him more, so I continued. "In the summer, sometimes I go to Tanglewood to hear classical music. Liam and I go every summer, since he was four. We sit on the lawn, light a candle, listen to live music. Total peace. Do you ever go there?"

"Naw. We like country music."

Then he swallowed a long drink of tea and I continued. "I have friends who live near there but I haven't visited them for quite awhile."

We'd ambled around the yard and ended up back at the picnic table. The Chief set his glass on a napkin and frowned. "Would that be the Jewdanos?"

Buhrman mispronounced the name without a hint of irony. "You mean the Giordanos." I laughed. "Yes. Giordano Brothers is my customer in New York."

"What kind of relationship would you say you have with Mr. Jewdono?

"What do you mean, Aaron?"

"Personal or professional?"

"Professional and personal. We're friends. I'm friends with all my customers. It's the key to my success."

He stuck out his lower lip and scratched his temple. "You know, I heard about this big competition you had with Greer, see who could sell the most tofu?"

"Yeah, a little game we played to keep things interesting"

"You won, right?"

"Yeah. What does that have to do with anything?"

"You win any prize or anything?"

He knew what I won and I felt so defensive I wanted to pick up the tea pitcher and pour it on his head. I was long done with Gianni and he had no right...but I had to play it cool.

"A trip to Cancun. Not only that, Charlie had to wash my car inside and out ten times."

"Jewdino give you the winning edge, did he?"

"You could say that. His sales grew fastest."

He stopped and breathed, letting his shoulders sag. Peering into his teacup and speaking as if he'd memorized a script, he said, "Can you explain to me if a personal relationship with a customer that brings you personal reward is not a breach of ethics?"

"What are you talking about? If you're in sales, you don't want customers, you want friends."

The Chief flabbergasted me. I had to deflect his aggression again. "Aaron, are you insulting me or accusing me of something?"

"Sorry, Jon-a. Just asking things. Need your help to figure out motives and such."

"What motives?"

He raised his brows and smiled without opening his lips.

I spoke in a soft, sisterly voice, as helpful as I could be. "Aaron, I'm afraid you're naive about business. Ever been in business?"

Clarity came into his eyes. "No, law enforcement was my calling, since I was ten years old."

"In business, it's not all tooth and claw. People help each other all the time. That's how it's done."

"They help each other break the law. Big companies, little companies...they help each other all right."

Exasperated, I continued, wanting to lecture him. "Anything I did with Giordano or any other customers that you might construe as personal, we always followed the bonds of propriety."

He nodded in agreement. "I believe you. Don't blame you for being upset with me, but it's my job to sniff around. Gotta stir things up to see what happens."

I laughed, trying to lighten up. "Like flour when you make bread. Stirring the flour so it rises evenly."

"I guess. Gloria takes care of our baking and cooking. I take her over to White Owl's, Wegmans or such, she and I shop together. She points, I pick up what she says.

"No doubt she's a great chef."

"The best."

We'd circled back to the garden. "Best smelling flower in the world, rose," he said. "I should come back in the summer to smell them."

"Please," I said, "come by any time. Some of these roses get as big as cantaloupes. You can smell them from the deck."

"Interesting," he said, distracted. He turned toward me, looking past, toward the house. "So anyway, Jordina. I'm going to visit him. Go down to Hunts Point and get a feel."

"When? Why?"

"No stone unturned," he said. "I told Greer I was sorry I had to interrupt with your customers, but, you never know."

"I better call him to let him know, Aaron. If you just show up, Giordano could get the wrong idea."

The Chief picked up his mug and sipped at the iced tea. "Sure, give him a call." He set the mug down. "Y'know, Jon, 'scuse me, Gen...life in Clement's real nice. Outta the way. Good place to raise kids..."

"Yes, Liam likes it here. The school's much better than his last one."

"My wife said she felt sorry for you."

"Why?"

"Said it must get lonely for a single woman, young professional woman like you. Good-looking."

"Thank you." I smiled as modestly as I could, trying to gain some control in the conversation. Politeness and form went a long way with the Chief. "Sometimes it's lonely. I'm not that interested in getting involved right now. Between my son and my work, who has the time or energy?"

"I don't mean to be invading, here, but you understand. It's complicated, this murder thing. Was it a murder? Here I can only go with my gut. If somebody gets away with it, everybody in town's in danger. Right?"

"I pray to God it's nothing like that."

"Me, too."

"Well, I gotta ask a few difficult questions. You're doing fine, like Gloria said you would."

I wondered if he thought what he'd already asked and implied was easy. "Shall we sit down, Aaron?"

"No, no. I talk better if I keep moving. Walking or driving. Don't have the cruiser or we could take a ride. Anyways, you have a nice yard."

I was sure Buhrman didn't consider me involved in the "murder," until his next question.

"Now what about this Benkowander Popov or Smirkov or whatever?"

"Gladonov."

"Gladenuff. Strange name. Guess he's a happy guy?" He barked a tiny laugh. "He's your friend, right?"

"Yes. I'm friends with the people I work with."

"I thought you weren't friends with the dead woman. She's worked there at least a year."

Flustered, I said, "Aaron, you're making me feel like you're accusing me of something and I don't know what."

"No, no. It's friendly. I just never did one of these murder investigations before. I had training a long time ago, but, you know." "Okay. No problem, long as you're not involving me."

Not answering directly, he went on. "We're not sure about this case, you know, but we gotta go on with the investigation: double murder, you know. Last thing—by the way, that salad wasn't bad—this Gladnuff comes over here sometimes?"

"Sure. I invite different people over from work. To try out recipes. Charlie likes me to. Says it promotes the team spirit. I'm a good team player."

He muttered, "I bet you are."

When he said that, I realized nothing I said would make him trust me. He fired his next question at me like a trial lawyer.

"Do you know where Gladenuff was the night of the murder?"

I ignored this continual reference to "murder." I hoped Buhrman was only a backcountry cop who identified with the prosecuting attorney on the TV courtroom shows and learned his interviewing techniques from them, but with every question, I doubted that more and more. "All I know is he said he was at the woman's birthday party."

"Yeah. Him and those other rowdies you've got working for you. Wild party, they say. If Gladkop lets anything slip, about the woman, anything, I'd appreciate it if you let me know right away. There's scuttlebutt around that he knew the dead woman, in the Biblical sense. He denies it. But I can't help wonder if that was a little Russky she had inside her when she died." He stood up. "Would sure make it easy if we had some way of telling."

"What about DNA testing?" I asked. "Seems like it's the latest thing."

"We're working on it. Takes time, is all. First the machines screwed up. New operators, they said. Probably some Chinaman just off the boat. Now they tell me it'll take a little while to match the samples with the results."

"Must really frustrate you, Aaron."

"Yeah, well, I'm used to it, small town, upstate and all. Good thing is, D.A.'s not worried. He's with me all the way. Jona... Gena...I'll get the DNA."

I smiled. "Does it really matter, Aaron?"

He stared at me, his mouth open, as if he couldn't believe such a foolish question. "It could be the key to the whole investigation."

"Oh." My smile disappeared. "Guess I don't understand these complicated investigations. Selling tofu is about as complicated as I can get," I said, playing his game.

"Well, don't worry about it. He forced a grin up at me with tight thin lips. "Thanks for lunch, Jona. Gloria must've told you about the tea? It was good."

"No sugar added, Aaron. Just good old New York clover honey. Straight from the farm."

"Everything lived up to your reputation, like Gloria said it would.

"I'll send her some of my recipes."

"No, you don't have to do that."

"No, really, I'll send them from the office."

"Maybe she'll change 'em, fix 'em up a bit for me." The Chief laughed, I laughed. "If anybody can make me eat that stuff, it's her," he said. "No offense."

He smoothed his thick black hair and said, "I know it's tough being a newcomer here. You've been here what? A few years? Gloria and I have lived here twelve years already. We still feel like the natives' favorite TV show."

"I've felt that, too."

"Yeah, you'd be surprised what people know about you," he said. "Well, thanks again. If you think of anything, let me hear from you."

"Good luck, Aaron. I'm sure you'll figure everything out before long."

He opened his car door and turned back. "Watch out for stray bullets," he said.

Taken aback, I said, "What?"

"The war, you know. Greer's tofu war."

I glared at him. "You scared me, Aaron. Don't do that."

He sputtered, "I'm sorry. Just trying to joke."

I paused and made what I hoped was a schoolmarm's face, admonishing him. He dropped his eyes.

"It's okay," I said. "I always think of Clement as safe—no guns, no bullets."

He stared away from me, nodding, then climbed into his car and rolled down the window. "I'm paid to keep it that way."

"Say hello to Gloria," I said, and waved good bye. As soon his tail lights disappeared, I went inside and made myself a cup of black tea and sat down to think.

***

The Chief had targeted every man in my recent life. Golman and the other men in town could handle themselves.

I didn't worry about Gianni. If he had to, he could prevent Buhrman from getting too close.

If the rumor about Charlie and Becky was true, Charlie could be in big trouble. Not for having the affair—that would color his reputation and who knows what Nora would do—but for denying it to the Chief.

Ten minutes after Buhrman left, I packed a bowl of tofu salad and got in my car to drive to Benko's. For all the reasons he'd fretted about, it seemed he'd end up bearing the brunt of Buhrman's scrutiny. He was foreign, he knew the woman, maybe too well. I'd have to ask Benko about his 'Biblical knowledge' of Becky.

As with the rumor of Charlie and Becky, I suspected the Chief was spreading hearsay, hoping to frighten Benko. Buhrman's suspicion about the 'little Russky' worried me but I didn't see how it was possible that Benko had been sleeping with Becky. I'd kept him busy most of the summer.

Right then Benko needed me to coach him in his dealings with Buhrman. If he reacted the same way that got him in trouble in Russia, or the way he'd promised me he would if he received the least threat from the Clement police, Buhrman would have him in jail in five minutes. He may not be deported, but he'd be back on the road in America with millions of other aimless immigrants.

I wanted to help him but, as I drove across town, the Chief's warning reverberated. "...you'd be surprised what people know..."

I had to be realistic. I couldn't take any sides here, except mine and Liam's. I drove by Benko's, turned my car around, and headed home. No matter how much I tried, I couldn't help Benko and he'd take on Buhrman as a personal challenge, anyway, no matter what I said. Benko would need all his survival skills and cleverness.

Now I had to to shelter myself from any trace of suspicion in Buhrman's mind. I had to distance myself from Benko and keep it that way as long as the investigation lasted. Chief Buhrman had just packed my sizzling summer affair with the 'Amazing Russian Sausage' deep under ice.

Chapter Eight

Genevieve

CHARLIE'S PECCADILLO

Charlie called at 11:00 p.m. the night before our quarterly sales trip to Philadelphia.

"Will you drive, Gen? My back's acting up."

The next morning, I rushed out of the house to pick him up by six. A big grin rolled across his face when he opened the door of my Volvo wagon. He'd spotted my running gear on the passenger seat.

"What's this?" he said, dangling a pair of my underpants between his fingers. "Ready for any emergency?" He scooped up my pants and shorts and bra and shirt and running shoes stuffed with soggy socks and tossed them into the back seat.

"You know me, Charlie—I gotta move. Since you've made me spend so much time in my car, I'm always ready to run. Sometimes I spot a lovely woods and I have to explore it."

I knew I didn't have any choice about the road trips. When Liam and I decided to settle in the country, I accepted the fact that

I might have to travel to make a living. Fortunately Liam liked staying with Carla whenever I was out of town. She let him play computer games until well after his bedtime, but I didn't really mind.

Charlie would do just about anything to keep me on the road, so it was easy to get him to pay her a stipend if I stayed away over night. When I drive alone on the highway, I never listen to the radio or CD's because my mind keeps me company.

But if I ride with someone, especially Charlie, I love to talk and tell him stories of my life. He believed I was the wildest, freest woman he'd ever heard of. Sometimes I wonder if he didn't ask me to go on trips with him just so he could listen to the adventures of my youth. This trip was different. He had to talk.

"I don't want to sound too personal? But have you had a lot of lovers?"

"Enough. Why?"

"I haven't had many. Really just Nora. I don't count the five before her as real lovers. They were more like warm-ups."

"Sounds like you have plenty of experience, Charlie." I didn't want him to feel lacking in the manhood department.

"Nora knows about them," he said. "We talk about everything. Well, almost. Some stuff, you talk about it? It takes on a life of its own nobody needs."

"What do you mean?"

"I'm tempted sometimes by other women," he admitted, "but not enough to take action. The kids are young and I wouldn't want to throw a monkey wrench into our marriage."

I kept my expression flat, incurious.

"Sometimes it's miserable. Nora's gone a lot now, golfing afternoons, taking classes at night. She's hanging out at the country club. We don't sleep together, you know what I mean, very often. When we do, though, it's still great. I guess that's what's most important. I mean, with the murder—the death, I mean—all the heat I'm taking."

Charlie rolled his window down and stretched his arm out, playing with the wind, swooping and slicing his open palm around, like a little boy. "It's a good thing we go to therapy every week. We work out most of our problems there. You know, I know you have a hard life, Gen, single mom'n all. Being married's just as tough. Still, I wouldn't give it up."

Since Nora and I had started running together, we'd gotten to know each other better. We found we could work out some of the stress the death had infected our lives with by slow jogging while we talked.

No wonder she spent so much time away from home and Charlie. When they were together, he probably moaned and groaned non-stop. She was reserved and the pressure of the investigation had started to show on her, but she opened up a little more with every run.

I didn't respond to Charlie's invitation to discuss his marriage, a subject I already knew too much about. We rode in silence most of the first hour, both of us half-asleep.

***

I'd been up late on the phone the night before, listening to Benko complain about work, about his horniness, about my cruelty for not letting him come over.

"You dump me, Genevieve. I don't like that. Not the kind woman you used to be. Not like Russian girls, all beautiful and mean. Sweet Genevieve. Sweet creamy Irish lassie." He laughed, then his voice turned sinister. "You leave me? Big trouble you never know."

I'd talked with him three or four times a week by phone since I stopped seeing him, mainly to keep track of him and to keep him on the far end of a string, a string I kept taut and tried to lengthen with every phone call, one that he tugged and tried to reel around his finger with his gruff charm.

The night I told him that we had to stop seeing each other because of the Chief's suspicions, he'd barged into my house, charging up my front stairs red-faced and growling. He refused to believe me about Buhrman's snooping.

I tried to gentle him with hugs and soft words. When I wouldn't kiss him, he threw me down on the couch and ripped at my shorts. I yelped, not loud enough to wake Liam, but sharp enough to surprise Benko.

Claiming innocence, he blustered, "Before, you like rough."

"Benko, get out of here right now."

He shoved me down again. "Don't play hard to get."

I pulled myself up and slid off the couch and ran to the phone. "If you don't leave right now, I'll call the police. You'll never see citizenship."

He got hold of himself, barely. Trembling and panting, he stormed around the room. "You be sorry. You're like every other woman. My big cock you want. You gotta have it."

"I want more from a man than his cock. I don't care how big it is." I was as angry as he was.

He ignored me. "You'll never see it again. Till you beg. For my sausage, you'll beg. I'll laugh." He turned and left, rattling the windows as he slammed the door. I locked it behind him and sagged to the floor, weak in every muscle. I slouched against the door for a long time, letting my heart settle down.

The phone rang. It was Benko. "I'm sorry, Gennee. You beautiful woman. I make you feel good. Not bad like I did."

"Benko, you scare me."

"I'll be good, don't worry. Fun we can still have. In more secret now. No Chief can catch me."

"I can't see you, Benko, somebody might see us. If the Chief finds out, we're both in big trouble. Besides, you scared me just now—you don't control your temper. If I say I don't want you to come over, you have to listen to me."

"Oh, Gennee, whatever you say."

"We can talk on the phone. Let's see how you behave."

"Honey. I know we'll be so close. Best woman I ever had. We have best phone sex you ever tried."

"We'll see, but I don't think I could handle that with you just a mile away."

"See what I mean? You want me."

"Good night, Benko."

"Tomorrow yes? Phone date?"

He hung up. Maybe I'd have to talk with Benko on the phone every night to keep him under control, but phone sex? I'd have to be so horny and lonely I couldn't resist. Then we may as well have the real thing.

***

I came out of my fugue as the car followed its nose toward the New Jersey Turnpike. We stopped for lattes at a rest area, and while we waited for service, Charlie launched into one of his obligatory management conversations. Every month he gave his managers a one-on-one pep talk based on *Harvard Business Review* or *Fast Company*'s lead article. That month it was self-forgiveness as the basis for top performance.

We got back into the car and he changed the subject to one of his favorite topics: the difference between men and women. As usual, I had to let him ramble on for a while until he wormed his way around to what he really intended to say. "You know, Genevieve, I could never be a woman. I'm not brave enough to go through birth," he began.

"Charlie, where've you been? You can be a woman and not have a baby."

"Would that be a complete woman?" he answered, challenging me. "If you can't fulfill your biological destiny, wouldn't you feel frustrated? Be maybe a little less than you can be, totally?"

"I disagree. Who says biological destiny is the most important destiny? Who says a baby is a woman's biological destiny, just because she can?"

Charlie stuck out his chin at the windshield. "If you don't give a hundred per cent of yourself, you'll never be your real self."

I waited. Charlie was wound up about something.

"Your real self is a moving target. In Zen, they say it's your original face. The one you were born with. I always wonder how that can be, especially after you grow a beard, or get wrinkles." He chuckled. "I see my baby pictures and say where'd I lose my original face? Maybe when I got married. Maybe it's the business. Maybe the time's coming for me to try out a monastery for a while. Let all this commotion go. Simplify. How do you keep your life simple?"

"I don't even try and don't think a woman has to have a baby to be her full self. You're really out of touch if you think that."

"Don't get mad. I'm a feminist."

"Sure you are. But for me what's true is, my raising Liam by myself is what gives me strength."

"I can see that. You face death square in the face when you give birth, you survive. You can handle anything after that. That's what I mean." Charlie grinned. "Bold. It's what you get when you go all out. Risk everything. You don't have a choice, so you give it everything you've got. Like being an entrepreneur."

I sensed Charlie tugging himself back on track to pump himself up with the self-esteem speech. He needed to listen to himself to find his own courage in the middle of the company's troubles.

"Genevieve, we have to have a serious talk for a minute."

"What have we been doing, Charlie?"

"About business, I mean. Meng and Giordano. What shall we do? You haven't told me what you think yet. It might be a bigger problem than we thought. I know you and Giordano are through, but I fucked up, too. Somebody outside my marriage. It's a little thing. You know what a peccadillo is?"

"It's a sex toy, Charlie. Everybody knows that."

"Don't mock me. It's a little sin, is all. Everybody does them. Maybe mine's worse than your affair with Giordano. I'm married." I kept my eyes on the road.

Charlie sighed and said, "I've been fooling around with Shu Ling Meng since last summer."

I slammed the steering wheel. "My god, how could you?" I had a feeling about that when he and Shu Ling came back from a 'meeting' and Charlie's face stayed flushed all afternoon.

"I'm afraid Buhrman's gonna find out and then the whole town will know. Right now he suspects that Chinese worker did the deed. He'll assume that I'm in on it. Then, 'That's all she wrote, Charlie.' I'm destroyed. Maybe it was the Chinese guy, but I had nothing to do with it." His voice pleaded.

"I know you didn't. Everybody knows you didn't. Stop saying you didn't. You're calling attention to yourself."

"What should I do?"

"Does Nora know?"

"No. Thank god."

"Does Meng? "

"I'm afraid he might. Maybe not. I hope not. I'm not gonna ask." "He'll keep quiet. He doesn't want his family involved. Make sure Shu Ling doesn't admit anything."

"She won't. She's a tough little empress."

"Empress? You're nuts, Charlie. Does she have kids?" I waited for Charlie to answer but he had rolled down the window and started playing with the wind again.

In a quiet voice nearly obliterated by the sound of traffic, he whined, "No. She doesn't want children."

Thank god, I thought. The last thing he needed was to get seriously involved with this spoiled witch. I grabbed his arm and squeezed it hard. "What about your kids? What about Nora?"

He shrugged his shoulders.

"Don't be stupid, Charlie." I squeezed again and he pulled away. "You have to stop with her right now." I was nearly screaming. "You said it. Stop and deny you ever had anything to do with her. Call her right now." Catching him while he was vulnerable and open, I handed Charlie my cell phone. "Hurry up. If you want to save your family and the rest of us, call her."

"Why? We messed around but we never slept together."

"Christ, Charlie. Wake up. Did you hear yourself a minute ago? It doesn't matter if you slept together or not. If the word gets out you were playing around with her, we're all screwed. I don't care what you do for yourself. Think of the rest of us for once."

"It's innocent. All about communication, not sex. Like the bonobos, those little monkeys? They never fight. Just caress each other, make love. If any one of them gets mad or hurt, they just fuck all their conflicts away."

"That's what you want to be, a bonobo?"

"No, of course not. But they're in our genes. They use sex to keep things in harmony. I call them the original 'Make-Love-notWarriors.'"

Impatient, I said "Did you ever hear about evolution? We're not apes. They're in your genes, not mine."

"In my jeans like my pants?" Charlie laughed hard, nearly choking. "Lighten up, Gen. Sometimes animals know more than humans. It's a game. I'm learning about communicating with women. Shu Ling's an expert."

I was as stubborn as Charlie was deceptive. I began to lose my temper. "Shu Ling's a little slut. She's got a hook in your dick and she's dragging you around by a line of bullshit." His self-justifying narcissism pissed me off as much as my ex-husband's.

"Why are you so upset, Gen? It's nothing."

"If you're a bonobo, Mr. Meng's the big gorilla and he'll bash your head. You're blowing it, Charlie. Remember, it's not just you involved here."

He groaned. "This is what I get for following my dreams."

"Stuff the self-pity and stop whining. Make the call or I will." I stared at him with all the fury and disgust I could shoot out of my eyes. Make Love Not Warriors?

He lifted the phone to his ear and then let it drop into his lap without dialing. "Do I have to do this?"

I screamed at him. "Do it and shut the fuck up." I'd never lost my temper with him before, but between his gullibility and Benko's bullying, all my patience was squeezed dry.

He dialed Shu Ling's number and listened for a long time and then left a message.

"Thank you, Charlie," I said, relieved that he'd taken the first step, but I had to keep pressure on him, or he'd backslide. "Keep trying. After our appointment, you take the car into New York to talk to her. I'll take a bus home."

"Jesus, Gen. A bus'll take all night. Fly."

At least he'd agreed to go to New York but, to break up with her? Or was this a good excuse for him to get laid? Maybe

I should back off and tell Nora and let her work it out with her husband.

"The company can afford it. Fly."

Charlie's compliance turned the tables on me, as if he were calling my bluff. I meant what I said and if he didn't break up with her, I was ready to make a change anyway. Tired of Benko, exhausted from keeping the business together, I was fed up with the Chief's antagonism.

"All right, I'll fly. But if you don't break up with Shu Ling right now in your mind and, and..." He nodded his head in time to a song playing on the radio, as if he were alone. "Charlie. Listen to me. You break up with her today, or you and I are done. I mean it."

He glanced at me then back at the highway. "I get it. It's important. But the movie..."

"The movie means shit to a dead company. Christ, Charlie. Where's your brain?"

He grinned, nodding and glancing down at his lap.

"Don't mess around with me. This is life and death serious," I said. Charlie was incorrigible. He thought he could charm his way out of anything.

"What's the difference between me and Shu Ling and you and Giordano? C'mon. I mean it."

He didn't need to know anything more about Gianni and me. "The obvious thing is Gianni and I ended it a long time ago. He cared about me. Shu Ling's using you. She doesn't care about you."

"Yes, she does."

"I mean it, Charlie. Don't bullshit me. I'll quit and tell Nora why."

"God, don't let the mice abandon ship," he mumbled.

"Shut up. I'm not going anywhere. I have to support my kid. Stop feeling sorry for yourself."

He sat staring out the window into the harvested fields. "I guess you're right. I feel relieved I told you about us," he said. Abruptly he turned to me. "Gen, if this works out and you get that cookbook done, you can have a twenty percent royalty on every copy we sell. Liam's college education will be all set."

"Just straighten out your fucking life, then tell me how much money I'll make."

Charlie told the truth—his brains hung down below his belly button. The only logic he understood was the yang of his balls and the yin of the Chinese girl's crotch. All Meng needed to transfer his business to the Canadians was a simple implication about Charlie's ethics. Worse, that would ruin us in the marketplace. Charlie knew it, he sweated it, but he kept seeing that woman.

"I'll go with you, Charlie. I promise I'll sit quietly and when it's done, I'll take you out for Thai food and a bottle of wine. We'll stay in the city and you can cry on my shoulder all night. I won't tell a soul in Clement."

"Give me a break, Gen. It's not that bad. Anyway, I need to do this with class, in private. Her and me. I know I have to let her go, but I want to stay friends. Her film might be worth millions in sales over the next few years."

I wasn't sure he would follow through, but I agreed to let him handle it, mostly because I couldn't stand to be with him that day any longer than I had to.

When we got to Philadelphia, Charlie couldn't focus on the sales meeting. He kept checking his watch, fumbling with his cell phone, generally ignoring what our distributor had to say. So I ran the meeting and we left with a commitment for business in a hundred new stores. Charlie was so distracted he didn't even comment or thank me.

On the way out to the airport, I broached the other taboo subject. "All right, Charlie. Truth or consequences. We have to clear up one more thing."

"What's truth?" he asked.

"Don't play games."

"I'm not."

"All right. The *truth*," he said, stiffening and gripping the steering wheel. "You can trust me. You know that. Better than anybody else. Maybe even yourself." He smiled but faced away.

The traffic was heavy and sometimes Charlie spaced out when he was driving. I asked "Shall we pull over? You make me nervous sometimes."

"I got a long trip ahead of me. Let's get you to the airport and I'll paddle on upriver to the Big Island."

"You sure you can talk and drive?" He'd always been an inconsistent driver, missing stop signs, weaving in and out of traffic, getting lost. Now he was deeply upset.

"Sure. Let's talk. We can talk anything now, Gen. We pretty much hit bottom."

"Maybe you hit bottom. I call it being smart. If you don't give up Shu Ling, you'll hit the real bottom."

"I know. I play it stupid sometimes." He grinned, trying to charm me into absolving him for his idiocy. "Thank god for my luck. And for you and Benko and Nora. Without you guys, I'd probably be in a nuthouse right now."

"We'll make it, Charlie. We're in this together."

"I'm countin' on it. Countin' on you. Sorry, Gen, but you're the best. Don't groan. It's true. That's truth."

"Don't flatter me, Charlie."

"Shut up, Gen. You said truth. That's it."

I spoke quickly in a matter of fact tone to keep him talking. "This is it: you and Becky. What happened?"

"Oh, shit," he said, rolling his eyes back and smirking. "I knew it. I've known it for months."

"The Chief says there's a rumor around town about you and her. Don't you see that's as bad as you and Shu Ling?"

"Sure I do. If it was true, it's worse. But you know who's spreading that rumor?"

"Who?"

"Our good old public servant, Aaron Buhrman."

"Why in God's name would he do that? He's an honest cop."

"Ambitious cop. He's trying to make up something to build his career on. He came up with that 'rumor' on the spot in my office after Becky died. Now he's using her to claw his way out of Clement to Albany, or some other ginned-up police station job."

Charlie might have Buhrman pegged, but he was too defensive. I wanted the full story about him and Becky. "The Chief's been straightforward with me and very polite and considerate with everybody in the company."

Charlie's teeth ground, sending ripples from his jaw up across his temples. "Here's how it is. First, he fucked with me. Then he fucked with all our workers, asking them about me and women, especially Becky. Can you believe that? Then he interferes with Meng, and Giordano. Now he's threatening you. Goddam slimy blight on society out to crush me on his way up!"

He was tailgating the car in front of us at seventy miles an hour. I shouted at him "Slow down. You're gonna kill us."

He slammed on the brakes and backed off from the car ahead and said, "Sorry."

"All right," I said.

"Don't mean to take my frustration out on you."

"Don't worry."

"Buhrman's on my ass and I don't know what to do."

"Stay cool, Charlie. He's trying to do his job and if he's a little dim and has to resort to rumors...don't take him so seriously. I don't."

"You don't?"

"It's gonna blow over. Relax. Let him do his cop thing and stay on course. Be smart."

"I'm trying." Charlie pulled over at the Continental Airlines terminal.

"Good luck in New York, boss," I said. "I'm with you. Don't think about the rumors. Nobody believes them."

"They better not," he said. "I'm gonna do this and I'd appreciate it if you let me tell Nora—when the time comes."

Always negotiating, Charlie stared at me as if we were ironing out the last details of a business contract. I nodded and said, "I don't want to mess up your marriage, Charlie. You do that on your own."

"Thanks," he said and pulled away, waving, a grim expression replacing his usual smile.

While buying my ticket for the next flight home, I realized that Charlie didn't answer my question about him and Becky. Either he respected me enough not to lie to me, or he feared me enough to evade telling the truth.

I called Giordano Brothers from the air to set up an appointment with Gianni. He'd mentioned a couple of jobs last year. They'd sounded good but at that time, they were too far away. Now, I had to be ready to get out of American Tofu. Either Charlie the bonobo or Benko the sausage is likely to wreck everything.

Chapter Nine

Charlie

IMPORTS FROM CHINA

gosling kicks, webbed feet
splash free, cold wind calls
strong wings storm empty blue sky

Driving north from Philly, I called Shu Ling and left a message asking her to meet me at the Empire Hotel, on Broadway across from Lincoln Center. I wanted to go down to Shu Ling's apartment but it relieved me when she insisted on coming uptown to my hotel.

I was afraid I'd lose my sense of purpose if I had the chance to sink into Shu Ling's black leather couch and sniff the perfumes of the exotic flowers that turned her apartment into a jungle. Her bedroom at my back would tantalize my mind with Simian Soles or some other tempting monkey love "practice" Shu Ling teased me with.

My other voice chimed in with Genevieve's hissing at me to break up with Shu Ling.

Forget Shu Ling. Calm Genevieve down. If she leaves you, bye bye American Tofu.

Jiminy's right, as usual. If Genevieve left while we're vulnerable from the investigation, we might lose Giordano. Since Giordano made way too much money from our products, he wouldn't fly the coop overnight. But I didn't need the uncertainty her leaving would cause.

Yet, behind her threat and the angst it would give me, I sensed that she might be the most crucial person to have on my side throughout the whole fiasco.

No matter what I did with Shu Ling, I faced an immense sacrifice. To save American Tofu, for my family, for eighty-three workers and their families, Genevieve insisted I had to give up the potential of the most amazing love affair I could imagine. I had to be a hero, but nobody could know but me and Genevieve, and it wasn't heroics to her.

I never thought of myself as any kind of Super Hero. I'd rather have a love affair with Shu Ling than leap tall buildings. Except for the investigation, tofu was getting boring and a life with Shu Ling would be wild and exciting.

Chuck, Chuck, listen to yourself. You don't know Shu Ling at all. Shu Ling's using you. Cruising you. Abusing you.

Yeah, I've been using her, too. So what?

She's too hot. She's the flame you can never tame. You'll have no money, no family, no fun, no fame.

I know. I know. Sometimes you have to take the heat.

Charlie Greer, fire fighter. You think you can piss on the fire and put it out? You got so much heat on you right now, it's singed your brain. Watch your life flow down the drain.

Even if I was willing to give up everything for Shu Ling, Could I survive in her world? Adventure, excitement, transformation into a wild Taoist lover? Am I thinking too short-term by sticking with the company no matter what happens? I don't have to worry about losing everything because I barely have any net worth anyway. Lots of people would want to hire me. Or I could start another business whenever I want. Nora? She would protect herself, but what about the kids?

I didn't worry about the kids. They were the most beautiful beings in my life. Chuckie made me laugh with his constant clowning around and his drive for soccer. He knew how to break out of the pack and score, sort of like his old man. Rissi... so precious, soft, snuggly. She already played the piano like a ten-year-old and she was in first grade. She could play ragtime

and Chopin well enough to make me cry. I'd stay in their lives
no matter what. I loved them more than I loved anybody else,
yeah, I hated to say it but it was true. I loved them more than I
loved their mom, so whatever happened, I'd be there for them.

Driving toward the city that afternoon, my mind spun out
of control. At one point, as I sped up sulfurous New Jersey
Turnpike toward the Holland tunnel, I made up my mind to
blow off everything. I'd sell the business to Meng for the best
price I could get and sign on as Shu Ling's manager. Then I'd
build her movie career into a spectacular success and she and I
would ignore her father.

Nora and the kids would have plenty of money to live on
from the sale of the company and based on the success I expected with Shu Ling's films, I saw myself a wealthy movie producer.

Traffic stalled while I sat in the Tunnel. Not another black-
out? No, the lights stayed on and the carbon monoxide seeped.
I gritted my teeth and tried not to breathe. I sat sucking down
noxious exhaust. I was an idiot for even thinking about selling
out.

I remembered how in therapy Deborah contended I let
my dreams and fantasies overwhelm my good sense. I agreed,
laughing a little self-defensively that my fantasies could change
my view of life as easily as calcium sulfate coagulated soymilk.
Toss a little bit of calcium into a tank of soymilk, make a huge
vat of tofu. From a vat of tofu, build a dynamic, world-shaking
company. My gift: Take a little fantasy, create a whole new happy world in my mind.

Tofu was real world stuff, Soy to the World come to life. I
didn't want to sell out. I'd given it my heart and guts and soul
for too long. It wouldn't be worth any real money for maybe five
years, but I had a payroll of more than two million dollars. Half
the town of Clement was eating sirloin and lobster because of
American Tofu. When I received a New York Entrepreneur of
the Year award, I think I blew all the town fathers' minds. Now

everybody in the Chamber of Commerce wanted me to speak or sit on their boards.

Now I had Shu Ling's documentary movie to promote me. Once she released it, I'd be a star of an industrial film. What better way to become known as the Henry Ford of tofu? I'd started with nothing and put tofu into the stomachs of millions. Who else can say that? Besides, who remembers the name of the producer of last year's big bucks blockbuster?

Bottom line? I was the boss now and I planned to stay the boss but what really pissed me off was that again, I had to make a choice between love and money. Between magical sex and vast power. Shu Ling or American Tofu.

I stewed in the cancerous vapors under the Hudson, the power of my anger infusing my muscles like a steroid. If Genevieve wanted to quit, let her. I'd find somebody else, somebody more beautiful, more charming. Maybe a woman who didn't have a kid so she could travel more often, really put American Tofu on the map. I could afford to pay somebody twice what she made, if I had to.

When the traffic finally moved and released me from the fumes of hell, I called Shu Ling to change our meeting back to her apartment. Instead of breaking up with her, I'd persuade her to give me one of her mystical lovemaking sessions. She didn't answer but she'd changed her voicemail message to say she'd see me uptown. I cruised up Tenth Avenue to the hotel.

I had time to shower and change before Shu Ling rang me in my room.

"Hi, Charlie. I'm here. Meet me in Hannigan's downstairs."

"Why don't you come up? I booked a beautiful suite, one of the best views in the house."

"Not now. I thought you had something big-time to talk to me about."

"It's changed. I think we have more fun things to do than talk." She laughed. "Crazy like always. I'll wait in the bar."

I spotted Shu Ling at a table in the back of the bar, her headphones on, eyes closed, nodding to the beat.

A gorgeous animal, a sleek feline beast. Slow down, Charlie. Savor the feast.

I slipped past the bar and stopped to soak up her beauty. She was radiant in a tight black silk blouse and her trademark crimson leather pants. Half the men in the place were ogling her. Sensing me, she removed her headphones, stood up and hugged me. We sat beside each other and she pointed to the glass of wine she'd ordered for me.

"Your favorite. A California Merlot. Guess the brand."

I had no idea but when she said, "Gosling," a smile as wide as the Hudson flowed across my face: A witty reference to her message on my voicemail after our *Marmoset* session, when she called me "Little Gander." I settled in for an evening appetizer of repartee and teasing. I was sure a sexual feast of "Orangutan Toes" was on the menu for the night.

"I'm glad you came to the city, Charlie."

"Me, too."

"You got my message?" she asked.

"Which one? I forgot to check my voicemail. I had a lot on my mind." Thirsty, I gulped my wine.

"We're still telepathic then. I called your office this morning." "What about?"

"Let's take a walk. I can't talk seriously in a bar, can you? Besides, you're too cute sitting there." She laid some cash on the table and stood up. "I like you without a mustache. I almost want to kiss your lips."

That she noticed I'd shaved off my mustache, and liked it, lifted my spirits more than anything since the last time I saw her. Shu Ling really paid attention to me.

I congratulated myself for my decision to let Genevieve go her way. I'd devote myself even more to loving Shu Ling and, at the same time, doing whatever I had to to save my company.

"Let's go," she said.

I squeezed beside her into the same compartment of the bar's revolving door and said "I've been thinking about our training program."

"Yeah?"

"I remembered an ancient technique, too. Goes way back."

"You can't be serious," Shu Ling said. "You never heard of Monkey Love before I told you."

"This is so ancient, so embedded in everybody's mind, we all know it. Only when you apply it to Monkey Love, you get the most erotic thrill."

"I doubt it."

"Quick lesson?"

"In public?"

"Nobody but us will know." I leered at her.

"Go ahead."

Waiting on the curb for the light to change, I stuck my tongue out at her. She wrinkled her face and tucked her chin in, wondering what I was up to. I stuck it out again. She didn't respond so I stuck it out once more and got the result I wanted: She stuck her tongue out at me, flipping and tasting the chill evening air again and again with her glistening pink tongue.

"That's it! You got it. See what I told you: everybody knows."

"Knows what, you crazy man?"

"Monkey see, monkey do. Now we go to bed and work on the kinks."

Shu Ling grinned. She grabbed my arm and tugged me across the street and we started uptown. The stores on the upper West Side sparkled with pre-Thanksgiving decorations and early Christmas lighting. Cold breeze blew steadily against us as we walked arm in arm up Broadway in the romantic evening twilight, belying how unsettled I felt. My nervousness forced me to keep wagging my tongue.

"After that, I have another one. Learned it from my mother."

"What? Get serious. Monkey Love is not perverted. The opposite: it's holy."

"So's this. Goes along with Orangutan Toes. Like this." I maneuvered us to the brick wall of the building and stopped. "I don't know if Chinese do this, but every kid born in this country knows it by heart. All we have to do is add our little erotic spin to it: Imagine I'm holding your bare foot in one hand and your toe in my other."

"As long as I don't have to take off my boots out here. It's cold."

"Here we go. Eenee, meenee, minee, mo, catch a monkey by the toe, If she hollers, make her pay, fifty kisses every day." I tried to kiss her but she averted her face and laughing, pushed me back and started walking.

"Charlie, you're goofy. I really like you. Sometimes you feel like my little brother."

I chuckled. "Hold it, Shu Ling. First of all, I'm older than you. Second, if that's how you treat brothers in China, no wonder you have such a population problem."

Grinning, she slapped me on the shoulder.

"Not that. I mean, how you respect me. How what I do impresses you. How you listen to me. How you trust me to try what I tell you to do."

"I told you I love you. Isn't that how a lover acts? Not just a little brother." I purposely let a hurt note shadow my voice.

"What I mean is, I have a couple of things to tell you and I don't want you to get mad. I want to stay friends."

I stopped in the middle of the sidewalk and turned her toward me. An old man in a shabby ankle-length coat bumped into my back, bounced off, and swore. My Chinese princess and I stood there, staring into each other's eyes. Here it comes, I thought, more bad news. What the hell.

"Let's keep going," I said. "It's easier to talk." We crossed the street between stalled cars. "Well," I said after strolling a block in silence and growing anxiety, "tell me."

"Real fast. Here goes," she said. "The film's off, at least the American Tofu part. And we can't see each other anymore."

I stopped again and stepped around, turning to face her. Speechless, I examined her eyes for the real meaning behind what she said. I saw moist anthracite pupils and yellow streetlight glints, but nothing deeper.

I'd made up my mind two hours before to fight for her in spite of the investigation, Nora, Buhrman, Genevieve, every possible obstacle a man could have. Now she was dumping me: No more Taoist sex, no Henry Ford of tofu movie, no future. Anger hissed into my voice.

"What the fuck do you mean? Do you know what it's cost me to help you make that film? I gave you thousands of dollars of my time...my company's time. I spread the word around the whole industry. Everybody knows I'm in on it. I'll look like an idiot."

"Sorry, Charlie. I can't help it."

"You can't help it."

"Either I pull American Tofu from the movie or ditch the whole project. My backers in Taiwan think all the bad publicity you've had will ruin the film." She kept her face turned away as she talked.

"I'll back your film myself, Shu Ling. It can't cost that much more."

"They're my distributors, too. They control the film."

When I didn't say anything, she stammered, "I can leave the AT footage in, and the shots of the water and the countryside, and say something like 'a typical American-run tofu factory...' That way, if everything blows over, we can change the soundtrack to identify your place."

"IF it blows over! IF it blows over!" I shouted over again and again, charging ahead, feeling the savage freedom of shouting on a New York street. Two or three pedestrians stopped to watch my performance but most put their heads down and trudged on. I turned circles on the sidewalk, waving my arms and shouting "IF, IF!"

I jumped up on the skirt of a light pole like some soap actor and grabbing the pole in both hands, I swung around and around. "If. If. If."

Shu Ling retreated to a storefront doorway and stared at me, giving me plenty of room, but she didn't run away. I stumbled down and climbed up on the bumper of a parked car, then higher, onto the trunk, then the roof. I didn't know what I was doing but it felt good to move and climb and ignore the rules. A guy came out of one of the stores and screamed, "Hey asshole. Get the fuck off my car. I'm gonna beat the shit outta ya."

I scrambled down and tripped off the sidewalk into the gutter, ignoring traffic. A horn blared as a taxi sped past inches from my outstretched hand and shocked me awake. I jumped back and found Shu Ling standing in the middle of the sidewalk, my true love, my betrayer, my teacher, my friend, shaking her head sadly as if she wouldn't be surprised if I tried to kill myself by falling into the grille of a speeding Yellow Cab.

Shu Ling circled my arm with hers. "You're acting like a chimpanzee. Don't be so melodramatic."

"That's me. Charlie the Chimp." I tried to jerk loose, but she held me firmly, turning us back into the uptown pedestrian flow. "No," I said. "Charlie the Chump. That's what Monkey Love does for me."

I resisted her until she leaned into me, tightening her fingers around my biceps. She absorbed my anger into her little body. My agitation began to subside and we walked silently for several blocks, her arm clutching mine as if we were lovers savoring recent love-making, unable to detach our bodies, or anticipating a night of intimacy that we'd begin with a slow stroll in each other's arms.

My mind calmed down and I put my arm around Shu Ling and dismissed my worries, enjoying what was probably my last date with her, at least until I figured out the next steps. I loved her and I knew she cared for me, in her little rich girl way, but my fantasies of a future unencumbered by my own baggage and hers looked really silly right then.

Still, I was in so deep with the Meng family, I had to salvage whatever I could from this bizarre twist of fate. By the time we reached Seventy-second Street, my well-oiled businessman's problem-solving mode kicked in and I realized that the movie itself played a minor role in my plans for expanding American

Tofu. When the fiasco settled down, Shu Ling would name American Tofu in the film, so I might as well wait.

Knowing when not to do something, and not doing it, is as important as knowing when to do it.

Wising up, Chuck? It's not too late. Maybe you can still change your fate.

We stopped at the light in front of the tropical green façade of Gray's Papaya Juice and Hot Dog store at the hectic intersection of Amsterdam and Broadway. I stepped away from Shu Ling and pulled her out of the pedestrian crush. Hoping I'd wrung the self-pity out of my voice, I said, "Why are you dumping me? That's the last thing I expected today. You hugged me, ordered that Gosling wine, walked arm in arm. I've never understood you. Do you really mean it?"

"I don't want to, Charlie. We'd never be able to have a true love the way you want it anyway. We're from two different worlds but we can still be friends." She pulled my hands from her shoulders and held them in her gloved ones.

As my fingers brushed the silky leather on her palms, I grinned. "What about *Tamarin* Toes? Maybe some *Monkey See, Monkey Do?*" Unfortunately, I humored myself more than her.

"That's over." She dropped my hands and shrugged her shoulders. "We can't see each other anymore."

"Who says?"

"My father."

I jammed my fists into my coat pockets. "I knew it. You're still under his thumb."

Meng sliced you, your business, your future. Time to close up the cut and tighten the suture.

His power reached into every single aspect of my life, whether he knew it or not, and I wouldn't be surprised if he did.

"Charlie, you don't get it. If I don't stop seeing you, you won't have your business. Not with him. Not with the others. He doesn't want me associated with you at all."

"Can't you stand up to him? I'm not afraid of him. Or Giordano. My business doesn't depend on them." My bravado sounded hollow even to me. I'd already given up but I couldn't show her how easily I'd been beat, then she stunned me again.

"My father didn't appreciate that article you published about the snake bar. A Taipei paper picked it up and printed it. Now my father's friends in Taiwan are laughing at him for bringing a crude American into their circle."

"I erased Meng Produce from the article."

"Everybody knows who you are over there. They keep track of who my father hangs out with. He's famous in their politics and the food business. He doesn't like the attention you bring him."

The story was my lead-off public relations article for the Soy to the World campaign. I thought I'd written it with panache and humor and respect for tradition, good P. R. for everybody.

"Not only that, your police chief's taken his snooping around to new levels. He asked my father if he was hiding the man who killed your worker. He threatened to call in federal agents to search the premises."

So, that was it. Meng hadn't rejected me only because I'd fallen for Shu Ling and might have an entree into his empire, he had his own big problem. He was hiding something foul and the Chief's stubborn nose had sniffed it out. "Yeah, I know. Meng told me Chinese don't do business the way American companies do. They have their own rules."

"That's right. You know why my father traveled with you to Taiwan?"

I waited but at that point I didn't really care what other excuse she'd make. My stomach rumbled and I almost asked her if she wanted a hot dog, normally, the last thing I would eat.

Shu Ling didn't notice my distraction. She plowed on with her story and though I was curious, I doubted she'd tell me the truth.

"He wanted to see if he could trust you," she said, "maybe let you in on his importing business."

"I know about that," I said. "I've never told anyone anything. I had my suspicions, but I don't know any details."

"The aphrodisiacs? The monkey brains? The bear balls and livers he pays Canadian trappers for? The deer penises he buys from hunters in upstate New York?"

"What? I thought it was mostly ginseng and maybe some rhino horn." Just as I'd suspected: Canada.

"Ginseng is the cover. They all want ginseng but the mainland Chinese are spending millions more for the animal parts. So much of the money they get for making cheap computers and things go for aphrodisiacs. Why do you think my father was such a foe of the Tian An Men Square leaders? They shut down his trade for a year. The Americans tightened import regulations and we lost millions."

'We' she said. She's Meng Produce, too. What an idiot, you. It was always obvious and you ignored it. Take what you can and hoard it.

"Charlie, I like you. I trust you. My father trusts you a lot, really. You've always treated me like a princess, so I'm going to tell you something you can never tell anyone."

Meng had set up this whole conversation. Now, Shu Ling had sweetened me up with her sincerity and flattery, she'd bring on the Big Lie, the falsehood Meng could 'trust' me with, because it didn't matter who I told. I could play, too.

"Once I tell you, you'll know why we can't see each other again. If you want the truth, you've got to promise."

"What? Your father's a sex slave runner?"

"Shut up, Charlie. Don't be an idiot. He's a good man. You know it. He's important. He saves people's lives. And he never wants credit for what he does. But—"

"I don't believe that." My bitterness spilled out. He'd just about ruined my life now.

"No, Charlie. You'll see."

At the green light, we crossed and walked north on Broadway, where she let me take her hand. I inhaled deeply, calming myself. The air across the street smelled strangely fresh, despite the evening traffic.

"Do you want to have dinner, at least?" I asked her. "Great sushi on the next block?"

"How can you even think of eating? But it's a good idea to stop for a minute."

I had no idea she was so upset. She pulled us into the alcove of an unlit storefront. I squinted through the windows and saw stepladders and paint buckets and boxes littering the floor.

"You're shivering, Charlie. It's not that bad."

Hunching over in my topcoat, I said, "It's more important to me than you know, Shu Ling."

"You can't tell anyone this. If you do, and my father finds out? I don't know what he'll do. If I tell you, will you keep quiet? Forever?"

"Forever's a long time. I'll have to think about it." Standing so close to her, I felt desperate and I couldn't keep an idiotic grin off my face.

"Stop playing with me, Charlie." She grabbed my coat collars. "I'm offering you the truth you always wanted. My father trusts you a lot. That's why he sent me to you, remember? But now, he can't afford to be involved with your destiny."

"Sounds like philosophical bullshit." She scowled, probably teasing me again. I'd listen and decide later what to say or what to believe. "All right. I'll keep it quiet, if it's so secret."

Shu Ling lowered her voice. "My father imports human organs. They're harvested from executed prisoners and other people. I think sometimes people sell their organs just to survive. Rich Americans who can't wait in the national transplant queue buy them. Livers, kidneys, lungs, everything. He keeps then in a special refrigerated room at Hunts Point. He says it's a logistics nightmare."

"Jesus! Is that legal?" I stiffened up and backed a step away.

"It's legit, totally safe," she said, letting me go. "I don't think the laws have been made yet. He works with the big pharmaceutical companies. Merck, Roche, doctors from Harvard, doctors from the University of Heidelberg, geneticists from Oxford and Stanford. He provides a service that saves lives. He's part of an international team that's decades ahead of ordinary medical practice, but it has to be under the radar."

"If it's only executed prisoners, that's probably okay. What kind of crimes did they commit? I heard people are executed just for their parts? Someone in the government must know about this," I began to feel numb. If the Chief found out, he'd find some way to implicate me in the organ business, too. Guilt by association.

Meng the murderer. Greer the corpse robber.

"I heard Chinese gangsters killed innocent young people for their body parts. Many families have babies just to sell them."

"That has nothing to do with my father. The people who supply the organs are what Americans call 'criminals,' but in China they're businessmen," she said. "My family has to pull together now, all because of your police chief and your big mouth. Soy to the World is getting too much publicity."

"Hey, Soy to the World helps everybody. It heals people!"

She glowered at me. "Meng Produce has a lot more to lose than you do. My father's friends could get in trouble, and he'd have to call in some big favors. You know my father. He doesn't like owing anybody anything. You'd end up getting investigated, too. Do you want that on top of everything else?"

I rolled my eyes.

"Do you want to be responsible for people losing their lives?"

"What do you mean?" I couldn't resist blowing on my hands and stamping my feet. Doing something, hunching down into my chest, warming my hands, somehow protected me.

"You're so dense." Shu Ling's voice began to break. "Without Meng Produce, dozens of people will die every year. If the cops investigate, the newspapers start mucking around in the governor's family, senators."

"Oh." How big was this?

"He saves lives, Charlie It's totally ethical, but it's got to be secret. America has a whole bunch of primitive laws and all those Christians who think anything with a neo-cortex and a shriveled penis is a saint. Remember the southern senator who supported that abortion doctor killer? That decrepit old senator who had the emergency kidney transplant? My father risked his life to get the kidney to that man. If he ever gets caught, he could go to jail and lose everything."

I stared at her.

"Charlie, just think about it. China executes more people than any other country."

"Yeah, except the U.S."

"No, China has lots more. You don't hear about them, that's all. They're criminals. The only good thing they've ever done with their lives is to give up their organs."

"Jesus, Shu Ling. Your dad must make a lot of money in this business." Tofu meant nothing to him. It was a front.

"Sure. He's a businessman, this is bio-tech. Imagine the delicacy of the surgery, the storage, the shipment, all the details. The timing has to be perfect."

"I guess you can't put a dollar sign on a life," I said. As we walked silently, I thought about the executed, and I was beginning to see Meng's point. This was how he had become so powerful. As long as Congress had an inside track to the organs, the government would never pass trade laws condemning China's human rights abuses. Meng was a master. The Henry Ford of organ transplants. I choked off a laugh. "You're sure the organs come only from prisoners?"

"Of course," she said.

Was she pleading or only trying to persuade me?

"It's only prisoners...convicted criminals, evil people. I told you my father runs an ethical, legitimate business. My father and his colleagues help keep the criminal element under control, both countries."

"In more ways than one," I said, suddenly more nervous than I'd been when I signed my first bank loan. "So this is 'The Special Fruit Company'."

"The what company?"

"Never mind." Whatever name Meng's organ importing company went by, now I understood why "The Special Fruit Company" sounded so hilarious to him and his cronies when I had dinner with them in Taipei.

Shu Ling kept quiet for a minute, then she laced her fingers into mine and gave me Meng's three demands and three offers.

"We have to stop seeing each other."

"What? At all?"

"At all."

I smirked. "I figured that. I'm too close for his comfort."

"Listen. If anybody asks, you don't know me."

"Everybody knows we did the film together. My whole town, half the tofu world. We had our picture in the Clement paper." "Professional's no problem. Personally I mean."

"Did you tell your father we did *Lemur Lips*?"

"Shut up, Charlie. This is not the time to fool around."

"I know, I know. I'm serious."

"Last thing. If anybody asks about your trip to Taipei, you tell them it was business and a cultural tour and you barely saw him."

"That's easy, 'cuz it's true." At that point I leered at her and tried to lick her ear. She stiff-armed me with both of her hands on my shoulders.

"You're acting so stupid."

"How else should I act?" I said. "This whole thing is ridiculous."

Shu Ling shook her head and blinked. "It'll sink in. You were a lot of fun and you did give me a lot of help on the film. I told my father you deserved a lot of credit."

"That's for goddam sure and not only your movie. I gave him the best of everything for seven years. I treated him like a friend, not a customer."

"He likes you."

She said that as if offering me a rare jewel, as if it could replace my dream.

"Business as usual. He'll keep selling your tofu, help you get some new customers, too. He'll ignore your Chief's insults, and he'll send out word to try to find Chen."

The full impact of her message settled in: Meng and I were done except for routine business. He'd never buy the company and I'd never be welcomed into the inner circle of power in the international produce world. Maybe I no longer wanted into that circle anyway. "What if I want to keep seeing you? What if I don't agree to all these conditions?"

"My father can't predict what might happen. He's protecting both of us, Charlie. Don't you get it?"

It was brilliant. Meng gave me no choice. A light as cold and pulsing as the black lights in the Taipei "barbershop" filled my head. I held Shu Ling and kissed her hard and long. I told her I loved her and I always would and, grinning, I guaranteed I'd see her again because she owed me an *Orangutan Toes* lesson.

"You agree, Charlie?"

"It's over with us, Shu Ling, but...who knows?" I flagged down a cab and put her in it. Before I closed the door, I said "Too bad your dad couldn't get everyone in congress a brain transplant."

She laughed. "No, but Denzel Washington's people have inquired about other parts."

"Sure," I said, waving good-bye and hustling back to the Empire Hotel.

Forget the Monkey Toes. You may love her, but you gotta let her go.

I began to mentally dismiss Shu Ling from my life. People who let me down, no matter how much I liked them before, they can evaporate,for all I care.

Shu Ling didn't really betray me, but Gen was amazingly accurate.

Shu Ling led you by your nose, your ears, mostly by the thing between your legs, the thing that grows.

Yeah, it was true. She used my lust to get what she wanted. She was always in her father's shadow and I was too drunk on my lust to see.

She didn't have anything I wanted now. For God's sake, I wasn't about to get into the human meat business. "Tofu: The Meat of the Fields" was as close I was going to come to being any kind of a meat distributor, I don't care how many lives I'd save as Meng's partner. How many would I have to take? Jesus.

Took you long enough to figure out what it's really all about.

If letting Shu Ling go was all I had to do I was glad to be free of Meng's schemes, as long as he kept ordering tofu every week and paying us on time. In the long run, it didn't matter much that Shu Ling and I were history.

***

Once I crossed the George Washington Bridge and headed north on the I-87 with the other late-evening commuters milling toward home, a state of calm settled over me. I stopped for gas and something to eat at the rest area just south of Albany. Ironically, after our exchange in front of the hot dog shop on Broadway, I gravitated to the hot dog stand.

I ordered the first hot dog I'd eaten in at least ten years, slathered it with mustard, and I sat down at the bar to eat. I loved it. I'd tried quite a few tofu hot dogs, but one bite of a real hot dog, and I knew the only way you could make tofu taste that good would be to add pig fat and sugar. So, what's the point? Cook tofu the way it's supposed to be, the old-fashioned Asian way, and when you want a hot dog, eat a real one.

Invigorated, I got back on the highway and set the cruise control at seven miles above the speed limit. The traffic was so light I leaned back and almost entered an alpha state. Sometimes I have to talk to myself out loud to know what I'm thinking or feeling.

I started a conversation with Meng that changed my whole attitude toward life.

'Meng, you old bastard. All I wanted was true love and you repossessed the only woman I really loved in the last five years. Yeah, I loved Becky, but our future would have been so crazy.

I'll admit it to you, she was a stand-in for Shu Ling, and now you've ripped her away. You broke my heart, old man.'

I listened as hard as I could, but he kept quiet.

'I know, you had to do it. You didn't really mind the article but the Chief is getting too close. He's a clever son of a bitch, isn't he? Brighter than we thought. Shu Ling and I were getting closer in a different way. But you have too much to lose. Your big secret. So you told me your big secret. Why?'

That's when I got it. Meng had given me something far richer than even the hand of his girl, a revelation a thousand times bigger and far more perilous than my little secret about Becky.

Meng maneuvered through his days at Hunts Point as if the organ smuggling business didn't exist, pretending he was a vegetable trader, keeping up an impeccable front, while fielding immense pressure from some of the most powerful people in the world. No doubt earning enormous profits.

His life wasn't so different from what I was up to, only we lived on different levels. His Special Fruit Company saved a few rich people's lives in the short run by providing them with healthy organs. I saved millions of peoples' lives over the long term by providing healthy food, not the poisons the mainstream food industry foists on people.

Who's got the most to lose? Meng or you? You choose.

As I stacked up our similarities and differences, at first it seemed that Meng did have a lot more to lose if the wrong people discovered his secret. In terms of money, yes, but family, self-esteem, reputation? Not really. In fact, he had more protection than I'd ever muster, more powerful friends, more options. In reality, I could lose everything if my secret came to light. And, worse, compared to him, I had far less to gain. He'd already entered the inner sanctum of the global untouchables.

By forbidding Shu Ling to see me, he'd severed our emotional ties and turned any future Meng and I had into strictly business. The truth was, now that I'd attained maybe my first rational view of him since I knew him, I saw that our entire history had been strictly and only business. Shu Ling was a wild card that the old man flipped out of the deck.

But, and this was amazing, when he ordered Shu Ling to tell me about the organ trade, he had Shu Ling tell me because it had never come up between Meng and me personally, and he could deny everything.

Meng would never know it, but by letting me know about the organ importing, he revealed how I could handle my secret: Live life the way I wanted to, ignore what society demands, don't ask permission. Meng had shown me the path to reaching my dream of freedom.

I drove home in a state of euphoria, fearless and eager, arriving in Clement at one a.m., focused, a man of mission. Meng's secret alchemized in my heart, radiating the power to change the chaos of my life into the pure gold of power.

Chapter Ten

Genevieve

GRACE UNDER PRESSURE OF DESIRE

Before I met with Gianni to ask for his help with finding a new job, I hadn't made love to a man since I sent Benko packing.

In my lonely musings, a storm of memories about men rolls over me, confusing one with another. One's long blonde hair curling on a bald brown one's neck. One's deep laugh roaring out of another thin chest, sauntering athletic hips angling toward me.

My imagination conjures these apparitions into my life where they surround me, offering me their airy love, their ghostly touches precisely on my perfect pleasure points, their pure attention until I wake out of my trance, unmoved, sick of their perfection, sick of creating spirit lovers to guide my hands over my body, resenting their ghostliness, grieving because I needed self-deluding sorcery.

It's their silence I can't bear. Beautiful, precise images I can summon, but sounds? As soon as I magicked my shadow men into speech, noise emerged from their mouths like ghoulish moans or dull commands that never found the shapes or tones that make sense.

Yet my dream-men satisfy me with their faithfulness, their loyalty to my desires. The men-in-bodies in my life always disappoint me. They're inconsistent in their affections and confused about their feelings. They all go by the same name: Mr. Ambivalence. They act muddled about whether they can love me as freely as they love, or hate, their mothers; mixedup about whether they love me or love themselves in my loving them, they have to follow rules and parameters to know who they are. Even the rebels and bohemians I've loved spend most of their energy in just another kind of obedience, proving to themselves the authorities have no control over them.

Even before the Chief scared me off, I'd begun to seek a graceful way out from Benko. I had to work too hard to ignore his boring narcissism and crude physicality. He and I didn't find much to talk about beyond work, food, and sex. As much as I loved and craved them all, Benko hadn't had a new thought or made an original move in weeks. He, his mind, and even that spectacle of a sausage began to bore me, and boredom depressed me far more than loneliness.

Buhrman's investigation gave me a good excuse to hang up my memories of Benko along with the photos in my 'Boyfriend Gallery,' a show nobody but me would ever see. There, the pictures I'd taken of his inimitable appendage would take their place among the other shots I'd taken of other men to portray rare gifts each of my lovers had given me.

Once I stopped seeing Benko regularly, he turned volatile and unpredictable. For a while, he completely stopped speaking to me in person. When I'd ask for help fetching samples or marketing materials from the warehouse, he'd walk up to me, thrust his eyes two inches away from mine and glare at me, breathing stale garlic into my face. He'd grunt and turn around and walk away, his neck muscles twitching.

Then, when I felt relief that he'd given up on me, he'd call. I'd lead him on, assuring him that I was still fond of him, always reminding him that he had to treat me right if he wanted to keep my friendship. I let him believe that after the investigation, he and I could rekindle our affair.

He ignored the implication that I might not want him.

"I want you always, Genevieve. I want you now. You make me too crazy to wait. But I'll be good. Damn Chief. Maybe something happens to him."

"Benko. Don't be stupid."

"Just play. Make you laugh. Too serious. Let's have fun."

"It's not easy, Benko. Best we take it easy like we agreed." "Sure, boss. When you say yes, my word is always yes. Don't know if I can control myself, Gen. I want you too bad."

"That's not 'friends.'"

"Friends need love. You need me."

"Benko, I'm gonna hang up."

He barked "No. Friends now. Later, later we go back to lovers."

I wanted to believe him, but I couldn't. Every once in a while, I called him. Telephone check-ins with Benko became my shield. A flimsy protection, but by talking to him now and then, I counted on being able to detect any overt hostility and keep him at bay. If I couldn't, I didn't know what I'd do.

***

In the airport the day Charlie revealed his affair with Shu Ling, I punched in Giordano Brothers' number. Gianni was out.

"I'm boarding a plane right now," I told his secretary. "I need his help with something. Have him call me as soon as he can. It's not urgent. He knows my number."

Once I made the call to Gianni for help, he reappeared in my emotional consciousness. With no other man to absorb my affection, my energy naturally flowed to reflecting on our time together. It had been more than six months since we slept together. So much had happened I barely understood where Gianni fit into my life any more.

Once, he told me he'd never loved a woman for her mind before me, and it was the hottest love he'd ever felt. When we separated so abruptly last spring, I wanted to kill him. My jealous mind seethed with every kind of revenge.

My favorite vengeance fantasy was watching the Berkshire house on fire, burning all the memories stored in the sheets, the couches, everywhere we made love. I could see that poor polar bear we'd lain on in front of the fireplace snarling as the place collapsed in flames.

During the first weeks of separation, I wrote Gianni letters and emails cursing him, but I never mailed them. I dialed his home number in Brooklyn at least ten times, always hanging up when anyone answered—it was always his wife or kid. In late April, I bought a dozen long-stemmed red roses and dried them in my oven. I wrapped the crisp, burnt petals in red silk, and mailed it to his office. His reply a few days later: A birthday bouquet with a sweet note. Of course he loved me—six months ago.

A week after I called him from Philadelphia, Gianni called. With typical grace, he apologized. "I'd have called from Buenos Aires if my secretary had forwarded your message. You know that."

That morning, I got out of bed with laryngitis. I could barely whisper. "I believe you, Gianni." My throat burned when I spoke, but I had to talk to him. "I have to talk to you, Gianni," I croaked. "As soon as possible."

"Right now," he said.

"I can barely talk. How about next Monday?"

"I'm coming to the Berkshires tomorrow, for the weekend. Alone. Do you want to meet met there?"

I knew what would happen if I met him there alone and I wanted it. "Are you sure? I just want to talk business."

"That's fine. It's better to talk business without any pressure. We'll just relax. You sound like you need a rest, anyway."

How can I relax with you? I thought. You'll just drive me out of my mind.

I mumbled, "I'm still mad at you."

"Good. You still have feelings for me."

"Forget it. That was a long time ago, Gianni."

"I have a perfect memory. With you, yesterday is the same as today to me."

"Tomorrow is different," I said. "I need your help and friend-ship, that's all."

"Anything, Genevieve. You know that."

We decided to meet at his home on Saturday noon for lunch. I told him that I needed to leave by three and that he should keep his chef on duty. "Being with you alone scares me, Gianni."

"I'm a bear cub."

"You don't understand how vulnerable I am."

"I'll be good, I promise. You're the one..."

I laughed. "We're both the one, so you better be good."

Protecting myself from reviving my deepest feelings for him, I concocted an escape plan. I would arrange to pick up Liam early that night so if I had to run from temptation, I could plea lack of childcare. If I was tempted to give in to the urge I'd feel on the skin of my thighs for the touch of the hair on his legs, I'd get in my car and drive away because I had to fetch Liam.

With Liam happy and safe at Joanne's with her son Nelson, my mind and heart were free for once.

Like the first time I stepped through the front door of his Berkshire home, the moment we looked into each other's eyes, probing to learn what depths we'd allow each other, we disap-peared into our enchanted mountain hideaway.

I'd mistaken Gianni's flirtation on the phone for superficial toying with our love. Inside the front door of his house, he drew me to him, kissing me delicately, almost shyly and I let myself fall against him, opened my mouth, hugged his body so tightly I felt him tremble.

"Genevieve, darling. Sweet Genevieve," he whispered, pull-ing back. "It hasn't really been six months. I feel like we just held each other yesterday."

He led me to the couch where we sat in front of an apple-wood fire, holding hands, staring into the flames.

The voice I'd regained chunks of that morning melted away again as I relaxed. For the first time in months, I felt safe. American Tofu, Charlie, the dead woman, Buhrman, Benko, my photos and cookbook, all the work seemed like minor scenes in an old movie. I felt I was home with Gianni and I dropped all my fears about losing myself in him. I didn't care what happened.

I gazed around the study, realizing for the first time I was a foreigner to this world, an interloper from the world of work. His riches surrounded us: the marble mantle with gold and crystal candlesticks ranked across it, the black and mahogany leather chairs and couch squatting like waiting pack animals, the slim lamps shining warm light through chafed cotton shades. I felt like I was in a movie set. I was the star playing the pretty servant girl he'd sneaked into the mansion when everyone else was gone.

"You want to talk?" Gianni asked. "No, don't answer."

I couldn't speak louder than a dull whisper anyway.

He scrolled through his music collection. In a moment, mellow saxophone notes surrounded us.

"Old Miles," he said. "*Love songs.*" He handed me a snifter of blackberry brandy. "This will cure you, if anything can."

I grinned, mouthing, "Family collection?" His family in Naples produced an elderberry liqueur that Gianni claimed tasted like the blood of resurrected Christ. I sipped it and as the creamy elderberry juice slipped down my throat, the alcohol vapors rose into my head and I almost swooned.

"In heaven yet? Take another sip."

"I'm afraid I'll never make it all the way up there," I rasped. "Way too sinful."

Mocking an amorous priest, he caressed my hand and whispered, "All can be forgiven, my child."

I watched him stir the embers and add several fragrant logs to the fire.

"It hasn't been easy, Genevieve," he said as he refilled our glasses. "I tried to be out of the office every time you came near Hunts Point. I feel so much for you, I often wanted to cash in, pick you up, take you off to Fiji. In my dream, we live the rest of our lives in paradise."

He stood up and paced in front of the fireplace. The chill November sun dropped in through the windows, stretched across the carpet, and climbed into my lap. At least he was opening up to me but I couldn't let him take control of us. I needed a simple little thing—his help getting a new job quick—if he couldn't help, so be it.

I watched the sizzling fire, listening to logs shift and fall, like American Tofu and my whole life in Clement, weakened and surrendering to the insistent flames that, once started, would have to burn themselves out.

"Let's have lunch," he said. "I'm the chef."

I swallowed the last of my liqueur and whispered, "You weren't supposed to give your man the afternoon off."

Gianni pulled me off the couch and led me into the kitchen. "I couldn't help it. On weekends, he works at his brother's shop in Lenox."

"Likely story."

"But true. He'll be home by five, and we have a lot to do, so," raising his eyebrows and winking, "we have to hurry."

He wasn't referring to getting lunch over with or discussing my new job. Heat from the liqueur rose up from my stomach into my face.

"You look like a Christmas cherub with your cheeks all red and shiny like that." He kissed me on my lips and twirled me into the kitchen where uplifting strings sang from invisible speakers.

"Albinoni," he said. "I can't cook without him." I watched him scramble eggs and tofu with leeks and elephant garlic in an elegant copper pan with the *savoir-faire* of a professional chef.

He tore chunks of bread off a loaf of focaccia and divided the pieces with his fingers. He placed the crusty sandwiches next to tossed salads on white over-sized plates, poured two mugs of coffee, and set our lunch on the counter.

"Mangé," he ordered, "mangé," smiling as if he'd just created a gourmet delicacy for the pope. Or the queen.

We ate in silence, smiling and chewing and swinging our heads and shoulders in time with the music, like casual friends. The kitchen gas fireplace roared, relaxing me even more.

"What a meal. I wish I could make that."

His face lit up and he bowed to his waist.

"You cured me," I said. My voice grated and skipped like an old man's straining to make a point. "My throat doesn't hurt and I can talk a little bit."

"Let's not get serious too soon," he said.

"I already agreed to that, last spring. Remember?" A note of bitterness crept into my halting words.

"Genevieve." He moved toward me. "I'm sorry."

I stepped back. "Gianni, don't confuse me."

"I just want to help," he said.

"It's so hot in here. Can we go for a walk?"

"Good idea." Gianni brought me my coat and said, "I like talking among my trees. Somehow the words sound deeper."

I saw him in a new way, as handsome and mature as ever, but he acted less sure of himself. He moved tentatively around me, as if he didn't know how to treat me without cues, as if he'd forgotten my body language.

Strolling in the cool sunlight, past fields dotted with fat, golden pumpkins, we lingered in the apple orchard and plucked mushy fruit from trees that were all but stripped of their boun-ty.

"Apple wood makes delicious smelling fire, doesn't it? When you have to sacrifice a few trees for the health of the or-chard, you don't even think about it."

Standing beside dried corn still not harvested, rustling in the breeze, we marveled at the sky's opalescent blues and the rich harvest his farm offered up so casually.

"I could never leave this," he murmured. "But I have an idea. It might work." He gripped my hand, chafing it to warm it, and we walked on. "You know I love you and respect you as much as anybody in my life. You need a job now. With all the craziness around the accident in your plant, your call didn't surprise me."

"It's been wild," I said.

"Your police chief has visited me twice and Charlie calls me way too often for my comfort. My comfort for you, I mean."

That was the first I'd heard of Buhrman's actual visits to him. I cocked my head, concerned.

"No problems," Gianni went on, responding to my gesture.

"He's just fishing. I like the man. Good country cop, doing his job and having a good time. Poor Greer, though. Buhrman's turned up the pressure on him."

We went back inside to his study. He banked the fire and poured us small snifters of cognac. He raised his glass, "La Vita."

"La Vita."

"Now, what shall we do?" he asked.

"First things first," I said, "like they say in business."

"Absolutely. The only way."

I loved jousting with him, tossing double entendre back and forth. Unlike Benko, Gianni was the Prince of Flirtation. A cloud passed over the sun and the room dimmed, not unexpect-edly, at the thought of Benko.

"I'm in a mess. Charlie's acting like an idiot."

"Idiot?"

"Messing around with Meng's daughter, pissing Meng off, freaking out."

"I could tell he's been on edge from his calls."

"I think he's going to lose Meng's trade."

"How serious are he and the girl?"

"It's over."

"Good. She's protected. Meng will be happy now."

"He's going through my files."

"He can, you know. Boss has the right."

"Gianni, who's side are you on?"

"Yours. What do you think? See it from his point of view. He's going through your files because he has to cover his ass, in case you leave."

"I never said anything about leaving. Well, I threatened, but he didn't take it seriously."

"He knows."

"How?"

"He's a good businessman, just covering his ass."

"All right. He's not the only problem."

Gianni sat back his chair and crossed his leg over his knee. Sipping his brandy, he waited.

"The guy I've been seeing since we split up?"

"The Russian. Low class, but what can I say?"

"Worse than that. He's a brute. When the Chief told me he was investigating him along with Charlie in the death? I told him I couldn't see him anymore and he pushed me down on the couch and I thought he would rape me or hit me."

Gianni jumped up from his chair and sat beside me, knee to knee.

"Do not fool around with this guy. He's a powder keg."

"You think? That's the whole point."

"Did you call the police? Do you want me to send somebody up to talk to him? I can."

"No, no. I can handle it. I've got him calmed down. He thinks the Chief has targeted him for murder, so he's keeping his distance from me, for now. But I want to get out of Clement tomorrow."

"Just quit. You can work for me in New York."

"I can't. Liam—"

"Telecommute. Start Monday."

"I can't. I owe too much to Charlie and Nora. I can't leave them like that. Besides, I have to give Liam some time to adjust. He's not a baby any more."

Gianni stood up and banked the fire again. "Are you sure you're safe?" The apple wood crackled and its heart-breaking sweet fragrance drifted into the study.

"Yes. I'm sure," I said, taking a deep breath.

"When do you want to start at Giordano Brothers?"

"Gianni, you're so sweet. I can't go to work for you. It would be pure misery to see you walk by my desk and know..."

He nodded his head and shrugged.

"Remember the guy you mentioned on the West Coast? The guy who did the new foods research?"

"Sure. You want to work for him? That's a long ways away. San Francisco."

He meant that San Francisco was a long way away from him. "I could use a big change."

He observed me for a long time then lay back on the couch and sighed. The leather crinkled and he made himself cozy. "All right."

"Thank you, Gianni. I'll start with him. I don't know what I'll do for sure."

"I can call him and set you up right away."

"Don't. Just give me his number and be my reference. That's all. I don't want to owe you more than I should."

"You won't owe me—"

"Gianni, thank you. Maybe you could give me a list of other names, too? Without mentioning it to anyone? I don't want word to get out that I'm job hunting until after the New Year."

"I'll have Jerrylyn email names of a few people you can trust. That's all?"

"That's all. I wanted to tell you about how scared I've felt lately. I needed to talk to somebody."

He sat up and pulled me to him. "It's all right. It's a big change, but any help you need, I'm here. You know that?"

"Yes." I kissed his ear. You're the sweetest. I only wish..."

"Mmmmmm?"

"You know. Can't go there."

"Guess not," he said. "Well, now everything's straightened out? Anything else?"

Raising my eyebrows and tsking my teeth, pretending to think hard. "Not that I can think of." My knees trembled a little and I felt my jaw quiver. The whole front of my body went warm, except my nipples. They swelled and stretched tight against my sweater. Gianni's eyes dropped to my chest.

"You came all the way over here for that?" His voice rose. Even he lost his grace under pressure of desire.

I said, "That and lunch." I shrugged and my nipples hardened further. "You know women. Talking in person makes us feel better." "You feel better now?"

"Much." I kissed him quickly on the lips and then on the nose and stood up.

"Gianni, do you know what an incredible life you have?"

"Yes," he said, standing up and crossing to the liquor cabinet. "You could stay here if you need to get out right away."

"I can't."

"Are you sure? Leave right now and I'll take care of your expenses until you get your new job."

"No. I have to give Charlie plenty of notice. Right now, I think he's on the verge of a nervous breakdown." The last thing I wanted was to take money from Gianni.

"What do you mean?"

"He's gone on a manic work spree. Ten meetings every day about things like bathroom policy. A memo every hour about nothing. He calls up the Chief every time he hears from a consumer and pleads with him to solve the crime or close the case." Talking about Charlie and work again dropped my temperature and I decided to leave.

"A lot of pressure. So far, I think he's done a good job." Gianni paused, gathering his thoughts. "If Charlie can't find anyone to try to fill your shoes...you move on to your new job by spring anyway? He won't complain. I've known plenty of guys like him. They're hard on the outside, they know it all. Inside, they're marshmallows."

I hugged Gianni, brushing his upper lip with a light kiss. I let my lips linger and he kissed back, but sweetly.

"I have to ask you something, Genevieve."

"Oh?"

"What about us?" he asked.

Feeling loose I said, "Que sera, sera. Right?" I touched his hand, raised it to my lips, then settled it over my heart. "Gianni, I know you can't change your life for me. I can't change my life for you either."

I started to feel light-headed. I would be free of American Tofu and Charlie and all the pressures. Gianni would be my friend and that's all I wanted.

"You'll find a new job ten times better than tofu."

"I know I will." I stood and tugged him up beside me, pulling us toward the stairs. "Don't you think we should celebrate?"

"I don't know," he demurred. "You're tired. Besides, you don't have a new job yet."

"Oh. Right. By the way, let's not tell Charlie or anyone until I get the job?"

"Of course not."

I turned, pretending I needed my coat. "Well, Signor Giordano, if we've finished our meeting, I guess it's time for me to leave. I have a child to retrieve from his computer dungeon before he gets captured by the evil terrorists on the tundra."

"Wait, Ms. O'Connor. There is one more aspect of this agreement I think we should work out before you leave. Do you have a moment?" Stepping back, he addressed me, politely, formally, his eyes twinkling. "Would you mind stepping into my private office. It shouldn't take long."

I pretended disappointment and glanced at my watch. "Well, let's make it quick," I whispered.

"I can't promise how quick we'll be. As you know, these important matters often take longer than you expect."

I ran up the steps and he chased me hooting. Stripping quickly in the chilly upstairs room, we slipped between cold sheets. The past, the demands of our present lives beyond the room, our possible futures, sank under our breathing and quiet moans.

I caught Gianni's thick gold necklace in my fingers, tightening it gently around his throat as he wound my hair in his fist, drawing my face into his. He tried to swallow me through my mouth, scissoring my waist and bottom between taut legs, squeezing until my bones ached.

We rolled and kicked and rode the bed like a raft in a storm trying to rip its anchor free from the grip of the rocks down below.

The last of the light sank with us into a place where nothing existed except our lips, our soaked bellies and thighs, the twists and arcs we threw our bodies into as we sought total immersion in each other's moans and laughs.

"You're too sexy when you groan," he said.

Our fingers and tongues swirled everywhere, moist weedy tentacles wrapping around thighs, licking down our necks and shoulders, tugging and tilting us back and forth across the bed.

He turned me on my belly and said, "Ssshhh." I shivered as he poured cool oil along my spine, his fingertips brushing it into the sweat on my back. He kneaded my long muscles, nipping folds of skin between his fingernails, a big cat teasing his willing prey, softening the last bit of tension out of my shoulders.

Pressing his elbows into the sides of my lower back, he elongated the rigid muscles that clung to my hips, then pulling them like taffy, he released the stiffness that thousands of miles of driving had bound like a thick belt around my pelvis.

He rubbed my bottom, gently at first, probing my soft fat with his thumbs, then he began to slap and pinch until I jerked away.

"Ssshhh," he said again. Soothing the warmed skin on my bottom, he continued massaging my thighs and calves. As he lifted my foot, blowing warm breath on my sole and licking the tips of my toes with his soft tongue, I drifted into a spell, floating on a cloud with angel wings nudging me ever higher into ecstasy.

I don't know how long I dozed, but I stirred when I felt Gianni enter me. Both on our stomachs, we lay languorous, our bodies shifting in tiny motions signaling the storm's potential return. As we began to move into each other more quickly, the friction of our bodies as gentle as two wide rivers joining courses, I heard Gianni gasp. A sob broke from his throat and I immediately began weeping. We rolled over and stared deeply into each other's streaming eyes as we continued pushing and pulling, ignoring ourselves, urging the other to climax.

We collapsed into a delicious nap under the eiderdown quilt, twisted into each other like a French braid of arms and legs. We woke and hugged each other as if we were the only people on earth. Then, still without speaking, we dressed and made our way down the softly lit main staircase.

Gianni offered me one last blackberry brandy toast and, handing me a bottle "Just like the pope's," he said. "Don't worry. You'll have the best job of your life."

We hugged like we'd never hug again, and I left. I drove down the narrow lane and pulled over before I turned onto the street, so I could cry.

***

I drove home with my windows wide open to the crisp night and the heater blasting a blanket of heat across my lap. The stars shone so brightly in the glossy sky each one seemed to beam a message to me. Love. Peace. Freedom. A bright new life. Even though I'd long before learned never to count on anything, I let all my worries and fears dissolve in the chilly breeze blowing across my face.

Eventually, my exhilaration faded and I began to feel incredibly sentimental about American Tofu. What an emotional wimp. But AT has changed me more than any other chapter in my life. I loved everybody I worked with, even that rat Benko when he backed off and treated me like a friend, and I would miss all my customer friends. The worst thing about changing jobs and leaving AT was that I didn't know how I'd break the news to Liam. He was finally feeling at home in Clement, happy with friends, winning meets with his swim team.

The other worse thing was that Charlie would hate me for leaving him in the lurch. What did he say? The mice were leaving the ship?

Once he knew about Benko and me, he'd probably fire him, but that wouldn't do me any good. Besides, he couldn't fire Benko before the next Chinese New Year anyway. The Year of the Rooster had his whole Soy to the World dream riding on it. I'd stick with him till we got through that and then, up up and away to San Francisco.

I stopped in front of Joanne's and sat in my car, thinking, before I went in to get Liam.

I had a clear mind for the first time since Becky died. That beautiful sex with Gianni this afternoon cleared my mind.

I did love them all at American Tofu. But I had to admit to myself I was really getting tired of Charlie's antics and Benko's bullying attitude. Trying to control them both was taking way too much out of me.

I wouldn't leave Charlie in the lurch, but if he gave me any trouble about my moving on, I'd walk out. Nora would have to deal with him on her own. And Benko, he's either an idiot in love with himself or a bully who knows only one way to get his way.

I picked up my boy and pulled into our driveway by midnight. I kissed my lovely, patient son good night and tumbled exhausted into my bed for the deepest sleep since Gianni and I first celebrated the Year of the Monkey, nearly a year ago.

Chapter Eleven

Charlie

A RIDE WITH THE CHIEF

blue lights flash, clever
cop angles for a big catch
charlie trout slips away

I came out of my office bathroom after lunch the Wednesday before Thanksgiving to hear my secretary say, "No problem, Chief. His calendar is clear this afternoon. I'll tell him you'll be by at two."

At that moment, the floor leapt up into my face. I closed my eyes and tried to breathe while my body swerved back and forth. I wanted to support my forehead against the wall of carpet, but when I leaned toward it, the carpet backed off, beckoning me to follow it down. Lucky, I stayed almost vertical.

I staggered to my office and collapsed on the couch, planning to lie there until I regained my balance. When I lay down, the vertigo disappeared.

Since I returned from Taiwan, I'd worked myself and everyone else to the bone. If I hadn't ignored the little symptoms of fatigue and stress, I doubt if I'd been able to drive Soy to the World beyond the idea stage. Talking, phoning, writing, following up, turning people on and keeping them fired up wore me out, especially since I was carrying the weight of the investigation on top of work.

I was lucky I didn't have to worry about managing the core of our business: the production. Benko had offered to run the factory, the warehouse, and the shipping department single-handedly. I gave him a nice bonus and let him hire a mechanic to help with maintenance. After his first successful week in charge, I called him into my office.

"Benko, you're saving my ass. I don't have the energy to handle all the details."

"That's fine, Charlie. My job. I do it, everybody's happy."

"Doing it right, too. I see the costs are holding."

"Good. I'm good."

"Here's a little present. We call it a token of appreciation." I handed him a bottle of Stolichnaya.

"You don't have to do that." He pulled the bottle out of its carton and unscrewed the cap. "Here. Old custom. Drink, we share." I drank from the bottle, not too deeply. He drank a long slug.

"Good stuff, Charlie. Only thing, next time. I like scotch. You know single malt? Laphroig? The best." He grinned.

"Sure, Benko," I said, not amused that he wanted a fifty dollar bottle of scotch rather than the twenty five dollar of vodka, but I had to admit he had balls to tell me what he wanted while he assumed there would be a next time. "Just keep up the good work and we'll see."

"Thanks, Charlie. I got it all covered."

"Great, Benko."

"By the way. Another Scotch? The MacAllan. I like it. Ever try it?"

With the way my head felt, if he kept things cool in the factory so I didn't have to think about them at all, I'd buy him a case of single malt scotch.

***

I'd been hungry for Thanksgiving like never before, not the feast, but the time off.

All I wanted was real down-time: raking the yard, taking the kids for a burger and the movies, maybe getting out the old Joy of Sensual Massage workbook with Nora. I usually hiked in the woods to relax, but since Becky died, whenever I'd tried bushwhacking in the trees, everything about her came back and that's the last thing I needed.

As I got out of bed in the morning, dizzy spells would strike. All day, at random, they'd strike. I'd walk to my car and the driveway would spring into my face. Or I'd drive down the block and the car would tilt sideways, and I'd wobble on two wheels, then I'd be fine for maybe a day. Eventually, one of the office ladies said they'd all been talking and they wanted me to take some time off.

"We can handle the business," she said. "You trained us good."

I was touched but I'd stay on deck until the Thanksgiving break even though my body shouted at me loud and clear: Charlie, clean up your act or I'm gonna scrub your insides so pure you'll never stop squeaking.

The one person I didn't want to see that afternoon was Buhrman. We'd already shut down production for the long weekend and the office staff would leave by three. I lay on my office couch preparing for him, resting my eyes.

The Chief was the most punctual man I'd ever met. He marched through the front door precisely at two o'clock. If I wasn't ready exactly on time for a planned meeting with him, he let me know his opinion that my work habits were slovenly and unlikely to ever lead to success. All my employees bowed and scraped before Buhrman as if he alone determined what happened to their futures. But not if I could help it.

From my couch, when I rolled up the blinds, I could see everyone who approached the front of the building. I watched Buhrman near the plate glass door and stop to check his reflection. He pumped up his brass-buttoned chest and tilting his hat back, ambled in like he was the headman.

The way he struts? No wonder you have a knot in your guts.

Once the investigation ended, I intended to do my best to have him demoted or transferred. I'd love to see him humbled in the local newspaper and retired as fast as possible to a parking lot security job in Miami. That afternoon, he pranced around the office like a proud tom turkey, the one who kept his head. His mood worried me.

"Hey, Charlie. Why's it so gloomy in here?"

I'd dimmed all the lights except my screen saver with its migrating flock of winged tofus.

"Let's go," Buhrman said in an unusually friendly tone. "Take a ride in the cruiser. You all right?" He stepped close, peering at my face. "You're pale."

"I'm fine. Just tired." Ignoring the hand he offered, I slipped off the couch and sidestepped him. The spell had passed, leaving me with dampness on my chest and a pain pulsing at the base of my skull. I switched on the overhead lights, trying to dissolve the gloom that had settled into my heart like a permanent November, the month of low skies, low sales, low energy. "I don't really feel like going anywhere," I said. "I was just about to go home for a long weekend. My kids are expecting me. Am I under arrest, or what?"

"Hey. Take it easy. I'm doing a patrol shift this afternoon. Thought you'd enjoy a quiet drive and a nice talk. Clear some things up before we take off for the holiday." He opened the office door, motioning me out.

Resistance would only antagonize him and though I didn't mind making him mad, I sure didn't have the stamina to deal with him the way I wanted to.

It's only a bluff. He knows enough. Show him you're not well. Have a dizzy spell.

As usual, Jiminy made sense. The vertigo might come in handy. Work with whatever you're given, another one of my business success mottos.

As soon as he settled in the patrol car, Buhrman switched on the flashing blue lights.

"In a rush, Aaron?" I asked, annoyed, but not very surprised at his adolescent ostentation. "I thought we're out for a peaceful ride." "That's right. The lights make sure nobody bothers us."

And they make sure that everybody sees us. Buhrman drove slowly, deliberately. The streets were empty, as if everyone had abandoned the neighborhoods to burrow in and wait out a storm. I hadn't seen the weather report.

"I hear you're a pretty good boss?"

He's using the old routine: Doodles and Dips. Gonna open up King Tofu's lips.

Not likely. "I try to be. Like any employer, I have some problem workers. The rest, you trust them and treat them like grown-ups, they like you. They do a better job than if you browbeat them." I kept everything simple with him, so his skeptical mind would miss any dubious claims in my philosophy: if something caught his attention, he'd consider it a clue.

"Yeah. Not like criminals. You have to stand over them all the time or they'll con you and rip you off before you know it." He paused. "You must know your workers pretty well?"

Leading by asking, the oldest sales trick in the book. I'd play along. "Pretty well. We check references. Regular evaluations." "How well did you know the MacDaniel woman?"

Jesus, I thought. He knows. Here it comes. Now I'm fucked. My other voice held its breath. "Not too well. Why?"

"We dug up some interesting new information. Thought you ought be the first to know. The first outside of criminal justice circles, that is."

"About the fingerprints?" I'd turn the tables on the interrogator.

"Naw. Didn't I tell you? No clear leads there. She must have had a doozey of a party. She knew half the people in Clement. You heard about the drug paraphernalia? We expected that, after the blood tests and all."

"Yeah. Wasn't that in the paper?"

Buhrman's image quivered and my stomach began to twist up again. Buhrman's voice developed a faint echo as if he called to me from across a wide gorge. Why didn't he tell me before now that my print meant nothing? Maybe he didn't have my fingerprint. If he did, maybe he was saving it for court.

"But before I get into the new info," he said, "I want to ask you something."

"Why don't you just tell me?" I groaned, unsure whether I'd tip over in the seat in a dizzy fit or whether I'd vomit on his radio.

"It can wait." Buhrman had developed an exquisite sense of interrogation timing.

He knows you're sick. Best time to trick you, make it stick.

"You still think it was an accident?" he said, a false note of incredulity in his voice belying his interrogation technique.

"Of course," I said. "There's no evidence otherwise, is there? No motive. Besides, I know my people. None of them are mur-derers."

"Well, Greer. Part of being a good boss is protecting your people. You do that?"

"Yeah. My workers are good people. I expect them to keep the law. The law's their final protection. This is America, Aaron. Everyone has rights. A whole Bill of Rights, in case you forgot. Did you forget that?" Buhrman's dogged hostility irritated me no matter how well-prepared for it I was.

"Hey, don't get mad. From what everybody tells me, your judgment's supposed to be pretty good. You seem like a straight enough guy to me. Been pretty helpful. So let's say I expected you to trust your people. I just want to know," he grit his teeth, "what about the one rotten apple that's all shiny and red, but under that skin, it's brown, turning black. Rotten to the core."

"It's possible. They'd have to be pretty smart, though. After a while, you work with somebody, you get to know them pretty well."

"Everybody's got something to hide. You can admit that." He caught himself in a statement and rephrased it. "Can you admit that?"

At that insinuation, I breathed deeply, pausing to let a wave of nausea decide whether it was staying or passing through. When it dwindled, I said, "It's not always that big a deal. Sometimes it's better to hide something."

Not bad, Chuck. Tell it true. Confuse this arrogant gumshoe.

Nausea tugged at my jaw again and something slipped up my throat. I had to slide down on the seat and the change in position shut me up.

"You sure you're all right?"

"Dizzy spell. Need some time off."

"Yeah, me too. This murder thing's a bitch. I never been so busy, mind never stops, paperwork, phone calls. I get why the smartest cop acts stupid, y'know. Old TV show—*Columbo.* You ever catch a re-run?"

He forgot I already called him a Columbo, but I just shook my head.

"No? Ya gotta see him in action. He's got so much going on upstairs he has to keep the info coming in at a speed he can manage. Sort, file it, move the pawns. That, and keeping criminals confused."

I was the last person in the world to sympathize with Buhrman's stress. Slumping, I stared at the a plastic replica of the town's emblem that was glued to the glove compartment, a blue hatchet crossed with a red plow on a field of triangular green pines. I supposed the town fathers wanted their descendants to remember who won the war between the savages and the farmers. The plow gleamed as if the Chief painted it with scarlet nail polish.

Chipper as the first morning of the universe, Burhman said, "Columbo's not like Monk. He's a normal guy, not some freak. He stopped talking and fiddled with his radio, reducing the volume on the static.

"One good thing..." he muttered.

I waited for him to finish his sentence. Then I caught on.

It's the old bait and switch. Maybe he has a snitch.

"Yeah?" I said. "Always a bright side to everything, eh, Aaron?" "That computer's becoming a friend of mine. Internet, downloading, email, Twister, MugBook. You must be into that stuff?"

"I got all the stuff. We're totally wired. You want to make money, you got no choice." My collegial attitude was starting to work.

Don't be a jerk. He's the one doing the work. On you.

"Charlie, I assume that anybody could have done this."

Watching him change direction like an angler dragging his lure across the current. "Anybody?"

"Yeah." He circled it closer.

"Not anybody," I said. "Even if it was murder, not everybody could do it. You ever meet a murderer?"

"Maybe. You never know. It's beside the point. In my line, you assume everybody can do it. Wouldn't you?"

I sat up and at that moment, the dizziness disappeared. Ready for a friendly argument, I said, "Maybe they can, just because they're human. As a human, you can say I can. As Charlie Greer, a specific human, I couldn't. Not only that, I wouldn't. How about you," I said, turning the tables again. "Can you kill someone?"

"Sure, if I had to. I'm trained to kill. I'm ready any time. It's not the favorite part of my job but if I had to uphold the law, stop somebody on a rampage? I'd do it. Decent people need protection. There's a lot of douche bag psychopath mental cases out there. What do you think they hired me for?"

I stared at him, shaking my head at the hypocritical twisted reasoning I'd come to expect from him.

"Don't look at me that way," Buhrman said. "Some asshole comes after you or your wife or kids? Don't tell me you wouldn't shoot him?"

"I don't own a gun."

"If you did, you would."

"Yeah, I would. No doubt. That's not murder. That's self-defense. It's legal. Society wants you to protect yourself and your family."

"What about the woman whose old man abused her for years before she finally shot him?"

"Sounds like self-defense."

"Jury disagreed. Second-degree murder. Gave her twenty years, said they'd thought about life, only it was second degree. I think the D.A. should have pushed all the way. She clearly premeditated it."

He switched on the siren and accelerated, passing a pick-up sagging with a load of firewood. As soon as he passed, he punched his steering wheel and the siren blurped into silence in mid-howl.

"What about that teenager in Florida? White guy shoots black kid. Self-defense?"

The Chief scowled.

Blue lights, speed, he's on a cops and robbers trip. Better bite your lip.

I deep-breathed a few times, showed him a poker face and said, "This discussion doesn't have anything to do with American Tofu, Aaron. Why don't you take me back to the factory?"

"You don't get it yet, do you, Greer?" he said as he swung the cruiser around in the middle of the street. "It looked like an accident, but it was too slick. Big woman. Strong. All the reports said you had good safety policies. Special training and all. You hadn't had an accident for what, 632 days straight? You posted the number for everyone to see."

"It's one of the best records in the food industry."

Ignoring my obvious pride in our safety record, Buhrman's zealotry twisted our competence into the realm of self-serving hypothetical mathematics.

"By my calculations, that makes a point zero zero one percent chance it was an accident. Those odds say we're on a one way street, my friend, straight down Homicide Lane."

He found a way to use my good business practices against me. Thank God I'd stayed in the saddle no matter how bad my body felt.

If I stayed home to heal my vertigo, Buhrman would snoop and claw around like some mutt with rabbit shit up his nose. He'd contrive some way to get at people and records and create so much fear that my employees would shiver when they saw him.

You stay home to satisfy your relaxation needs? Facts about you and Becky will sprout like weeds.

"I love statistics, Charlie. They reveal a lot of secrets. How about this one: nine out of ten of industrial accidents happen to men. So, repose that one and you get a one in ten chance Mac-Daniel should have an accident. See how it's addin' up to murder?"

His scatterbrained mathematics flummoxed me. He was so crazy maybe I should let him have free rein. Let everyone see him for his true Nazi persecutor self.

But, the fact was, everyone did have something to hide, including me, most of all, so I let my better judgment prevail. Nobody, nobody, never, ever needed to know anything about my harmless little affair with big strong Becky MacDaniel.

In his insistence on a conviction, Buhrman would weave a motive for Becky's death into his suspect's every ordinary, grubby deed and he'd have the support of the district attorney who didn't have an idea what Buhrman was up to. Lawyers be damned, I'd bust Buhrman as easily as he could bust me.

You ain't used to squirming. Why do it with Buhman?

I'd always been boss and whenever I wasn't top dog, I left the squabble. I couldn't leave this one, so I decided to take back as much control as I could. An image of Meng crossed my mind. How would he handle this conversation? Gambling that Buhrman didn't know a thing about my affair with Becky, I went on the offensive.

I sat up straight, my head cleared, my gut tightened. I felt buckled into the cruiser seat like a captain in a cockpit. I turned toward Buhrman and noticed how small he was. Narrow shoulders, thin thighs. He had to scoot the seat up as far forward as he could to reach the pedals.

"Yeah. We run a tight ship," I said. "Of course, you never know what can happen to your employees, on or off the job. Ask anyone in manufacturing, ask any employer. Do you follow up every accident at Pulzewski's Sausage Factory across town with a big investigation?"

He turned to me and slowed the car.

You're on a roll. Let yourself go.

My anger was coming on strong, sharpening my mind and tongue. I attacked. "Did you know the meat packing industry rips arms and heads off innocent people every day all across the country?" I paused, hoping it would sink in.

Buhrman dawdled along Main Street, listening, his chin jutting ahead under thin lips. The day's few pedestrians turned toward the cruiser, curious about the flashing lights.

I had the momentum. "A point zero zero one percent accident rate ought to win us an award from OSHA. It's so low, it's Guinness Book of Records. Go back and check your calculations before you make your conclusions about the street we're headed down."

He smirked.

"By the way," I said, with a calm, neutral tone, hoping he'd hear me without defenses and get the point right in his flat little gut. "Didn't I hear that the new deputy you hired for the night shift shot himself in the leg a few weeks ago? Was it an accident? Maybe somebody else shot him? Did you check his references before you hired him?"

Buhrman muttered, "This is not about the police, Greer."

"It might turn out to be, Aaron, if you don't get off this witch hunt. You still don't have any hard evidence, do you?" Now I had a chance to expose the one threat he could nab me with, the thing that was beyond my control, a possible fact. I asked, "What about that stuff under her fingernails. Did you get the DNA report?"

"Yeah."

I caught my breath. "Well?"

"Can't tell you."

"Christ, Aaron. I want to clear this up as much as you."

"Gotta save it for court, Charlie."

He's got nothing new. Back off, let him stew.

I let out my breath. The fake bait he flaunted in front of my face—"new information"—slipped right off his lure and the clever Charlie fish wiggled away, for now.

The "new information" I gave him about the meat industry and the accident in his own office should make him think before he waltzed onto my turf again as if he owned it.

Stay on course. Show him you can ride any bucking horse.

"One last question, Aaron," I said, maintaining the offensive. "You've never said why you think someone would kill Becky. Without a motive, you can't prove anybody's guilty, can you? With no motive, every lead or idea you have sends you on a wild goose chase. Basic logic, right?"

"Whad'ya mean?"

"Remember that first time you came to my office? You said you'd find a motive then you'd find the killer?"

"Charlie," he said, using my first name in a transparent effort to discount my points, "you're right. We don't tell the public we have The Motive. Why would we? You don't understand police work. Why do you think I have to investigate every angle? What you think is a wild goose chase is just solid old-time Beat the Bushes, Scare the Snakes. Do you know how much work that is?"

His narrow shoulders sagged and the beginnings of a wattle showed under his chin. The investigation had taken a lot out of him, too. Buhrman dropped me off at the factory and wished me a nice Thanksgiving. I watched him speed down the street with the cruiser's lights strobing violet shadows through the bare branches overhead. As he turned the corner, his siren wailed and retreated toward the center of town. I thought of the turkeys arriving at the chopping block suddenly understanding what their lives were all about.

***

I carved the turkey and ate Thanksgiving dinner with Nora and the kids, and went back to bed. By Saturday night, after seventy two hours of forgetting about my problems, I felt strong enough to go out for pizza and the movies with Chuck and Rissi.

Rissi and I sat down in our regular booth by the window at Jumbo's Pizza parlor while Chuckie climbed up on the bench behind me.

Rissi giggled. "Daddy, there's Chuckie."

I swung around and saw Chuckie's face mashed against the etched glass booth divider making a chimpanzee face at us. Rissi and I laughed together and Chuckie came and sat down beside his sister.

"My silly little monkeys," I said.

Rissi said, "Do monkeys cry, Daddy?"

"No, honey. Animals don't cry. Only people."

"Mommy says Chuckie's an animal and he cries."

Chuckie poked her in the shoulder. "No I'm not."

"You eat like one. Mommy says."

Chuckie stuck out his tongue and began licking Rissi's arm and neck and cheeks while she squealed and pushed him away. After they settled down to wait for our plain cheese pizza, Rissi studied me with her frank six-year-old's stare, then she said, "Daddy, did you have a fight?"

"Why, honey?"

"You have two black eyes."

I hadn't realized that the bags under my eyes were so dark.

Little kids see the facts. You can't fool your girl with your public acts.

I'd been slugging it out, now taking a break between rounds thirteen and fourteen of a battle that would go on till the last man standing.

With the comforting odors of sizzling cheese and sweet dough baking, my seven year-old son traced a maze in the chili pepper flakes he'd poured on the tabletop, listening to us while his eyes focused on the peppers. I appreciated the sweetest lovingest little girl in the world who worried about her old papa, and my heart creaked. Tears leaked from my eyes.

"What's the matter, Daddy? Why you crying? Do your eyes hurt?" she asked. Chuck snapped his head up from his pepper play and frowned when he saw me crying and smiling at the same time. "No fights, honey," I said. "Daddy's been working way too hard." "Why you crying then?"

"There's happy crying. You know happy crying? I'm so happy to be sitting here waiting to eat the best pizza in New York with the two most beautiful smartest kids I love more than anything in the whole world."

"When Mommy cries, she's sad. I guess it's different for girls and boys."

She's wise. No surprise.

I laughed and sniffled, wiping my eyes with a napkin. "You said it, Rissi. It's different for girls and boys."

She changed her tone and aimed a disapproving, purse-lipped stare at her brother. "Daddy, if Chuck licks his fingers now, he'll burn his tongue. Mommy always tells him to leave the peppers alone."

Chuck immediately stabbed his fingers between his lips and shoved his face up to his sister's, twisting his hand around the inside of his mouth as if he was unscrewing a bottle cap. In two seconds, his eyes bulged, he coughed and gagged and panted. He poured his Seven-Up into his mouth and over his lips and chin, splashing his shirt and the table, then he grabbed my water and sloshed it down. "Chuckie," I said, laughing, "go to the bathroom and wash your mouth out with cold water until it stops burning."

"It's her fault," he said. "Don't laugh at me." Big tears flowed off his cheeks. Rissi and I raised our eyebrows at each other and shrugged our shoulders as he dashed off to the bathroom.

My son, I thought. My beautiful son and daughter.

Protect their innocence. It's the only way you can make a difference.

That night, after packing the kids off to bed, Nora and I stayed up late in bed, reading, but we never opened the massage manual. She practiced some acupressure on my forearms, to dispel the stale chi that was stuck in my body, she said.

"When you get dizzy, it's old chi trying to move. Somehow it gets stuck in your head, like some dam's in there holding it back." At least she must have been reading the massage book.

"I watched a video about this. When you move, old chi wobbles like a big pot of soup and makes you dizzy."

I thought her diagnosis was as good as any. She squeezed and pressed a couple of sensitive spots and then said, "Can we talk?"

Nora and I had avoided serious conversations outside of therapy and I was actually sick of talking about what's for dinner, what did the kids do in school, how're sales, did we hire any new workers. Now that I'd let my Shu Ling fantasies go, maybe I could open up to Nora for serious talk, if that's what she wanted.

"Sure but, remember, we agreed we won't get heavy just before we fall asleep." I reached out and put my arm around her, pulling her toward me. She lay her cheek on my chest.

"Sometimes you suspend the rules," she said.

"Yeah. We gotta get this investigation wrapped up. If it went away, we'd be fine."

"Would we? Is that all it is, Charlie, the investigation?"

"That and work. Soy to the World is the biggest marketing project I've ever tried. It could change the face of the industry."

"I know, I know. But I'm worried about you, honey."

"Oh, thank you, baby. I'm all right. Little tired is all."

"I'm more worried about us."

The relationship. To a woman, everything else is just a blip.

"That's why we're in therapy, sweetie. Working things out." "We're not making much progress. I don't think you're really present in therapy, any more than you are at home."

She was right. I opened myself up as little as I could get away with but I said, "What do you mean? I haven't missed one session." "You sit there like a lump of dough."

"C'mon. We have great talks."

"You talk. You can always talk. I don't know what you feel. I can't tell any more." Nora pulled away and stretched out on her back. "I'm so sad when we're together."

I turned on to my side and propped myself up on my elbow. "Sweetie, I don't know. I've been out of it. Give us some time. We can get through this. Think of the kids."

"I think of myself, the kids, you. I think of everything, Charlie. I always have and you barely think about anything except your work."

I noticed I was clenching my jaws and breathing quicker. The last thing I wanted was a fight on the first night I'd been relaxed in weeks. I lay down on my back and said, "Can't we do this in therapy? I'm sorry, honey. I've been a lousy husband."

"You didn't used to be."

"There's hope, then, right?"

"I don't know, Charlie. We've fallen so far apart, we'll be lucky to make it back."

"Hey, that's enough. We've still got two months of Year of the Monkey luck."

"Some luck."

"Luck's not something you know you have while you're having it, Nora. You see it when you review your life later."

"Oh, Charlie. I'm too tired to listen to your pontifications." She snapped off her bedside light and rolled onto her side, facing away from me.

With my hand on her back, I said, "Let's go away, after the New Year. How about Spain or someplace warm but not too hot?"

"We can talk about it later."

You can still make it, even if you have to fake it. You know you should. It'll feel good.

I scooted over to her and spooned my body into hers. We fit perfectly. I cupped her breast in my hand and moved my pelvis against her bottom, wondering if she would respond. She swiveled her neck and kissed me on the lips, then turned back and sighed, falling asleep in about ten seconds.

That night, I slept without waking up once. That was it for my dizzy spells, except for one last small one the next afternoon. I think it came from eating too much whipped cream on the last three pieces of Nora's left-over pumpkin pie.

Chapter Twelve

Genevieve

WHERE'S LIAM?

Wegmans Markets in Rochester had always been my best customer. As I learned from Gianni, Wegmans "...owns Rochester."
When I told that to a seatmate on a plane once, he replied, "I
thought Kodak owned Rochester." We laughed and agreed that
between the two companies, Rochester was thoroughly owned
by some powerful masters and Kodak was great in its day, but
now it's history. Wegmans will always be around.

The most relaxing part of my job was giving tofu cooking
demonstrations in supermarkets. I put on a good show because
I wanted the store managers to value me as entertainment for
their customers. Modern food store marketing assumes that
people hate having to shop because no one has time to prepare food any more. So if you showed them a good time while
they did their chores, they'd feel better and spend more money.
When I put on a lively demo, I built my reputation as a top performer with the corporate office and it didn't matter to them
what I was touting as long as it sold.

I staged my best demos in the Wegmans stores. I'd arrive
on a Saturday morning, load a cart with pots, an electric wok,
a toaster oven, and roll it into a bright spot in the produce aisle
somewhere between the potatoes and the bean sprouts. I'd
prop up my easel and sign, and start chopping tofu and vegetables. No matter what recipe I demo-ed, I sautéed clove after

clove of garlic, so its aroma would waft over the whole store, advertising my demo, enticing the hungry as well as the curious, all with shopping dollars lurking in their purses waiting to leap out. My bait wasn't tofu, but the exotic.

My message to the shoppers was. 'I'm just like you. I can chop and stir and talk and smile, all at once, like any mother, like everyworking woman anywhere." I wasn't acting—maybe just a little to keep the show entertaining—and the shoppers respected me for showing up with the real Gen. That made demoing a pleasure. Usually.

At the beginning of my tofu demos career, I'd compose recipes like "Tofu Dengaku" or "Gohiji Dofu." The novelty appealed to people but too many sampled without buying. The authentic Chinese and Japanese recipe names sounded strange and impossible to prepare.

At one demo, a produce manager, flirting with me, asked me if I could fix him scrambled eggs and fried potatoes, to "bring out the men."

So I did, except I made scrambled tofu with turmeric added to give it an eggy color. He couldn't tell the difference between scrambled eggs and the crumbled, yellow tofu. He wolfed it down. When I told him he'd just eaten half a pound of tofu and reduced the cholesterol in his blood by 50%, he laughed and promised he'd never let me trick him again. I noticed that he stuck a recipe brochure into his pocket.

After that, I created and demoed recipes any American could recognize. Charlie loved my marketing slogan: 'Tofu the American Way.'

"Why didn't I think of that?" he said. "It's so obvious. Gen the Genius strikes again."

Sometimes I didn't know if Charlie praised me or mocked me so I let it slide. He painted the company trucks with the phrase and we used it in all of our sales literature.

***

Since Becky's death in the factory, I'd been so busy that Liam and I had less time than usual together. When I asked him if he'd like to do a demo with me in Wegmans Superstore in Buffalo, he said, "Sure, Mom. I bet I sell more tofu than you."

He and I made an irresistible sales act: Working Mom and Charming Son. I taught Liam that, as long as we told the truth, we could sell anything. We proved it. As we handed out samples, I'd say things like, "Yeah. We work Saturdays so we can be together." Which was true. Then Liam would offer someone a taste of tofu, chiming in with, "Gotta save up for college." That was true, too.

I didn't tell him that just because he was with me, people would buy two packages of tofu rather than one.

Between bursts of customers, Liam roamed around the store, chatting with managers and stock clerks usually ending up hanging around the in-store bakery. The bakers in the Buffalo store insisted that he gorge on cream horns and sticky buns as a reward for helping me and for having to eat so much tofu. I let him eat as many as he wanted.

Three weeks before Christmas, we put on our last supermarket demo of the year. I'd contrived a cranberry tofu Christmas dessert that sold ten cases of tofu before lunch. Liam left our little stand just before noon to visit the bakery for a special lunch treat. He'd had a swim meet the night before and felt a little tired, so I told him to take an hour off. By one o'clock, I was serving Working Woman's Quick Casserole to a flood of customers, so I couldn't shut down the demo to find him. When the crowd thinned, it was already one-thirty and I wondered where he was. I unplugged my pans and covered my cart then hurried to the bakery.

He wasn't there. They'd given him two bear claws around noon, and he'd taken them and gone. I circled the store, checking every aisle, visiting every kiosk. No one had seen him and I asked all the clerks and shelf-stockers to watch for him. Fear began to claw at my chest.

I burst into the walk-in cooler, calling "Liam. Liam. Are you in here? Come out."

The absolute hush of cheese wheels and milk crates and beef haunches answered me. Breathlessly, I raced through the back room, slamming open the freezer door, fearing I'd find him locked in, stiff and lifeless on the floor. Thank God, it was only boxes of microwave dinners and ice cream perched on shelves in dim light.

I ran to the customer service desk and asked them to page him to the tofu demo. I raced up and down every aisle, bumping into the backs and butts of foraging shoppers, tripping over their carts.

I asked everybody "Have you seen a 12-year old black-haired boy wearing a red sweatshirt?"

They all gawked at me with wide eyes.

"No."

"Sorry."

"Sorry."

"No."

"We'll watch for him."

"I thought I saw a kid in a red sweatshirt. Back at the meat counter."

"Yeah. At the bakery."

"Maybe he's at produce?"

"Did you check the parking lot?"

"You'll find him. My grandson always wanders off."

"Wish I could help."

"Good luck."

The supermarket pager called his name over and over into the emptiness. My heart raced and I sprinted back to the demo to wait for him.

A knot of women clustered around my table, expecting me to begin cooking.

"I'm sorry. I can't demo right now. My son disappeared. Have you seen a black-haired boy wearing a red Bills sweatshirt?"

Most of them were mothers and they said they'd help. The sympathy in their eyes made me feel more scared, but I showed them the picture of Liam that I carried in my wallet, then they fanned out across the store. Two women volunteered to scout the parking lot and another said she'd check around the recycling bins. "They're always full of things boys like to investigate," she said, stroking my arm.

By two o'clock I was in the store manager's office, on the phone to the police. I called Charlie at home, leaving a message on his machine that I'd stopped the demo because Liam had taken off and I couldn't find him. I asked him or Nora to call me as soon as they got the message. The police showed up in ten minutes, but the pity on their faces tore my heart out.

I started having trouble breathing. Burning air caught in my throat, gagging me. I willed my chest to relax while all around me, people faded into a fog and sounds dulled to a grating wind that cut through my body, chilling me. I don't know how long that lasted, but eventually, my chest began to loosen up and heave and tears gushed from my eyes. Trying to speak, all I could do was cough and grunt.

A big, motherly woman sergeant-in-charge sat beside me, pulling me into her soft shoulder with one arm, pushing my hair off my forehead and dabbing my cheeks with a Kleenex.

"Don't worry, Genny," she said, rocking me in her arms. "We'll find him, honey. We have plenty of time. Probably wandering around the neighborhood. You know boys, always curious."

Her warm voice comforted me enough that I emerged from near total numbness.

"I'm Darlene," she said. "Got kids of my own. My Bobbie, when he was twelve? Vanished on us one afternoon in the State Park. Gave us the shock of our life." She squeezed my arm. "He came back. Thought he saw some deer. Wanted to get closer. Time he noticed where he was, it was twilight. That's when we panicked. All of a sudden, he comes strollin' up the hill from the lake like a ghost."

I barely heard her.

"When he got closer, he laughed at us. At first, I wanted to slap him silly. Then we hugged and hugged, and cried and cried. We ended up stayin' till the Park closed, burnin' marshmallows and fillin' our faces with S'mores like we'd never tasted anything so fine."

I smiled weakly but she interested me only for as long as she was telling me her story. I was glad she found him, but I'd heard too many stories about kids who never came back. I pushed her away.

"I'm fine. Can't we get to work finding my son?"

For what seemed like hours, she and her staff interviewed me, customers, store managers, clerks. They asked if we'd seen any suspicious characters, if we had any relatives in Buffalo, whether Liam often went off by himself.

"Of course he does. He's a boy."

Their list seemed endless and I had no idea how it would help. Right now he was in danger and all their questions did was stall. They persisted: Was he a curious kid or did he stay close to home? Was he into music? What kind of rules did I have about his not taking rides from strangers? When they asked the manager did the store have any security discs we could review? I got excited. He went to check and came back in five minutes carrying three tapes.

He shoved the first one into the DVD player. It flickered on. An overview of the whole store, it showed an empty produce aisle. I read the digital clock in the lower right of the screen. "04.27.29."

"That's this morning," I said. "The middle of the night."

Embarrassed, he ejected the tape and inserted the next.

Same view, different time. "05.33.47." We watched it turn to "05:44.00" before he ejected it.

"This should be it," he said. "Unless they fucked up again. 'Scuse my language."

"Just play it," I said.

Same view. "06:53.21."

"Shit," he said. He turned to me and Darlene, his face red and scrunched up like he was about to cry. He grabbed the phone and started hollering into it. Everyone else in the office started talking at once. Standing around and talking.

Finally, I screamed. "God damn it! Do something! Don't just stand there blabbering! It's my son's life!"

They tried to calm me, offering me a Valium and Darlene tried to hug me again, but I shrugged her off. The store manager slipped a cup into my hand. "Drink this," he said. "It'll help."

I sniffed the liquid—straight bourbon. I narrowed my eyes at him, letting him know what I thought of his competence as a store manager, and I gulped the whiskey down.

I'd never felt more helpless in my life. Nora wasn't home, no way would I call Liam's Dad. Robert would terrorize me for the rest of my life about this. I wished I could call Gianni. He'd understand but what could he do? I almost called Benko because I just needed somebody, anybody I knew, to be with me. In that helpless afternoon, I realized how all-by-myself I was in life. I knew hundreds of people, had dozens of friends I would do anything for whenever they asked. But in reality, I had nobody but Liam, and nobody who cared about him the way I do.

Liam's disappearance galvanized everyone in the store into some kind of action. A grocery bagger came up with the idea of making blow-up copies of my wallet photo of Liam and posting them around the neighborhood.

One of the women who'd come to the store just to attend my demo offered to call her son-in-law who worked at a local TV station. She wanted to fax him the photo and have him run it on the news. That was one of the best ideas I'd heard. She left with a photo of Liam cradled in her hands, his beautiful smile glittering with silver braces, his eyes shining with mischief.

I couldn't sit still. Darlene stayed beside me wherever I went, circling the parking lot ten times, peering into every car, handing out copies of the photo with my and Darlene's cell phone numbers written on the back.

I jerked apart every column of grocery carts littering the lot. Darlene had the warehouse clerk call up the trucking companies that had unloaded earlier, but since it was Saturday, only three trucks had stopped by the store. All of them were gone before Liam and I had arrived.

My mind boiled with images of Liam laying twisted in a ditch, filthy water flowing over his head. I saw him chained in the back of a dented, rusty van, surrounded by brutes prodding him with knives. I saw his picture on a milk carton on the kitchen table in his friend's house where he should have been having breakfast after a sleep-over. I saw his empty grave in our family cemetery on the Connecticut coast, right next to my mother's tombstone...

I began to offer God anything He wanted if only He'd bring Liam back. I'd spend every weekend at homeless shelters...I'd adopt a meth baby...I'd teach cooking classes at the Senior Center...I'd have sex only if I was engaged to somebody...

"God," I bargained, "give me this one little miracle and you can have me for the rest of my life."

The police organized some store employees into a search team that went out into the neighborhood, knocking on doors, pinning Liam's face up on all the telephone poles. An ambulance sat quietly parked next to a fire truck near the front entrance to the store. Police cruisers roamed back and forth regularly in front of the store.

A crowd of catastrophe vampires had gathered nearby. Every now and then, one would shout something encouraging like "Hang in there. He'll come back." Then a woman bellowed at me: "Kids run away from mothers who beat them."

When I heard that I tore loose from Darlene. I would have killed the woman if one of the policemen hadn't held me while another escorted her to her car and guided her out the exit.

About the time the lights came on over the parking lot, my lungs seized up again as the dusk settled around me like a shroud. If Liam didn't come back before nightfall, I was afraid I'd never see him again. I leaned against Darlene as she escorted me to the ambulance where the EMT's laid me down and put an oxygen mask over my face.

Within a minute, my head cleared and my terror ebbed. I sat up and tore the mask off. I stepped out of the ambulance's rear door just as Liam emerged from between some parked cars and headed for the supermarket's front door.

I screamed "Liam!" and flew across the sidewalk. He glanced around, then spotted me and gave me a big smile. The crowd parted for me as I rushed to him and grabbed him, hugging him, picking him up and pressing him into my body as if I wanted to stuff him back inside where he'd be safe. The crowd burst into applause.

I felt Liam's heart beating fast against my chest, his quick breaths chafing my ears like brushes. I heard the clapping from each pair of hands, the pounding steps on the asphalt of police and the employees as they ran to watch us. The parking lot lights cast a moist yellow halo around Liam's head.

"Oh, sweetie. God. You're safe. God. Thank you." I blubbered and grinned and cried. Sounds of sobbing rose from the crowd.

Liam pushed back against my hands. "Mom, what's going on?" He stared at the police and the EMTs. "Why are all these people here?" Attracted by the blinking red lights of the emergency vehicles, he tried to turn around to see through the surrounding mob.

I gripped Liam's shoulders as hard as I could, holding him tightly, but pushing him back to arm's length. "Where have you been, young man?" I said, still breathless.

"You know. Niagara Falls."

"Niagara Falls!"

The words "Niagara Falls" rippled through the crowd.

"Niagara Falls! How did you get there?"

"I'm sorry, Mom. I thought it'd be okay."

With him in my arms, my fears washed away. Anger began to rise into my face. "How did you get there, young man?"

"Benko. You know."

"Benko?"

The word "Benko" echoed out of the crowd.

"He's your friend, too, Mom."

All I could say was "Benko?"

"We went and came back as fast as we could. I'd never seen it from Canada before. You always said it's good to try new things. It was beautiful. All ice castles and stuff."

I shouted for the policewoman. "Where is he? That asshole. He can't do this to me! Darlene, find the man who kidnapped him." "Where is this Benko, son?" Darlene asked Liam.

"I don't know. He let me off in the parking lot."

Darlene put her muscular arms around both of us, pushing us gently into the store while the police dispersed the crowd of shoppers. She signaled to one of the EMTs to follow us. In the store manager's office, Liam sat shirtless on the manager's desk while the EMT examined him for marks.

"I'm fine, Mom. Don't make such a fuss. I was having a good time."

"You were having a good time?" I shouted. "What kind of time do you think I was having? I was afraid somebody kidnapped you. I thought I'd never see you again." Now that he was back, I released the hysteria I'd bottled up since I noticed he was gone.

"Mom, take it easy. I'm back. I'm all right."

I refused to let him console me. "You're in big trouble, young man. The whole city of Buffalo was on alert for you."

"Didn't you get my note?" Liam asked.

"What note?" I said, a shudder streaking up my back.

"The one I left in the bakery with the cookie lady."

Having listened to us intently, the store manager immediately called down to his bakery supervisor. Liam's sniffles made the only sound in the room while we all waited for the supervisor to find the note. In a minute, the manager, still on the phone, nodded to me, grinning like an idiot. His job was saved. He told the employee to bring the note to his office.

"I'd never split without telling you," Liam said, tears flowing again.

"I know, honey," I said, hugging him. I felt relieved and confused. I blamed myself for not being careful, for mistrusting Liam. "That's why I was so worried."

The bakery supervisor entered the office, handing the note to her boss. She said, "It was laying under some wax paper. I'm surprised we even saw it." He read it and, with a sour face, passed it to me.

Mom I'm going to Canada with Benko to see Niagara Falls It's gonna be LOUD

Back later to help you pack up

Your son Liam

P.S. You win the selling contest!!!!

"I gave it to somebody standing there. I asked him to give it to Nancy. He said he would. I'm sorry, Mom. I didn't want to get you upset."

The manager threw his hands up and announced to the ceiling, "She's fired. They're fired. What a mess."

"No, don't fire them. It's not their fault," I said.

"It's nobody's fault," Liam said.

"No. It's somebody's fault." I seethed. "Benko had no right to take you without speaking to me."

"Do you want us to arrest this Benko?" Darlene asked. "You can charge him with any number of things. Up to kidnapping. Could be Federal. Going into Canada, doesn't matter he brought the boy back. Least you can do is scare the devil outta him."

"I'm tempted. I want to. I don't know." I thought for a minute. "Do I have to make up my mind right now?"

"Give yourself some time to calm down. We got twenty-four hours at least, maybe longer, 'less he runs. Lemme know tomorrow. If I were you, I'd give this Benko somethin' serious to think about," she counseled. "It's up to you. Was me? I'd have him in jail in five minutes."

"It's not that easy. I can't think straight. Maybe it was innocent. He was my old boyfriend."

"Did you dump him?"

I nodded my head yes.

"Worst kind. You better take care of this," Darlene said. "Your son could be in real trouble."

I had to find out what was going on. Liam liked Benko and lately, Benko had been calm and friendly on the phone. The night before when I told him we were going to Buffalo, he did ask what store we'd be at, but if I threw him in jail, what would happen when he got out?

In another hour, strength returned to my adrenaline-drained muscles. Liam and the bakery crew packed up our demo, telling me it was the least they could do. I thanked everyone.

"We're happy everything turned out all right," the manager said. His voice was pinched, holding back anger, and I expected I'd hear from the Wegmans front office before long. No doubt the manager was calculating how much money this distraction had cost the company and how much it had reduced his bonus. I was sure I had a good enough reputation with everyone in the store as well as the company headquarters to withstand their dissatisfaction. Besides, if anybody asked, I'd tell them what fast, caring response they'd given to a mother in distress. Publicity like that was priceless, so I wasn't worried about the manager.

I doubted they'd have much more to say to me than "Be careful" and send out a memo to all food demonstrators: "Leave your children home!" Charlie would hear from them, for sure. That was the last thing I cared about.

⁂

That night I sent Liam to bed as soon as we got home. He protested that he didn't deserve a punishment. It wasn't his fault that the man in the bakery forgot to give Nancy his note. "I always wanted to do something with Benko so I figured this was a good time. I'm sorry I left you all the demo work."

"It has nothing to do with the work, Liam."

"Benko said we'd see the purest water in the world. You always said American Tofu was made from the purest water."

"Liam!"

"I would've come and told you but you were too busy—you had a hundred ladies crowding around your table. I couldn't get through. Benko said a note would be good enough. You should see those ice palaces and caves. Everyone says this is the best time of year—"

"What? He told you not to tell me in person?"

"I tried," he moaned.

"You didn't try hard enough. Besides, who does Benko think he is, telling my son how to behave with his mother? Not even your father can make up rules for you when you're with me. You know that."

"Mom, I'm growing up. I can do a lot of stuff on my own."

"You're not that old that you can go running off in the middle of a strange city and leave me alone wondering where the hell you are!" I spun around and left before I lost my temper completely. "You're grounded until further notice."

Leaving Liam sobbing in his room, I immediately called Benko. "Yes?"

"How dare you take my son without telling me! You can't do that! I could have you arrested. They'll deport you back to Russia where you belong!"

"Genevieve. Wait."

"Who do you think you are? You can't just take him someplace because you want to! I could charge you with kidnapping! The police are on my side. They want to pick you up right now. You'd be in jail in ten minutes if I wanted it. I could have you deported!" The phone was silent. "Benko! Do you hear me?"

"Don't bring cops into this, Genevieve. Real bad if you did."

"Bad? For who? For you! Liam is my son."

"Genevieve, a minute. Wait. He's all right?"

I fumed, not answering.

"Answer me."

"He's okay."

"He had good time. Yes?"

I admitted that, too.

"So, what's your problem?"

"You didn't get my permission. You can't do that. This is America. We respect mothers here! You abducted him!"

"Need your permission? You're so busy, I figure, help her out.

Take kid for a few minutes. Give him good time. She'll like me better."

"Like you better? I almost had a heart attack."

"Can I take Liam anywhere I want? Sure, you know. With me he'll go, anytime. For a father, he's starved in his life. Like you, for a man, you're starved. But smart, Liam he's real smart boy. Not like mother." His voice seethed with bitterness.

"Shut up! Listen to me. I can call the police and they'll have you behind bars before you can hide your vodka."

"Don't. You'll be too sorry."

"Just leave us alone."

"I'm giving you a present—break from every minute child care, that's all."

"That's nice, Benko. If it's true, you have to talk to me about that."

"Sorry you're upset. Right now I come over. Make you feel good."

"I'm in no mood. I'm still thinking about calling the cops."

He gentled his tone, his words almost purring in his rumbling register. "How do you think I feel? You don't want anymore to see me? Little police chief scared you? He's prick. Tiny cock. No balls."

His voice deepened further, growling with menace. "You know, Disney World? He'd like to go, Liam said. Good plan, taking him. Let's go to Florida, Gen."

An icicle fell from my throat into my stomach. My jaw went numb.

"Gen?"

Had Benko purposely taken Liam to get revenge on me for dumping him? He just told me he'd steal Liam again if I didn't change my attitude toward him.

I imagined Benko drunk in a chair with a fire raging around him, licking at his clothes and hair as he lay unconscious, burning him out of my life. Then, I saw him lying lifeless, crushed under a big machine in the factory. I shivered.

"Genevieve, are you here? You need little hug." He purred. "It's been long day. After demos, I know how tired you get. I remember after one demo you had me come over for long nice foot rub. What about tonight? Nice rub, start with feet then all over?"

I tried to figure out what to do. I could have him arrested. Then, as soon as he was released, I'd suffer his fury and I had no way to predict how bad that would be. I could get a restraining order but that would was enrage him. Benko would probably come after me just to prove I couldn't control him, even with the law on my side.

I was afraid. Still, I had to veil my anger until I could make sure Liam and I were safe. "Benko, you know I didn't drop you. I had no choice. It's for your own good as much as mine. That Chief snoops everywhere. Once this blows over, well...A foot rub would be nice," I said, trying to cajole him, "but I'm totally wiped out tonight."

"Ah, Genevieve. Gentle little rub. Nothing else? I bring you to life. Your skin wants my 'silky' touching?"

"Benko, I'm out of it." I inhaled. With as much friendship in my voice as I could muster, I said, "Do me one favor. That's all. Until they close the case on the MacDaniel woman, please, stick to our agreement. We can't see or talk to each other."

"What about work? I'm nicer to you at work now, right?"

"Yes. At work. In public. But don't come around Liam."

"If you say so, beautiful woman. You know, Liam comes to me, what can I do?"

"He won't."

"You don't know. He's growing up. Twelve? What they want, boys start to do what they want—not what mother wants. Disney World he talks about. I like Florida, too. Warm. Sunny. Nice place for kids."

"Benko, shut up. Good night."

"Genevieve, I'm sorry you got so upset. Take it easy. For your health it's way bad."

He laughed. I ended the call, my hands shaking. The adrenaline seeped out of my muscles and I collapsed again, weeping, my arms and legs trembling. He hadn't really threatened me or Liam directly, but I felt us in danger.

Maybe I was just so exhausted that I didn't understand him. Did he take Liam to Niagara Falls because Liam asked him to? Maybe the offer of a foot rub was genuine. I didn't want to make him my enemy but I couldn't trust him now. My mind was totally befuddled and half-paralyzed with fear. I had to get out, or I'd go mad. Or worse, I'd hurt somebody, somebody named Benko.

I'd just survived the most harrowing day of my life. I flopped down on the couch, waiting to sink into the soothing arms of sleep. But Benko's gravelly voice saying "...boys do what they want" and "I like Florida, too" echoed through my brain until finally, not even my fears for Liam could keep me awake.

***

Sun pouring through my window sent me into a dream of sweating in the desert and woke me out of a deep sleep. An English muffin spread with my favorite strawberry jam and a steaming cup of Irish Breakfast tea sat on the coffee table next to me. Liam sat in the rocker, the comics in his lap. Love for him bloomed in my chest and throat, sprouting petals of tears from my eyes.

He glanced up and sprung off his chair. Wrapping his arms around my neck, he said, "Don't cry, mom. I'm sorry. Next time, I'll tell you in person. I promise."

We hugged and I stopped crying. I pushed my rag of a body to sitting position and offered him a bite of the muffin. He'd laid the strawberry jam on an inch thick, something I'd never do, but I relished Liam's caring. We read the comics together on the couch and I asked him about Niagara Falls. He didn't want to say much, but when I encouraged him, he became so excited, I promised to take him back in the spring.

"Can we take the boat under the falls?"

"If it's not too cold," I said. "But Liam, promise me one thing?"

"What?"

"Don't ever go with Benko or anybody else again."

"What if I ask you first? I have to go places with somebody," he said with all the logic he could muster. "You're not around all the time."

"That's true," I said. "But for now, until I get over what happened, ask me way ahead of time. Do you understand?"

"Sure, mom. Will you tell me when you're over it?" he said, squeezing my hand.

I heard my own optimism and persuasiveness in his voice. He'd learned well. Right then, I wished I'd taught him to be a little more afraid of the world.

Chapter Thirteen

Genevieve

CONFESSION IN THE KITCHEN

It's impossible for a mother to know just how much damage a child can inflict on himself and still be normal. If he gets hurt, should she blame him, bad luck, or herself?

Every few months, Liam hurt himself badly enough to go to the emergency room. He bruised his shin at soccer so deeply that he had to wear a plastic cast. Then he launched himself over his handlebars while he was biking in the woods, landing on his shoulder and head. Thank God he'd paid attention to me and worn his helmet. He sported the six stitches in his chin like a combat medal.

Then, the week after the Wegmans incident, when Liam sprained his wrist playing volleyball at gym in school and the school sent him to the ER for treatment, Ron Michelson, the emergency room doctor called me asked me to come in for a talk about Liam.

He was one of the Clementines who'd asked me out. He was too short for me, and every doctor I'd ever gone out with jumped me almost before they said hello, so I told him I was involved with someone from out of town. I thought I'd let him down gently but after the interview about Liam, I wasn't sure.

"I just wondered if there was anything wrong at home?"

"Nothing unusual, Ron," I said, taken aback.

"I asked only because when a kid shows a pattern of accidents, sometimes he's acting out emotional troubles. If there's something going on, and we can help...Well, you know, we're here to help."

The last thing I needed was the medical authorities prying into our life. I started to smolder. "You think he has a pattern?" He may have been well-meaning and I didn't want to appear guilty by reason of defensiveness.

"Well, we do see him a lot."

"What do you expect? He's a lively kid. He thinks he can do anything."

"Maybe you should slow down. He's probably just modeling you. How have you been feeling?"

I really didn't like him telling me what to do, but I thought he might have a point about Liam. He needed me to be home with him. "You know, I've been a single mother for twelve years now. Maybe Liam has grown up faster than other kids his age. He's still a new kid in town. Bound to show off sometimes, take it over the top."

"I just had to ask," he said, taking my hand. "I want to make sure you're doing well, too."

I hoped he wasn't planning to ask me out again. I didn't want to reject him, but I resented a sneaky power play.

"You know one of our workers died in the factory?" I said. "Who doesn't?"

"That's put a lot of strain on me," I said, withdrawing the hand, but smiling, encouraging him to continue his mock-compassionate tone.

He nodded sympathetically. "I bet."

"Liam's probably feeling some of that," I said, intending to assuage his concern about my flakiness with a gentle reminder that I was in the middle of a crisis.

"That could do it," Ron said. He urged me to take some time off and to relax with Liam.

I worried that Ron may have had a point about Liam's accidents. Just because he wanted to go out with me didn't mean I should ignore warning signs, especially since I could be responsible. After Wegmans and my constant distraction with Benko and the fact that I'd begun to lean on Gianni to get me a new job, I didn't doubt that Liam had picked up my worries. I hoped Liam hadn't created a pattern of hurting himself to bring my attention back to him.

Before I left the interview with Ron, his caring questions convinced me that Liam might have a problem.

I met with Liam's counselor at school, told her my fears, and asked her to try to find out whether my son had any issues I didn't know about—with his friends, teachers, any weird thing that could happen to a beautiful child who might be afraid to reveal it to his mother. After she and Liam talked several times, she reported that, as far as she could tell, Liam was just a rambunctious kid.

She had to hug me for five minutes while I sobbed my relief into her shoulder. Surprised by the depth of my anxiety under the tears, I decided to take Ron's advice and go on a real vacation over the Christmas holidays when Liam would go to Robert in Boston.

***

Despite a week of vegging-out, long slow swims at the club, and silence at home, with no stimulation other than my daily phone calls with Liam, Christmas vacation ended with me tired, not in the best shape to start a six-week Chinese New Year push of sales. The low skies and sub-freezing temperatures made me want to get on the first plane to Miami.

Then the one warm star in my life came home from spending his Christmas vacation with Robert. Liam limped into the house with a broken toe.

"Me'n Dad were swimming at the Y. Dad tossed me up and I came down a little crooked. Banged my foot against the side of the pool.

"It's nothing, Mom," he said. "The doctor says I'll be running on it in a few weeks. Relax. It wasn't Dad's fault. I was trying a flip."

I couldn't help worrying, no matter what the counselor said about his high energy level. What next?

That night over dinner, Liam asked me why I was upset.

I said, "No reason, honey."

"Mom, you always bite your lips and hunch your shoulders when you're worried. Tell me. I can take it. We're friends, remember?"

Liam's reading of my feelings brought tears to my eyes. "I have a lot on my mind right now. The next month or so we won't be seeing each other so much and I don't like that."

"We'll talk. I'll be fine."

He meant to assure me but I didn't like pressuring Liam with my melancholy, even though the most important teaching I could ever give him was emotional honesty.

"I know, honey. I'm just glad you're home safe with me again." "You'll still come to the regional swim meet, right?"

"Nothing would keep me away. I told Charlie I have priorities."

Liam reached over and caressed my cheek. As we started to eat, tears dripped off my chin into my tortellini. He handed me his napkin. "Take this for your nose. You're gonna make your pasta all slimy."

He made me laugh deeper than anybody in the world.

***

Liam, me, Charlie, Nora, a lot of the workers who'd had accidents on the job, Charlie's kids who'd been sick off and on for two months—all of us were victims of some toxic cloud of grief and doubt raining misery on us since Becky died. It poured on Charlie and splattered off his broad back onto the rest of us. Our record days without an accident was ancient history.

Charlie's distress fueled his determination to make a huge recovery from our poor sales in the fall. Out of guilt about my upcoming departure from American Tofu and loyalty to Nora and Charlie, I let Charlie pile on more work than anyone in her right mind could handle. For our Year of the Rooster tofu promotion, he arranged a seven-city media tour for me with eight TV and six radio shows and who knows how many newspaper interviews, all crammed between January nineteenth and twenty-ninth.

With his inflated plans, Charlie settled the future of the company on my shoulders. A few months ago, I might have welcomed it, but now, my to-do list hung over me like a tipping boulder about to fall.

I couldn't believe it once I wrote down everything I had to do. Sixty-five supermarket sales phone calls, five dozen demos to schedule, 2000 posters to design, photograph, print, distribute, not to mention all the TV and radio shows to prepare for, and the hotel reservations. How was I going to find good hotels in cities I'd never been in? Plus, I had to make arrangements for Liam while I was gone, not to mention the blog and Facebook.

I knocked on Charlie's office door and without waiting for him to say "Come in," I barged in and laid my five-page to-do list on his desk. I'd written the last item in red magic marker. *Benko! Keep him away from me!!!!*

Standing in front of Charlie, I raised myself up as tall as I could so he would have to sit back and see me staring down at him from the ceiling.

"Talk, Charlie," I said. "I'm trying to make this your best year yet, but how do I get everything done? This list. God and all his angels couldn't get it done in four weeks."

He scanned the list. "Good planning, Gen. You've become an excellent manager. Sit down. We can figure this out."

I hated it when Charlie patronized me with his management bullshit. I growled but he pretended he didn't notice.

"Seems you thought of everything. Now, add the amount of time you need for each step and chart it into your plan. It's not too bad. I have a list like that every week."

Yeah, right, Charlie, I thought. You sit around and make up lists and give them to the rest of us to do them for you.

"Why don't you hire a helper?" He surprised me with that, but it's what I wanted. "You need to be fresh for the TV shows."

When I glowered at him, he said, "Just kidding. I don't want you to overdo it. Get somebody good to take care of the admin stuff, the calls, reservations, minor things."

I sat on the corner of his desk to make sure he heard me. "I'll need a full-time helper, somebody who's good. I don't have time to train anybody."

"Try one of the office ladies. Sheryl? Maxine?

"Thanks, Charlie. It'll help. I can't guarantee perfection."

He held my hand in both of his. "Everything will be fine. It'll all work out."

When he said that, it sounded like an echo of Gianni assuring me about us against our impossible odds. Charlie dropped my hand and stood up. He almost pranced around to the front of the desk. His eyes shined, as if he were about to cry. I stood up to face him.

"By the way, Gen the Genius strikes again. Your to-do list just gave me an idea. Why don't we call our employee Chinese New Year part a *Tofu To-Do*? The Year of the Rooster!"

He crowed the four high notes of "Tofu To-Do. Tofu To-Do. Tofu To-Do." He laughed, whistling the notes over and over and we high-fived and low-fived. "Maybe I'll write a Tofu To-Do Tune," he said.

I couldn't believe him. He'd rope me into handling all the food and drink for the party, as usual. "Great idea. All I can say is you do the cooking. I won't have time."

"Nora will take care of it. All you do is supply the recipes and show up and enjoy yourself."

I felt relieved that he'd heard me and offered me some help. Given the realities of the upcoming month, I couldn't feel too comfortable, no matter what.

"By the way, what's up with Benko and you?"

"He's a creep. Because of him, we almost lost Wegmans as an account. My best customer!"

"Gen, you have to feel some responsibility for that."

"What? A mother's working her butt off for the company and a guy comes and takes her kid without telling her? I'm responsible? Don't make me any more pissed off than I am."

"Okay, okay. We've been over this. I understand how scared you were, but Benko said he was doing you a favor."

"Some favor. I could have him arrested-"

"Wait a minute-"

"Keep him away from me and my kid. If you don't..."

Charlie sat back on his desk. "I told him if he ever did something like that again, it would be the last thing he did as an AT employee. He was contrite. He said he was just trying to help you. I believe him."

Benko had Charlie as fooled as everyone else.

"We all have to work together, especially now when so much hinges on the next couple of months," Charlie said.

"When did I ever not pull my share of the load?"

"Gen, you're the most important person working here. Don't worry, please. If Benko annoys you, tell me and I'll take care of it. Give it a little time. Things can heal."

"Charlie, that's half of it. The worse half. I'm nervous about the media trip. "

"You'll have them eating tofu from your fingertips."

"I don't mean that. I mean Liam."

"Oh," Charlie said. "Yes. Anything we can do to make sure he's in good hands? Anything. We'll do it. He'll be totally fine. Hey, he can stay with us. I'll ask Nora."

I said I'd make arrangements for Liam, but I'd keep his offer in mind. Before I left his office, I told him if he wanted a miracle New Year sale, he had to carry some of my load. I must have come across as so desperate or angry that he agreed to handle some of the radio and newspaper interviews.

"Anything, Gen. We'll do this together."

Together to him meant he'd make big money and I'd get a paid comp time off. I wanted to resent Charlie, but at the bottom of my heart, I couldn't. I'm too forgiving. But I couldn't help myself. I felt bitter. I was not looking forward to all the travel and handling the inevitable tofu jokes with all the media.

At that moment, I resolved to give notice on Chinese New Year day. I'd give him four weeks, maybe stay on a few more to train the new person. Gone by lilac season.

It was my fault that Charlie expected miracles because I'd always given him way more than he asked for and now he demanded it. Not only that, but he planned for it. He spent so much money on this promotion that if we didn't do as well as he assumed the company might not be able to recover fully.

Later the afternoon after our meeting, Charlie buzzed me and asked if he could see me in my office. What now? "I've only got a few minutes," I said. "I just figured out the amount of time all these jobs will take. If I don't have any glitches, I'll be done in six months, a little late for New Year."

"I've got something to make it a little easier," he laughed. "I'll come to you. A two-minute meeting."

He sat down in my office's guest chair.

"Genevieve, you're better than the best salesman any company could have. After this is over, I'm sending you back to Cancun to recharge. The company will pay. I know you'll need a rest."

I heard Nora's urging behind Charlie's offer.

"Plus, you'll get a nice bonus this year."

At that point, I didn't care about the money. I just wanted to get the next month over with, but the vacation sounded incredible. Charlie must have read my mind or my face. A vacation in the sun. I needed it to carry me through the agony that work had turned into, then I'd have fresh energy to leave the company.

"Sounds beautiful, Charlie. A good vacation's just what I need." I fiddled with my pen and put the most elfin twinkles I could find in my eye. "One thing. Does it have to be Mexico?"

Charlie slapped my desk, laughing. "That's what I love about you, Gen," he said. "Always negotiating." He hugged me. "Go anywhere on the planet. No problem. Just come back."

I let myself sag against him.

"Go someplace hot and wet." He held me for a minute and raised himself on his tiptoes to kiss me on my forehead, like a father.

As soon as Charlie walked out of my office, I called Gianni. "Do you want to go to Saint Thomas or sailing in the Virgin Islands? He didn't miss a beat. "Let's go. When?"

"I surprised you, didn't I?"

"It's your late birthday present?"

"No, but Charlie's giving me a trip to someplace warm after the Chinese New Year. I'd hate to lounge on those beaches, all alone, wearing my iridescent green bikini."

"You'd better be all alone," he growled.

"There's one way you can make sure of that."

We laughed. Tears came to my eyes. I'd just agreed to be his mistress, for one glorious week, at least. I didn't want to talk about it, but sometime after our trip, we'd come to our new arrangement for the Year of the Rooster.

***

The first thing I had to do was to finish the new recipes for the promotion. Nora volunteered her gourmet kitchen as our recipe lab. She used it for her occasional party, otherwise she and Charlie and their kids could get by with a breakfast nook.

My kitchen was too small to spread around all the ingredients and dishes I'd need for the trial and error, splashing and spilling, recipe development required.

Work always energized me, so I was grateful the night of January second, when I shopped for two hours then hauled half a dozen grocery bags filled with enough wonton skins, Chinese herbs and spices, chicken and pork and beef, and vegetables to test a dozen new recipes.

I loved cooking on her restaurant-sized gas stove. She owned every kitchen implement and top-of-the-line brand machine known to modern woman. Mixing eggs and tofu and flour in her custom-thrown bowls gave me extra confidence in my baking. Best of all, leaning on a high-backed wood and leather-seated stool, I relaxed when I stirred and simmered in her designer copper and stainless steel pans and pots. I anticipated our intense but satisfying work, no phones, no problems, just me and food and her, and some laughs.

Nora had other things on her mind than the joys of dicing and stirring. We unloaded the groceries and set up the cutting boards and knives. I had at least three feet of ginger root that I would hack into half-inch slices. I laid out onions and garlic and the ginger and began peeling and chopping.

Nora stood beside me at the counter with a listless knife her hand and said. "Charlie's been acting so weird lately. Not just his dizziness, that's gone. You know, last summer when Benko called and said that a woman had died in the plant? Charlie thought it was you. He said if it had been you, he'd throw in the towel. He can't get along without you. None of us could."

I winced. Did she intuit my plans to leave?

"And now you and Benko are so estranged. Charlie says you're so mad at Benko you don't want him near you."

"You know why. You get it. Anybody who threatens your kid is no friend."

"I can't believe he meant it."

"He meant it. He did it to scare me."

"Why? He's a rough character, but why frighten you?"

"That's a long story. I'll tell you later. Right now, let's just chop and enjoy ourselves and forget about business."

Normally, Nora would stop everything and question me and sympathize and lead me on until I told her the whole story. Not that I usually held back on any subject, except Benko, she knew everything about Gianni. So, when she ignored my unwillingness to talk, I was relieved but surprised until she changed the subject.

Nora stared out the double bay window over the sink into the white January yard. "Charlie and I have been married for what, almost ten years? We had great sex for the first six, until after Rissi was born. Since then, it's pretty flat. But lately, y'know? He can't stop bugging me for it."

"Is that a bad thing?"

She ignored me. "He didn't want to touch me all last spring or summer. A lot of nights, we didn't even sleep together. Now, the more intense things have gotten, since Becky died, the Chief and all, the more he wants."

"It's a good tension reliever for men."

"Women, too," she laughed. "But I'm just not interested right now. It would be too much."

I peeled and diced the garlic while I listened. Sitting in a warm working kitchen with a friend makes you want to give up your deepest secrets and when you do, you feel so satisfied. Maybe because in a kitchen you feel safer than any other place in the house, or than in any other place in your life. I do.

Asking her to mix it with the ginger, I handed Nora the garlic and began sifting the won ton wrapper dough, listening, my nose now irritated by the bowl of chopped onions. I sniffled and let tears dribble down my cheeks.

She went on. "Charlie's not that bad a lover."

I rolled my eyes and arranged the bok choy and water chestnuts for their turns under the cleaver.

"It's just that I can't keep my mind on two lovers at once."
"Nora. The painter is back?"

"No. Somebody else."

"Do tell." God, she and Charlie are just alike. If it's not one, it's the other.

"In therapy we'd been talking about the idea of an open marriage." Nora paused, expecting me to ask her who her lover was. When I didn't answer, she went on. "I guess I decided to try it out."

Then I asked. "Should I guess who it is?"

She grinned, then blushed, bracing her arms on the counter and closing her eyes, she said, "Benko."

I dropped my knife on the floor, jerking my foot out of the way just in time. "I can't believe it"

"'S true."

"How long?"

"Since last spring." She starting crying. "I wanna get out now, but it's so messy, y'know, how can I?" Fat tears rolled off her cheeks and splashed into the ginger she was slicing. She turned to me, lay her head against my breast and wept.

I circled around the end of the prep island and put my arms around her, clamping down hard on my anger. That son of a bitch, I thought. Lying asshole. I said to Nora, "All you have to do is stop. Right now. You can't see him anymore. Tell him to leave you alone. The only way."

"O my god. You don't understand. It's not that simple. He can cause a lot of trouble. I really fucked up. I shouldn't have ever looked at him a second time but he's so handsome. His voice melts me. I love the way he makes machines work, just by touching them."

What was it about the way he handles metal that turns women on?

"The first time we did it was last May, when Charlie sent him over to fix my bread baking machine. The way he touches me sometimes, like I'm a delicate flower. We have the same birthdays. October 10. Ten Ten. Same year. Like we know each other inside out like soul twins. He's so kind, usually...but I really blew it."

I raised my eyebrows.

Self-conscious, she chuckled. "No pun intended."

"Everybody makes a big mistake sometime," I said. "Just tell him you're done. It's all over. It was fun while it lasted but things have changed. You've said it before, every woman has."

Nora and I gave up on slicing and chopping. We sat down at the kitchen table. No doubt, Benko reveled in his duplicity. He'd conquered the two most important women in Charlie's life, and not only that, he probably slept with both of us on the same day, maybe more than once.

I knew I'd have to tell Nora sometime that she and I had been sleeping with Benko at the same time. A confusing mixture of anger and humor came over me. I felt like a fool. While I raged at Benko, I had to laugh at myself.

"But I'm afraid of him, y'know." Nora said.

"Don't be," I said. "He's a nobody. No friends, no money. If it weren't for American Tofu, he wouldn't even have a job. Tell him to leave you alone or he's out of work."

Nora's eyes narrowed. "You don't know him. He's crazy. You think what he did with Liam is bad. He'd try to destroy Charlie and me. He'd probably accuse us of murdering Becky."

Flabbergasted at that idea, I said, "Who'd believe him?"

Nora hung her head, dropping it onto her palms, lost in her feelings. "He's not always gentle," she said, "The first time he hurt me. I wouldn't do it without a rubber." She spoke into the table. "He wanted to feel the real me, y'know."

"What happened?"

"He forced me to. Grabbed my wrists and held me down. I fought. He ripped my pants off and fucked me. I fought him and then I gave in. It was the most amazing sex I ever had. I held on to him so tight and screamed and screamed. Afterwards he said he was sorry. All I could do was lay there in a daze. I didn't want him to know how much I loved it, y'know. Said he was only playing." She lifted her head. "He said he knew I'd like it a little rough, especially after being married to such a wimp. I got mad and said don't ever try that again and don't talk about Charlie. O my god, I was pissed." "Why didn't you stop then? That would have been smart."

"He apologized. Such a cuddly bear. A giant panda bear." She sighed. "He's got the biggest penis I ever imagined. I couldn't believe it would fit inside me, y'know. Must be a miracle, how it did. That thing's a log." She spread her hands to show me how long it was. "But I don't feel any more inside than I do with Charlie."

I didn't believe her but I said "Then you can get rid of him."

She didn't want to listen. "Another time he wanted to do it on my and Charlie's bed. You and Charlie were on some sales trip and the kids were staying with my mom. He practically dragged me into the bedroom by my hair. I yelled at him and he let me go. I thought he was following me into the living room and then he picked me up and threw me down on the bed."

"Nora, do you hear yourself? This guy's a beast."

"He's not. He's more like a teenage boy. He didn't really try to rape me that time. He never hit me or anything. He's passionate. He loves me." Her eyes pleaded with me to sympathize with her. "He's the most passionate man you can imagine."

"What if you told him no?"

"I don't know."

"He'd hurt you. You know he would."

Nora cried. "Gen, I'm afraid."

"You should be. What if Liam had an accident when Benko drove him to Canada? He scared me half to death. He's evil. Get rid of him. Right now." God help us, I prayed. Forgive us for all the stupid things we've done and don't let anybody get hurt. Please.

Nora said, "The worst thing? Now all he wants is to do it from behind. He makes me come to his house and strip while he sits on the couch. Then I have to kneel down in front of the TV, y'know, while he watches a movie. He puts his bottle on my back while he fucks me. It spills all over me and he licks it up. I feel like a pig."

I pulled her toward me. "Honey, this is serious. You've got to get out."

"I know. I don't know what to do."

"Sweetie, wake up. Stop seeing him. Why don't you come and stay with me and Liam for a while. Send Chuck and Rissi to your mom. She'll be happy to have them and they'll be safe from Benko. Maybe you should go out of town for a while."

Telling me her horrendous story had put her in some kind of a trance. Sniffling against my shoulder, she rambled on.

"I can't. You know that. Charlie would never let me go until I told him why. I'm not the only one in American Tofu either. Benko told me all the women in factory came on to him. He said he couldn't resist a couple of them. When he first came to Clement, he didn't know anyone. He just wanted to make friends and that's how he tried to do it. You have to admit he has great sex appeal."

"Did he tell you who else he slept with?" I hoped she didn't know about him and me.

"Well, he told me about a couple of them. I didn't want to hear, y'now. He told me I was the only American woman he could ever love."

Memories of his pledges to me, his passionate yearning gazes, his desperate lips that gnawed on mine like a starved child's, dropped to my stomach like scalding tea. Should I tell Nora? I had to...but not yet. "God. He laid it on thick."

"I got a phone call a couple of weeks ago. Bernice, the part-time night shift woman? She's done some ironing and house-cleaning for me, y'know? We're sort of friends. She called.

"'Don't mess with Benko,' she said."

"She told me she'd been his lover, he'd hurt her with his thing. Bernice is tiny. Not only that, she wouldn't do some things he wanted, so he hit her."

"Sounds like somebody better go to the cops."

"She said he was seeing Becky when she died."

"Shit."

"I asked Benko if it was true. He said yes, but not then. A couple of months before, she seduced him in the warehouse. He resisted but she reminded him of a Russian woman. When she hugged him and panted against his chest, he lost all willpower, y'know. He said he was sorry. He didn't want to cheat on me, it was only once. It's just, y'know, I was out of town and he felt so vulnerable and alone. He has a hard time with redheads."

My own red hair felt like flames rising from my guilty skull. "Did you fall for that crock of shit?" By now, I was fuming at

Nora and Benko, furious with myself. What did her comment about redheads imply?

"Gen, you don't know the half. Don't get mad at me. I finally told my therapist and she's helping me. After Bernice called, I stopped sleeping with him. Not because I don't want to—I still want to. I do. Nothing to do with him being a great guy or a great lover, y'know. I don't know why. Maybe I feel sorry for him, maybe it's only chemicals, maybe it does mean something great. If it wouldn't wreck everything, I'd sleep with him to-night, right now. I love his hand pressing on my stomach. It's better than a blanket."

"You've lost your mind, Nora. You can't be in love with him. He doesn't care about you. He just wants to fuck every woman who crosses his path. He's a predator. What's there to feel sorry for?"

"I can't help it. He has a sweet side, y'know. Did you know he was sexually abused by his uncles? His father wouldn't be-lieve him when he told him. I feel so sorry for him."

"Do you believe that?" I couldn't believe Nora was so gull-ible. "He'll say anything to get what he wants. You're smarter than this." "I believe him, Gen."

Her face went slack, adding years. Since Becky's death, Nora had begun to age. I saw her as an older sister, tortured by her effort to break out of her good girl role.

"He told me the details. It went on for years. They nearly killed him."

I didn't react, she continued. "You're right. He's put some kind of spell on me. Maybe some Russian magic. Last week he asked me for thirty thousand dollars for his mother in Russia. She needs heart surgery but only people with money get opera-tions in Russia. I almost wrote him a check. I have the money in my private account. Maybe I should have."

"I hope you're talking to your therapist about this." We clenched our hands together, our nails digging deeply into the pads of our fingers and palms.

She nodded yes. "Whenever I need to." She sighed. "He said, after Becky seduced him? She wanted a raise and a promotion. He didn't give it to her, y'know. She didn't work hard enough, he said. Then she threatened to tell Charlie Benko was sleeping with one of his workers. He gave her the raise so she would keep quiet. Sometime after she died, Benko snooped around her house, found her diary. He says the diary tells Becky was sleeping with Charlie right up to when she died."

"O my God!" I stood up, not totally surprised but now that it was in the open, at least among us, my heart went out to her. "I can't believe it. The Peyton Place of tofu. Everybody's sleeping with everybody?"

"I never thought Charlie would go through with 'open marriage,'" Nora said. "I let him say it because he needed to feel free. I didn't want him to leave our marriage because I controlled him and shut him down, like his mother did when he was a kid. He still resents her. But I was stupid and thinking too much of myself."

"Now Benko could stop all the bad publicity the diary would bring. All he has to do is keep it quiet or give it to us. If the press ever finds out? Can you imagine the headlines. 'The Boss and Me: Tofu Tigers in Bed!' It'd ruin us."

"Good god, Nora, Benko's grabbing you by the hair and fucking you like a mad dog. Does he sound like somebody who gives a shit about you? If he keeps things quiet, it's because he just wants to preserve his harem. You and every other woman in the company were his captive prey."

I changed the subject quickly before I got reckless and gave in to my anger at Benko and confessed my affair with him. I didn't want to hurt Nora any more, and if she knew, I was afraid she'd fall apart, so I asked, "Why did he wait so long to tell you about the book?"

"I asked him that and he said he was waiting for the right time." "The right time? Time for what?"

"I don't know. I think he wants a lot of money for it."

"Sure he does, that asshole." I grabbed her by the wrists and squeezed. "Nora, what on earth makes you think you can trust him at all?"

"I don't know. He said if anything ever did happen to Charlie? If the news got out about him and Becky, y'know? And Charlie went to jail or anything, Benko promised he'd help me run the company. He'd handle the workers and the factory and I could take care of the money part of the business. You'd be vice president of sales."

"Nora, he wants to take over everything."

"He's not that bad. Remember how much time he spent with Becky's kids after she died? He took them to the movies, stayed overnight a couple of times? He'd never hurt Liam, I'm sure, Gen. Deep down, y'know, he's a decent man. Just messed up about sex."

"I'll never trust Benko around my son again. I always wondered why he got involved with the MacDaniel kids. So he could snoop around her house? Or was it something else? The kids themselves?"

"That's stupid. Don't think that." Nora wandered over to the sink. She yanked the faucet on and swabbed at the counter with hard, skittering swipes. "He has his own kids in England. He misses them." I watched her, waiting out her thinking.

"Did Benko ever want to take your kids on a trip?"

Nora turned around. "What do you mean?"

"Face it, Nora. After what Benko did to me and Liam, he could do it to you. I'm worried about your kids."

"Ridiculous. He'd never touch a child."

"He kidnapped Liam."

"He brought him back. He told me he was just trying to help you."

"You're lost if you believe that. Benko's so clever he could convince the President to change parties."

Nora flopped down into the soft rocker next to the bay window. "You hate him, don't you?"

"I'm furious at what he did to you and to me and Liam." I paced around the kitchen. "If I were you, I wouldn't trust his production reports, either. I bet he's stealing from the company." As I spoke, I understood how thoroughly I feared him. "Nora, listen. You've got to make sure your kids are safe."

Her eyes glazed over as she tried to comprehend my anger and pleading. She lay her head back on the chair and rocked. "Maybe it did have something to do with his affair with her or the diary..."

Nora was smart enough to suspect Benko of the worst, yet she couldn't stop herself from defending him and putting herself and her kids in real danger.

I'd begun to give up on her, thinking I should tell her about my affair with Benko just to shock her awake when she said, "If I try to break up with Benko, he'll take the diary to the police and incriminate Charlie in Becky's death. I know he will. Charlie'd get charged with murder."

"God. If Benko did that, we're all finished. Did you ask Charlie if he slept with her?"

"I couldn't. He'd ask me where I got that idea. After Benko told me about the diary, Charlie came home in a rage. I asked him what happened and he told me everything."

"What?"

"Benko asked to meet him for lunch to talk about some production problem, but he really wanted to tell Charlie he had the diary and he knows about him and Becky."

"No wonder Charlie's acting weird."

"Charlie said he kept cool. He denied anything about Becky while he figured out how to handle Benko. Then, he said he couldn't help it, he asked Benko point blank how much he wanted for the diary. Benko grinned at him and said 'How much is worth?' Charlie said he wanted to slam Benko in the jaw but he forced himself into 'negotiation mode.'" Nora tipped a glass of water back and drained the whole thing.

"You gotta hand it to, Charlie," I said. "He's a wild man but he's consistent." I'd seen 'negotiation mode' plenty of times in sales meetings and he was so obvious in his insincerity. Not that sincerity would matter between him and Benko.

Nora put the glass down. "So Charlie says 'It's not worth anything.' And Benko says, 'I could get you in big trouble, Charlie. Be careful. I know you did it.' Then Charlie got up from the table and said, 'You show me this diary you claim you have and then we'll talk.' And Charlie comes home."

I couldn't believe Charlie would let Benko keep the diary, if it was true about him and Becky. If Benko had it. "Did you ask Charlie then if he'd been sleeping with Becky?"

"Yes. He admitted to it once or twice. A few times. Said he was drunk."

"Oh, no." Thank God I'd had the sense to start looking for a new job already.

Nora slumped back onto the chair, trying to burrow into the seam. She picked up a pillow and hugged it and rocked hard. "He couldn't have killed her. You know that. Charlie wouldn't do something like that. Besides, she was at her birthday party and he was with me that night, y'know..."

I was astounded at the thought that Charlie might have killed Becky. Impossible.

"If it ever went to court? I'd have to kill myself or something. I couldn't lie."

"What do you mean? Lie about what?" Nora could lie. She lied about her first lover, the painting teacher, she lied about Benko. "You can lie real well."

"The morning after the death? I found Charlie's clothes in the hamper. His pants and shirt were wet and muddy."

"So?"

"I asked him about it. He said he went out to the river for a few minutes while the kids were asleep. To meditate."

"Charlie meditates?"

"He goes out into nature and thinks about business, and things. Writes haiku, y'know."

"Still? What's the problem?"

"I don't know. He was lying to me about something. I'm afraid if the Chief or a lawyer asks me, I'll be the one to convict Charlie of something he didn't do. It's so fucked up, Gen."

I stood up and walked to the refrigerator and extracted a bottle of white wine from a loaded shelf. I filled two glasses and offered one to Nora. As I sipped mine, I said, "It's odd, but it's circumstantial. I don't see any relationship between Charlie's muddy clothes and Becky's death in the factory. Really. Think about it."

"You're right. But something's wrong."

"What's wrong is we know Charlie lied to everybody about him and Becky. But don't be ridiculous. Benko's a pathological liar, twisting your mind as bad as he's using your body. It's just as likely there is no diary. Does Charlie know you slept with Benko?"

"No way. That's the last thing I can tell Charlie. He's a mess. At home, all he does is sleep and complain. He's constantly plotting on ways to get the diary from Benko and shut him up."

We sat in silence, listening to the soup water boil. While she'd told her story, I'd forgotten where we were. Nora rose and with her head down and tears soaking her blouse front, she began cleaning up our half-finished recipe.

Her helplessness infected me with deep sadness for all of us. I wondered if we should just call Benko and tell him to go ahead, take the diary to the police, and let the chips fall where they may, get this over. I'd have to leave town sooner than I planned but Liam could handle withdrawing from school a few months early. We'd call off the Chinese New Year media tour and still have good enough sales. Charlie and Nora could hire the best lawyers in the state so they'd come out of this fine, a little dirtied, but they'd survive and so would the company.

As I heard myself tempted to give in to Benko, a criminal predatory rapist I'd had inside my body, willingly, enthusiastically, a few months ago, a sociopath, a conniving abuser of women, a kidnapper, I wondered how I could have fallen so low in my choice of men. I went from Gianni to Benko, a friend of the pope to the friend of the devil. A harsh laugh erupted from my chest.

Nora threw me a foul glance. "How can you laugh?"

She dragged around the kitchen, sponging the counter, the picture of a woman scorned, a woman beaten. She sniffled, wiped her nose on her apron, glanced at me, and smiled as if she understood that it was funny in a hopeless, tragic way. She walked in front of the refrigerator and stooped over to pick up ginger peelings from the floor. From over her bent back, Rissi's crayon drawing leapt at me off the refrigerator.

Ragged Christmas trees lit with bright yellow stars rode on the backs of horsey creatures whose heads sprouted antlers. Christmas tree bulbs decorated the borders of the drawing with red and green and orange patterns. I stared at the drawing. I breathed in and held it, letting a surge of anger rush from my nostrils down into my belly.

Listening to Nora's whole sad tale, I began to lose my temper. I was mad at Nora. Even madder at Charlie. I was enraged with Benko that he dared blackmail Nora and Charlie, everyone who worked in the company, so he could slam his cudgel dick whenever he wanted into a sweet woman whose mind he controlled in a way I knew too well.

"Nora, it's already 10:30. I'll finish up here, You go up to bed." "Charlie said he'd be home about two. He's driving in from Cleveland. I could help till then," she said.

"No. I'll take care of it. I can concentrate better if I'm alone. I'll be done by the time he's home. Only...I might not get everything cleaned up."

"No problem, sweetie. I'll call Sonia in the morning. She won't mind cleaning the kitchen. I pay her overtime."

Nora and I hugged goodnight, and she left the kitchen. I washed my hands, turned Nora's Pandora on to a Caribbean reggae station, and let the beat take me to work.

Scents of sautéing ginger and garlic rose around me and my knife danced with the leeks and chicken breasts. I sprinkled five spice powder into simmering sauce as if it was fairy dust transforming the world into a safe, happy, delicious place.

For the next three hours, I was all by myself, chopping, stirring, tasting, forgetting how lost we were, absorbing myself in the only dependable place I ever find peace, in the pure heaven of creating new dishes.

I left Nora's by 1:30, with three recipes finished and no Charlie in sight, thank goodness. I couldn't face him that night. He'd taste my gorgeous new dishes, mumble some compliment, then comment on how much money they'd make us.

Charlie was so predictable. If he only knew what was really going on.

Chapter Fourteen

Charlie

NOBLE GIFTS

flinging white robes into
the lap of the valley,
winter hills shrug night off their shoulders

I stopped taking business phone calls at home because I had to have peace someplace in my life. We got an unlisted home number for important calls about the kids or from her mother or our friends and we ran every call through voice mail. Nora and I changed our cell phone numbers and gave them out to a few key people.

One of the people I gave my new cell number to was Buhrman, another was Gladonov. Before either one tried to do something ridiculous to me, I wanted them to be able to give me plenty of warning. I never answered the phone when it rang but I checked the message immediately.

I thought Gladonov was my friend, a business friend but a friend, who I trusted enough to assign a critical piece of the operation making him as important to me as anyone. Somehow, I misinterpreted his management skills as a sign of his dedication to me.

If he was remotely a friend, even a loyal employee, he'd hand the diary over to me with the understanding that we were allies, together through the thick and thin, hanging in for the long run, building the business together, fighting back to back against the real enemies out to take American Tofu down. Instead, Gladonov showed his true colors by threatening me, and I was glad he did. Knowing where he stood and who he really was gave me an advantage, if I could only find it.

Except for necessary business meetings, Benko had kept to himself since he laid his diary scam on me. I expected him to offer it to me any time now for an exorbitant amount because he didn't really have any other play. He could take it to the police, but he obviously didn't care about being the hero.

Maybe Becky wrote something about him in the diary. Why not? He's her boss. If she did, he was either too worried or too clever to hand it over it to the police. Besides, the diary was circumstantial evidence. She obviously didn't write anything after she died. At worst, it would be embarrassing. Still, if it went public, I'd be mortified.

With relief, I realized that Gladonov had started to blaze a trail of possible guilt that my lawyers might be able to use to deflect suspicion from me, if they ever had to defend me. For a start, I'd have somebody research his immigration status.

Of course, if Gladonov furnished the diary to Buhrman, I'd deny I had anything to do with Becky. Women always fantasize about having affairs with men in power and this was one of those cases and besides, a diary was a pretty weak argument for conviction of a death.

I had to make sure Nora stayed away from Gladonov, too, in case he tried to intimidate her into offering too much money.

"I have it under control," I told her. "Gladonov's a complete liar. If he approaches you, don't say anything about my affair with Becky. Tell him you don't believe it and I denied it. I'll deny it until I see it written in her handwriting."

"I hope I can lie without him knowing. I'm a rotten liar," she said.

"For God's sake, Nora. We have to walk on eggshells around him until we get through the New Year. You know we need him to run the plant and we have to have the cash from the sales before we can do anything. I'll figure this out. I always do." Who was I bluffing? Not Nora.

I couldn't fire Gladonov for a lot of reasons. He had to handle the two week-long twenty-hour day production schedule coming up for our peak sales during the New Year. He must know that once the New Year push ended in February, I could fire him. Then, if things worked out the way I hoped, I would offer him a good severance package in exchange for the diary. If he didn't give it to me, he'd get nothing but the boot.

Blacklist him in New York State. He's made his fate.

***

I returned to my office from the gym one afternoon feeling unusually relaxed. My new personal trainer had started me on some stretching and breathing exercises that soothed me as much as a massage. I lounged on the office couch, studying the latest promising sales orders for the Year of the Rooster, when Meng called.

"Hello, Charlie," he said in a flat voice.

"Hello, Meng. It's been a little while. How are you?" The psychic infrared I've always had for bad news began blinking, sending a current to every fight and flight center in my brain.

"Good, Charlie. I want to talk for a minute."

"Sure. I have all the time you want." An icy tube of fear shot down the center of my body and my breathing went shallow.

"Charlie, starting March first, Meng Produce will stop doing business with American Tofu."

"What?" I doubled over my thighs with a pain in my stomach that felt like Meng had just kicked me. Our whole growth plans for the next year depended on Meng's opening of the national oriental markets. If we lost Meng, who knows who else would abandon us? I creaked my body upright and leaned against the soft couch back. My stomach ached.

"You can't. I mean, what did we do wrong, Meng? Give me a chance to work it out."

"It's already decided. I like you personally and don't want to hurt you. That's why we're waiting until after the Chinese New Year."

I should have paid more attention to him during the last month. The dizziness reduced my productivity to almost nothing.

He went on. "My farewell gift will be record sales for you during the month of February. I will pay everything I owe you as soon as I've shipped to my customers."

"But, Meng, we have the best product on the market. We can work on the price. Maybe we'll go to an Everyday Low Price for the Oriental market."

"Charlie, it's over."

"We could make you a private label. Your brand for your customers."

He paused, controlling the conversation. "Your tofu is fine. I don't need my own brand."

"What did we do...?" I waited in the silence. The phone dragged at my wrist like a twenty-pound weight.

"There are other reasons."

"What reasons? Who's taking over?" I wanted to shout at him. "You motherfucker. You just killed me!"

"I'm sorry," he said. "I don't want to discuss the reasons with you. The Quebec company will become my partner in tofu and other products."

"We had an agreement, Meng. The three-part agreement I worked out with Shu Ling? I haven't seen her for months."

My hand crawled across my desk top to the lucky pile of soybeans I kept in a raku pot. I picked up one bean and rolled it between my sweaty palms. The outer skin of the bean shriveled and slipped off the seed. I threw the naked bean as hard as I could across the room.

"It's all over, Charlie. I have appreciated our long and happy business relationship. Perhaps in the future we may do business again."

I'd remember that. "Shu Ling said you'd keep buying American Tofu." I let my voice drop before my obvious desperation humiliated me.

"Things have changed, Charlie. We can no longer abide by that agreement."

I didn't know what else to say. I lay back on my couch with one arm across my forehead, the other hand holding the phone to my ear. Thoughts and images of Taiwan reeled in my head. Nighttime Taipei spilling across my inner eye in oily neon rainbows...the Big Buddha's nostrils exhaling thick smoke... rats scuttling around the yard of the primitive tofu factory...the barbershop girl searching my crotch with her rubber glove...the carrion reek of the snake's blood rising up my nostrils...

Had I failed the test in Taiwan? I told him I'd consider importing for him. Or did Meng think Chen killed Becky and he was cutting his losses? Buhrman. He soured the whole thing. Did he sick the FBI on Meng? It had to be something out of my control. Should I play my ace and say something about the human organs? Or was it too late for that, too?

While my thoughts whirled, Meng waited silently on the other end of the line. In a minute I recovered enough composure to know if I wanted to preserve any positive relationship to protect myself, I had to retain face and to give him face.

Not only that, if Shu Ling had told me the truth, Meng was tied into powerful circles I could never hope to access. Circles that he could tighten around my neck if I wasn't careful.

I gave up trying to stop the inevitable. I couldn't do anything so I'd do nothing. Good old non-action: wu wei, the best martial arts move made the best business move. A graceful retreat was my best counter.

Standing up, I said, gagging at first, "Thank you for your gracious call, Meng." I got control of my throat. "All of us at American Tofu appreciate the business you've given us over the years. Your current decision is the best decision, I'm sure."

"You're welcome, Charlie." He sounded relieved.

I stiffened my voice with as much formality and objectivity as I could muster. "And thank you for staying with us through the Chinese New Year. That will help."

I quickly thought of a way to regain a little balance and salvage some pride. Almost casually, I offered him payment terms that he couldn't resist. "Pay us when you can, Meng. I'm never worried about payment from Meng Produce," I said. "Take as long as you wish to settle accounts."

He would understand the subtlety of my generosity: I determined the final form and the timing of his decision. But more important, I demonstrated that I was above business. My life, my world, would go on regardless of Meng's actions. Besides, it's a small world.

"Thank you, Charlie. Good luck." Did I hear a smile in his voice?

"Good luck to you, Meng. We'll probably see each other sometime. May the best man win." I couldn't resist challenging him. "Please tell Shu Ling hello from me." That was risky, I thought, but from now on it was simply Meng and Greer speaking man to man, so nothing rode on my keeping secret my friendship with Shu Ling. What the hell, this is how I wanted it, even though my knees were shaking.

"I will, Charlie. Good bye."

As soon as he hung up, I dialed Shu Ling. It rang twice before I put down the phone. She'd be no help now. Maybe she'd even been the reason Meng had gone with the Canadians.

If Meng didn't understand me, a unique individual with my own way of living life...like him...if he can't do business with somebody who has different values...who sees things his own way...an independent like me...eventually our relationship would have fallen apart anyway. It's better to get it done and let him bring in record sales.

Then, flash–I got it.

The Canadians will import the body parts. Good. Stay away from raw human kidneys, lungs, hearts.

Meng made a lot more money from kidneys and lungs than from tofu and bean sprouts. Shipping the organs through a Canadian customer would give Meng another layer of protection in case someone, maybe even Buhrman, stumbled onto something dicey, blew his cover.

I called Nora and Genevieve and asked them to come to my office. I broke the news and we all grumbled and stomped around and reassured each other. When they realized the dimensions of what had just happened to us, we all hugged. I made tea and we moped around my office until Genevieve came up with a great idea.

"Charlie, you should visit Gianni in person to tell him. He'll help, I'm sure. He'll sell to your old customers. They're used to American Tofu. Don't worry. This won't be as bad as you think. Thousands of refrigerators out there have to have their weekly supply of American Tofu. Don't be so emotional."

As usual, I followed her advice. That woman really knew how to sell.

***

Giordano had no time to see me at his office in New York before the end of January but he invited me to an early breakfast the next week at his estate in the Berkshires.

I'd suspected that Giordano was one of the richest men I knew, but I had no sense of the vastness of his wealth until I drove up to his estate that morning. His mansion perched on a hilltop, white and radiant among huge pines and bare-limbed oaks, above a snowy valley. I later learned that he farmed and forested several thousand acres in Massachusetts, Connecticut, and New York.

Seeing his riches, I felt curious, maybe even a little scornful, about his showing up for work every morning at Hunts Point. I'd be traveling Asia, windsurfing Hawaii waves, or strolling the streets of Rio if I were him. I'll never understand the rich.

Giordano's butler, a tall West Indian dressed in a purple velvet sweat suit, greeted me.

"Hello, Mr. Greer. My name is William, Mr. Giordano's assistant here at Lenox Farm. He asked me to beg your pardon for not being here, but he insists you stay for breakfast."

I almost turned around at that moment.

"Mr. Greer, please. Mr. Giordano apologizes. He instructed me to give you breakfast. He said he hoped you wouldn't be upset."

More than the butler, my stomach convinced me to stay. I might as well eat, no matter how disappointed I felt. In the foyer, he waited while I slipped out of my coat.

After hanging it up in a closet concealed behind a gold-framed floor-length mirror, William handed me an envelope. "I'm sure Mr. Giordano explains everything in the letter." He backed out of the foyer.

"I drive all night to meet with him, and he leaves me a note? He could have called me on my cell. My time's valuable." I ripped open the envelope.

First good friend Meng, now buddy Giordano. More good news? Keep singin' the blues. The note's gonna say he hired Genevieve away.

Numb, I sat on a mahogany bench to read. In his handwritten note, Giordano apologized profusely. He had to return to New York for an emergency breakfast meeting. He said he wished he'd had my cell phone number but he didn't want to wake up Genevieve to get it.

Considerate jerk, I thought. I read the rest of the note.

I read that and fell in love with Genevieve for the tenth time. She handled Giordano far better than I ever could. She was a better tofu sales person than I, no matter how she did it. She just did it, that's all I cared about. Besides, Giordano didn't need to meet me in person for me to achieve my goal of securing his ongoing commitment. My years of unrelenting service to his company proved to him how loyal I was and now, he proved his loyalty to me. This is why I love business.

His loyalty to Genevieve, Greer. That's what I hear.

We hit the bottom with Meng. Now we're on the way up.

Don't bet yet. Nothing's set.

William returned and invited me down a long, softly lit and paneled hallway into a bright dining room. He served me fresh-squeezed orange juice and espresso at an elegant setting on a long and heavy polished wooden table. Probably a Colonial antique, I thought. As William unloaded my breakfast from a filigreed silver tray inlaid with mother-of-pearl in the shape of a flock of chickens, I relaxed, Giordano's subtle humor surprised me, and I imagined owning a mansion like this when American Tofu became the largest tofu company in the Western world.

"Mr. Giordano had the chef prepare something special for you," William said. "He's quite well-known. Came to us from Il Pecadillo in Rome. I believe this is an original recipe. He told me to tell you he will send the recipe home with you if you like it. I'm sure you'll enjoy it."

"What is it?"

"Mr. Giordano said I was to surprise you. Do you prefer any particular music?"

My taste in music ran from U2 to Mozart, and not much else. Lately, I listened to hip hop, Becky's favorite music. I like the beat.

"What do you like, William?"

"We were listening to Cape Verdean tunes before you arrived."

"Sounds great. I've never heard that before. But, Mr. Giordano may have told you I like new things. I'm like your chef that way. Let's listen to it."

I devoured an exquisite meal of asparagus omelet with tofu bacon and fresh Italian bread. The tofu tasted far better than any bacon I remembered eating and the whole thing fit right into my new diet. While I chewed along to simple rhythms with bouncy singing and upbeat guitars, my eyes scanned the room, but the speakers were artfully hidden.

What else don't you see? Wealth has secrets, don't you agree?

Giordano's breakfast nook was a simple white room with a cathedral ceiling. From my chair, I looked out a bay window as the sky began to whiten. On each of the other walls hung a Norman Rockwell painting. Originals, too, I supposed.

The one I recognized showed a little boy and his puppy, sitting soaked and shivering next to a stream. A lump rose in my throat as I watched the boy and the dog gaze into each other's eyes like long-lost brothers. Maybe I'd get a dog for the kids.

Grateful that Giordano had been called away so I could enjoy a fantasy dukedom of my own, I lingered over a third cup of espresso and a snifter of the smoothest fruit brandy I'd ever tasted.

"Mr. Giordano wants you to take a bottle with you. It's from the *Giordano Collection*."

"I'd love to."

He changed the music to a throaty diva singing heart-wrenching blues. She suited my mood perfectly. Prolonging the moment of opulence and melancholy, I gazed into the broad valley outside as shadows slid back into the woods, leaving the valley floor clear and radiant.

Another ache formed in my throat as I realized that if I wanted my children and grandchildren to have even a sliver of the security and prosperity Giordano's family felt, I'd have to hang on to my company no matter what happened. I'd have to ride out any accusations, revelations, embarrassments, expenses, customer betrayals.

If the worst happens, I'll survive, I thought. No one will understand me, what I've gone through, who I really am. I'll be lonely, but so what else is new? I'll survive.

***

Groggy and road weary, I dragged myself into the office that afternoon with a brandy buzz. As I drove home, I'd sipped at Giordano's Collection, the smoothest, headiest liqueur I'd ever tasted. A different universe from anything Scotch, Irish, Russian. I wondered what other amazements Italy might have to offer.

I flipped on the lights in my office, planning to check my voice-mail and take a nap. A large FedEx package lay on my desk.

From Meng.

God, I thought. What now?

I peeled off the brown shipping paper. Inside a cardboard liner was a beautiful wooden box lacquered in black with scarlet designs in the style of imperial China. I held the box for several minutes, again recalling my trip to Taiwan, the tour through the bazaar, the temples, the girls. My fondness and desire for Shu Ling fluttered in my stomach like a promise of a wonderful vacation. I'd suffered strangeness and embarrassment during my association with Meng, but he'd brought excitement into my life like nobody else.

I lifted the painted lid with all the care an Imperial treasure deserved and, peeling back a wrapping of crushed red velvet, I saw what was inside. I immediately closed the lid.

What is he up to now? What did Shu Ling tell him about me? Did Buhrman get to him? Was he threatening me with something else?

I set the box on my desk, and made a cup of tea, lacing it with a big shot of my office brandy, not so fine as Giordano's— I'd save his for ultra-special times—but just the ticket. I'm not a drinking man so brandy at breakfast, brandy before lunch, brandy before dinner dulled my normal keen senses. My mind wandered. Maybe I should call Shu Ling...or Buhrman...or Genevieve...anything new out there in the stores? What was Nora up to?

Sipping tea in silence, I pondered the box. If I had to, I could probably sell it for a decent price to some sinophile, although I didn't really know any besides myself. Let it go on eBay if I had to.

It's a matter of pride. Hurry up. Look inside.

I raised the lid again and stared at the huge snake's head that lay cushioned in black velvet, its polished nose aimed at me with its toothy jaw propped half open and yellow glass eyes gleaming back, vengefully. It was as big as the anaconda whose blood I'd drunk and whose liver I'd chewed. Was this the same head that clenched mine between its jaws in old Taipei?

A metallic odor rose from the box, the same stench that plagued my nostrils for days after my visit to the snake house. As I bent closer, remembering the bizarre euphoria I'd felt when we all stood around slick with blood, guffawing and sipping snake blood cocktails, I noticed the snake's tongue curled around a rolled piece of paper.

I peeled the tongue back and, careful not to snag my fingers on teeth, I extracted the paper. It was a note in Meng's handwriting.

Charlie, I trust this will settle our accounts. Sincerely, MENG.

PS Big Man sends his regards. His business has never been so brisk. He's naming a new breed of snake after you. Charlie Yu. "Happy Charlie." Big Man told me next to the president of Taiwan, Charlie Greer is the funniest man he's ever met.

What did he mean? Did he think I made a fool of myself in Taipei? I bet they laugh their heads off every time they talk about Charlie, the clown from New York.

Meng was acting out of character. He could be covert, but never mysterious or, on the other hand, really forthcoming. I thought maybe the box itself was worth a few thousand dollars at most. I guessed that was about what Meng Produce still owed American Tofu for 30 days of past business, but the snake's head puzzled me. If I showed it around, I'd have to have a story to go with it. I'd never be able to tell the truth, but I'd have no trouble making something up. If I told it like it happened, nobody would believe me anyway.

I decided to make the best of it. I'd just call Meng and thank him, hoping he'd reveal his secret message. If not, at least I had a couple of new conversation pieces for my office.

I tugged the anaconda head gently, pulling it out of the box. Some of the velvet lining stuck to the scales so I dragged it out, too, intending to separate it once I laid the head on my desk. I gathered some flaky scales into a heap and unstuck the cloth from the snake. I picked up the case.

Eight thousand dollar bills lay on the bottom of the box. Oh, I thought, this is the settlement. Cute. I reached in to withdraw the nice little offering Meng had made. A deep pile of thousand dollar bills lay under each one of the top bills. I counted a pile—thirty nine bills. My palms began to sweat. I peeled away the layers of thousands, counted them all. My god. Three hundred twenty thousand dollars.

I peered at the face on the bill. William McKinley. Homely guy. What did he do to have his mug engraved on the thousand-dollar bill? Who cares? Meng gave me more than a year's profits on the business I used to do with him—in cash. Tax free? Maybe. It had to be. If I booked it, Buhrman could subpoena my records any time he wanted and learn way too much.

Jesus, now what did Meng want? Was he paying some kind of retribution because he thought Chen killed Becky and caused me all the pain? Was Meng feeling guilty that he'd given the future profits from my tofu business to the Canadians? I doubted that.

Don't be in such a rush. It's for the human organs. Give back the cash, or all you can do is shush.

Obviously, even though he'd brought me to the brink of ruin, Meng wasn't all bad. In spite of the fears that Shu Ling had planted in my heart, I saw, and decided to believe, that the Emperor of Hunts Point was acting as a consummate politician. He knew we'd meet on the fields of business for years to come and he didn't need me as an enemy. Besides, American Tofu was a perfect place to dump extra cash.

Three hundred twenty thousand was a nice sum, but not nearly enough to be a perfect bribe. Between Nora and me, we make almost that much in a good year. I felt the urge to call Meng and say, how about five hundred? If you want me to shut up, let's make it worth my while. How am I going to deposit this anyway? It'll take me six months to bury it in the business.

Of course, Meng was a master dealmaker. I couldn't call him now to talk about the gift. At best, I could thank him for the souvenir and the lovely antique box. In typical Meng fashion, he'd countered and upped the face-saving ritual I began when I told him to take his time paying his bill to AT, and he'd done it for a more than reasonable cost.

I'd keep quiet about the organs since, in actuality, transplants were common in modern medicine. It was only their source that the mainstream didn't approve of. Where would I be anyway if I did what middle-of-the-road people expected?

Meng knows you too well. He's sure you won't tell.

Once I accepted the money, I gave up any reason I had to seek revenge. Since it was significant but small, the amount felt almost like an enticement to respond with a more outrageous act. I had to hold off making any moves until I saw how things worked out with putting my business back on track through Giordano. This money was the sign I needed: once Becky's death was a closed case, everything would be normal.

IF, Greer. Remember the big IF here.

I thought about what to do with the money. I had enough to buy the diary from Gladonov with plenty left over. I could use a new car—my Jeep had nearly 200,000 miles on it. The Beemer was eight years old. One of the guys at the Y had bragged about his Lincoln LX. Best American car in history, he said. Mine would be a pure white cube of class: the new "TofuMobile."

Before I spent the money on myself, I thought I'd better bank some of the cash in the AT account to clean up the Meng Produce Bill. Then I realized a really odd thing. Meng had promised to do business with us through Chinese New Year. In fact, I had a huge tofu order from Meng Produce sitting on my desk that would mean even more profits.

I had to do some good with all this money, not just spend it on myself. I'd made a huge mistake, but with this money I could make up for it, at least a little.

I decided to put fifty thousand in the MacDaniel kids' fund, an anonymous cash donation. The local food bank always needed money. Another fifty thousand to them, mailed in cash from an anonymous donor in Rochester. I'd put a big chunk into my workers' year-end bonuses.

Maybe I should have been more suspicious of Meng, but when somebody loads your lap with even that much cash, no questions asked, you take it with a smile. Nobody needed to know about it. This was between Meng and me. In fact, it was only between me and me. "I and I," like those reggae singers say. Now I had cash—the unstoppable power source. Before long, I'd have the diary.

Finally, my luck was turning. Amazed, I bowed my head and imagined the Buddha's golden nose beaming at me. I whispered "Thank you."

Chuck, having fun? Don't get chill. We're far from done.

The End

Book Two

The Special Fruit Company

THE HOUR BETWEEN ONE AND TWO: BOOK THREE
A DARK COMIC MYSTERY
DOWN AT THE RIVER
THOMAS TIMMINS
TOFU NOIR

Chapter One

Charlie

BLACKMAIL

we knew it was coming
but what could we do? he
thinks he's got me, ha!

A few minutes after I got back from lunch, Benko walked into my office without knocking. I spotted his shoe so I knew it was him before he came all the way in. He shut the door, and locked it behind him and I kept my head down, watching his reflection in the stainless steel base of my desk lamp. He stood leaning against the door until I finally said, "Yeah?"

"Production's going good, boss."

"Yeah, Benko, I know. That's your job. What do you want?"
"About that book? You got a good offer?"

I flashed a cold look at him, in his stained production whites, wearing short sleeves to show off his muscles, with a floppy net holding his hair off his forehead. I said, "Get that shit-eating grin off your face. I don't have a number for you because you don't have anything for me."

"You don't believe that. You know what I have and you need it. I give it to you. Cheap. Five hundred."

"Five hundred?" I said, half in shock. I thought he'd ask for ten thousand at least. "Go home right now. Get that book and bring it back and I'll have five crisp hundred dollar bills waiting, right here on the desk."

He laughed and laughed. Then he sat down on my couch
and leaned back and crossed his legs. He spread his arms across
the span of the couch and clenched his cucumber-sized fingers.
A pulse rippled up his arms from his wrist to his biceps and
disappeared under the sleeves.

"Thousand, boss. Five hundred thousand."

Flabbergasted, I sat still and closed my eyes.

"Cat got the tongue?" Gladonov said. "Five hundred by February."

He's playing a power card, but hang in, be hard.

"You're an idiot, Gladonov. You want to blackmail me, go
ahead. I was thinking ten thousand was a high number."

He laughed again. "This is big company, boss. Make lot of
tofu, lot of money. I see my workers' payroll every week. Figure office pay is pretty big. You, Nora, Genevieve, me, we make
good pay. Right now, it's a record sales. You skim a little, hand
it over to Russian friend. Save your ass."

"I'm not rich, Benko. Everything that comes in goes out the
next day to pay bills. Anything extra goes to paying our people
good wages, benefits, schooling."

"Bullshit. Your house, this factory. Record sales."

"Not bullshit. If you knew anything about business, you'd
know we have assets, all mortgaged, and we don't have cash. I
couldn't even get you fifty thousand from profits."

Benko leaned forward with his paws gripping his thighs
and stared at the floor. As he pushed himself to his feet, he said,
"Sounds like we're close," then he walked away. As he unlocked
and opened the door, he said, "Four hundred, done deal. Like
they say."

"Fuck you, Benko," I said.

"We talk later, Charlie."

He left my office and just before he closed the door, he
shoved it open again.

"I like you, Charlie. Very nice wife. Nice kids, too. You don't
want jail. It's bad place for soft guy. Tell you what? Make business deal: I run production for Chinese New Year, you make big

money. Give me two-fifty at end of sale, another one, one-fifty in a month, I go. You stay out of jail. Deal?"

We were getting somewhere, and I figured he'd take two hundred, maybe one-seventy-five by the time we finished dealing. I might be able to handle one fifty if I hocked everything and tossed in some of Meng's boon, but at that moment, he disgusted me and I lost my temper. I snarled at him. "Fuck you. You're fired."

He grinned and came back into the office. "Be careful, Charlie. Nobody makes production hum like me."

"I'll appoint Jorge or, hell, Nancy can do everything you do. I'm not stupid, Gladonov. I have back-ups in place."

He knew I was bluffing.

"Sure. Tell me about it. Who knows electricity? Who keeps steam boiler up when electricity goes down?"

Only one guy in the whole company could keep the electricity running. The same guy who could shut it down and keep it off. If he didn't get what he wanted in cash, he'd take it some other way.

I stared at him until he said, "One last thing. You don't want the diary, you know who does. I don't mean Nora."

He closed the door quietly, whistling as he went down the long hall toward production.

***

I called Nora and told her to take the kids to her mom's. I'd be home in twenty minutes. We had to talk.

As soon as I came in the door, Nora said, "What happened, Charlie?"

"Benko," I growled, taking off my coat. I was fuming.

"Benko? What did he do? What did he tell you?"

"He didn't do anything, yet. It's what he plans to do. He wants five hundred thousand dollars or he gives the diary to the Chief. He might sabotage the plant, too."

"Five hundred thousand? Where does he think we'll get that?" Nora's voice trembled.

"I'll tell you when I get home. Take the kids to your mom's. I'm almost finished here and I'm out the door."

***

An ugly sky squatted on the tops of the house and the bare syca- more and oak bordering our property. At least the low-pressure system raised the temperature above freezing for the first time in a month. All of upstate New York could get a foot of wet snow during the night.

Nora was in the kitchen brewing coffee when I came in. Without speaking, I hung up my coat and hat and walked over to her. When I hugged her, trying to establish our togetherness against Benko, she didn't stop shivering. It was infectious and shudders ran through me, too. I turned the thermostat up to eighty.

We carried our cups into the living room where Nora had built a fire in the fireplace. I spiked my coffee with a shot of Maker's Mark and stared into the flames. Nora sat on the edge of her chair, tapping her heel on the maple floor. I inhaled the sweet peppery fragrance of the burning birch and turned around. She was still shaking.

Nora stood up and crossed the room to the liquor cabinet. "I better join you for this one." She poured herself a splash of the bourbon in a glass. "Sit down, Charlie. You're making me way too nervous standing there."

"I don't know if I can." I sat down and got right back up. "I can't talk sitting down."

Nora shrugged and raised her glass to me. "Whatever. Walk. Talk. Tell me what's going on."

"He sent an email asking for a meeting. I knew what it was about. Let him come, I thought. I told him to see me in my office after lunch—my turf, my time."

I told her the whole story, ending with his threat to disable the factory if I didn't give him the ransom.

"He has me by both balls, now. The plant and the Chief."

Nora ignored my comment and said, "Is it true? Is he the only one who can handle the electricity?"

I snapped back. "Yes, goddam it. It's complex. We're too small to afford two skilled electricians on staff."

"I wasn't accusing you."

"Benko meant if I fired him, he'd sabotage the plant, cut the electricity."

"He wouldn't."

"What world do you live in?" For all her numbers and business acumen, Nora could be so naive about people.

"I'll talk to him," she said, pouring herself another finger of whiskey. Tossing a log onto the fire and settling herself on a footstool in front of the fireplace, she stared into the orange blaze. "He'll listen to reason. He and I have always had good communications."

"Stay away from him. I don't trust him. If he comes near you, call me. I'll handle Gladonov."

I hadn't told her about the cash Meng sent me, and before I dipped into it to ransom the diary, I'd try waiting Gladonov out. I'd had twenty years of negotiating experience and, unless he resorted to violence, I was sure I could beat him down to a reasonable fee. I might have to pay, but I'd pay as little as I could.

As I started toward the liquor cabinet, Nora rose and put her arm around my waist and lay her head on my shoulder. Her breath smelled sweet with bourbon.

"We'll figure it out, Charlie."

"It's a business battle, Nora. We win this one, we're home free." I lifted my arm over her head and dropped it around her, pulling her gently to me.

After a minute, she said, "Hey, look out the window. It's started."

In the west, the sky had turned blue but over our house the clouds had opened. Fat snowflakes sputtered down with deceptive delicacy.

I said, "I bet we'll get a foot by dawn."

With her ear still pressed against my chest, over my heart, she said, "Let's go for a walk before it gets dark."

"What about the kids?" I said, not wanting to leave them stranded during a blizzard, even with grandma.

"We'll walk first, then we'll pick them up, come home and roast marshmallows."

"God, Nora. I don't know how you can be so playful at a time like this."

"Don't worry, Charlie. I'm not feeling playful. This is survival. Hunker down with family on a snowy night. That's common sense."

***

I checked the thermometer outside the kitchen window. The temperature had dropped to twenty-three, perfect for an all night snowstorm. I retrieved Nora's and my down jackets and brought them to where she waited.

"You know, honey. It's strange," I said. "I feel good, well, not exactly good, but mentally clear. Benko started the bidding, laid out his hand, and said, come on, Charlie, your bet. Now I know about what he wants and his position, we have a good chance of working this out."

Nora sat down on the stool she kept by the serving island in the kitchen.

"Hey, let's go," I said, tossing her a coat. "Before it gets too slippery out."

She caught the coat and lay it on the island. "Take your coat off, Charlie. Sit down."

"What? I thought you wanted to go walking? We can figure out a plan to get the diary."

"Not yet. You said you knew a lot more about him? And that improved our odds?"

"Of course." Nora had become her serious and distant self again. "Don't tell me you know something else, something I don't." I sat down and bounced back up, searching for my glass.

When I couldn't find it, I went over to the island and sat on the stool across from her. "So?"

Nora raised her eyes to the ceiling, then, with her chin in her hand, she glanced around the room.

"You're making me nervous now, Nora. What?"

"All right," she said, her brown eyes liquid and sad. "You have to know this."

My heart started thumping in my ears. I was afraid of what she would say.

"I'm really sorry, Charlie. You know how I didn't come down on you when you told me you slept with Becky? I kind of accepted it and said let's make the best of it?"

"Yeah. By then, what else could we do? Benko had the diary." "And I'm one hundred per cent supporting you in the investigation?"

Uhoh, here it comes. Fee fi fo fum, don't get yourself bummed.

"Why are you saying this?"

"Remember, I never tried to hurt you. I made a mistake but it wasn't because I had bad feelings about you."

"What mistake?"

"I slept with Benko."

"You slept with Benko?"

"I'm sorry. Yes."

Could it be any worse? Only riding in the back of a hearse.

My throat clutched and I gagged. Sputtering, I groaned, "How could you? How could you? Gladonov?" She tried to take my hand but I jerked it away and slammed my palm into the refrigerator door.

Nora called after me, as if I were already out of the house. "I couldn't help it, Charlie. You weren't interested in me. He paid attention to me. I wanted a summertime fling, that's all. You had one. Yours ended in total disaster."

How could I deny that? I didn't try. Instead, I shouted, "The lowest snake in the grass is fucking my wife. How the fuck could you do that with that criminal?"

Nora stayed quiet, sitting at the counter. She'd laid the coat on her lap and was playing with the fur collar while I ranted and raved.

I felt about an inch high but I wouldn't let her see that. "Where did you fuck him? Here? Right here on that fabulous oak island I had hand-made for you for five thousand dollars?"

Nora stood up. "Stop it, Charlie."

"Sure, I know where you fucked him. Right in front of our romantic fireplace?"

"Stop acting like a two year old. I'm sorry. It was a big mistake. It's over. It's been over."

I swung my arms and picked up my coat and threw it as hard as I could at the cupboards. Then I faced her and growled, "I bet you did it on our bed."

"No, never here," Nora said. "We only did it a few times. Like you and Becky."

The words I'd used to minimize my affair with Becky flew out of Nora's mouth and slapped me across my jaw.

I recoiled. "Oh. Like me and Becky ... like me and her."

No surprise. It's the old new age. You got it: open marriage.

I laughed, not a funny laugh, but a hard, sad laugh. "Nora, you and me," I said. "A couple of losers. We should never have got married. No wonder you wanted that open marriage crap."

"You're right. I know. But we are married and we both screwed up big time. I'm sorry. You're sorry. What else can we do?"

"All the time we're in therapy you're dicking Gladonov. Such a liar." She had me completely fooled. What's worse, Gladonov knew I didn't know about him and Nora. No wonder he smirked at me when he asked for half a million dollars. He'd already conned me out of something far more valuable.

Nora came across the kitchen to within a few feet of me, ready to don boxing gloves, if I wanted to, though she knew I'd never strike her.

She said, "Don't start that hypocrisy thing, Mr. Hypocrite. I was stupid, I admit it. But you were in therapy with me when you were fucking your employee. What's so honest about that?"

Our anger escalated and we started shouting until Nora walked out to the back yard and stood in the twilight, hugging herself. I watched her while I cooled off.

She said it was over with Benko. She wasn't leaving me for him. We were still a team. I wanted to keep it that way, at least until we got the diary. We'd get Benko gone and then we could sort out our lives.

I picked up her coat and slid down the back steps to bring it to her. I brushed the snow off her hair and sweater and settled the coat on her shoulders. I snugged it closed around her and said, "Look at us. What a strange pair."

For the first time, she started crying. I pulled her against me and said, "We can get through this somehow, Nora. We've made it this far. But it's gonna cost us."

"I know," she said. "We have to pay Benko now, don't we?"
"Pronto," I said. "The only question is, how much more?"

Chapter Two

Genevieve

"DRAGON STEW"

The Year of the Rooster started at dawn every morning that January. I didn't stop moving or talking all month as I clucked Charlie's Soy to the World message like a chicken gone berserk. Half the time, I wondered if I still had my head on my shoulders.

My sense of humor saved me. I told my men produce buyers they could call the promotion the Year of the Chick if they thought of me and made out big tofu orders.

I created a dozen new recipes for the Year of the Rooster, traveled the whole Northeast from Philadelphia to Portland, with side trips to Chicago, Denver, Miami, and Atlanta, appeared endlessly on TV and radio, talked non-stop with customers, all because Charlie had dedicated American Tofu to a life or death mission.

I had to create widespread positive feelings about the company that no matter what happened regarding Becky's death, the company would live on as the only brand in our customers' minds.

Every night until my trip began, I stayed close to Liam, helping him with his math project or reading with him or cheering at one of his swim meets. When he and his friends raced back and forth across the pool, I forgot all my worries. Screaming with all the parents perched on the bleachers beside the pool, I felt like a normal mom, enjoying the chill of a damp but proud swim team parent.

The morning I left town, I planted Liam with my friends Carla and Denise who promised they wouldn't let him out of their sight, and he'd never know it. I crossed my fingers that Benko would keep his distance, now that he was so occupied in the plant.

On January twenty-third, almost a week into a grueling trip, I fielded an emergency call from Nora just before I went on Providence public television's cooking show.

Nearly hyperventilating, she gasped. "Thank God I had your itinerary, Genevieve. Benko is gonna do it. What should I do now?" "Benko. What?"

"He'll take the diary to Buhrman unless we give him five hundred thousand dollars."

"Five hundred thousand dollars?"

"Charlie won't give him the money. He says we can't."

"Doesn't the company have it?"

"Not even close. Charlie says Benko doesn't deserve anything." Nora began crying. "I know we don't have all of it, but Charlie says he won't even negotiate. I told him to sell his new SUV for cash and he refuses."

"You have to tell Charlie about your affair with Benko," I said. "If he doesn't know that, he won't know how demonic Benko really is. He thinks he's got Benko under his control because he writes his paycheck."

Nora didn't reply for a long minute while she thought it over one more time. She and I had rehearsed how she would tell Charlie, but she never committed to it. She was afraid Charlie would hate her because she'd betrayed him when he needed her most.

"I told him," she said.

"What happened?"

"He was furious. He stood there in the middle of the living room like I'd smacked him on the head with a hammer. His face went completely white and he started biting his mustache."

"Did he get physical?" I asked, fearing the worst.

"Charlie would never do that." A defensive note came into her voice. "He's not that kind. Besides, he feels so guilty about Becky, he almost said he understood about me and Benko. I know he hates me, though. As soon as he heard about our affair, he said we had no choice. We have to give Benko the money, as much as we can raise. It's the only way. We have to get Benko out of our lives."

"Stay calm, honey. It's between Charlie and Benko now. Nothing will happen while the factory's so busy. They'll try to psyche each other out, but I don't think Benko will make another move right away."

"I hope he waits," Nora said. You were right about my telling him. "He threatened to shut down the factory if Charlie didn't give him the money."

"Benko's not stupid. He won't bite the hand of the dog who feeds him."

Nora said, "That's what Charlie thinks, but you can't predict Benko."

"Maybe. They're calling me, Nora. Showtime in thirty seconds. I'll call you tonight." I hung up wondering what ruins I'd find when I returned to Clement.

***

I came back from the tour and shut out the world. I didn't unpack my clothes or organize the rolls of film I'd shot or sort out the videos of my TV shows. I collapsed.

The first night home with Liam, we celebrated with a dinner of hot fudge sundaes and big mugs of hot chocolate. He insisted on popping caramel corn for desert. Liam had sculpted a miniature set of red and blue pots and pans out of Femo to commemorate my new fame as a TV tofu cook and I gave him a little souvenir from each city I'd stayed in. He liked the miniature Liberty Bell best because it had a tongue that clanged the bell in high C.

"When I shake it fast, it sounds like the 'Next Level' magic gateway chimes in 'Ace Blastforce and Company.'"

As soon as I tucked Liam in and kissed him goodnight, he fell asleep, and I called Nora.

"Oh, sweetie. I'm so glad you're back. Charlie said you knocked 'em dead in every city on the East Coast."

"I brought back a lot of video and audio tapes. We can watch them together."

"Let's have a show for the employees. They can see what marketing does to keep them in jobs."

"That'll be fun."

"Gen, this Benko thing is driving us nuts. I haven't slept in a week."

"Nora, please, I'm wrecked. Let's not talk about business or Benko or anything bad. I can't take it. Right now, I feel like a bowl of beef consommé that's been left out overnight."

"Gross. Let's pretend everything's fine. I can't get the diary and the money off my mind and I've lost ten pounds since you left and if Charlie wasn't out somewhere I'd come right over."

"Ten pounds? You don't have ten pounds to lose."

"I've got the new foolproof diet. Call it the Benko Plan. You're so afraid you don't eat."

We laughed a little. "I've been on that one myself. But right now ... I'm gorging on family love. The only thing that really works in the long run."

"I wish I could," Nora said. "How is Liam? Did he survive without mom's cooking?"

"Didn't miss it. He's great," I said. "Made me a little Femo cooking kit for a welcome home."

"He really loves you. So grown up."

I replayed the media tour for her, regaling her with stories about the egotistic media chefs and TV personalities I'd met, the camera men at every station who offered me carte blanche with their lives, how my recipes were big hits everywhere, especially with the crews I fed after the shows.

"After Philly, I had my closing pitch down cold," I said. "I left them with a tofu cooking idea anyone can do."

"The stir fry thing?" Nora asked. "Throw it in a hot pan with veggies and plenty of garlic and stir?"

"Even that's too complicated. No, what I said was, 'Take your favorite recipe that uses a hearty sauce, spice up the sauce twice as much as usual, saute tofu in cubes and toss them into the sauce. Simmer and serve. Presto."

We talked and talked about anything except Benko and Charlie and the business. For that half hour, I felt ten years younger, as if Benko didn't exist, as if my whole life lay in front of me with a certainty of happiness for me and Liam.

***

Over the weekend I plotted the details of my exit from American Tofu. A few more weeks of watching the fruits of my Year of the Rooster toil pour in, one more recipe demo shin-dig for Wegmans, and I'd begin my permanent vacation from the world of soybeans, rapacious Russians, and small town police chiefs watching every move you make.

I stayed in bed twenty-fours hours, regaining my strength, then Nora and I met for lunch at her house to talk about Benko. I doubted we'd find anything funny now that I'd come back to reality. She presented me with a mug of fresh carrot-beet-ginger juice.

"I think I need something stronger."

We laughed. She opened a bottle of red wine and poured two large goblets. "Cheers."

"Cheers." We held hands and sipped our wine.

"Things are out of control with Benko," she said.

"I was afraid of it."

"Charlie's totally consumed by the blackmail." Then Nora suggested we move into the dining room where we sat at the round table and sipped wine.

She said, "Ever since I told Charlie about me and Benko, I feel like I'm barely in touch with the ground. My head feels like it's either behind or ahead of time. I'm here but only part of me."

"Sounds like jet lag," I said. "I feel that way after road trips."

"Charlie and I haven't talked about it since. We're sleeping in separate bedrooms now, but at least we're civil. He couldn't say anything to me about the affair and I didn't tell him any of the down and dirty."

"That was smart. If you did, he might have confronted him."

"I'll never tell Charlie the details," Nora said. "He'd lose his mind if he heard some of the things we did. He'd have Benko killed. He'd torture him first. We'd lose everything."

We both swallowed deep drinks of our wine. The cuckoo clock on the wall ticked as we leaned on our elbows. I chewed my lower lip. Nora wrung her hands.

"We negotiated the ransom to a hundred fifty thousand," she said, "down from his five hundred thousand. Then he raised it to a hundred-fifty plus all the company cash on hand, whatever's in the bank or at the office."

"Charlie told him we'd have to sell our house and get the bank involved because I had to use our property as security for the money we borrowed to buy the new tofu equipment. Our credit cards are maxed-out. He told Benko it would get really complicated and it might take twelve months. Benko believed him. Said he'd take a hundred-fifty as soon as Chinese New Year production was done."

"That's a lot," I nodded, glad that I wasn't an entrepreneur, always having everything I owned on the line.

"We have no choice," Nora said. "It's all set. Charlie plans to use the profits from the Chinese New Year sales. That's about half. He said he'd find the rest someplace else. We told Benko nothing could happen until March first, when the returns from the business would be in."

"That gives you a little time."

"He wants it by February tenth. Charlie thinks he'll sabotage the factory."

"The asshole. That's the end of next week. Do you have it?"
"Charlie says don't worry," she said. "I don't know."

"Have you seen the diary or a copy of it?" I asked.

"Charlie asked Benko to prove he had it, to show it to him. Trust me, you can, he says. What a laugh. But like Charlie says, what difference does it make? I had the affair with Benko. Charlie had the affair with Becky, so we might at well pay for our sins. We'll have the diary in our hands once we buy it. If there's no diary, better yet, Charlie says. He can beat Benko at any game he wants to play."

"Jesus. Pure testosterone talking."

"That's Charlie," Nora said. "He's not always the smartest when it comes to money."

I almost said, "Or women," catching myself before I belittled Nora. Instead, I asked, "If Benko's bluffing, why doesn't Charlie go to Buhrman, tell him everything? He can fire Benko and charge him with blackmail."

"Neither of us want our reputations ruined. Would you? The media was a flock of vultures when Becky died. What do you think they'd do if they found out about the diary or Benko and me?" Nora finished her wine with a big gulp.

"Yeah. I know. Biggest scandal outside Albany for years."

"They'd find out all right. The Chief would leak it and we'd lose the business. No customer would stay with us if they thought the owner was a womanizing murder suspect. Everyone would think Charlie killed her. We'd lose everything." She'd thought through all the sorry consequences. "What would you and Liam do?"

"I don't know." I wasn't ready to tell her that I'd be leaving Clement before long. I had to keep that secret until I landed a new job. I knew Benko hadn't revealed our affair to her because if he had, she'd have said something by now and Benko would have bragged to me that he told Charlie and Nora. He'd enjoy my shame about not letting my close friends know the whole foul truth about all of us.

"What if he takes the money and hands the diary over to the cops anyway?" I asked, moving the conversation ahead, wanting to slide by the possibility that Nora might know about Benko. If I were in her shoes, I'd expect her to tell me. On the other hand, I said to myself, I'd want to keep the situation as simple as possible. Besides, my affair with Benko had nothing to do with the blackmail.

Nora smiled at me, her eyebrows raised a fraction. "That's where we're hoping you'll help us."

"Help you? How?"

"We want you to make the exchange, the cash for diary."

A fist of fear thumped into my abdomen.

"Will you?" she asked, squeezing my fingers.

I stared at her, my stomach rumbling with wine souring the carrot juice. "I'm as scared of him as you are," I said. "When he kidnapped Liam at Niagra Falls, it showed he'll do anything."

"It was Benko's idea. He said you're the only one he trusts."

Benko had cornered me again. Maybe he had kept our affair secret, so far, but now I wondered. If Nora knew about us, would she tell me or would she play it the same way I did, keeping it secret?

Once I got involved, Benko would want something else from me besides Charlie and Nora's cash. Still, I had an irrational feeling I'd be safe because Benko would call me his only friend in Clement. If I was the money-bearer, he'd have to back off from me and Liam. So, always a foot soldier in the tofu wars, I agreed to carry the ransom and retrieve the diary.

Now that I entangled myself in whatever happened with the blackmail, I decided Charlie and Nora needed to know about my affair with Benko. If I didn't tell them soon, before the exchange, with the pressure they were under, they'd think the most paranoid thing possible: I was in collusion Benko.

When they heard, I expected Nora would feel hurt and Charlie mad, at first, then they'd understand how Benko had swooped through American Tofu like a raptor, piercing every little mouse and mole with his voracious beak, and dragging us away, bleeding and crying like the sorry prey we were.

Every winter, on the night before Chinese New Year, Charlie threw a party for the employees. That year he wanted something unforgettable, something to make everyone proud and steep them in American Tofu's mission.

A few nights after Nora asked me to carry the ransom to Benko, we sat in their living room, drinking tea and designing the menu, putting the final touches on the Year of the Rooster "Tofu To-Do" company bash. They'd asked me to make a photo documentary of the party for the company newsletter and web site.

"I will," I said. "But if the party's anything like last year's, I better shoot before they empty the punch bowl. We don't want everyone to look smashed out of their minds."

Charlie and Nora laughed. "Take a few later on, too," Charlie said. "For kicks. We won't publish them, but some of the crew might like to see themselves cutting loose."

I described the "Dragon Stew" I wanted to make for everyone.

"After tasting a bowl of the stew, the guys at every station claimed they could feel dragon energy in their ... You could see color rising in most of the women's faces, too."

Charlie just stared at me, a sour expression on his face. As he tossed back another slug of his drink, he muttered, "Sounds uplifting."

"We'll need to have our spirits uplifted after I tell you guys something you don't want to hear," I said. Without waiting for them to prepare themselves for bad news, I went on. "Benko and I had an affair last summer." I gazed at Nora with sorrow in my heart. "The same time you were doing it with him."

I felt sorry for Nora. Every person she loved had betrayed her: her best friend - me, her idiotic husband, her cruel lover. Worse, her own feelings for a scheming monster had nearly brought her and her family to ruin.

Nora opened her mouth and put her fingers between her teeth. Shivering, she sagged in her chair and bawled. Charlie's eyes blazed.

"This is fucked," he said. "Totally fucked. I should have known it. That settles it. We're all in this shit up to our throats."

"We can't blame ourselves," I said. "He's good. He fooled all of us. He played on our weaknesses and got what he wanted. We just have to be smarter than him from here on in."

Nora asked sadly, vaguely, "I wonder who he's sleeping with now?"

"It better not be you two!" Charlie shouted, standing up. "Tell me. You're not still fucking him are you?"

"Settle down, Charlie," I said, standing to face him. "You two are so emotional about this."

"God dammit, Genevieve. We're gonna get tarred and feathered. I end up in jail, my family's homeless in the middle of winter-you want us to be logical! Wake the fuck up!"

I barked right back. "Go work out your feelings with your therapist." Charlie could be so dense. "Benko is brilliant. Cold. We have to use our heads or we'll all lose everything. Not just money."

Charlie poured himself a drink of whiskey. Nora and I declined his offer.

"I have just as much to lose as you two. Think about it."

We sat staring at each other. Charlie gulped his drink.

"Yeah. All right," he said.

"Let's be rational," Nora said.

I doubted "rational" was possible for either of them. For me, either.

Charlie swilled the rest of his whiskey. "Right. Rational as chickens with a fox in the coop."

Nora's question about who he was sleeping with now gave me an idea. In the short time since I'd unloaded my secret, my mind had cleared. Benko was going to get away with the money. Was he getting away with murder, too? I hoped not. Becky's death had to be an accident, but at that moment, I couldn't put it past Benko.

"That's a good question, Nora," I said. "Who is he sleeping with now? It's got to be somebody. That pole he's got hanging between his legs runs his life. Have you talked to Bernice lately?"

"I'm too ashamed. I'm afraid she'll gossip about me." She sat on the couch, her knees tucked under, holding herself in her thin arms.

I never expected Nora to fall into self-pity. I pushed against her paralysis. "Forget it, Nora. You've got to risk the gossip. Call Bernice right now. She's our best bet to find out any rumors we can use against Benko. Get her to start telling you everything she knows about him. I'm going to listen in on the other phone."

"Me, too," Charlie said.

"You just sit with Nora while she's talking to Bernice." I had to order Charlie around, keep him in the background or he'd try to take charge and end up forgetting what's important. Playing macho man, confronting Benko, Charlie would lose. "I bet we hear some shocking things about our long-dong blackmailer. Your wife needs all the support you can give her. Maybe even some love, if you still can."

Chapter Three

Charlie

EVERYBODY KNOWS ALREADY

The one guy I trusted, the jerk I depended on to keep my factory pumping out product, the sleazebag ends up as the guy who stabs me in the back.

I can't believe I missed it. Gladonov's practically running my business, I'm giving him bonuses, I'm laying on the booze and all the time, he's fucking my wife. Not only that, he was bonging the only woman I ever had a true love affair with, right while she's sleeping with me. If this guy'd had a chance, he'd have jumped Shu Ling. Maybe he did? My trusted second mate.

In my own house, when Genevieve revealed that Gladonov had been doing her, too, I lost faith in everyone.

Being one of the liveliest and most talented women I'd ever met, I'd always thought Genevieve was the most independent and powerful. I liked her as a saleswoman because she was used to getting whatever she wanted. She controlled her environment and the people in it and everybody loved her for it. When she'd told me about her affair with Giordano, I silently congratulated her for her guts.

A single mother living in a god-forsaken little town in the middle of nowhere, working her tail off, driving her car into the ground, Giordano could have meant total freedom for her. If Giordano wanted, he could support her in any way she desired, out of his petty cash, and never notice it. For her sake, I half-hoped she and Giordano would get permanently involved. For our sake, what better way to guarantee long-term tofu sales than to have your sales manager intimate with your best customer?

But when I heard she'd been involved with Gladonov, at the same time Nora was, I said to myself, why does everything come back to the pecker? He's a nothing, a flesh-and-blood wrench, a worker, a factory man, that's all. A big baboon nobody would ever miss if he was gone from the earth.

I'd never felt hate until I found out the truth about him and women. I wanted to kill him. Not only that, I had a duty to get rid of him. His death would solve all of my problems, the company's problems, save all the women in town from Gladonov's berserk prick.

I had three or four options, people who could help me make the contact. Giordano, Meng, a guy I knew from the Philadelphia produce market, or I'd take care of him myself.

Assign him some hazardous job at work, say, repairs to the 440 amp electrical service. Hit him "accidentally" with enough voltage to fry him to a cinder. We'd celebrate the Year of the Rooster by roasting that arrogant cock in his own juice. Or I'd get him under one of our trucks to fix the transmission and somehow knock it off the jack, squashing him like the roach he is.

As thoughts of revenge jetted around my brain, I realized I didn't know enough about the factory machines or trucks to entrap him. Besides, another dead worker in the shop could be the company's funeral. I decided on the straightforward, anonymous way: have him shot.

Under an alias with a New York City address, I would subscribe to a UPS box number in Albany and write to a classified in Global Mercenary that advertised "discrete jobs."

You're going too far, it's crazy, man. Do this, the Chief will have you rotting in the can.

I thought of going online until I realized how easy it would be to trace any emails back to me, if something went wrong. People were already watching me, I thought. Just because of the publicity around Becky's death.

Still, I didn't think anything short of putting Benko out of his misery would save any of us, until Genevieve persuaded Nora to call Bernice.

We all sat in my living room listening to Nora interview the woman like a professional reporter. Even though Nora said nothing about the blackmail, Bernice understood the stakes were high.

She told us everything she knew about Gladonov. He seemed distracted lately, she said. He'd bought a car and spent a lot of time out of town. Bernice claimed she didn't know who Benko was sleeping with now.

Genevieve passed Nora a note to ask the woman if she knew anything else about Becky and Benko.

"I told you about how she couldn't get him off her back?" Bernice replied. "All I know is she told me she was thinking about charging him with sex harassment."

"Bernice, did Becky ever say anything bad about Charlie?"

I almost peed my pants when she brought that up.

"No. She loved Charlie. She'd never had a better boss. Becky would have done anything for Charlie. We all would."

"Are you sure?"

Nora, I thought, stop pushing.

"Why do you think we put up with Gladonov? Charlie must have a good reason for keeping him. We can't figure out why he doesn't get rid of Benko. We don't need him. We can handle any production problems and fix the machines ourselves. Benko treats us like dirt. We want a little decency."

"I'll tell Charlie," Nora said. "I'm sure he's working on it. He'll be glad to know how much you trust him."

Bernice cheered me when I heard her say "Charlie knows already, Nora, I'm sure he knows. We saw how broke up he was when Becky died. How good he treated her kids."

The conversation stopped while Nora read another note from Genevieve.

"Can I ask you one more question?"

"Sure. Anything to help."

"Did Becky ever show you her diary?"

"Diary? No. That's funny. Did she have a diary? She told me everything about herself, so I'm sure I would have known about it. She was a lot like me. We don't like to be alone and we like to talk. In a lot of ways, we were each other's diaries."

Nora thanked Bernice and said that she was so sorry that she'd lost her best friend. She asked her to keep their talk just between themselves.

"It's important for the company's future," she said.

"I get it, Nora. Don't worry. Nobody needs to know everybody's dirty laundry."

"You're such a good friend, Bernice. I'm sure Charlie will do everything he can to get a better plant manager, real soon. Ask everyone to be patient for a little longer."

She's no dumb broad. You oughta be proud.

The way she handled the interview, I'd be lucky to have her run AT's human resources full-time.

After the call, we all felt better, especially me. My people were still with me. I'd just found seventy allies I didn't know I had. The people were my production crew, not Gladonov's, and I'll let them know in spades tomorrow. I'd have plenty of character witnesses if Buhrman ever indicted me. I was sure Bernice's praise made Nora feel proud of me.

"You know," I said, "you were great, both of you. Great questions, great interview. I feel good."

"Don't get too secure, Charlie. Bernice knows you were sleeping with Becky," Genevieve said.

"What? She didn't say that. How do you know?"

"You better learn to listen between the lines. Becky told her everything? They were each other's diaries? Get it? She also said she wouldn't tell anyone and that means Buhrman. If she knows, I bet half the factory knows. We better hope they can all keep their mouths shut."

She held out her glass and I refilled it with *Gato 999*, one of my finest wines. We were drinking up my cellar, but what difference would it make if we didn't get Benko out of our lives.

"It doesn't mean Becky told her anything. She promised me she wouldn't." I glanced at Nora, sad to admit the depths of my deceit. Staring hard at Genevieve, she ignored me.

"Before you pay Benko off, get that diary," Genevieve said. "In fact, you better get him to show it to you before you agree to do anything. You better make sure it exists. If Bernice is right, the diary's just another Gladonov bluff. If it does, he must have made a bunch of copies."

We sat up past midnight talking and finished two bottles of eighty-dollar Cabernet. Our involvement in Becky's death and the paths we had to take to extricate ourselves had evolved into a complex maze of 'ifs' with no clear path out.

Genevieve's opinion was we didn't have proof that there was a diary. If as Bernice believed, Becky had plans to file a suit against Benko, that would be in the diary and he knew it. He'd be implicated in the death by her words.

Really good news was that if we got rid of Gladonov, whether we paid him off or he had an accident, no one in the plant would mind. In fact, they'd probably rally behind me and whatever I wanted to do. It wasn't a case of my honor—this was pure survival.

I tried to "listen between the lines" as Genevieve spoke. I thought I heard her imply that I, or someone, should go ahead and eliminate Gladonov. I was tempted to tell her about the steps I'd already decided on.

Nora suggested paying him off as soon as possible and telling him to stay out of our lives forever.

"We can pay him money," I said, "but if we don't have the diary, I'll never sleep at night".

Genevieve said, "We have to see that diary. If he doesn't have it or she didn't write anything about Charlie, we have a whole new future. Get him to show you a photocopy. At least a couple of pages."

"Yeah," Nora said. "If he really has it and we get it, we know who's in trouble, Charlie or Benko."

"Or both," Gen snapped.

I said, "I'm way ahead of you guys. I asked him for a copy to prove one really existed. He said he'd show one to me for a fifty thousand."

"Maybe it's worth it," Nora said.

"Maybe. Worst case? I give him fifty thousand dollars for blank sheets of paper. He wins big."

"But we'd know for sure."

"Not only that, we all know, he makes a bunch of copies. Then he blackmails us for the rest of our lives," I said.

"It's worth it," Nora said.

"You write him the check from your account, then. I won't." After listening to Bernice, I was sure Gladonov was bluffing and I wasn't about to pay him a cent for anything less than the real thing and proof we had all the copies, paper, on his hard drive, in the cloud. I'd have to have my genius IT guy make sure.

Gen got up out of her chair and knelt down between us, taking one of our hands in each of hers, lacing her fingers into ours and clenching.

"All right. Stop it. You're both right. Let's just get this over with. I'll be the transfer agent," she said. "It scares me to death. I give him the money, he gives me the diary. You be close by, Charlie, in case he tries anything funny. If he does, we'll give him the money and run as fast as we can."

Chapter Four

Genevieve

THE "TOFU-TO-DO" BASH

The night before our "Tofu-To-Do" party at Charlie's house, Jorge Riviera called me from San Francisco. He offered me the job of Vice President of Marketing and Research of his company *New Old World Foods*.

"Our friend Giordano told me I'd be crazy if I didn't hire you," he said. "So, if you want, the job's yours. I personally think this is one of the most exciting jobs in the whole food industry."

"It sounds great," I said.

"You'll have a chance to influence people's eating for years to come." His exuberance inspired me to imagine the new life he offered me. I saw myself zooming all over the world exploring every continent for exotic vegetables, fresh tastes, bringing back old ways of cooking and transforming them into modern menus. I'd photo-document them and publicize them on the internet the way I did the small farm women's lives and foods.

Liam would come with me on our mission to find original foods that humans have eaten for centuries and bring them back to the twenty-first century.

Barely on the ground, I said good night to Riviera and began to let my fantasies about San Francisco fly. I wandered to Liam's room and leaned against his open door, watching him sprawled in sleep, wishing I could wake him to tell him the news. Living in the Bay area had always been a dream of mine and I knew he'd learn to love our new life there.

When I tell my customers I get my inspiration from my son, I mean that I do what I do for his sake, but I also mean his energy and love of life excite me. He'd dive into San Francisco with the same zest he dives into the pool or makes friends wherever he goes.

I'd decided long ago that Liam would go to high school some place other than Clement. He deserved more than football, beer, and cruising the mile-long downtown strip for his adolescent education. With the salary Riviera offered, Liam would still be able to see his father as much as he wanted. My main worry was that when I traveled, I'd have to find somebody I could trust to stay with him.

Only two things stood in the way of a smooth transition to the new life. One: The Year of the Rooster, and that was just about done, as far as I was concerned.

And Benko. More than anything, we had to get Benko out of our lives.

***

Benko the swindler, acting the martyr, sought sympathy from everyone. He claimed he was so busy filling the record sales orders for the Chinese New Year he might not be able to come to the company party. He'd tried to have it postponed until after the New Year, so "the workers would be fresh" he claimed. But Charlie authorized as much overtime for all the workers as they needed to finish work well ahead of the party.

Charlie was sharp about his employees. With big checks and a party coming, the factory workers would be in great moods and they'd be on Charlie's side no matter how our scheming about Benko worked out.

I tried to stay away from Benko completely. When we accidentally saw each other in the factory or near the office copy machine, he always grinned and caressed my whole body with cold eyes. The first time he did it I turned my back.

"Nice bottom you have. Always my hands you can feel them good on it," he whispered.

"Shut up, Benko. Leave me alone."

If he came into the office to talk about some production issue, I kept my door wide open. We'd stopped talking on the phone once Nora told me about how he treated her, but I could feel his twisted mind calculating the best way to handle me as he carried out his plans for extracting the money from Charlie. I felt relieved he'd decided that putting pressure on me wouldn't help him with Charlie.

Once, approaching me in the warehouse and smiling, tossing his long hair like a whip, he said, "I'm available. Always for you, Genevieve. How about tonight?"

The way he snarled my name sent prickles of fear up my neck. After that, for the first time in my life, I locked my door every night.

***

Charlie called me into his office. I sat down on the couch and sighed.

He sighed with me, but held his body rigid in the chair.

"It's a bitch. The worst."

He looked to me for sympathy. I felt for him and Nora, but I couldn't afford to be emotional now. None of us could. We were past that. I nodded and reached over to hold his knee for a couple of seconds. Charlie relaxed a little.

"The Chief started another round of interviews with the staff," he said. "Some crazy idea he learned at a conference. He's asking everyone to submit to hypnosis. The hypnotist is going to take them back in time."

"That'll never hold up in court, Charlie."

"Doesn't matter. He'll scare the hell out of them. Everybody has secrets. He told Bernice everything he learned about the workers would be secret. Irrelevant. Unless of course someone admitted to a crime."

"When's this supposed to happen?" I needed to know so I could get out of town before the Chief had someone put me under.

"Right after the New Year. Buhrman said the shrink who's gonna do the hypnosis said it's more effective when everyone's rested. Less resistance to the hypnosis. Christ. What next?"

"I'm surprised he hasn't called us all in for a lie detector test."

"It gets worse every minute," Charlie said, kicking the coffee table. His precious bowl of lucky soybeans tipped over, spilling the little tan globes across the carpet.

"So much for Soy to the World," I said, making a weak joke. Charlie gripped my hand and stared into my eyes.

After a long silence, he said, "It's not done, Gen. Never give up." I hugged him and eased out the door. Back in my office, I wept.

Charlie, Nora, and I devised a plan to find out if Benko really had the diary. If he did, Nora and I wanted to read it before Charlie gave him any money. In his high anxiety, we doubted he could tell the difference between a forgery and the real thing.

None of us could bear being with Benko alone. Even Charlie had taken to writing him memos and texts for all of their business communications. So our plan was to use the hubbub of the party crowd to protect Nora as she talked to him.

She'd tell him they had to read the diary before they could give him any money. Once they read it, he'd get half the money, as they agreed. The rest would come on March first. He could keep the diary until the final exchange of cash for the book. If he didn't let them read it first, he'd get nothing.

"What if he says 'no'?" Nora asked, her face tighter, revealing lines I'd never seen. She couldn't eat. She hardly drank water.

I said, "Then he's bluffing. Charlie should just fire him."

"Wait a minute," Charlie interjected. "He's way too tricky. I'm afraid even if we get the original diary, he'll blackmail us with a hidden copy whenever he needs cash. We're his freaking pension."

"He'll have to give me his hard drive. And any copies he has around," I said. "You can have your IT guy track down anything in the cloud and get rid of it."

Charlie looked doubtful. "He'll hide a copy somewhere."

"What other choice do we have?" Nora said.

She'd become so pessimistic and dispirited, I wondered if she could handle any conversation with Benko.

When Charlie muttered, "There's other ways ..." I said to myself, Shit. Don't let Charlie try something stupid. He doesn't understand he can't play the violence game with Benko.

"Let's just work our plan, like we do every day in business," I said. "If Benko says 'no,' we'll figure something out."

"Goddam it," Charlie said. "We can't cover all the bases. No matter what we do, it's risky. With enough money, we can handle Benko. I'm worried about the Chief if he ever hears anything from the crew about me and Becky. Jesus."

I picked up their hands again, held them like limp empty gloves. "We'll just have to do something and pray Benko takes the money and runs as far away as he can."

They both gripped my hands, both with weak, hopeless smiles on their faces. Even if our plan worked, we all knew Benko might come back for a second installment. At least by then, I'd be far away, living a new life. Even if I had to change my and Liam's names.

***

On party day, Nora had a migraine and she spent the afternoon in bed. She planned to greet people at the door, but then she would leave with the kids for her mother's where they'd spend the night. The closer party time came, the worse her head ached. Charlie drove her and the children to her mother's an hour before the first guests arrived.

I steeled myself to play Nora's role in the negotiation with Benko. Midway through the evening, when the noise level began to rise with the hard-driving dance music and high-pitched talk, I approached Benko, keeping my fear hidden behind an amiable face. He'd spent most of the evening sitting alone next to the piano, sipping from a half-concealed flask.

"Did you like the Dragon Stew?" I said.

The piece de resistance of my new recipes was a spicy tofu and seafood dish that was meant to fill you with euphoria. By the happy faces of everyone else in the room, I thought the recipe had worked.

"Didn't try it yet. My own 'Dragon Blood' I like very much," he said, pointing to the flask in his paw.

"By the way," he continued, "congratulations on selling so much tofu. Only you, in all the world, beautiful woman. You convince supermarket guys to buy so much." He smiled. "Of course, to get man to do whatever you want, you know how. I know." He grinned. He lowered his voice and leaned toward me. "Your victim any time. Just say."

Tempted to reply to his banter, I inhaled instead, and smiled warmly. "Benko, I know everything about you. I know you're a ten-faced hypocrite. You were never my victim. You're the one who has victims."

I felt half the people in the room watching us, turning their heads, glancing, turning away, and glancing over again. The buzz of talk diminished. Charlie stood behind the bar with his back turned, laughing loudly and clapping one of the men on the back. I turned my back to the party and whispered.

"Nora's sick, Benko. She asked me to talk with you." He nodded, still smiling, still playing along for the audience. "She said they'll give you the money you want tomorrow but you have to show them the diary first and let them read it." He stopped smiling and glanced toward Charlie. "Then if everything's cool, you'll get the rest on schedule. If not, too bad."

He finished the half-glass of vodka he'd held buried in his paw. "Thank you so much, sales woman." He stood up, shoving his face close to mine, and mumbled so quietly only I could have heard him. "I have enjoyed our talk. Immensely like my heart enjoys you. Almost like I have enjoyed your mouth around the 'Amazing Russian Sausage.'"

I turned my head away from his septic breath, but he pinched my chin in his hand and turned it back, pulling me even closer.

Smiling as if he were telling a happy secret to a good friend, he groaned into my ear. "Same pleasure perhaps you can offer me again? Before I hand over diary. Why don't you check your book so we can arrange time. You can always find me in factory."

Fine drops of his spittle landed on my cheek. I expected vile comments, but he nauseated me to my toes.

"Excuse me," he said, still smiling, dropping my chin and turning around toward the bottle. "King Tofu I must speak with himself." His fist seized the vodka and he meandered through the crowd calling cheerfully, "Boss. Boss."

Charlie spotted him and tilted his head toward me, mimicking a question.

I raised my eyebrows and mouthed "I tried."

Benko and Charlie disappeared out the back door. While I waited, I stirred the remaining Dragon Stew. Bernice, a petite brunette wearing an iridescent blue body stocking and a white cashmere vest, worked her way toward me through the munchers at the counter.

"Benko is so hard to resist," she said as she ladled some stew into a bowl, "even if he is evil." She watched my face, holding my eyes in a long, knowledgeable stare. "I really like these scallops," she said casually, breaking the spell. "They taste so fresh."

I filled a small bowl and waited for her to go on. I had nothing to hide from Bernice. She was our secret ally.

"I can't talk with my mouth full," she said. "I wish I could cook like you, Genevieve."

"I'm coming out with a cookbook. I'll give you a copy," I said, keeping the double talk going.

"Oh. I always wanted to know how to make what I fix taste the way I bet you do." She moved closer to me, as if she wanted to speak in secret.

"It's easy." I went on. "You can make it taste like anything. That's how I sell it."

"People like your recipes. I never saw so many tofus fly out that factory as this year. Good overtime for all of us. We owe you."

"No. I'm just doing what I'm hired for."

"Ain't we all," Bernice said. She pulled me by the arm into the empty kitchen. "When are you going out of town again?"

"Soon. Why?"

"I'm just glad things are slowing down in the plant," Bernice said, running water from the sink spigot into her glass. "It's been awfully crazy in there lately. Some of the guys were worried about one of the grinders. They think Gladonov needs to put some time in on it. There's some real necessary work they've got to do. In a couple of days, then ... you're out of town?"

"Always on the road," I said.

"Everything will be all right, Genevieve." She smiled, caressed my cheek with her callused little hand, and said, "Have a good trip. I'll see you when you get back."

Before I could say anything, she slipped away and disappeared into the living room, letting a burst of music pound into the kitchen before the door swung shut behind her, leaving me alone with the dulled thud of percussion.

What was that all about?

If she and the other workers were planning to take Benko into their own hands, I'd better warn her. I doubted any of the factory workers were clever enough to corner him. Not only that, if he saw them coming, he'd incite someone to attack so he could hurt them, badly, claim self-defense, and somehow, find himself free and set up for life by lawyers and American Tofu's insurance company. Bernice and the crew deserved a warning. I pushed my way back into the party, searching for Bernice just as Charlie came in from outside, alone.

Jovial, carefree, he hugged half a dozen men and women as he made his way toward me. He reeled into my side, lodged a finger in my belt, whirled me around, and gave me a huge squeeze. Charlie and I were sometimes affectionate at work, so nobody paid any attention to us. I thought he'd drunk way too much for a company party with the liability he could have.

He held me as he whispered, "It's all set. We'll know in the morning." He kissed me vertically, half on the lips, half on my chin, and pirouetted away.

Momentarily relieved but doubtful, I snagged his collar and hauled him back. "What do you mean?"

"I'll tell you later. Don't worry. It's fine. I'm not drunk. I'm saving that for tomorrow night. Let me go. I gotta show everybody a good time. We meet Gladonov at his place at five thirty in the morning."

Charlie wove his way from person to person until he staggered onto the dance floor. I watched from the door for a while before one of the young warehousemen asked me to dance. We bounced around the room, bumping into everyone we passed, all in momentary release from our problems, whatever they were.

Bernice hurtled by me and I slipped away from my partner and angled myself in front of her. With her eyes half-closed, she was working hard against the blasting beat of some reggae star. I gripped her shoulders and put my mouth against her ear. "Don't try anything with Benko. He's dangerous."

She grinned and tickled my ribs with both her hands and whirled away. I watched her snuggle into a man's arms and grind her pelvis against him. I watched all the revelers, cutting loose in the boss's house. Ah, Chinese New Year's Eve. East meets West in rural New York and anything goes. For the rest of the party, American Tofu crammed itself into Charlie's living room to jerk and sweat and whoop out the old year and call in its own special New Year.

Charlie avoided me for the rest of the party, except to thank me when I came to say good-bye just before midnight. "Leaving so early?" He tried to slur but I could tell he was acting.

"You're picking me up before dawn and Liam has a swim meet tomorrow night. His mom needs sleep so she can cheer really loud after working a long day."

"Thanks for everything, Genevieve," Charlie said, walking me to the door. "I mean everything. The stew, taking Nora's place. The sales. The sales." He started to wax drunkenly rhapsodic. "If you hadn't sold so much, we'd never have had this party."

"We all did it, Charlie. Now," I said, gently circling my arm around his shoulder and pulling him close for a confidential chat, "what deal did you make with Benko?"

"The money for the diary. Like we said."

"You told him, first the book, then some money, right?"

"Well, I have to give him some of the money first but if he doesn't show me the diary, he won't get the rest." Charlie puckered his lips in a show of determination.

"When will you see the diary?"

"I'm leaving the money—."

I interrupted. "You're leaving the money? How much? Will you see the diary or just leave the money?"

"Twenty-five thousand," Charlie said.

"*Only* twenty-five?"

"It's all I'm willing to give him. "

"Why give him anything without the diary?"

"I didn't have a choice."

I kept shaking my head.

"Don't worry," he said. "It's only money. Think of it as a sales deal. Give a little, get a lot. We'll know soon if he has the diary or not." His cheeks flattened and he sobered up. "Nora and I are together on this. I'll pick you up at five fifteen," he said. "Be ready."

"Just don't oversleep."

"Don't worry. This is the last appointment I'd miss," he said, and then he kissed me, leaving a burning whiskey smudge on my cheek.

At midnight, our three Tibetan Buddhist workers lit a bundle of firecrackers and shot off bottle rocket rainbows and fountains of sparks. They showered across the sky then vanished like stars crossing the moonless February night.

As we watched and cheered the fireworks from the front porch, the freezing night air seeped into our sweaty clothes. Huddled together, tangled in tribal palhood, we sought warmth in each other's folds and angles.

One of the women crooned a caricature rendition of 'Soy to the World' anthem until everyone joined in. Soon, a boisterous choir harmonized to the Christmas melody.

Soy to the World, the beans have come.
Let earth receive her seed.
Let e-ver-y hear-ar-arth prepare its pots and pans
For tofu and tempeh
For soymilk and agé
Let heaven and nature sing Let A T and nature sing
Heaven and heaven and American Tofu sing

Then, party energy transported the song into howling cheers of uninhibited release and I slipped down the side porch stairs to my car.

Exhausted from the tension, the cooking, the party, dreading what I'd have to go through with Charlie and Benko in the morning, I climbed into my car. I heard Charlie bellowing "Happy New Year" to the workers as they wobbled around his wide Victorian porch. If the deal he'd made with Benko didn't work out, Charlie would have to change his anthem and everyone at the plant would be singing "Oy to the World."

As I pulled out of the driveway into the street, the employee chorus gathered for another chorus of "Soy to the World." A police cruiser pulled up and double-parked. I stopped to watch. The Chief got out and walked to the porch with a smile on his face. The employee chorus faltered for a minute then, when Charlie waved his arms like a conductor, they burst into the refrain one more time.

Buhrman walked up the porch steps, wagging his head back and forth. Charlie greeted him in the same effusive spirit he'd displayed all night.

He and Buhrman talked for a minute then Charlie turned to the crew. He shouted, "Now, that's a party, folks. When the Chief himself comes out to complain, you know it's a party." Charlie lowered his voice and semi-slurred. "Chief was wondering how all you happy people were getting home tonight. Told him don't worry. Didn't he know about the shuttles?"

Like a tipsy magician, Charlie swung his arm around toward the street. A caravan of a dozen vans and taxis crawled down the street toward his house. Charlie stepped onto the sidewalk and waved. In unison, lights flashed and the cars slowed down. Charlie bowed to the singers on the porch.

"Step right up, folks," he said. "Door to door delivery for the greatest tofu makers in the world."

I watched the laughing crew stumble toward the vans' open doors as I drove off in the opposite direction.

After I'd locked my apartment door behind me, I got a glass of water and went into the living room to sit and relax a minute before I dropped into bed.

"Hello, Genevieve."

Benko's voice rumbled out of the shadows. I leapt out of the chair and switched on the floor lamp. He sat a few feet away, on the couch, leaning back with his legs up, resting on the coffee table. He propped a half-empty bottle of vodka on his lap, holding it like a tumbler between his massive folded hands.

"Get out!" I growled at him, controlling my voice so I wouldn't wake Liam up. "Get out!" I hissed. "Right now! I'm calling the cops."

"Don't. It's not worth it," he said. "Take it easy. I'm your friend."

"Benko. You're a bastard. You're nobody's friend. You're drunk." I started for the phone. As if in slow motion, he glided off the couch and grabbed me by my belt. I gasped and swung my arm around to hit him.

He laughed and pushed me onto the couch. "Relax. Easy as a baby bottom. I'm not hurting you. Everything Charlie and I worked out." He sipped the vodka, then tilted the bottle toward me.

I glowered at him.

He shrugged and pulled at the bottle again. "It's win-win, Genevieve." His demon eyes gleamed.

"What do you want?"

"That's it. You know," he said, grinning, his words dripping from his mouth in bitter clusters. "You want it, too. Admit it. Let yourself. Smell it, sweet flower smell. Your breath. At the party we talked so nice."

"I'm giving you one minute then I'm screaming."

"Wake up Liam? He needs sleep. He has swim meet tomorrow?" His voice resonated between real menace and fake concern. I had to get him out, fast.

"One last time, Genevieve. Unforgettable one more time. Nobody will know. I go away and you remember me."

I glared. I wanted to try to cajole him but I couldn't control my reaction. Panic was climbing my back. Breathing deep, hard, I readied myself to launch the most blood-curdling yell I could.

"My beautiful long-haired redhead. You're so tall and fine. Perfect hourglass shape. All men want that. Liam's fine. A good looking boy. Smart. Friendly, like his mom. He's safe. His bedroom door is shut. He sleeps deep, I know. Him nothing bothers."

I screamed. His hand came down on my face like a hard pillow. I kicked and bit at his fingers and clawed at his face. He held me easily, pinning me down but letting me breathe. He smiled almost wistfully. His calm horrified me.

"Liam's fine," he said again. "Be quiet? I'll show you."

I nodded. He raised me, and with his palm loosely covering the lower half of my face, he walked me to Liam's room. Cracking the door, he let the living room light shine on Liam's bed. My son lay on his back, his arms and legs splayed out of his covers, his face all dreamy.

Relieved, I sagged against Benko, but immediately bolted up straight as I felt his pelvis slide and rub against my hip.

He closed the door quietly and spun me back toward the living room. "Will you be quiet if I let go?"

I nodded my head vigorously, scraping my nose against his callused fingers.

We sat down on the couch, side by side. He retrieved his bottle and gulped. I couldn't move or say a thing.

"I'm sad, tofu queen," he slurred. "Beautiful loving, eating together. My sausage once upon a time you never got full. You don't want me now. Makes me sad."

"Benko, please go. If you go now, I won't say anything to anyone."

"It's problem like everything now. All a problem. I hoped we could tell everyone we love each other how much you can't count. Like silo of full of beans." He snorted and coughed. "Maybe we marry? Liam likes me. You know." His head dropped onto his chest. He seemed to fall asleep. "You could have saved me," he mumbled.

"Too late. Way too much has happened."

Adrenaline poured through my body and mind. How could I convince him to go? He could control me physically, so the only power I had was words.

He straightened up and moved his face close to mine. His vodka breath stank. "Too late. Yes. The light. Too bright."

He leaned away and reached up, easing the table lamp's rheostat down until we sat in shadow. The room was so hushed I heard the second hand from my armoire clock skidding click by click into the past. Benko's body shuddered and slumped, his head fell back onto the couch and the bottle slipped from his hand. I let it fall and watched vodka dribble out onto my carpet. A snort erupted from his nostrils.

Afraid to disturb him, I sat for a long time, exhausted from our encounters already that night. I extricated myself slowly, hoping I could get to Liam and escape with him before Benko startled awake. I began to stand up and his arm clutched mine and I fell back. Rigid, I banged into his side.

"See," he said, "how our bodies fit so nice? Bolt and nut in factory we say."

He let me go and bent over to pick up his bottle. He poured the dregs into his mouth and mumbled, "Now I'm going. See how nice I am?"

He lurched to his feet. "All worked out. His bargain if Charlie keeps, win-win. Happy?"

If he was leaving, my best strategy was to stay quiet. He went to the kitchen sink and turned on the tap. Returning to the living room twilight with a glass of water, he signaled for me to stand up. "I'm not happy why? You know?" His voice cracked.

He drank and slammed the half-full glass onto the floor. The carpet's thick nap softened the fall and the glass bounced, unbroken. "This piss tastes water!"

I kept myself still as a rabbit caught in headlights. Totally at the mercy of whatever alcoholic mood possessed him, I was afraid that any response now would provoke his rage, but his melancholy calm returned.

"No. No. Truth? I miss you." He stumbled around the room, bumping into chairs, finally bracing his back against the wall. "One time sausage you couldn't keep hands off, yes? Now lost." He laughed. "Not even one more time. Tonight no chance. That's problem with vodka. After two liters, all you do is sleep. Used to take four. I'm getting old."

"Why don't you go home and sleep it off."

"I came to say good-bye."

"All right." I said. "Let's good-bye on the porch," I said, tugging at his sleeve. "You need some fresh air."

"I need more something. You," he said, putting his palm on my breast.

I winced and stepped back and he laughed again.

"Give me something to remember."

Whatever I could give him to get him out the door was fine with me.

"What about this necklace?" I said, starting to unfasten the clasp. "It's gold and it has a yin yang symbol. You can remember me and tofu."

"You keep your gold. I want something about you. More deep." I waited. His eyes widened as an idea came to him. "What color underpants tonight?"

"I don't know," I said. "I didn't notice when I put them on. Blue, I think."

"Let's see," he growled.

I lifted my crimson and emerald Chinese party skirt up as modestly as I could.

"God," he said.

"Yeah, blue," I said, dropping my dress.

"Blue sky. Like I feel flying with you. Let me have them."

"Will you leave?" I said, bargaining.

"Maybe. Yes. Give me. I'll go."

I started to slip out the underpants but he stopped me.

"Let me."

He sagged to the floor and fell against my knees. He straightened himself and ducked under the hem of my skirt. I kept my eyes closed as his whiskered jaws scraped the flesh on the inside of both my thighs. Leaning his head against my knees, he reached one hand up behind me under my skirt and yanked my pants down halfway. He jerked his head back and pushed them down to my ankles. I stood rigid, my thighs clamped together.

"Help Gen. Gen, you have to."

I lifted one leg to step out of the pants. He pulled them out from under my shoe and jammed his head between my legs.

"Be nice," he muttered.

I wanted to slam my knee into his face, but I resisted and clenched my jaw as his warm tongue slid up my thigh. His two hands clutched my naked bottom and he pulled my pelvis into his face. His hot breath sent a flutter of pleasure into my stomach and then he began to lap at my clitoris. He probed and pushed and nibbled. He began to lick at my labia, sticking his tongue into me as far as he could.

I slapped at his head through my skirt. I clenched my thighs and he squeezed me tighter. With one hand, I reached around to try to peel his fingers off my bottom, but he'd sunk them into me so deep I couldn't pry them out.

With both hands, I hammered my palms onto the top of his head through my skirt. He didn't respond. I started to topple back so I opened my legs to get a foothold and regain my balance. He rammed his head into me and began vibrating his face back and forth, like a mechanical loofa sponge scraping my thighs and my labia.

I pounded and pushed his head. I pushed so hard, the waistband of my skirt tore and I slipped and fell backwards. My neck banged against the arm of the couch and he fell on top, pinning me. He lay across the lower half of my body, his head wrapped like a turban in my Chinese skirt, snoring.

My labia burned. Agony racked my head when I moved it but I had to get up. I wiggled and slithered out from under him. I rolled him over and began to creep toward Liam. I stopped to pick up the phone.

Benko's huge wrist grabbed me by the ankle.

"Don't go."

I struck at him with the phone, but he caught my arm.

"Be nice, Gen. I just want to show you love."

"I hate you. Get out."

"I'm drunk," he said, grunting. "We'd have great time." He held on to my arm and pulled himself up.

I backed away, but he pulled me toward him. His eyes closed and he fell against me again, drooping his head across my shoulder. I waited, wanting to let him fall into a deep sleep before I shoved him away and ran. I waited too long.

He raised his head, bringing his eyes to within a few inch-es of mine. "Good. You're still here." He blinked, struggling to stay awake. He gripped my forearm so tightly, my fingers went numb.

"I'm going now," he said. "You don't want me. I'm going." Without letting my hand go, he pointed to the floor. "Here. Pick up."

I saw my underpants hanging from the tip of a rocker arm on the rocking chair. I bent over and picked them up, deposit-ing them on his broad palm. Slowly, he raised them to his face and inhaled deeply. He shivered and gasped like a dog splashed with cold water.

Dropping my arm, he grabbed me around the waist and bent into me. Slobbering a kiss on my face, he snickered.

"I kiss real good. Right? Nora taught American kissing. I like fucking her, but you. Over all them I take you."

He let me go and taking time to stuff the pants into his jacket pocket, he jerked open the door and backed out. His heel snagged the doormat and he stumbled to his knees. Coughing into his fist, he picked himself up and hobbled off the porch into the night.

I slammed and locked the door and shoved a chair under the handle. I ran to the back door, jamming another chair against it. I checked Liam again, examining every window lock, and went to the phone.

I called the police and told them I'd heard strange noises outside and would they send a patrol car into the neighbor-hood? I'd heard them before, I said. I was afraid.

I sat with the lights on, watching and listening. I prayed I'd seen the last of Benko for the night, but unless he'd passed out from drinking, I couldn't count on his staying away. After the third approach by the police cruiser, I lay down on the couch. I lay there with my eyes and ears wide open until I heard a car pull into the driveway.

I picked up the phone and went to the window and pulling the drapes apart, I peeked out. Freezing rain had smeared a coat of ice on everything. With his arms flung out for balance, Charlie worked his way up my ice-crusted sidewalk. He slipped from side to side, sliding along like a kid skating across a pond.

Chapter Five

Charlie

BECKY'S DIARY

deep as midnight, wet
to my bones, i sink,
dive down, rise on swelling waves

The morning after the Year of the Rooster party, I showed up right on schedule at Benko's house. Genevieve waited for me outside in my old nondescript Honda. I parked down the block, so she could watch the door from a fairly safe place.

If something strange happened, she'd call the police right away. If I came out and Benko didn't, everything was fine. If he came out and I didn't follow him within two minutes, she'd call the police.

"The whole thing should take five minutes. Keep the car running."

"I should come with you. He's probably drunk. When I came home last night, he was waiting for me. Drunk. He tried to rape me but he couldn't he was so lit."

"Jesus. Did you call the cops?"

"Yes. But I didn't say his name. Just I was scared somebody was stalking me."

"Good. He'll be inside then. Whatever you do, don't come inside," I said, counting on my own booze bravado to compensate for the bravery I'd left back in my bedroom.

I'd had a couple of shots of whiskey to chase away a bloom-
ing hangover. I barely slept all night and I'd had three cups of
coffee already so I wasn't worried the whiskey would make me
too drunk to make the deal. I had ten thousand dollars in cash
and a twenty-five thousand dollar bank money order. First, I'd
give him the ten thousand in cash, show him the money order,
and after I read the diary, I'd make it out to him. He'd get the
rest later, when he handed over the book and any copies. And I
was sure I had everything.

The money was a lot less than he wanted, but I gambled
on his desperation to get out of town. Tried to rape Genevieve?
He'd lost any edge he had over me.

His little house was set back from the road like most of the
homes in the neighborhood. I scuffed up the slick driveway and
knocked on his side door.

He growled, "Come. Come." He sounded impatient.

I walked into the dingy kitchen. The ceiling hung down less
than a foot over my head and he'd drawn the shades down over
the two small windows beside the sink. A low-wattage bulb
glowed over a sink piled with pans and dishes. Benko sat at a
round table in the middle of the room with a half-full amber
glass in his big paw. His head bobbed and his eyes glazed.

I blurted out, "Where's the diary? I have the money."

Pie-eyed as I'd ever seen anyone, Gladonov grinned and
raised the glass to me. "Come in. Sit down. Time to talk." His
chin tilted down and he yanked it back. He smiled at me again.
"I don't bite."

"Gladonov, I came to do business, not to argue with a drunk
criminal about what belongs to me."

"Insult get you nowhere." He offered me a glass.

"I don't get drunk at sunrise, my friend. I don't need to be
drunk to get through the day." Gladonov's attempt to distract
me from our business raised my suspicions even further that I'd
leave empty-handed, because he had nothing. A frisson of pleasure rolled up my back: He was bluffing about the diary.

"You know, Mr. Big Man, you got one thing I want: money. You can have Nora."

The son of a bitch. "Leave Nora out of this, asshole. I worked my ass off for the money you're robbing."

"You worked? You slave driver. You're a good one, Charlie. Everybody thinks: Charlie honest and kind. I know you crock of shit."

"Benko, let's get this over with. Cut the lecture and give me the book. If you have it." My next move would be to turn around and head for the door.

"You're no better than anybody, Greer. You got money, that's all." He swallowed half the whiskey remaining in his glass, coughing a little. "Inherited from the wife? Good luck, eh? Now who's got the wife?" He laughed, coughing and hacking.

"Leave the wife out of it, I said. You fucked her. So what? You sneak around my back and fuck my wife. It means nothing in all this except you're a traitor. I did everything for you and all you want is to fuck the Greers."

He hefted himself up from the table and stumbled over to me. "Let's see cash."

His sour boozy breath nearly blew me over. Bloodshot eyes squinted out of his puffy face the color of a raw scab. He spread his legs to balance himself and leaning back, he clutched the table.

"Let's see the diary first. You know the condition."

"Fuck with me?"

He picked up a wrench from the table and gripped it hard. The veins in his arms bulged. His face reddened.

I opened my briefcase and pointed to the money.

He indicated that I should lay it on the table. "Count it," he said.

I counted out the bills, piling up ten stacks of ten hundreds on the floor of my open briefcase, and showed him the check, gritting my teeth to keep from chattering. "This is yours, too. Let me read the diary and I'll sign it over to you."

"Money order? Idiot. You don't have to sign it. All I do is write 'Tofu King Charles Greer.' Bank says 'Benko, take money.'" He laughed, grunting like a dog.

I backed away from the briefcase with the money order in my hand. "Show me the diary, Gladonov. Then you'll get the check."

"You crazy fuckin'. I want the money, I take it." He wagged his head back and forth, incredulous at my stupidity.

Without the booze in my gut driving out all my common sense, I'd drop the briefcase and split, but I stood glued to the floor, focused on taking the diary with me.

Without turning around, Benko reached behind his back to retrieve a half-full whiskey bottle. "Here, boss. Last chance. Drink with me. Celebrate. Laphroig. You bought it."

"I won't drink with you."

He had the wrench, he was crazy, I knew he'd take all the money as soon as he wanted but I had nothing to lose and I doubted he'd try to kill me. He might hurt me a little, but he was really only a con man who couldn't get it up any more.

Gladonov wagged the wrench up and down, as easy as shaking a fever thermometer. Watching my reaction, he swallowed the rest of his whiskey. "Where's all the money? I said fifty thousand right now. Fifty," he said in clear, simple American English. "Where is it? Don't make me mad."

"I told you, Benko. Give me the diary, I'll give you the whole hundred."

Considering his next move, he poured himself another glass of Laphroig and toasting me, he said, "Okay, boss. Hundred fifty, right?"

He wavered between amiable cooperation and angry threat. He wasn't sure whether I had all the money or not. We both had to keep our options open until we had a little more information about who had what to give.

"Diary, sure. I'll get it for you. Like always, no problem. You're the big boss. Honest Charlie. You give me fifty now. Hundred this afternoon."

He shuffled into the living room and fumbled in one of the stuffed chairs. When he came back holding a book, my knees wobbled.

She must have bought it in a supermarket. A mottled green-and-white school notebook lay across his hand like the Book of Revelations. I reached for it.

He pulled it back. "Wait. My fifty. Then you get the book."

"Jesus, Benko. I told you. Here's twenty-five now and the rest soon as I can. I can't have it for three weeks. We gotta wait for the customers to pay us."

"Shit tough. I'm in the air today. Gone. With all my money. I knew Charlie Greer would try to fuck me, like you did poor Becky." "Shut up, Gladonov. Take the thirty-five and get out."

"I need one more thing, Mister Tofu King."

"I don't have any more money. Ten dollars maybe." I reached into my pocket and eased out my wallet. "Here's twenty one dollars, all I have. Now give it to me."

He slapped the bills away. "You got something more. Your car." "My car?"

"LX. TofuMobile. Sixty, seventy thousand you paid? I'll take LX."

"You'll never get away with my car."

"Give me keys."

I backed away.

He shrugged. "No problem. Let's make it easy. Here. Read diary. Then you give me keys. You'll get down on your knees, beg me, take the keys, Benko. You give me whatever I want now. How about blowjob for book? You ask me, 'Take my wife, take anything.' Soon as I hand over Becky diary, its winwin. One hundred fifty, plus one car. Like I say, fair deal."

I grabbed the diary from his outstretched hand and opened it. "Sure. I'll read. If it's real, you get the keys. First I read the diary."

"Smart man." Benko slouched in his chair and slugged more scotch.

The diary entries were printed in round, childish letters. I'd never seen Becky's handwriting, but it could have been hers. The cover was scuffed, but the most terrifying and telling thing was its smell—Forest Rose, the perfume she always wore, and I always had to wash off before I came home.

"It's not hers. You bought this and wrote in it. I'm not giving you any thing."

Gladonov seemed to sober up. "No," he glared. "It's hers. No way I wrote it. You want the Chief to get it? That's all she wrote for Mister Tofu King."

I sat down at the table and opened the next page. Benko filled his glass and sat down across from me to watch.

"You don't think she wrote it? I guarantee it's hers."

"Your guarantee's worth a piece of used toilet paper."

He laughed.

Of course the diary was Becky's. As I smelled the perfume rising from the pages, her face appeared out of the gloom, smiling at me with those mischievous blue eyes. I listened, expecting her to crack a joke or giggle. She didn't, and her image faded and my eyes fell on the book. I forced myself to open it, and read.

Becky had written several notes on each page, dating each one and pasting a red heart beside several entries. She'd told me she stuck little heart stickers on anything she loved. I'd seen them on her kids' room door, on photos of her family and friends, on the dash of her car. She'd even tagged my bare chest with one. It was Becky's all right.

I squinted at the first page.

> *apr 7 trying out a diary—my sister got one—said she learned so much about herself reading what she wrote—every night I'm supposed to write something—it's amazing she said—lets see how it goes*

> *apr 8 Bernie told me she has crush on new production manager—the Russian—good looking for sure—I told her be careful*

    apr 14 Ralph called—drunk—I wasn't in mood for arguing—that's what always happens with him—i'm no good at writing—only wrote grocery lists and kids notes since high school

I thumbed ahead and started at what I read.

    may 20 Charlie looked at me again—I know what he's thinking—Me too—I like the way he walks—not much of a butt but he has long legs and the way his thighs bulge a little give me shivers—

    may 21 I told Bernie if Charlie ever came on to me I didn't know what to do—she said he's married—but what if he came on to me I said—I dont' know—play it by ear—He's cute she said he is cute—we've been looking at each other a lot—everybody's excited about being in the tofu movie—we're supposed to bring the kids in tomorrow—we came up with the idea at lunch one day to show AT as a family company

I flipped forward to the night we made love for the first time. No entry then, but two days later, she sealed my fate.

    jun 21 great company party other nite—so good I'm still messed up—not by beer or weed—Charlie—Charlie Greer the boss—the owner of the company and me—he brought me home & the kids weren't here & we fucked did it made beautiful love in my bed—he's sweet—I love his laugh—he never smoked hash before!—he said I don't want any bath salts or meth—I said don't be silly—I hate meth or stuff that makes you addict—he said ok I trust you—when he said that it made me shiver—trust   love!!!—I've never had a man who was so careful to make sure

I was happy and boy did he make me cum—about ten times!!!! at least !!!!—too bad he's married but o well—he didn't just fuck me, that's for sure!

The diary had to be real. Gladonov couldn't concoct this whole thing. The date of our lovemaking was too accurate. Why did Bernice say Becky didn't keep a diary? Maybe she never told Bernice about us. I hope not. Maybe nobody else knows. I shouldn't have told Nora and Gen.

"Good reading, Boss? Romance story, all women love romance," he mumbled. "You know, I'm best fuck they all had. Me, my giant prick. Nora must have told you about it. We did it five times a night. She wears me out. 'Benko's magic wand,' she calls it."

"Shut up, asshole. I don't care who you fucked or how big your flabby dick is."

"Genevieve. Oh her. I love her. I can't count the times she came every time I did her. Never had better piece in my life."

His narcissism showed me a weak spot. "Tell you what, Benko. This might be the real thing."

"S'real," he slurred. "I found it af' she died. Before cops came. Under bed. Idiot cops."

His stared at me cock-eyed as only a drunk can, then his head swung toward the side of the room across from the sink. His monitor and keyboard sat on a low table, propped up on an empty plastic shipping crate. The production office scanner perched on top of the monitor.

"You brought the scanner home?" I knew why.

He grinned but didn't reply. I understood immediately that my worst fear might come true: even if he sold me the book and disappeared, who knows who he emailed a copy of the diary to?

So far, I could explain the diary entry as her fantasy. After all, when I came home that night, Nora was sound asleep and I'd told her that I was home by midnight, a few minutes after I dropped off our inebriated employees at their homes.

I paged ahead in the diary and stopped at an early July entry.

jul 12 Benko stopped me in the locker room—he asked me to have coffee & I said no—Then he said he wanted to show me something—Come to his house—I said no—I told him not to but he came to mine—unzipped his pants—he has the biggest henry—we did it—he didn't come & neither did I—won't tell Bernie about him—she'd get furious—she already knows about Charlie—she thinks I should play my cards and not be an idiot—that means sleep with Charlie and wait for him to get a divorce—sure

july 25 I told Benko to leave me alone—I'm gonna file a sex hairassment case if he keeps coming on—

jly 31 I did it with Benko once more—last time—even if I like it, next time he tries, It's LAWYER time—I told Bernie and she knows a good one—only thing is if Charlie found out, I'm sure he'd never see me again—Charlie's why I don't go to the lawyer right now—he'd dump me and what else? he'd have to fire me and Benko—then what?

I raised my eyes. Gladonov's chin bobbed against his chest. He snorted a few times as if he were in a deep sleep.

"She hated you, Gladonov. She was gonna file a sexual harassment suit. She didn't because she was afraid I'd find out."

His head down, he muttered, "Fucked her good. Gave her good job. Her kids like me. Not like you, big boss. Money. She fucked your money."

I had what I needed now. I should have left but I couldn't stop reading. I flipped ahead to the last entry halfway through the book.

aug 19 guess what?—I can't believe it—I'm P-G!—I hope it's Charlie's—Bernie says get rid of it—I'll wait and see how I feel in a few weeks—who knows, maybe if it's

Charlie's, me and him will get married—he's almost good as divorced

I knew it. She acted so strange when we did it the night before she died. A loopy grin curling her lips, she squirmed when she whispered, "Don't use a rubber tonight, Charlie. Anything that's gonna happen already did. We don't have to worry."

My denial firewall kicked in and I didn't go there. Not about to deal with anything scary, so I used the rubber. I'm sure I used a rubber that first night, too. I had to. Why didn't she tell me that night. Oh, I get it. That's it: It was going to be her hobbit's birthday present.

aug 22 Bernie says maybe the baby is Benko's—I took a PG test but it can't say how old baby is—could be his—shit—I'm gonna have to get rid of it—unless Charlie wants to keep it

aug 26 thinking seriously about this. If Charlie and me get married, I don't care if his wife gets half his money—by law, that's all she gets—I love him—does he love me???? I think so. He said it once and the way he holds me is definitely more than just sex.

aug 31 birthday party tonight—Bar B Q for the Big 3-0— Charlie's coming over after!—I told everybody the party's over at 9—I need time to get ready for work—sober up :-) Charlie has a present for me & do I have present for him—What's he gonna say when he hears I'm P-G???—I'm sure it's his baby—it's gotta be—I want to keep it—anyway— Happy Birthday to me!

That's it. This diary's going into the furnace, or I'm going to hell in a handbasket. I stuffed the book into my briefcase and stared hard at Benko. He snored. If he wasn't deep asleep, he seemed so drowsy I thought I could escape with it before he managed to get out the door.

Hurry up. Take the book and run. Get going. He might have a gun.

In case he heard me leaving. I wanted something to throw at him, to slow him down. I saw the whiskey bottle on the counter. I glanced at Gladonov as he snorted again and raised his head. His eyes were so glazed, I didn't know if he could focus, but he started to get up. I had to take a chance. I stood up and turned around, taking two quick steps to the counter and reached for the bottle. I clutched it by the neck and tensed to turn and aim it.

I swung around with the bottle in my raised arm in case he'd heard me. He had. Benko stood up and charged around the table, lifting his wrench. I tipped the briefcase over in front of him, spilling the bills and the diary onto the floor. He kicked it aside and, before I could hit him, he lashed at me, just missing my head. I smelled the grease on the wrench as it whooshed past my nose.

He regained his balance and stood there, the wrench raised behind his head. "You killed her, Charlie. I know."

"You don't know shit, Benko."

"You," he mumbled and the wrench drooped a little, then he woke up, sober as I'd ever seen him. "You fucker Charlie. You dumped Becky in my bean tank so cops think I did it. You didn't want that little baby, did you?" He sniggered. "She had my baby. She wants you, *Mister Money King*, to marry her. Not me."

He spit at me. Missed.

"You don't know shit. I slipped and she fell."

Goddam it. What am I saying?

"I had nothing to do with it." I was breathing hard. "It wasn't my baby. Was it yours? You raped her and knocked her up. Don't try to blame me for anything."

Benko's nostrils flared and his lips bulged, then his head rolled back.

He's drunk as a skunk. Do what you want with this piece of junk.

Now was my chance to turn the tables on him. "You sound like you know something. You know too much. You killed her. You hit her on the head and stuffed her in the bean vat."

He stepped closer. "That's what you want them to think. I know, ever since I called you at home. Waiting for me to call, eh? Clever as a rat. Mother fucker." He raised the wrench and lunged, slashing at me again, this time catching me on the chest and left shoulder, knocking me back but I stayed on my feet. Maybe the booze made him weaker than I thought.

He raised the wrench and I slammed head-first into his exposed chest. We crashed to the floor, two drunken sleep-deprived, raging animals. I felt I had the advantage because my whole body filled with hate. In reality, he had the upper hand and he showed it to me with a blow across the back of my head with his fist.

I lost consciousness. I came to with his fetid breath in my face and his hands digging in my pockets.

"Keys. Give me the keys."

I struggled to sit up. He shoved me back down.

"Give me keys. Shut up. Be quiet. Your kids. You want happy kids? Give me LX keys."

One of his gargantuan hands closed around my throat and squeezed my larynx and spine together. I started to swallow my Adams's apple. Pain drove my head against the floor while I kicked and pried helplessly at his fingers.

Gasping and pitching my head back and forth, I saw the kitchen door open and Genevieve flash into the room. Benko pounded his fist into my stomach. My body bent and I almost puked into his face.

"Benko. Get off him!" Genevieve ran over to us and started beating Gladonov on the back with her fists.

I called out, "Go away. Get out of here."

Gladonov swung his arm back, blocking her blows. He stood up and turned around, catching her by the hair. "Cunt."

She kicked at him. He slapped her on the head. She buckled and staggered. The fight went out of her.

"Charlie first. Then, I'll fuck you. Good. You'll come twenty times." He pushed her in the shoulder and she stumbled backwards, banging her head on the refrigerator. Then he turned back to me.

"Stop it, Benko," I groaned. "You have the money. Just go."

"LX keys." He shoved me down again and knelt on my chest to finish frisking me.

I tried to call to Genevieve, to tell her to give him the keys. We could let him go, I had the diary, but his knee had driven the wind out of me so I couldn't speak.

Genevieve pushed herself away from the fridge and picked up the whiskey bottle Benko had knocked out of my hands. She raised it in both hands over her head and with a crimson bulging face, she hammered it down on Gladonov's skull.

He collapsed onto my face, nearly smothering me. I jerked away trying to catch my breath. I turned and thrust as hard as I could and finally pushed him off into a puddle of glass shards and smoky scotch. A long splinter of glass sparkled from the top of his head like an icicle.

Gen and I sat on the floor, hyperventilating. We couldn't move. Finally, she whispered, "Is he dead?"

I crawled over to his face and put my fingers under his nose. I felt his moist breath.

"No."

"Check his pulse."

I lay my fingers against his neck. A slow pulse beat through his carotid artery.

He must be fakin', his eyelids're shakin'.

"He's alive."

"What now?"

"I don't know. Should we call the cops?

"Let's just get out of here," Gen said. "They'll think he had a brawl with some drunk friends."

I started to come to my senses. I noticed the diary in the shadow under the table. Gen didn't know I had it but Benko knew.

"What if he tells them it was us? We don't have an alibi."
"We could say we left town early to go on sales calls?"

"Sure," I groaned. "Perfect alibi."

She stared down at him. "Maybe he'll die."

"We'd be so lucky," I said.

"I don't want to kill him. I couldn't take that."

We stood up and brushed glass and spatters of blood and scotch off our jackets. We stared at him, our terrifying adversary reduced to a pile of sodden rags and sagging flesh. He lay with his prehensile hands folded over his crotch the way a child sleeps holding his genitals.

"We can't let him tell the police it was us. Buhrman will figure some way to arrest us. He'll charge us with at least assault and battery with a weapon. Maybe worse." Her face stiffened. "Did you get the diary?" she asked.

Should I let her in on the whole story? What good would that do? If she read the diary, she'd know about the baby. If anybody finds out about the baby, they'll put two and two together and think I killed Becky on purpose. "Uh, no. No diary. It was bullshit. He wanted the money and my new car. Like you said, it was bullshit blackmail. When I wouldn't give him the keys—you had 'em in the car. He came at me with his wrench."

"He's good with his tools," she said.

"Don't be funny. He tried to kill me."

"Funny? Don't be stupid." she said.

"We have to get rid of him," I said, looking around for something to give me an idea.

"Yeah. Easy to say."

"Throw him in the river? If we sink him under the ice, nobody would find him till spring."

She raised her eyebrows. "Jesus, Charlie. He's still alive. What if he comes to?"

"Yeah," I said, disappointed. "They'd find him."

"Yeah," she said. "We can't let anybody find out it's us."

"Another fucking investigation? More Enquirer? We lost Meng from the last one. What if we lose Giordano? We'll lose everything."

When I said "Giordano," her eyes fell.

"Maybe we could bury him?" I said half-seriously.

She turned back, pained, her shoulders bent inward and her face pale. "Alive? Charlie, listen to yourself. What are you saying?" "The ground's too frozen anyway."

Gladonov stirred and we jumped. His body spasmed for what seemed like thirty seconds. Glass shards fell off his shirt, his head lifted up and his eyes opened.

We gasped. Then, his head dropped and everything went quiet. "Check him," Genevieve said. "Did he die?"

I checked and felt his chest rising and falling. His breathing was regular but shallow. I was amazed at how little blood seeped out of his head. The glass must have barely penetrated the skull. He was probably just unconscious from Gen's crack on his head and passed out from all the booze he'd drunk since yesterday. If he came to, he'd probably attack like a wounded bear.

"Whatever we do, we better think fast. He might wake all the way up."

"I can't think. I laid on the couch all night worrying about him coming to kill me or Liam. Now this nightmare."

I stepped across Gladonov's body and bent down. He reeked of alcohol and garlic. Gen had dosed the Dragon Stew with garlic for the Rooster party.

If we didn't make Benko disappear, I doubted any of us would survive. Nora and the kids would never recover. They'd live in misery and shame and poverty. All because of one asshole with a prick bigger than his brain. I noticed the blood had stopped leaking out of the wound.

"Gen, at least we have to tie him up. If he wakes up ... Go find a rope or chain or something. He's gotta have some."

"What good will that do?"

"I don't know," I said. "Give us time to think?"

Slowly, she dragged her feet but found the door to the hallway. I heard her snap the light on and go into the back room. "Ow. Shit," she said. "Tools everywhere."

I knelt down and crawled under the table, retrieving the diary and stuffing it into my briefcase. Then I sidled over to Gladonov and put my hand on his forehead. It was sopping wet from our fight. I slid my hand down over his nose and mouth. Should I? If I smothered him now, no one would know. I pressed down. His head jerked.

I snatched my hand away and sat back on my thighs. No. I couldn't do it, not on purpose. I'm no killer, I don't care what kind of psycho he is. I'll take the diary and money and get out. We were never here. As long as I have the diary, he couldn't prove anything.

I'd have to take his computer and scanner. Christ, would this never end?

We were back where we started, but now, with the diary in my hands, I was in at least a litte more in control.

I watched him and sighed. We'd tie him up and get out and then wait. I'd check on him later. I propped my arm on the table and levered myself up. I turned to find Gen and get out of there when Benko groaned and grunted, an urgent wheezing. His legs bent at the knees and shot straight out. His body quaked, bouncing up and down.

I knelt back down and grabbed his chin in one hand, felt around the floor with the other for something to stick between his lips to stop him from biting his tongue.

His arm flopped and he reached up, clutching at my hand, trying to peel my fingers off. Then his legs dropped to the floor with a thud. A rill of trembles flooded his body, it jerked and quieted, oscillated again and went still. His arm sagged and his hand splayed palm-up big as a dinner plate beside my knee. He hadn't opened his eyes since he went down.

Genevieve's voice came from the hall doorway to the kitchen. "I've got an extension cord. Will that work?" then, from beside the body she said, "Charlie, what are you doing?"

I held out my hand to her and she tugged me up and I stepped back from the body. "Checking his breathing. He's gone. He must have had a heart attack or something."

She stared at me, then at him. Her eyes narrowed.

"He started jerking again. Kicking and shaking his head. A fit. Epilepsy or something. He pissed himself."

She hunkered down beside the body and, grimacing, she passed her hand in front of his nose. She held her fingers there for a long minute. She felt for a pulse in his neck. She felt for it on the other side. Then she laid her head on his chest while shot a narrow look at me. Her eyes glazed and she closed them, listening. Eventually, she reached out for my hand for help in getting up. I pulled her to her knees and held on to her hand.

She knelt beside the body, shaking her head. She gripped my hand, digging her fingernails into my wrist.

"O my God," she said. "I killed him."

I knew it already.

"Check him again," she said.

I knelt on one knee and put my ear on his chest. His green flannel shirt stank of sweat and grease and a harsh stink of urine underscored his helplessness. He lay totally still. Now what?

I slumped down beside Benko and let tears of shock or relief flow. Gen watched me coldly and she didn't try to comfort me and she didn't cry. When I stopped and wiped my eyes, I felt wide awake. She squatted across from me, with one hand on Gladonov's back, her eyes now closed, rocking her whole body on her ankles.

I picked myself up and circled around his body. I pulled her up by her shoulders. When she was fully up, we leaned into each other and moaned and whimpered.

She had trouble catching her breath but she didn't cry. "I didn't mean to. He was on top of you and I didn't know how to get him off. He's so strong."

I tried to comfort her. "It's all right."

"It's not all right. He's dead."

"I mean you didn't kill him."

"Oh, Charlie. He's dead. I hit him with a bottle and smashed glass into his brain. That's why died. If he really had a seizure, I gave it to him."

I held her against me as tight as I could. She didn't believe me that he had a seizure. She hit him and saved my life and I wouldn't let her think she killed him. Or she could think what she wanted but I wouldn't say anything about it. He was dead and the truth was, in one way, we both killed him. I didn't do anything that would make him end up dead. But I was in this all the way with Genevieve.

The kitchen was still dim but I noticed the sky beginning to gray outside the living room window. We had to get moving. We let go other each other and stared at the body.

"We gotta agree on something," I said. "He can still fuck our lives. We gotta get rid of the body and it's getting light out."

"I know. Where?"

"Maybe we can throw him in the lagoon behind the factory and he'll rot," I said.

"He'll float. Somebody will see him."

"So what? He fell in when he was drunk."

"If they drag him out, they'll see the gash on the back of his skull."

"Shit."

Another useless idea. We couldn't get rid of him underground, we didn't have a good place to give him a water burial. Staring down at the corpse, we let our brains whirl, trying to make sense out of the utter chaos of the last half hour. The universe was starting over again and we had to do something pretty amazing to make sure this latest Big Bang didn't blow us to oblivion.

My mind slowed, no thoughts, no Jiminy voice, no ideas. I wanted to drop to the floor and fall asleep. Fatigue washed through me and I didn't care if Buhrman walked in.

After a moment, Gen said, "This may sound stupid, but, what about the okara tank?"

"You mean throw him in?"

It was brilliant. She was brilliant. Pitch him in, let the okara, the day's soybean waste cover him. Then in the course of the
day, we'd ship him off to the hog farm we called Hog Heaven
where the boars and sows would enjoy a gourmet Russian dessert.

Nobody ever checked inside the rail car, except Gladonov
now and then when he needed to see whether he should move
another car into place.

"Yeah," I agreed, adrenalized. Sober and sharp. "Sure. Let's
do it."

"Wait a minute. Are you sure? What about his shoes?"

"Those hogs? They eat anything."

"Won't the farmers see him?"

"No way. One farmer for two thousand massive hogs. They
dump the whole rail car on a moving trough. Everything's auto-
matic. The hogs'll scarf him up before any human comes around.
I've seen them devour a whole rail car of okara in half an hour. "

"All right. Let's go. You take his head and I'll take his feet?"

"No way. I got him.

"You sure."

"Yeah. Don't worry."

I was about to do almost the same thing with Benko's dead
body I did with Becky's—bury him in beans. Only Becky's were
fresh and Benko's were ground up, the leftover lees of beans.
Like Benko himself. A used-up husk of a man. The dregs.

Chapter Six

Charlie

THE BURIAL PLOT

I gathered up the hundred dollar bills scattered around his kitchen and I jammed everything into my case along with the diary. I don't think I got all the bills, but I would come back and clean up later. Then I plucked the slightly curved four-inch blade of glass from the top of Gladonov's head.

I wiggled it and it slipped out like a knife out of Jell-O, clean except for a smear of blood. Thick red fluid gushed out of the wound for a few seconds, soaking his blond hair so I put my finger on the cut to staunch it. The skull felt soft and, when I removed my finger, the juice continued to seep.

Gen handed me a kitchen towel and I wrapped it around the head and wiped my hand on his shirt and lifted him onto my shoulders. I hoped the blood didn't spill on my clothes. I'd burn them anyway.

Staggering under his weight, but feeling the kind of strength a life-and-death situation fires your muscles with, I carried him to his car and lay him on the back seat. Checking the towel around his head for leakage and finding none, I slid back to the house. Gen was standing just inside with my briefcase. I reached for it.

"I'll take it, Charlie," Gen said. "You've got enough to carry. I'll put it in your car and you can get it later."

"That's good. Let me have my briefcase." I said. "I have a knife. Might need it to cut something."

She gave me the briefcase. I found the knife and shut the case. She reached for it. "That's all right. I'll take it."

She shrugged and walked slowly down the driveway to my car to drive it to her house where she would leave it for me to pick up when I was done with Benko.

After she changed her clothes, she'd leave town in her car, stop in to some of our customers' grocery stores along the way and talk to the managers, then she'd meet me later. In the meantime, I'd take care of what I had to do, drive Gladonov's car back to his house, walk home to pick up the Tofumobile and head out of town in the other direction.

By the time I left Gladonov's driveway, it was almost six and the gray sky had started fading to white. Looked like it would be a beautiful day.

Holding my breath and steering carefully on the slippery road, I drove the two miles to the factory in six minutes and parked at the rear of the building, out of sight from the street.

Nobody here. Damn lucky, Greer.

Because of the company party the night before, we'd scheduled the morning shift to start at ten, which meant that the first person wouldn't arrive at the factory until eight. I had two hours.

The parking lot was iced over so when I tried carrying his body to the rail line at the rear of the building, I staggered and slipped, falling flat on my back with Gladonov in my lap.

Risking a trail in the ice, I decided to slide the body across the slicked asphalt to the okara car. I hoped the sun or the warming air would melt the ice. If not, I only had a few minutes, so too bad about the trail.

I grabbed his ankles and dragged him to the railroad tracks. I stood over him, panting a dense cloud of breath around my head that seemed to drift, not rise. The mist blurred my vision for a moment while I considered my next step. One mistake now and after a whole year of dodging the Chief, I'd take a fatal dive.

I decided I'd better not trust the hogs to eat Benko's clothes. When I imagined the body cruising along the feed conveyor in Hog Heaven, I saw a riot of three hundred pound carnivores snuffling and snorting and ripping at the flesh, but ignoring the cloth.

No one would discover the corpse unless the hogs missed a knuckle or a rib, which I doubted. After a steady vegetarian diet of soy, those porkers would relish the meat treat.

Squatting down, I untied Benko's boots and tugged them off. One rank blue sock, one black, typically mismatched by a drunk. I quickly unbuttoned his reeking green mechanic's shirt. Once I pulled it off and dragged his soaking t-shirt over his head, his chest and belly steamed, releasing his last vital heat.

When I tugged at the cuffs of his black trousers, they slipped off, revealing red boxer briefs that bulged in the middle. Feeling squeamish for the first time, I grabbed the shorts by their sides and yanked. His penis flopped free and wobbled, half-erect, a sparse vapor rising from it.

Holy shit. Never seen nothing like it.

I immediately understood the women's fascination for him. His was easily twice as long and wide as mine and blue veins circled the shaft sort of like spirals on a barber pole. I wouldn't want to carry around a shillelagh like that banging against my thigh with every step. I'd have to learn to walk in a whole new way.

I was tempted to grab it just to feel what it was like to have such a honker. I reached for it, but it seemed to quiver. I came to my senses and jerked back from his godawful legacy, then turned and tended to business.

I piled the clothes and boots in a heap beside the tracks. Bending over him, I slid my arms around his sides. In my hands, his flesh was dense and firm. Hard muscle.

I heaved him onto my back in a fireman's carry and started up the icy ladder to the open top. I gripped the icy rung with one hand, held his arms around my neck with the other and stepped up on the bottom rung. I promptly slipped, tearing my hand loose from the ice, dropped the body, and this time, I fell on top of him, slamming my forehead into his jaw and my knee into his belly.

The blow shocked me wider awake. Morning became luminous. The bare branches of the trees shimmered like velvet wrinkles in the pale sky. The okara car loomed over me, a vast rusty hearse waiting to convey another wasted life to its next station.

I pushed off the body, rolled away, and stuck my burning hands into my gloves. As puffs of my warm exhalations evaporated in front of my face, sunrays struck my breath-clouds, tinting them with pale rainbow sparkles. I smiled to myself as if I'd risen early just to watch the sun rise.

Leaving Benko on the tracks, I climbed up the ladder, kicking and stubbing patches of ice off the steel rungs, to reconnoiter. The sun worried at the morning haze, so I expected it to wipe out all traces of my having climbed the ladder and the tracks in the parking lot Benko's head and shoulders had scraped in the ice. Sunlight was a double-edged sword right then. I had to hurry.

You got a break, Jake.

Jiminy was back. Somehow it was comforting. I wasn't the only one in this.

Back on the ground, Benko lay in a sunbeam, his face serene and golden. I saw the corpse as a young man: handsome and alluring. The wrinkles had disappeared from his forehead and his mouth hung open as if he were singing an endless one-note song. The little cannon propped in his lap had lost its loft, but it maintained its aim as if hopeful of one last shot.

I bent and hoisted him up again and draped him across my back. Climbing about as fast as I could, I trudged up the rungs, slipping a little, taking forever. At the top, I leaned over and folded myself over the three-inch wide steel lip and, turning sideways, I twisted quickly and heaved.

He slid off my shoulder and fell six feet with his head down but once his legs followed his trunk, he somersaulted, landing on his back with his arms and legs sprawled across a beige cone of ice-coated okara.

When he hit, his body whoomped like a small bomb striking and he crashed through the frozen soy pulp, exploding it into shards of ice and clumps of okara and a cloud of rancid steam.

Sealed under a coat of slush and ice, the tofu production waste had fermented at one hundred twenty degrees, souring into tangy hog chow. Once Benko's body shattered the frosted crust and cold air coupled with the hot moist pulp, a cloud of steam billowed up, hiding Benko's body in a small fog bubble. Then it floated up and away from him, some of it dissipating into the air, some forming crystals on the walls of the rail car.

With filaments of steam rising around the inert body, it seemed to smolder. If I were superstitious, I'd say I was watching his soul take a slow exit. His sallow skin and tawny hair blended into the tan okara as if he'd already begun to dissolve into his elements. Even the eager devil in his crotch had given up its ghost and lay between his thighs shriveled as an old banana.

I propped my shins against the top rung of the ladder and rested. Benko, as a human being, had deserved a better life and a better death. Benko as the particular human being he was deserved nothing better than a violent ending and this humiliating burial in waste. Not one twinge of regret, remorse or guilt bothered me.

Better Benko than you, my friend. You're breathing, he's met his end.

If this worked, Benko would become my best friend.

My ex-best friend.

I waited for the body to sink out of sight under the surface. It settled a little, but didn't sink. It must have compressed the okara where it landed. If I climbed into the tank, I'd make such a mess of the surface that anybody checking the level of the okara would notice and wonder what had happened. If I didn't force his body all the way down into its temporary grave, anybody who happened to see into the rail car would see the body.

I let myself down into the car as gently as possible. Naturally, I sank to my crotch in the hot muck. Sucking at me like quicksand, the okara scalded my thighs and formed a mist around me, saturating my pants as I slogged through. Starting with the feet, I shoved the body down into the steaming pulp, burying it as deeply as my arms could reach.

I plodded through the soy muck to the other side of the car to reach the ladder and I dragged myself back up. When I climbed out, my coat and pants and shoes had gained half an inch of okara insulation. I was soaked and steaming in the morning light like a primeval swamp creature rising into his first sunrise.

My pants and jacket began to stiffen in the sub-freezing air. I shivered, remembering myself as a kid playing in mushy snow then scraping toward home stiff-legged for supper. I walked into brush beside the tracks and bounced and stamped and scraped off the loose okara. With a stick, I scraped my clothes down, and with Benko's gear in my arms, I slipped and slid across the parking lot, oddly lighthearted, to the building where I let myself in through the employee entry. I dropped Benko's clothes beside the door.

In the employees' lounge, I removed my pants and jacket I ran into my office and pulled on the spare pants and shirt I kept in the closet.

Back in the factory, I grabbed a parka from the hook beside the walk-in cooler. I hurried back outside, my feet cold and wet but warming up. Along the way, I stuffed my wet pants and coat into a plastic garbage bag along with Benko's stuff.

I didn't have time to burn them. If I took the clothes home to hide them, I'd risk Nora's finding them. Hauling them to the refuse area out back, I chucked the bag into the dumpster that was emptied daily at ten a.m. with fifty other trash bags from the previous day's production and unloaded into landfill before noon.

Easing myself into Benko's car seat, brushing the soles of my shoes off into the parking lot, I drove Benko's car back to his house.

I parked the car in his driveway and walked home in watery morning light, carrying my briefcase like a city commuter heading for the train, slipping several times and taking a pratfall on a pool of black ice lurking on the sidewalk.

I bounced up, adrenaline still coursing through my muscles. I wanted to run, but forced myself into the scout's pace, fifty steps jogging, fifty steps walking, counting to keep me distracted and aimed to my safe and cozy house fewer and fewer blocks ahead.

I showered, changed into my grey suit and tasseled black loafers, swallowed a cup of orange juice, and left the house in my camelhair overcoat, ready for customers, just as the kids and Nora started making noises in the bathrooms.

I noticed that the ice had melted off the street where the early traffic wore it thin. Grateful for the clear asphalt underfoot, I walked along in the car tracks toward Genevieve's neighborhood. Her car was gone when I climbed into the Honda, and backed out of Genevieve's driveway at 7:30, steering east, toward my alibi. A fit of anxiety struck me and I swerved around, driving back toward the plant. In my euphoria at getting rid of the body, I realized the danger I'd left myself exposed to: Benko's and my clothes into the company dumpster, leaving a confession right under Buhrman's nose.

I slapped my cheek a dozen times to punish myself for setting myself up again for my destruction. Two blocks from the factory, I turned the car around. The startup crew was paid a bonus to be obnoxiously punctual. No doubt they'd punch in ten minutes ahead of time, even while sobering up from the company bash. I couldn't risk having one of my employees see me digging around in the trash.

If anyone found Benko and called the cops, they'd search the plant's premises, for sure. Even though the Chief was much smarter than before Becky's death, the odds were in my favor that they wouldn't catch on to anything suspicious before the garbage truck hauled away State's evidence number two and number three, our clothes, with Benko's corpse being number one.

I thought of calling off production with the excuse that everyone deserved more time off. I could retrieve the clothes when the plant was vacated. But then the hog farm wouldn't get its scheduled load of feed and they'd call the morning shift supervisor. He'd have to check the car, see some strange pattern in the okara, and all hell would break loose.

I was confident that no production worker would check the rail car to see if it was full. That was Benko's job and when the okara rose high enough to ship out, an electric eye read the level and shifted the okara exhaust pipe to the next car. Benko's coffin car and one other would fill and ship out by early afternoon.

I had to handle the suspense for a few more hours. As I drove, I puzzled out my solution to Benko's scanning the diary into his computer. I knew Benko didn't have any great skills so he would use the basic techniques anybody would. I knew how to erase that from his hard drive, but he may have known more about computers than he let on. I was a fair hand at computer security, and I counted on being able to trace any emails he may have sent with the diary attached: the last loophole that could strangle me. I'd count on my IT guy to sterilize everything. I wasn't finished with Benko yet.

***

At two in the afternoon, Genevieve and I sat exhausted in a Starbucks in Albany, picking at crumbs of our muffins. We barely spoke while we ate. We'd each visited several supermarkets and seen customers to establish alibis.

I ordered another cappuccino and made a call. When I brought the coffee back to the table, I said, "It's over, Gen. I checked with the factory. The okara shipment left on schedule half an hour ago."

"Thank God," she said. "We're free."

"Not totally. We have to make sure no one saw the body at the hog farm. Four hours from now, poof. Pig poop."

She wrinkled her nose and grit her teeth. "All right," she said. "We have no choice."

"Don't worry. I'm not." She needed to see me confident and so did I. Play it till you lay it.

I watched the other customers chewing their rolls and slurping their lattes, prodding their torpid minds into a couple of hours of semi-alertness. The same thing I needed.

Genevieve covered my hand with her cool palm. "I believe you. Now, I have some more news."

"Good, I hope."

"It is. Really. You'll understand."

My blood sugar was so low, I was wrung-out and half-asleep, so whatever she reported, I barely cared.

"After my Hawaii trip, I'm leaving American Tofu."

I sat up. How could she leave now?

"I have a job that pays twice as much and it's a long way away from all this. I'm going to San Francisco," she said. "I want to raise Liam in a city, not this hick town. Anyway, after this morning, how could I stay at Tofu? I'd always be thinking about what happened."

"Yeah. I see that."

She's known it for a while. Strategy's her style.

In about two seconds I realized that she'd planned this. I didn't blame her. If we hadn't vanished Benko, he'd have made her life miserable. Now she'd be so traumatized, she'd be useless at work anyway. Not that it mattered. Her customers loved her so much she could only do right.

"I'm not surprised," I said, "only sad." I could barely croak loud enough for her to hear. When he choked me, Benko had burned his fingerprints into my neck. I expected to have to wear turtlenecks for a couple of days, and I couldn't let Nora or the kids see me without my shirt on. "I wouldn't mind leaving, too. But I gotta stay and forget about it. Honestly? I tell myself what happened had to happen. The world's better off without him. But how am I gonna build the company without you?"

"You'll hire somebody better."

"I'll miss you so bad." I squeezed her fingers. "Nora won't be able to get along one minute without you."

"I'm sad, too, but I have to go. You'll be fine."

"We'll be fine, especially when we hear the hogs enjoyed their gourmet lunch. I know you'll be fine, too. San Francisco. What will you be doing?"

"It's a good job. I'll tell you all about it, but now there's one thing we have to do."

She seemed to know she could ask me for anything, and right then, with the vision of the blade of glass jutting from Benko's skull fresh in my mind, she could. "Jesus, what now, Gen? I barely have enough energy to drink this coffee. Look at me. Half-dead myself."

"This is easy. No, hard, but we have to: Never talk about any of this again. Wipe it out of our minds. I can't stand thinking about him. The sound of that bottle smashing. It's the pigs that gross me out as much as anything." She pulled her coat tight and zipped it up. Steam condensed on the windows and it must have been eighty inside the Starbucks.

"Oh, not talk? Maybe that's best." If she was gone, it would be easy. That was another good reason for her to go. She was so smart.

She laid her hand on my cheek. "Let's go. I gotta go home and climb in bed and stay away from the shop. I'm sorry."

"Take tomorrow off," I said. "Nobody will think anything weird. Then you show up and announce your fantastic luck with a new job and pack your stuff and say good-bye to everybody. You can put up an act for a couple of weeks. Make a smooth transition. In pain, but normal. Everybody will understand. We're all gonna miss you."

"I'll try, Charlie. For you and Nora and Liam. I need some sleep now to help me get my spirit back. I still feel like a boiled wonton. I don't know if I'll ever be able to see a bottle of whiskey again without seeing his body flat on the floor."

"I'll miss you, Gen."

"I'll miss you, Charlie. You were a bastard sometimes, and an idiot, but you were real and I always loved you for not pretending to be somebody better."

"You know what?" I said, sitting up, embracing with my eyes this woman who I owed so much to. "You and me? We're closer now than most husbands and wives. It's wild how Benko finally brought us together."

"What do you mean? This is about as romantic as a compost bucket."

"I don't mean romantic. I mean we're closer than almost anyone can be. We'll never be the same because of him."

She pursed her lips and sat back. "Lots of people will never be the same."

"Not the way we will."

She nodded, "Yeah, it's true," and stirred her coffee.

"The worst thing about this?" she said. "I mean, except Becky died? The sad thing is we really do have to forget each other. I'm sorry. I can't get the sound of the bottle smashing out of my mind."

"It'll take time for that. I won't forget you. I could never forget you. After everything we've been through?"

"I don't mean really forget each other. Once I leave? Not see each other. Maybe never again."

She started crying and I tried to smile reassurance. I offered her my napkin.

"Never say never. Long time, yeah, that's all right, but never?" I groaned. "I love you and I'll have to find out how you're doing?" How could I not love her after all we'd been through. Comrades-inarms. Captains in combat.

She leaned over and kissed me on the cheek and sat back and blew her nose.

We finished our cappuccinos and found our way to our cars. She had stopped at the Genesee Street P & C and talked to the produce manager, and I'd stop at a couple of Shop Rites and independent stores. In case anyone asked, we'd be covered. Plenty of witnesses observing us do our regular routine of customer visits.

We walked arm in arm across the parking lot. Before we separated, I said, "Meet me back in my office at five. I want to give you something."

"What about my day off? I don't know if I can last until five. I gotta sleep."

"Yeah, I forgot. No hurry, I just want to make you feel better. I'll call you tonight, say eight o'clock? Let you know if I hear anything. Any problems at the farm, we'll know for sure by then."

"All right. I'll be asleep so let it ring," she said. letting her head rest on my shoulder.

I leaned my cheek against her hair and closed my eyes. We could have fallen asleep standing right there.

After a few steps, I opened my eyes and lifted my head. Pulling her closer, I said, "I'm a little nervous. Something weird could always happen. I'm not too worried. But if they find him, we have nothing to do with it."

"I know. I've seen the way those hogs gorge themselves. I hope none of the farm hands are watching."

"Tiny chance of that."

"Right now, I'm so wiped out I can't think about it." We let go of each other and, after a long hug, she got into her car.

"Drive safe," I said. "Wait till you get home to fall asleep."

"Drink hot lemonade with fresh ginger. It works miracles for a hoarse throat." She sighed and rolled up her window and drove away.

Always thinking about others, that woman. Hot lemonade with ginger. I may have to try it if I don't get my voice back.

Chapter Seven

Charlie

FAIR SHARES

*I turned everything
over, upside down no
diary to be found*

That night, after drowsy, achy hours of driving around, staying out of sight, I trudged home to a quiet dinner with Nora and the kids.

"No diary," I said, as I sat down. "Everything's fine. He's gone. He took ten thousand and screamed at me and cursed and said he was leaving town. Didn't care what happened at the factory."

Tears streamed down Nora's smiling face. Chuckie scowled and Rissi said, "Mommy," and jumped out of her chair and ran to Nora.

"I'm fine, honey," Nora said. "Daddy told me good news, is all. Makes me happy."

Rissi pulled back and frowned at Nora. Then she smiled. "You're like Daddy now Mommy. He cries when he's happy, too."

I burst out laughing and Nora followed. The kids gave each other mocking faces, rolling their eyes, probably agreeing that their parents were crazy. After dinner, I said I had to go into the office for a while. I drove car to Benko's neighborhood and parked a block away. If that's what she did when she was hav-

ing her affair with him, maybe the neighbors were used to seeing the car.

I let myself into the house, found a broom and dustpan and
swept up all signs of the fight, dumping the glass into a bag I'd
throw into a trash bin at a rest area on the interstate. Benko's
blood had stained the brown carpet with a smudge as big as
a watermelon. I washed it as well as I could and prayed that
when it dried, it would blend into the nap like old ground-in
dirt. I stuffed the rags into the trash bag with the glass.

I found the nine hundred dollar bills that were missing from
the count I'd made earlier, then I started Benko's computer. Before I went to work, I activated my cell and called the hog farm.
Rare, but I'd checked on okara shipments in the past. Thank
God, the farmer had nothing to report. I called Genevieve.

***

"Gen. Sorry to wake you." "What?"
"All clear.
"What?"
"Go back to sleep." "Thanks. I thought so." "We're clear."
"Yeah. What time is it?" "Nine."
"Mmmm."
"See you in the morning?" "How about, after lunch?" "Sure."

***

By midnight, I'd cleaned Benko's hard drive of all evidence and
echoes of the diary. I printed out a list of Benko's few email
communications since August. He'd made all of them from the
factory since he didn't have an internet connection at home.
He'd sent a half dozen notes to Genevieve, bought several cases
of vodka and scotch on-line, downloaded some porn, joined a
dating website. It seemed the scanned diary was unmoved from
the hard drive, but I'd have to search all his emails. He must
have had a hard copy somewhere. I hoped not.

I checked the company cloud storage and found nothing personal for Benko, as expected. He'd told me once he didn't want to be traced every time he hit a key on the keyboard.

I returned the scanner to the production office at the factory and deposited Benko's computer with the other old office equipment in a storeroom in the company warehouse. I'd pour through his little office as soon as I could. I returned to Benko's house for one final inspection.

As far as I could tell, he managed his home like any bachelor drinker with dirty laundry strewn around the bedroom, an unmade bed, grimy dishes in the kitchen and on the coffee table in front of the TV, newspapers piled up.

Wearing gloves, I poked around under the bed, under the mattress, in the closet corners, every shelf and cupboard, even in the toilet tank. No copy of the diary. I went through the whole place a second time.

After thinking about it, I left the heat on and the door unlocked, and eased my way casually back to Nora's car and drove home.

Nora and I sat up for two hours, crying, laughing, holding each other. I told her that when I called Benko's bluff about the diary, he'd struck me with his wrench and run out of the house.

"I followed him, but he disappeared."

"Where could he go?" she wondered.

"Some woman's? Who cares. Soon as he comes in tomorrow, I'm firing him."

"What if he won't leave? What if he attacks you again?"

"I'll fire him in public, in the production room. The workers will protect me if he goes nuts."

"I'm still scared." Nora cuddled up and threw her legs across my lap, squeezing me as hard as she could.

"If he loses it, I'll call Buhrman. He needs to put his energy into something worthwhile." I tried to joke but Nora ignored me.

"C'mon. Let's go to bed," I said, more spent than ever in my life. "When he shows up, I'll give him his Chinese New Year bonus early and three months' severance. He'll be gone by noon. I'm not worried."

Way to cover your tracks, but don't think you can relax.

***

I arrived at the factory at 1:30, still groggy with a sleep debt hanging over me like a concrete cloud. Gen lay on my office couch with my grandmother's orange and green afghan pulled to her chin and her arm thrown over her eyes. I closed the door and tiptoed to my desk.

"You're late."

"Sorry. Slept late, then got tied up on the phone with production. Without Benko here, we had to make sure the schedule was set for the rest of the week."

Genevieve sat up and folded the afghan and lay it over the back of the couch. I switched on the lights.

"I need a lot of time off, maybe the rest of my life."

"Me, too. But everything's fine now. All we do is act normal."

"What's 'normal,' Charlie? How can anything be 'normal?'" She tossed aside the blanket and stood up and paced. I felt as bad as she did, I'm sure. Who wouldn't? But I was so relieved, I wanted to laugh and shout. If Benko hadn't bruised my chest and shoulders so badly, I would laugh.

I rose and put my arm around Genevieve, tugging her close. She sniffled into the tissue I offered her.

"Does Nora know anything?"

"No way."

"What about the factory workers?"

"They think he's still sleeping off his drunk or so hung over he can't get out of bed."

"Two days in bed?"

"Everyone at the party saw him staggering out the door barely able to keep his head up. It's as good a theory as any."

She held her breath. "The farm?"

"Business as usual. It's done, Gen. Life goes on." I smiled. "The hogs are happy."

She grimaced.

"Our future is wide open," I said. "We can relax."

"Relax? What's that?"

The ordeal had wasted Genevieve. Not only Benko's death, but the Chinese New Year road trip must have gutted all her reserves. "You don't need to mourn him," I said. "He was evil."

"Mourn him? Shit, Charlie. You don't know half."

"What d'ya mean?"

"Forget it," she said. "He's gone and too much of us went with him."

She hated him, I thought, but love's always buried somewhere inside fury. Once you taste passion, you can't resist it, no matter what shape it takes. Love, hate, grief. It's a lot better than feeling numb. We both sat down and I reached into my briefcase and pulled out my wallet.

"Don't take this wrong, Gen."

I opened my wallet and removed a one hundred thousand dollar bank draft and offered it to her. She didn't respond so I closed her fingers around the check. She tried to give it back but I wouldn't take it.

"It's money I set aside for emergencies," I said. "It makes me much happier to give it to you. You suffered plenty from him, too." Easy come, easy go, I thought. Thanks, Meng.

A tiny curve of smile trembled on her lips. She stared at me with moist green eyes. She finally folded the check but held it between her fingers like a card she didn't know whether to discard or bet. "This goes right into Liam's college account."

"Good. Anything you want to do with it. It's yours."

"You're sure?"

"Yes. It'll cost you plenty to move across country. Get yourself a nice place in San Francisco. Besides, money makes money."

"This is my Soy to the World sales bonus, right?"

"No. You'll get that when the customers pay their invoices. This is my personal appreciation. It has nothing to do with business." She unfolded the draft and stared at it. "I don't know. Are you paying me off? Was this the money you planned to give Benko?" "Genevieve. No. You can use the money."

"It feels scuzzy."

"It's yours. If you don't want to cash it for Liam, give it to some homeless shelter or something." She and I stared into each other's eyes for a long time. Behind me, my email pinged twice into the silence. I watched her make up her mind.

"Thank you," she said as she inserted the wrinkled draft into her wallet. "Tell Nora thank you."

"She doesn't know about it. If she did, she'd expect me to give it to you. You know that." My voice caught in my throat. The words scratched across my larynx and emerged barely above a whisper. "I'll tell her."

Genevieve stood up again and stepped around the coffee table to my chair. She squeezed my cheeks in both her hands and tilted my face up to hers. "You gonna be all right?"

"I never felt better."

I lay my head against her firm belly and let the tears flow. She brushed her fingers through my hair, her nails caressing my scalp the way my mother used to. I pressed my head against her hopelessly. When I finally won her, I lost her forever.

She goes, you stay on the home turf. You both get what you deserve.

A fantasy about Genevieve that I put aside two years ago floated to the surface of my sorrowing mind: If I were her one and only, my life's purpose would be met. We could never live together, but this feeling's not about marriage or family. I've known ever since she first applied for the job that she and I had a special destiny and it had nothing to do with romance.

Nora says that we have all kinds of soul mates, not romantic love partners. Genevieve and I are definitely soul mates. I'm sure I'll see her again. After she's settled and thriving in her new life, I bet she contacts me. If she doesn't, it won't be hard to find her.

***

On the third day of Benko's absence from work, I called Buhrman to let him know Gladonov hadn't come in to work since the Year of the Rooster party. If I waited any longer, he'd think I was hiding something. Once I told him, Buhrman went to Gladonov's apartment where he found Gladonov's car in the driveway and his apartment empty.

By then, I'd scoured every drawer, file folder, bookshelf, garbage can and box in his office. I turned everything over in his workshop. No copies of the diary anywhere. I didn't feel free yet, but my neck and jaw loosened up a bit. IT gave me the all clear. The headache I'd had for three days faded.

When Buhrman stopped into the factory to give me his latest news, I insisted that he put an all-out effort into finding Benko. I told him Gladonov had acted irrationally at the party and went home drunk. I needed him to run my factory and the least Buhrman could do now was help us find him. I had no idea where he went, but rumors had started to fly around the factory crew that he disappeared to escape suspicion that he was involved in Becky's death. I wanted Buhrman to think he'd found the hot trail of the elusive killer at last.

"What d'ya think we are, Charlie? New York City? You some kind of celebrity? I'm supposed to hire somebody just to go after him so you can make your toad food? Show me where that's in my budget. You've already cost this town plenty."

Buhrman almost drooled spite but the disappearance of one of his main suspects must have given him a sense of self-justification. He could give the D.A. a pretty good ending to the murder story.

Chief's a good cop, you gotta admit. But the bad guy's gonna come out on top.

I asked him, "My wife's nervous about Gladonov. So's Genevieve. Ever since Gladonov disappeared with her kid in Buffalo, she and my wife worry he might come back and they're afraid for the kids. How about posting a patrolman outside our houses until we're sure he's gone?"

He sputtered but without scorn. "Never heard of such a thing." "Just until we're sure he's gone."

"My overtime since last summer is more than your property taxes for a year, Greer. On your factory and that McMansion of yours. Sorry to say, but this town's gotta raise its taxes so guys like you pay their fair share."

Buhrman enjoyed playing the bumpkin, but he was so easy to see through. I wouldn't let him get under my skin any more. Besides, now we were negotiating the price of his special service.

He finally agreed to put a man on the factory premises and assign one to drive by my house and Genevieve's every half hour around the clock but, he said, if Gladonov showed up tomorrow after sleeping off a binge, the police department would send American Tofu the bill for every second his man spent on the case.

"What do you think about a hundred bucks an hour, Greer?" "Fine, Aaron. Whatever it takes to keep the kids safe and the mothers happy."

"Plus expenses."

"That would be donuts and coffee right?" I said.

Buhrman smiled and touched the bill of his cap and left, the humble, obliging civil servant.

Chapter Eight

Charlie

ASHES ASCENDING

by the icy stream, I
light the pages—
smoke drifts up, fades away

I burned the diary.

One afternoon, I loaded kindling and firewood into my LX and drove out to the river. I wanted to have my private ceremony, honoring Becky and closing this chaotic chapter of my life. I scraped a clearing in the snow with my boots and built a fire on the shore.

By now, I could almost recite the diary word for word, I'd read it fifty, a hundred times. If only she'd told me about the baby. Honestly, I don't know how I'd have reacted, but I know myself well enough to be sure I'd have done something honorable.

Standing close to the blaze so I could feel the heat on my calves and knees, and coughing in the smoke, I tore the diary apart, page by page, and set it on fire, offering it to the Buddha of good luck or whatever ironic god had mercy on me at the cost of two lives and who knows what other damage.

A wave of black burnt paper flowed toward my hand as a low orange flame followed it on each page, transforming the paper first into dark filigrees of ash then casting off white flakes into the rising air currents. They fluttered and bobbed and some of them brushed my hair and face and jacket like tatters of a shroud so fragile they disintegrated when they touched me.

The diary's cardboard covers guttered. Not wanting to leave any traces, I ripped them into pieces and while I bounced down the rough gravel road, I opened my window and sprinkling them little by little, I let them drift away.

For most of my life, I'd made denial my masterpiece. I was so good, I managed to turn my talent for denial outward and convince my wife, the Chief, my bankers, my customers, even my kids that I was who I was not. I did a beautiful job of convincing myself, too. While part of me played the role of the innocent, I willed the whole of me to believe it.

Perhaps being with Becky would have shown me the illusive real me. Becky, a simple woman who loved me, a simple man, and that might have been enough. Maybe she'd have died in an accident anyway. She had her fate.

You thought you were smart cuz you knew she was a tart.

Maybe if I'd been smarter about my motives, maybe if I'd given more to my marriage, maybe if ... aaah ... who knows?

I can handle more change than most people, and I don't regret risking everything to keep my family and my life intact. I did all I could to minimize the damage I'd done by falling for Becky and submitting to passion's reckless ultimatum: love or nothing. But where did I get the guts and brains to survive the Chief and Benko?

Underneath all my battling and tricking and deceiving had to be something like love, a desire for joy and connection, showing itself in other guises. The pure love I have for my kids, the responsible love I have for my employees, and yes, the married love I have for Nora.

Still, I have to admit, I loved myself more than any of them. The last thing I could do was live the rest of my life as infamous Charlie Greer, the guy who knocked up his employee and then she died by accident, ha, ha. Charlie Greer would not survive that.

Only you know who's to blame. What a shame.

As I neared town, my eyes dry in the cold breeze of the open window, I scattered the last pieces of the diary until all but a few were gone, each scrap taking the place of a tear falling.

Back in my office, I hid the remaining shreds in the lacquered box Meng gave me, concealing them inside the anaconda's jaw, my personal monument to love and ecstasy and survival. I locked the box in my desk expecting to feel closure or tangible release from my constant wariness, but trust in the way things were escaped me.

So I would go on, meeting whatever showed up next. That I could do this now, I was thankful for.

***

About a month after Benko sacrificed himself to the sausage lovers of America, Buhrman called. "I want to give you the update. My tentative final report before I back-drawer Gladenuff, least until we catch him in the flesh."

In response to my request that we talk now, he said, "No, I can't do it over the phone. Never know who's listening in. I'm going to a police chiefs' convention tomorrow, so let's handle it this afternoon. I'll be by quarter after one. Give you time for lunch."

He pulled up at exactly 1:15. I got in the patrol car with him.

"Security purposes," he'd replied when I asked him why we always had our meetings in the cruiser lately. "Gladenuff's our man, whatever his name really is. It sure ain't Benko Gladenuff. He's got a string of aliases as long as your income tax form."

The Chief cackled at his joke, staying on my case, letting me know he'd snooped into my tax filings and seen the novellas I submitted every April.

"The ID report on your boy finally came in. I can't believe how slow those guys in Washington are. They're supposed to have this immigrant tracking business under control by now. But they got a good excuse on this one: no immigrant. Ha!"

What did he mean? Gladonov wasn't from Russia?

The Chief rambled on. "Clement's just a dinky little town with no influence. I'm gonna let all the chiefs around the state know about the FBI's farting around while a murderer gets away. Don't know what good it will do, though."

Letting him vent, I rolled down my window and sniffed the moist, sparkling air. Whatever strange news he had couldn't faze me now. I don't know if I was still numb from all the stress or if I accepted deep-down that everything was all right now, but I'd become indifferent to the whole investigation. Whatever Buhrman knew, I couldn't do anything.

"No wonder Immigration couldn't find him. The file traces him back to New Jersey," Buhrman burst out, as excited as when he began the investigation. "It says he's Polish, born in Newark. His birth name is Robert Drinski. How do you like that?"

"Amazing." I sat up, clapped him on the shoulder, pretending enthusiasm. "Good job, Aaron. I wish I had you to check on all my employees with accents."

"Yeah," he said, so wrapped up in his story he missed my sarcasm. Just as well. I didn't need to maintain my adversarial attitude toward him any more. He was dismantling the entire case he'd built against me. "Jerk spent a couple of years in lock-up in Newark when he was a kid. He must have learned a few tricks there. Once he got out, he developed a nice career as a thief and credit card con under the names like Peter Gleeno, Josev Frunoosky, William Vallerie, who knows who godforsaken else? Spent more time behind bars. He sure sounded Russian. Where'd he get the accent?"

"Who knows?" I said. "Who cares now?"

"Faked it really good."

"He spoke English like an ape," I said.

"Sounded Russian enough to me. Don't know too many foreigners, though. Puerto Ricans, Frenchies from Quebec, some of them Vietnamese. My wife gets her nails done by a little Vietnamese gal."

Buhrman slowed down and stopped for some pedestrians. He waved and smiled at them. They waved back and he said, "I wish he was a Russky, be easier to take. Gotta admit, he's one tricky asshole. Didn't know Polacks were so clever."

"Like I said a while back, he fooled us all. Don't feel too bad about it, Aaron."

"Feel bad? I don't feel bad. He's a social pathawlic."

I laughed at him. "Whatever he was, he was good at it."

"Fell out of sight in '97. Showed up in New York again. Detained at Kennedy Airport in 2000. When did he start working for you? Did you ever call any people he worked for? Try to find out who he really was?

"I told you the company in England gave him a stellar reference." "Probably a phony company," Buhrman grunted.

"How would I know that, Aaron?" I started to heat up. It felt good. I started to feel like my old self, wide awake and ready for anything. "Now what are you accusing me of?"

"Nothing, Charlie. Calm down. We just got conned. The Mac-Daniel woman got the worst of it." He'd driven us to the outskirts of town and pulled into the abandoned drive-in movie theater lot. He began circling the weedy field and slowly curving around and between bent and rusted poles that held the car speakers in the drive-in's hay-day.

We've all got our own ways or working off tension and if the Chief wanted to pretend he was a test driver weaving through an obstacle course, let him cruise the Clement archeology of the last century.

"What pisses me off is that I should have known. Nine times out of ten, it's the boyfriend. Soon as we knew he was screwin' her, we should have closed in. He just knocked her on the head and tossed her in the tank to make it fool us. Trouble was, she didn't have any signs of recent sexual penetration."

"It could have been an accident. We don't know if he did it. You're too emotionally involved. Stay objective."

He'd used every subtle form of intimidation and threat to throw me off base during his investigation and I intended to make sure the town council knew how he'd treated me.

"Bullshit. You have to be emotionally involved in a murder in your town. You have to care if you're going to get anywhere. If you don't, nobody will. Except maybe the victim's kids. Think about it, Greer."

He spun out of the drive-in parking lot, spraying gravel behind us like a hyped-up adolescent rebel.

I waited to speak until we cruised smoothly down the highway. "All I'm saying is, do you have enough proof?"

"We got more than enough circumstantial. Here's what happened: He bumped her off. Brought her into the factory to set up the accident. The Chinaman saw him. He threatened the Chink or paid him off to get out. All those foreigners connive together. I had him scheduled to come in for a second interview. If hypnosis didn't work out—I never figured it would. It was some fancy bureaucrat in the D.A.s office came up with that cockamamie idea."

"I wish you'd done it. I've never been in a trance before," I said. "I hear it can make you feel real good."

"Yeah. If you mean how good you feel if you stop smoking. Anyway, I planned to polygram the weasel. I told him I wasn't gonna wait till the hyp-nutter waved his watch. So when the heat started coming down, Gladpop split. We almost had him."

"Sounds feasible," I said.

"District Attorney likes it, too. It's true. That's what counts." "But it's just your opinion, Aaron."

"Charlie, when are you gonna get it? I'm a professional police officer," he said. "My opinion is the second most important thing in an investigation. The facts is first. Smell the coffee, Mr. Tofu Head. If you don't have a strong opinion about things in this world, the way it's changin' so fast, you're just a sheet flappin' the breeze."

"All right, Aaron." I didn't feel like arguing, but I let slip some words I almost regretted. "If you knew the truth, you'd be surprised."

"What d'ya mean?" snapped Buhrman, ever suspicious. "What're you saying, Charlie? Do you know something you ought to tell me?" He stared at me gimlet-eyed, as if he still held the power of threat over me. "I haven't closed the case yet. No statute of limitations on murder, y'know. Don't hold back any information. We're still all in this together. D. A.'s thinking about posting a national wanted bulletin on Gladenuff. If you have something, say it."

Our eyes locked. I shrugged. "I mean, everybody's a mystery, when it comes to who they really are. You never know what makes people do the things they do. Anyway ..." I stared out the windshield wondering how to neutralize the Chief's willingness to ride the case into the ground, with me under him. I saw why the District Attorney had stuck with him, even when he had only his hunches. So I said, "I don't know anything you don't."

He slowed the car and squinted at me, figuring some way to regain his authority over me. Then he shrugged and gave me a flat smile as if I'd never see the truth, even if I was knee-deep in it, smelling it stinking up the room around me. "We have one witness," he said, "only one, but she might be helpful someday."

"What? Witness to what?" Did someone see me that morning? "A neighbor. Mrs. Brakefield, lady who lives across the street.

She must be ninety-five. Never sleeps." He watched my reaction. "Did she see him leave or something?"

He's leading up to this. You were careless when you dragged Benko out of the house.

"Naw. Too bad. Nobody saw him leave. Can't figure out how he got away. No cab, no bus out of town, no plane flights under his name. That's no surprise. Left his car to fake everybody out. Guy musta had friends from out of town, picked him up and spirited him away. Probably a woman."

"What did the neighbor see?" This worried me.

"Women. Lots of women coming and going at all times, day and night. Two in particular. One of 'em big and fat. It was winter so I thought maybe she was wearing a parka or something. Other one she saw quite a bit last summer, she said. Little, long black braid, maybe brown. Old Mrs. said she was a runner-type, shorts, shiny headband."

That one could have been Nora. She liked to run the streets of town early in the morning or just after dusk. When she ran, she braided her hair and wore a reflective headband.

"Any idea who these women were?"

"Could be anybody. Maybe there was only one, the deceased. She had the long brown hair and the old lady got mixed up. She's not really a good witness. I talked to all the other neighbors, but nobody saw anything unusual. 'Course, he could have taken off with one of those women. Pity her."

"So it's over? You're done."

"Not quite. Too bad I don't have his DNA. Too late now to make a match to the fetus. That would cinch it, I think. Disrict attorney says he doesn't have the budget to scrape around his apartment and send it out. Until I have his confession, I can't say it's over. Like most of these cases."

"So I hear." The Chief belonged on the criminal investigation unit of some city where he could dog a dozen cases at the same time, pressing on until he earned the satisfaction of filing at least one of them in his "Closed" drawer. I wouldn't feel totally easy until he left Clement and forgot about the case of the 'murder' in the tofu factory.

As he pulled to the curb outside my office, he said, "About the other DNA? There's one thing you might as well know. Just keep it to yourself."

I waited.

"You heard we had some trouble with the lab?"

"They got the samples mixed up?"

"Right. Those Puerto Ricans got themselves so discomboobulated with their paperwork they forgot to do the real testing. I'da known it was a dead end if they'd done their job right in the first place. D. A. understands. He promised to handle it. But he's not gonna spend any more budget on Gladnoof."

"What are you talking about, Aaron?"

"That flesh we found under the MacDaniel woman's fingernails?"

"Yeah?"

"It doesn't tell us much."

I caught my breath. "It wasn't Gladonov's skin?"

"Naw." He drove in silence, glancing at me several times before he went on. "It was hamburger."

"Hamburger!" I coughed, covering my shock.

"Yeah. It must have gotten stuck under there when she made the patties for her birthday party."

"Jesus. Aaron, do you know what that means?" I clenched my stomach muscles to prevent a bitter laugh and to stop myself from snapping, "You built the whole investigation around some hamburger?" I couldn't hold my laughter in and I burst into a belly laugh, throwing my body in wild shakes.

Embarrassed and solemn, he said, "I'm charging you officially to keep this quiet. You must know what it's like to be surrounded by idiots, being in business, so many employees and all."

I inhaled a deep breath to cover my glee, and followed it with another and another. I turned my face to the window so I could roll my eyes and drop my mouth and let my face contort while I held the laugh down in my diaphragm.

He went on. "Once we find Gladpop, or Drinkski, or Popsicle Pete, whatever, we'll need him to think we've got DNA evidence."

"I don't know if you can bluff those guys, Aaron," I said, snorting, coughing. "They're sharper than your average Clementine."

"That's true. We're not innocents up here, but we aren't citified. We plan to keep it that way, however we can. We don't blame ourselves for getting stung by a pro. Next time, I'm gonna stick with tradition—work the boyfriend first and foremost."

"Good idea, Aaron," I said, chuckling as we pulled to a stop in front of the factory. Little did he know, he'd been working the boyfriend all along.

"Did you ever figure out the motive?"

"Ah, Greer. You're dense. The cupcake in the oven. He knocked her up and she wouldn't get rid of it. She had morals, that one."

"Plausible," I said.

"Yeah. Kinda weak for murder, I know. What else do we have? The guy was evil. DA says pathohawlics don't need much of an excuse."

Buhrman sat up straighter, bracing his shoulders back, staring through the windshield. We rode in silence for a few minutes.

"By the way, I heard that sales lady of yours left the company. Nice woman."

Did he think it an odd coincidence that Genevieve had moved out of town a few weeks after Benko left? The truth was her best cover. "It wasn't easy trying to build sales in the middle of your murder investigation. Still, she did one hell of a job. Time came for her to move on anyway. She got a great job out West."

"Go West young lady. I liked her."

I opened the car door. "Thanks for the ride, Aaron. I'll miss our afternoon excursions in the cruiser. Think sometime you could take my kids for a jaunt around town with the lights flashing? I told them about the big gun and the radio."

"We'll see. I gotta think what the taxpayers would say if I was tooling around with rich kids in the squad car."

I grimaced but shook Buhrman's hand and gave him the thumbs up sign with my other hand. As I climbed out of the car, he flicked on his blue lights and gunned the motor.

"One good thing came out of this," Buhrman said. "I'm a lot smarter now. It ever happens again? I'm on it day one."

"Glad to hear that, Aaron. Makes me feel a lot safer." I grinned at him and slapped the top of the cruiser as he squealed away with the lights flashing, siren starting up.

As the Chief dopplered away toward town, I strolled around the factory, noting a few repairs we'd do once spring bloomed. Replaying the Chief's revelations, I laughed to myself, giddy as a head case. Shivers ran up and down my back and I ran to the building, scrambling up the four-story ladder to the top of our refrigerated warehouse where I could luxuriate in full March sunlight.

On the roof, higher than the old oaks and pines that bordered our lot, I clambered on all fours up the shingles, scanning the empty fields beyond American Tofu as I climbed. At the peak, I perched and raised my arms and stretched them out wide. For that moment, if a strong wind blew my way, I could fly.

Epilogue

Charlie

DOWN AT THE RIVER

bad luck, an accident
it wasn't my fault it
was all my fault

I didn't kill Becky. We had an accident, that's all. I couldn't help it.

If anyone else knew what happened, I can understand how they might think I was responsible, and in some way, I was, but not guilty of any wrongdoing. You could blame it on lust or tequila, or on the night, for that matter. Hell, you could say the moss on the rocks was lying there all slippery, waiting for us. You could take it all the way back to the beginning of our lives and say dying's what we're born for.

But the truth is, when it comes down to blaming, you can only blame it on bad luck.

I was just beginning to love her, this natural, light-hearted woman who surely loved me already.

Since we fell for each other, we'd kept our affair secret, totally undercover, because I was a married man. We—that is, I, had too much to lose by announcing I'd fallen in love with my employee and was leaving my family for her.

After a couple of months of seeing each other, she became my favorite person, the one I could tell everything to, and she was the best lover I'd ever had. Not that I'd had many, but she made me open up and praise whatever God there is for turning me all inside out and washing me in light and then putting me back together as a better happier person.

I picked her up at nine thirty, after her birthday party with friends. She'd told them to go home early because she had to be at the plant by two and she needed a few hours of rest. Little did they know she'd saved her real celebration for me.

I'd called our sitter but she couldn't come over so I had to leave the kids sleeping. It wouldn't be the first time their mother and dad were gone at night, so they wouldn't worry if they woke up and found themselves alone for a few minutes.

Becky jumped into my old Cherokee as excited and happy as I'd ever seen her. We drove out of town and down a pitted gravel road that followed the river, bumping along under a thick forest canopy drizzled with so much moonlight I crept along with my lights out. Warm breeze and gurgling sounds from the shallow river seeped into the car as we approached our favorite parking spot.

Before we climbed out of the car, Becky put her hand on my arm and asked me, "Don't you feel like a fish tonight?"

Joking, I said, "Not really. More like a stallion." When I reached to touch her cheek, she caught my hand in her chapped fingers and held it in mid-air.

"No, seriously. I mean, right now, see those shadows? How they wiggle between the moonbeams? Like we're sitting in a fish net made of light and dark."

Her imagination astounded me. I'd always wanted to be a poet, and I wrote haiku all the time, but Becky saw magic in the world that every grown-up had forgotten long ago.

She uncapped her thermos of frozen margaritas and we sat drinking and toasting each other. Before long, we started giggling and laughing like idiots, as we always did. I never had more fun with anybody in my life.

We hopped down the root-stairs on the riverbank and stood in the shade of an enormous oak. I told Becky I wanted to cross the river so I could give her my present in style.

"I have a wonderful present for you, too," she whispered, kissing my ear.

"Hobbit's birthday present?"

"How did you guess? Just like a hobbit, on my birthday I'm giving you a present."

A jumble of rocks and boulders colored pewter by the moon lay exposed above the August brook. After hanging out at the river for so many years, I was used to stepping from boulder to boulder to cross the shallow riverbed, so I whispered the most disastrous words I'd ever said.

"Let me carry you over."

"Like a groom?" she said. "Or like a stallion?"

We laughed until we bent over, bouncing off each other. At the riverbank, Becky leapt up and swung her legs around my waist. Holding my neck in both hands, she threw her head back and howled. She was small but she felt heavy and a pain nagged at my lower back so I flipped her around to hold her lying across both of my arms, like the groom.

The first rock was dry and flat. The nearly full moon painted such a clear path across the riverbed, I could have danced on the rocks with my eyes closed and never missed a step.

Hugging her tight, I stretched across the wide gap between flat boulders near the middle of the river. As my foot touched down, my heel skidded out and shot across the rock. My leg slid off the boulder and slipped down into shin-deep water, my legs splitting apart and my arms flying up. I tried to angle myself under Becky so she would land on top of me but she pitched out of my arms and dived head-first into the stream shadows. I fell on my back, landing on a flat rock and snagging my ankle in a cleft between two others.

I sat there, my ankle and back throbbing, letting the tequila fog clear. "Becky. Becky. You okay? I hurt my ankle." She didn't answer. As I observed her sprawled on the exposed riverbed, water filled my shoes and soaked my shorts. A hot ache climbed my calf from my ankle, stabbing deep inside my kneecap like a thorn.

"Must have been moss on the rock. I'm sorry," I said, calm as the night was warm. "Hang on, I'm coming."

She lay glowing in milky moonlight with her head and hand thrown back into the darkness on the other side of the slippery granite. "God. Becky. Becky. Are you all right?"

She was unconscious. I crawled across the rocks as quickly as I could and picked her up, lifting her high, holding her back to my chest and slipping and sliding my way five or six painful steps to shore where I lay her out on the stony beach. Raising her head to check for blood or any crushed bone, all I found in the dim light was a bump about the size of a thumb tip beside her left eyebrow.

She lay too still, so after tapping her cheek and calling her name, I pressed my ear to her chest. When I heard her heart beating, I sat back on my haunches, relieved, but still worrying. Even if her head was uninjured, what about her back?

The boozy haze had settled in again so I slapped my head to clear it while my mind raced senselessly. I knew what I had to do, but my arms and legs could barely move. I had to get her to the hospital and damn the consequences. Just let her be all right. I'd figure out a believable story later. Just let her be all right.

The brook struggled among the rocks, gurgling and choking its way downstream. Every few seconds, I glanced over at Becky. I could barely see her chest rise and fall.

I caressed her cheek again. Kissing her eyelids, I slid my fingers into her damp hair and lifted her head gently. Kissed her on the lips again. Did she kiss me back? I thought she did. I finally lay her head back on the ground—it flopped to the side.

At that, my lungs quivered in my chest and began to tighten up as panic stole my breath. After hacking as hard as I could and pounding on my chest with my palm, my throat finally loosened.

When my breath came a little easier, I tried to find her pulse in her wrist. Nothing there, so I touched her neck, seeking her carotids on both sides. Her skin felt clammy and spongy so I yanked my T-shirt off and patted her neck and face until it dried. Then I listened to her heart again—nothing.

A relentless homophony of crickets jangled the cool river air, distracting me for a second with an illusion of tranquility. Then, a bullfrog croaked from the weeds a few feet away. I jumped up and stumbled around, peering into the frightful night, expecting someone to step out of a shadow.

I knelt back down, and forcing my ear deep into her chest between her breasts, I listened for a long time. Nothing.

Opening my mouth and placing it around her nose, I wanted to feel her breath, to taste it. Under my hand, her chest didn't move and she didn't make the slightest sound.

"Jesus. O my God. O shit." I opened my mouth and screamed but caught myself and shut up, then listened for her heartbeat once more, for a long minute.

Nothing.

I lay my head on her stomach, my legs spread out on the stony shore.

I tried my version of CPR, breathing into her nose and mouth then pressing down on her chest. The slow rhythm calmed me down a bit, but she wouldn't respond. Finally I pushed myself away and stood up, tiny stones and pebbles stuck to my sweaty thighs. I brushed them off, slapping at them and picking them out of my kneecaps one by one, listening, waiting for something. Becky to wake up? Time to stop? The river to reverse itself and flow upstream? How could this happen to me? What did she do to deserve this? What did I do?

I carried Becky to my car and lay her in the back seat, the last place we'd made love. In death she had shrunk somehow. Her body fit between the doors, making it easy for me to wedge her against the crease between the bench and the seat back.

I started the car and turned around on the moonlight-mottled road and, bouncing on potholes, we headed toward the emergency room that wouldn't do any good. Every few minutes, I twisted around to check on her.

Every time I glanced back, she lay there, eyes closed, one arm hidden under her, one arm splayed toward me, her legs bent and leaning against the seat. I reached and felt her pulpy hand as if I could assure her everything was going to be fine.

I loved her more on that drive than I had ever loved her and felt so pissed off at love that it couldn't bring her back. Pure, spontaneous love for a woman, a woman I wasn't married to, a woman I shouldn't have fallen for, but a woman I couldn't resist because she didn't care who I was or what I did or when I came home, the kind of love I had always wanted and didn't know how badly.

Now that love would wreck Nora's and Chuckie's and Marissa's lives, too. Would my business go down? Would I lose everything? What about Becky's kids? Who'd take care of them now? They were my kids' age and their father had left them years ago.

I drove, still dizzy from the tequila, thoughts hurtling through my brain. My natural skepticism and caution spiraled into a full-blown paranoia, thinking through the possible questions the police might come up with.

The police? My God, the police would get involved. It was an accident, no matter how it happened. People die in accidents all the time, car accidents, falls. What about the thousands of people doctors kill by giving them the wrong drugs? My problem was not the accidental part of her death—I wasn't supposed to be with her. If people found out, that's all she wrote for Charlie Greer. The cops would want to check my story out to the nth detail. They were paid to distrust me and not believe anything I said.

Boss and pretty worker, happens all the time. When they got that, I rise to the top of the suspect list.

I told myself over and over I should just tell the truth right now and accept the misery. The divorce. The humiliation. Lose everything and everybody. I'd never be able to hold my head up in public. My God, the headlines: "New York Entrepreneur of the Year Indicted for Murder." These small towns have infinite memories, especially about scandals like this one.

The Charlie Greer everyone knows and loves would not survive. If I told the truth, I might as well end it all myself.

Maybe Becky wasn't as virtuous and loving as I thought. Maybe she wanted my money. Maybe she thought of herself as the next Mrs. Charlie Greer, queen to his kingdom of tofu. I heard the last thing she said to me again: "Like a groom?" If everything went according to her plan, I'd be supporting her two kids and mine and paying alimony and giving half my hard-earned income and the few assets I have to Nora.

I crept along below the speed limit. My mind slipped off into anxious reveries and then I'd come to, my teeth clicking, goose bumps skittering on my arms and shoulders, my car crawling along at ten miles an hour down streets I'd driven a hundred times before. But that night, I'd never been there before.

At least I didn't drive off the road and crash into a tree. Maybe that's how I should handle this, wreck the car, bloody my head and let Becky get thrown out onto the pavement where she smashes her head and dies?

The idea tempted me. Becoming lucid for a moment, I realized that if I tried that, first, I could get hurt and the situation would then be totally out of my control with gossips and cops having their way. Second, if I didn't get hurt, with Becky dead, people might guess it was a staged accident.

The closer we came to the hospital, the woman in the back seat became less Becky and more a body, a dense thing, the worst possible luck a man could have, short of losing his children. That body didn't belong on my earth. The inert flesh and bones back there reviled me no matter how much I'd loved the woman.

We approached the blinking yellow light at the hospital corner and I slowed down further.

I shivered and turned the opposite way and accelerated away from the hospital. No matter what happened now, old Charlie had to handle it on his own.

***

I pulled into my driveway and parked beside the garage on Chuckie's basketball court. I backed in, angling close to the tall lilac bushes.

Before climbing out of the car, I squeezed Becky's hands and legs. I guessed I had a few hours before rigor mortis set in. Rolling the body into the leg space between the seats, I covered it with the picnic blanket.

Limping inside, I swallowed four ibuprofen and showered in scalding water for as long as I could stand it. I still had half an hour before my wife showed up. I paced around my bedroom in the gloom.

I noticed the leather Bible Nora kept in her bedstead. I opened it to Samuel saying "God do so to me, and more also ... " I threw the book down. I didn't need an eye-for-an-eye judgment in my own bedroom. The outside world would supply more than enough.

Spotting my favorite haiku collection, I picked it up from my bedside table. I thumbed it open to tragic old haiku man Issa and read "In the heart of this everyday world we stroll along the roof of hell gawking at flowers."

Unable to bear literary truth, I dropped the book and went into the bathroom again. I turned on the bright make-up lights over the mirror and palmed a circle clear of moisture left over from my shower. I wanted to see my face, to assure myself that whatever happened, I was the same Charlie Greer, a man who met life's uncertainties head-on—Charlie never flinched.

My face resembled the same guy of a few hours ago whose biggest problems in life were making money and finding love, but I barely recognized him. His baggy eyes bugged out and glittered like a scared, pissed-off cat after some kid threw him in a tank of cold water.

I checked the kids in their rooms, imagining what it would be like if they grew up with their dad in jail for killing somebody. Whether he meant to kill or not, it wouldn't make any difference to them. "Killer's kids." They'd have to move far away and they'd never be able to visit me.

I knelt beside Chuckie's bed gazing into the face of inno-cence; nothing bothered him in his dream world. On the bed-side table, the illuminated clock face shone through his trans-parent bowl of sea monkeys, his latest favorite toy. He'd raised three batches in the last month, and none had survived to jump around his room, as he insisted they would, if only he found the right food. The latest batch lay inert, clumped together at the bottom of the bowl.

I kissed Chuckie on his hot cheek and pulled his blanket down so he wouldn't overheat and have nightmares.

Rissi heard me come through her door.

"Daddy?"

Her voice opened the floodgates on the pond of sorrows I'd stored up for my whole life. As a rivulet of tears pressed up and leaked out of my eyes, I coughed, "Hi sweetie."

"Hi Daddy."

She turned over and hugged her 'Georgie,' the sock mon-key her grandma made, her bedtime companion since she left Nora's and my bed four years ago. A beam of moonlight shined through the gap between the window shade and the sash and fell across her baby face, a blessing from the all-loving night.

My baby girl, my princess, safe and peaceful and gorgeous and all the world waiting to give you love and happiness. Oh, baby, I have totally wrecked your life. God help me.

I kissed her on the chin, then on the lips. A single tear dripped off my eyelash and fell onto her face. It rolled down her cheek and she brushed at it, like at a mosquito.

I stood there, trembling, and the thought of Becky's little girl came to me, motherless, red-haired like her mom, sleeping at some aunt's or friend's house with her doll tucked under her chin never again having a mother to watch over her and kiss her good night. I sagged against the wall wanting to let myself slide to the floor and fall asleep, forgetting all the misery I was causing.

Instead, I went back into the bathroom and stuck my head in the sink. I ran icy water over my skull and neck, chilling back tears and shrinking the puffiness around my eyes, in case Nora noticed. Then I climbed into bed and turned onto my stomach with the sheet pulled up to my ears, my mind now half-paralyzed from sorrow.

At exactly eleven thirty, Nora's car turned into the driveway. She came into the house and upstairs to the bedroom where I was faking sleep with a pillow over my head. She climbed in beside me. Thank God it takes her two minutes to drop into an eight-hour coma.

The customary sound of her breathing started to lull me into an alpha state and I almost faded out. Forcing myself to stay awake, tossing and turning with eyes open, I imagined Becky lying in my car. I could almost hear Becky calling my name.

'*Charlie? Come get me. It's cold out here. I need your arms around me. It's my birthday, remember?*'

I bolted up in bed. What kind of present was she going to give me? Did she leave something in the car? I had to make sure I cleaned out mud or leaves or her smell on the blanket—I'd have to throw it away. Did she have a purse when I picked her up? Did she tell anybody she was going out with me tonight? One of her girlfriends? Shit. I hoped to hell I didn't leave the margarita thermos at the river.

If someone's in the know, where you gonna go?

It was true, I had no place to go. If I disappeared, I'd be admitting guilt and be running for the rest of my life. Maybe I should just take her home and dump her in her back yard. Let somebody find her and the cops will figure that somebody at her party killed her.

Too many lights in her neighborhood. A lot of people in Clement would recognize my license plate "Tofu 4 U." No way I can drive up to Becky's front door in the middle of the night now and carry her body over my shoulder into her house.

Maybe I'll take Becky to the river and lay her on the rocks. Come back and get her car and abandon it there. Make it seem like she went out there by herself after her party and she slipped and did herself in.

I almost got out of bed until I thought, Stupid, how're you gonna get out to the river, do whatever, and walk back to town to get Becky's car? Too complicated. Somebody will see you wandering around the streets.

Bad luck Charlie Greer. All you can do is cry a tear.

Had to get myself under control and make a plan but my mind was paralyzed.

She ain't comin' back from the afterlife. You better figure out how to make the deal of your life.

Panicked whispers flooded my mind. I listened hard but all I could make out was a rush like wind in the trees. The sound soothed me. For a moment, I calmed down and I drifted toward sleep again, giving in to everything that had happened. I stretched my legs and tensed all my muscles, then let them go soft, allowing my body to separate from my head so I could think clearly.

At that moment, it came to me: I saw exactly what I had to do. It was what Becky would want me to do. Because she loved me, she wouldn't want me or my family or hers hurt any more. My heartbeat quickened and my thoughts cleared as I understood that if I played my cards right, I could make everything turn out the best way it could, for all of us, except Becky, of course.

She'd had an accident. Yes. Simple. Only it was an industrial accident—factories are dangerous places, everyone knows that, even tofu factories. For the next ten minutes, every step of a risky, but doable plan unfolded as I watched and listened and tweaked details. I checked at the clock. Twelve seventeen. I'd have time. It would take less than an hour to pull off what I decided to do that night—for Becky, for our kids, for all of us.

*****

I climbed out of bed, as I did in the middle of many nights. If Nora noticed me gone from the room, she'd think I was downstairs, maybe in the yard.

Checking the back seat, I felt relieved, almost happy, to find Becky's body still there. Wincing at my morbid reaction, I got in and saw the margarita thermos on the floor of the passenger side, but nothing else. No purse. Things were looking up.

In ten minutes, we arrived at my tofu factory where she was due for work at two. The sour smell of her clothes overwhelmed the naturally rich perfume of the leather upholstery.

I circled the parking lot to make sure all the night shift cars had left. Every night, for the hour between one and two, the building was completely empty.

I pulled up close to the factory side door and punched in the security code. I tugged Becky out of the car and hoisted her over my shoulder and started across the production room, a walk I'd taken almost every working day for the last seven years. The pain in my ankle had subsided and the bang on my tail barely throbbed.

Inside the hollow factory, the hideous moonlight shined down through the windows near the ceiling and glinted off a forest of stainless steel tanks and pipes, disorienting me again.

I shuffled through the murky plant, passing from shadows into slanting silvery beams and back into the gloom. I slipped once or twice on the floor, nearly tripping on the puddles. My steps scudded across the tile, sounding distant from my body, as if the echoes of someone else's feet followed me.

I entered the women's dressing room and flipped on the light and lay Becky gently on the floor. While stripping off her shorts and blouse, I avoided her face. She wore a lacy black bra and black silk bikini panties.

I sensed her spirit lingering near us the way they say they do when someone dies violently and unexpectedly. I don't believe in ghosts, I don't believe in any afterlife, but if, just in case, her life force hadn't evaporated and it could sense my intentions, I felt she'd do everything she could to help me, to protect me, as long as I still loved her and handled everything the best I could.

I noticed my watch and saw that I didn't have much time before the crew arrived. I stood up and nearly fell over. Not the booze this time. I waited with my eyes closed and my stomach clenched, but nothing came up.

In a minute, I opened Becky's locker and slipped her white production uniform off the hanger and pushed and tugged it up over her legs and arms. My fingers trembled so fiercely I could barely button the blouse. I arranged her cold, sodden party clothes on the hanger and hung them in her locker. They reeked of smoke from her barbecue.

I lifted her up and held her in a tender hug. I kissed her rubbery cheek and her cold nose and lay my lips against hers. Her icy mouth stung and I jerked away, gagging.

Buck up, Chuck.

I blew hard out my mouth, spluttering and spitting. I had to overcome my body's reaction to the dead body, my fear of what was coming. I had to get back to work.

I bent over to throw her body over my back and I eased my shoulder under her middle and tried to straighten up. She was wasn't too heavy but I was weak-kneed and my sore ankle buckled and my chin slammed into the floor. Groaning, I grunted and eased myself up.

I plodded out of the dressing room into production area trying to hold her away from my body but with every shuffling step I took, she flopped against me.

We approached the huge vats of soaking soybeans. Softening for processing, the beans smelled like yesterday's oatmeal.

I climbed up the steps to the open top of the five hundred gallon bean immersion tank. Four tons of hydrated soybeans lolled plump and ready for transformation into tofu. I opened the hinged lid and hefted Becky's body up over the lip of the tank and heaved, pushing her head, face-first, into the beans in the center of the tank.

As soon as I let the body go, it floated, bulging above the beans like a bubble of gas. Her hair, buoyed up by the two inches of water that covered the beans, spread into a dark red halo rippling around her skull.

I leaned over, bracing my knees against the wall of the vat and pressed her shoulders and head down into the beans.

One forty five.

As I rushed across the production room toward the glowing red exit sign, I glanced back at the bean soaking tank and its tragic contents. Silhouetted against the gleaming white wall, Becky's boot soles appeared above the vat staring at me like Kilroy eyes.

I laughed. A bark echoed back at me from the across the room. I stifled another laugh rising from my belly. I was losing it.

I let myself out, punched in the code, and drove home, my teeth chattering all the way.

In my yard, I sat in the kids' swing set until I calmed down. Listening to the crickets call incessantly for their mates, I gave in to prayer.

> *Becky, there's no way but please forgive me. You know we really fucked up. I didn't mean it. You were too wiggly. Your kids, O, my god, please forgive me. Nora, you can never know about this. Please forgive me. Jesus, Buddha, Great Spirit if you're there, please let me survive. Let us. Help me find a way to make this right.*

> *Anything, I'll do anything. Just let it go away. Don't let my kids ever know about this. Do with me what you have to. Let me make it up to you some other way. I'll do everything I can for her kids. Please.*

Finally, I realized I'd better go inside and pretend to have a normal night sleeping in bed with my wife. Hand over hand on the banisters, I hauled myself up the stairs and into the bedroom and stripped and threw my clothes into the hamper. I'd have to wash them myself before Nora saw them and got curious about the mud.

I glanced up the street out the bedroom window, convinced that someone would drive up the road looking for me. The pale light obscured the borders between trees and hedges and their shadows. I sank onto the mattress and worked my legs under the sheet and lay limp beside Nora feeling like I'd run five marathons. My thigh muscles fluttered.

I willed myself to fall asleep but Becky's sad face lying on the riverbank glowed inside my closed eyelids. My sweet little Rissi's moonlit sleeping face alternated in my mind's eye with Becky's beautiful dead face. Tears flowed down my temples into my ears. Shivers ran through my scalp.

I held Rissi's image in my mind, focusing on her smile, because I was afraid to think about what would happen tomorrow and she was the most wonderful thing about my life, my purest inspiration for anything good about me.

Eventually, exhaustion saturated every nerve and I went numb. I lost sight of Rissi as a cloud passed over and swept her image into shadow.

The leaves in the maple outside stirred and a damp breeze blew through the open window. I pulled the sheet up to my chin and glanced at the clock: 2.04. I had a little time until somebody called from the plant with the bad news. I rolled over on my stomach and tried to sleep.

Charlie

THE EMERALD TINCTURE

down at the river
where all my tofu starts
my secret wrongs, my sacrificial rites

I took a few days off after the Chief suspended the case. One cloudy afternoon, I found myself parked at Becky's and my favorite spot along the river. Plows had piled the snow four feet high on each side of the road and the wind scattered random flakes across my windshield.

I shut the car off and slogged over the snow banks and slid down the icy root staircase to the stream. Two or three courses of unfrozen water weaved among the boulders and flowed downstream to the reservoir that fed the tofu factory. All American Tofu was made with pure water from this little river.

That morning, I'd retrieved the maroon velvet jewelry case from my safe deposit box. Inside, I kept the birthday emerald earrings I never had a chance to give to Becky.

I stepped onto the ice, crossing the rocks, retracing my blundering steps when I'd held her warm living body in my arms. In a fit of self-punishment, I slipped both feet into the stream. Standing there, I cupped the earrings in my fist for a long time, then I opened my palm and stared at the sparkling green stones, the only color in the day.

A cold ache rose from my soaked feet up into my shins. My knees shook. I squatted down on the same flat rock I'd slipped on last summer and gazed for a long moment at the black water.

Just a matter of time, you'd end up at the scene of the crime.

A gust of frigid wind nearly knocked me backwards off my heels. I clasped my hands together over the jewels and rolled them back and forth. The earrings bit at my chilled skin, but the friction heated and softened my palms.

A crow flew by, wondering if the crazy human would leave any tasty morsels. He squawked and winged off.

I checked the earrings once more and joining my palms, held them in front of my chest and shook them together, hard. Like tiny dice, they clicked, but so softly I barely heard them above the splashing water.

I opened my hands for a last view of the fatal jewels. Then, I stretched my arms out and tipped my palms inward. The earrings slid into the indifferent river. They seemed to float for an instant. My fingers darted out, but the jewels sank into oblivion.

Now, all the tofu we make has water infused with the Becky MacDaniel emerald memorial. Everyone who eats American Tofu carries the mystical essence of Becky in their cells. It's a bizarre way to give somebody immortality—only in my mind.

No way the tincture's enough. Soy to the World? No. Nothing could ever be enough.

But what else is a tofu man to do?

Letter from San Francisco

Dear Charlie and Nora,

It took me a while to want to get in touch with you guys, but you understand. I think about you and AT and everything a lot and my therapist told me I'd probably be able to make peace with American Tofu in two years or so.

So now it's been more than two years, and I'm not ready to make full peace but I do want you both to know I still love you and most of all, I forgive all of us — well, there's one person I'll never forgive no matter if it corrupts my soul.

I forgive you Charlie for being an impulsive crazy ambitious narcissist because you have guts and you go for what you want and you do care about everyone else, even if it's in your own odd way. Maybe you've learned by now that just because you want it, it's not necessarily the right thing.

I forgive you Nora for being so complacent and not grabbing Charlie by the ears a long time ago and insisting he be honest with you, and for you being so dishonest with him, as if you guys had such a stable marriage you could weather any problems, like stupid affairs. Not that I'm innocent in the world of affairs—

Speaking of marriage, here's some cool news: I'm engaged. Not the ring way, with big wedding plans. No. We're totally heart to heart, nothing held back. Nothing. (Except one thing)

He's a combination painter-sculptor and biomedical entrepreneur. He's 45, has 2 kids by his baby-making marriage, loves me and I love him. I could go on and on about the handsomest man on the planet, Roberto Daniel Murakami. But I won't. Neither of us believe in marriage, but we believe the two of us (often the five of us) can create and live a beautiful life together for the rest of it.

Best news: Liam is now sort of in ninth grade—I'm homeschooling him with ten other families. Liam has the run of the city, or better said, the skateboard of the city. He has two wonderful close friends and countless other kids he spends time with. If you haven't already, you could check out his website and Facebook to see the beautiful wild videos he makes with his friends. He has the photographer's gift of perspective and structure, but his imagination is far cleverer than mine. He's happy.

So am I. My home is great—on Linda Street, a quiet little street in a nice section of town. I work a lot from my home office. My boss owns the house but he's giving me equity for my rent. Not bad. Needless to say, my job is perfect. I'm about to publish a cookbook (finally) featuring fusion recipes with vegetables and fruits and sauces very few people know about yet. I spend about eight weeks a year traveling, meeting chefs and farmers and ordinary people on four continents so far. They share their recipes with me—sort of like cooks did for me with the tofu cookbook. I often supply the recipes and voila! It'll be called Genevieve's Kitchen – Palette of the World. Pun intended, Charlie.

Remember when I used to play with romanesco and samphire? Well, get ready America—Gen's genius has finally been freed. By the way, Charlie, I love what dragon fruit and tiger nuts do for tofu. (I know you're going to come up with some crazy tiger nut promotion Charlie but please don't ask me to create any more tofu recipes.)

Gianni is still my best friend, tho we haven't seen each other in person for a while. We still talk almost every week. He mentioned American Tofu seems to be taking over the universe. You're all over the country and shipping to Mexico?

Okay, you guys. How are Rissi and Chuckie? Show them Liam's work. They'll be inspired and will get it better than we do. They'll know how to get in touch with him if they want to.

Most important, are you being good and loving to each other?

I'm still not ready to see either of you—too much trauma trigger. I've only been sleeping all night for a few months, so …

I just want you to know I love you both. Please write me especially with your kids' news and a little bit about how you are. I'll write back but let's not rush communications.

I'm sure you're still in recovery mode, Nora. I'd appreci-ate a short note about how you're doing.

It sounds like Charlie, you're still a mad achiever, must be your own brand of therapy. Not so sure if it goes very deep, but you're your own guy, one of the most unique characters I've ever met.

much love, your friend always

Genevieve

The End

Book Three

Down at the River

THE HOUR BETWEEN ONE AND TWO

The author

Thomas Timmins has published and performed his poetry and short fiction in person and in print across the U.S. and on the internet. He founded Fractals, a literary tabloid, cofounded and ran Poets & Players, a performance venue, developed and taught writing and coaching programs for inmates, published commercial writing, and founded and managed small business-es ranging from soyfoods to ice cream to telephone fundraising to biological pest control to a video game start-up to energy efficiency retrofits and a media company.

www.thomastimmins.com